Mystery Buehler, L

14 Day

Buehler, Luisa

The lion tamer : a caged
death

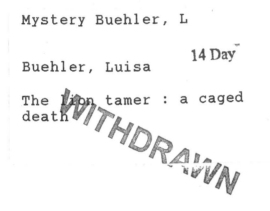

WITHDRAWN

Praise for...

The Station Master: *A Scheduled Death*

"Time for Janet Evanovich to take a lesser seat–to move over for Luisa Buehler...simply enthralling...Buehler has cooked up an excellent dish for her fans...unique sleuth, strong voice, and crisp storytelling." –Robert W. Walker, author of *City for Ransom*

"Cutting-edge cozy. *The Station Master* is filled with long-buried secrets, elaborate twists, and nail-biting suspense. Buehler and Marsden just keep getting better and better." –J.A. Konrath, author of *Bloody Mary*: A Lt. Jack Daniels Thriller

"Grace Marsden returns in Luisa Buehler's charming *The Station Master*...a fine blend of intrigue, vivid description, and quirky but compassionate characters. Don't miss it." –Libby Fischer Hellmann Author, the Ellie Foreman series

The Rosary Bride: *A Cloistered Death*

"...a stylishly written novel evocative of Barbara Michaels...a fascinating cast of characters, an engrossing tale of old wrongs, long-kept secrets, and murder." –Denise Swanson, author of the bestselling Scumble River Mysteries

"...a twisty, taut, compelling story of love gone wrong, a fascinating, haunting tale." –Carolyn Hart, author of *Engaged to Die*

"My favorite kind of book–old sins cast long shadows. When a long-dead woman is found behind the fireplace at Rosary College, new crimes begin to happen...suspenseful and poignant." –Barbara D'Amato, author of the Cat Marsala series

"A taut and suspenseful whodunit laced with a healthy dose of the supernatural." –Lee Driver, author of the *Chase Dagger series*

Books by

Luisa Buehler

The Grace Marsden Mystery series

The Station Master: A Scheduled Death
The Lion Tamer: A Caged Death
The Rosary Bride: A Cloistered Death

Coming Soon

The Scout Master: A Prepared Death

Luisa Buehler

The Lion Tamer:
A Caged Death

Book Two

Grace Marsden Mystery series

This is a work of fiction. Names, characters, places, and incidents are products of the author's imagination or are used fictitiously and are not to be construed as real. Any resemblance to actual events, locales, organizations, or persons, living or dead, is entirely coincidental.

Echelon Press
9735 Country Meadows Lane 1-D
Laurel, MD 20723
www.echelonpress.com

First Echelon Press paperback printing: October 2004
Second Echelon Press paperback printing: February 2006

10 9 8 7 6 5 4 3 2

Cover Art © Nathalie Moore
2004 Ariana Best in Category Award winner

Printed in the United States of America

Dedication

To the docents at Brookfield Zoo, whose mission to guide visitors to education through experience makes them pioneers on life's journey to harmony with nature.

Acknowledgments

My thanks to Kurt Hill for his help and expertise with diamonds, to my reading group, Kay Payne, Gary Ritter, and Lee Williams, for their honest and constant critique, and to Gerry Buehler and Christopher Buehler for their steady encouragement.

8512

Chapter One

The message on my answering machine played simply enough. Nine single syllables that conveyed a volume of possibilities. I replayed the entreaty three times, "Grace, I need your help. Call me at home." Normally a call from Karen Kramer, my best friend, didn't send me into a state of confused hopefulness. Karen and I had met at Regina College more years ago than either of us admits to easily. Our friendship started for all the right reasons and remained steadfast through every crisis.

So with that said, why were my fingers fumbling with the replay button? Karen and I hadn't spoken to each other in three months. My mind raced from one plausible possibility to the next, in the few seconds it took Ameritech to spin their fiber optics and connect my call. It rang, once, twice. Maybe she wasn't home. As fast as my mind ran down the possibilities, my fingers flew over a length of yellow yarn tied to the telephone cord. I am obsessive-compulsive about some things. When I'm nervous I calm my jitters by braiding. Phone calls can bring unsettling news, ergo the braid on the cord. I twisted two previous cords into grotesque uselessness before I added the yarn. Three rings. My underarms tingled with the sudden release of sweat. "You have reached 555…" Thank God, I thought. Her machine picked up. I took a deep breath to calm my voice as the message continued and waited for the beep. "Karen, this is…"

"Grace, don't hang up. I'm here."

"Hello," was my tentative approach. I wasn't feeling brilliant.

"Thanks for calling back. I mean, I wasn't sure if you would."

"Sure I would. I'm surprised to hear from you…but happy."

A soft chuckle greeted my response.

"How are you?" I wondered if Karen heard the caution in my

voice.

"It's still hard, without them, you know. I'm getting better. I've wanted to call you for awhile now, but I wasn't sure what to say." Her pause was so long; I felt I should say something soothing or conciliatory. Karen's voice filled the line before I could speak.

"Anyway, Hannah is in town for a few weeks. Of course, you know that. What I mean is, she said I should call."

This time I didn't wait for the pause. "I'm glad you did. I've missed you."

"Will you meet me at Braxton's?" Karen asked. "I want to see you."

"You bet. Name the time." I beamed at the receiver in my hand. We agreed on a time and I reminded Karen to exit south on Route 83 to get to the Oak Brook restaurant. She was lousy with directions.

"Thanks, Grace. We can catch up and I can tell you why I need your help."

"My help?" I had forgotten the message.

"Oh yeah," she answered. "This is right up your alley. A skeleton surfaced at Iroquois Lake at the zoo. See you at three o'clock."

A skeleton in Iroquois Lake…too bizarre, I thought as I rushed up the spiral iron stairs leading from the kitchen to the second floor of our home. I figuratively pat myself on the back every time I dash up those service stairs and save the fifty odd steps it takes to reach the oak staircase between the living room and dining room.

Our semi-wooded lot includes a twelve room house, a three car garage, carriage house, and small stable set out on three acres out of over one hundred acres of reclaimed swampland about twenty-five miles west of Chicago. My husband and I share this development with five other families and *Broken Feather*, a Pete Dye golf course. I love the solitude and space.

I grew up in Berkeley, Illinois, where I shared a three-bedroom bungalow with four brothers, two parents, and one uncle on my father's side. Our home had one bathroom with a busy and closely timed schedule tacked to the door.

Now, I could choose from one of *three* bathrooms. I usually choose the one in the master bedroom. Harry's toiletries are Spartan compared to mine, so I use all of my space and most of his; an allocation that works in our walk-in closet as well. Men don't seem to require as much space. At least my man doesn't; a fact, which deepens my esteem for him each time I need an extra shelf.

Three o'clock gave me a little over an hour and a half to meet Karen. The Braxton wasn't a blue jeans kind of restaurant. I pulled olive green, woolen walking shorts and matching tights from the drawer. A mustard colored turtleneck and a tweed jacket that picked up both colors completed the ensemble.

A quick glance in the mirror assured me I needed more than a quick glance. Mascara smudged the tops of my not so high cheekbones. Pretty Eyes advertised that swimming wouldn't smear their product. It didn't say anything about crying. Maybe tears are more potent than chlorine. Maybe if I'd paid attention to Sister Bernard in remedial Chemistry, I'd know the answer.

My fingers dipped and blended across my face making the necessary repairs. Lavender eyes, flecked with gold, now filled with tears again as I thought of how much I had missed Karen in my life. "Oh, stop it," I scolded myself. "You'll never get out of the bathroom at this rate." I blew my nose and reassessed my image.

I wear my hair one length cut at my shoulders for one reason. I'm lousy with hair. My parents' Irish-Italian gene pool designed thick sable brown hair. Unruly waves framed a fair complexion into which their genetic coupling had placed lavender eyes that turn pansy-purple during mood swings. Hair was the problem today. I bent over from the waist and brushed my hair vigorously, then straightened up. When the blood settled and my vision cleared, I looked like Simba in *The Lion King* pushing his head through a bush. I reached for a green woolen cap with a brown suede bill. With the cap on, I could push my hair behind my ears and have half a chance it would stay put.

The finished image was a lot of green and someone who looked ready to go walking over the moors. I lacked only a walking stick and sensible shoes. "Check, check, and done," I pronounced as I flipped off the light switch. I penned a quick note to Harry, jammed a piece of purple yarn in my pocket, and turned my thoughts to a skeleton in Iroquois Lake. *Too bizarre.*

Karen and I claimed Oak Brook as our meeting place since the exclusive suburb sits half way between Pine Marsh and Oak Park, where Karen lives. I secured a small table at the front of the restaurant in the lounge area. The wing chairs felt absolutely homey after a few cocktails.

I ordered a vodka and tonic and waited nervously, looking up each time the door opened. Lunch crowds already a memory, most of the wait staff looked longingly at the doors. Their raised heads met Karen's level gaze as she entered. I waved my hand to direct her. Dumb move; there were no other customers in the bar. I was nervous.

A smile spread across her face and jumped to her soft brown eyes. She looked a little thin, but at 5'10", she was always slim. Karen still looked much as she did in college. Her dark blonde curly hair framed an impish face. Tortoise shell glasses saved her from looking like Doris Day. She ordered a Tanqurey and tonic from a loitering waiter and sat down.

"Grace, thanks for coming," Karen greeted me. "I've been awful about this whole thing."

"Karen, don't," I interrupted. "You weren't yourself. Let's forget it."

"Forget it, after what I said to you? It wasn't your fault. You were almost killed. Forget it?" Karen's usually clear voice clouded with emotion.

"I know neither one of us can forget what happened. Let's get past it. I'm glad we're back." I reached across the table to squeeze her hand. My jacket cuff pulled back when I stretched my hand, exposing three tiny scars on the inside of my wrist. I regretted the movement, but it was too late. Her eyes stared at my wrist then looked at my face for confirmation.

"Did I do that?" she asked softly.

"It doesn't matter. I hurt more inside when you weren't around. Trust me, it doesn't matter."

She touched the scars gently and believed me. I could tell she did by her posture, as though a weight had eased from her. I ordered another round of drinks and then zeroed in on Karen.

"Now give. What's all this about a skeleton?"

"I knew you couldn't resist." Karen smirked. "Dee Sanders called me last night. We're on the board at the zoo. Her particular committee is working on fundraising for the new wetland exhibit. "As part of the *shtick* several community leaders with connections, captains of industry with deep pockets, and media crews with rolling cameras, were invited to a ceremony at the lake. Earlier in the week, divers with the Army Corps of Engineers discovered an old circus wagon buried in marsh up to its crown. Someone in Public Relations thought it would be great publicity to film the recovery of the wagon as a special interest event." Karen paused to quench her thirst.

"Were they able to raise it?" I prodded.

"Oh, they raised it all right. PR thought it went without a hitch."

"I haven't heard anything about this on the news."

"That's because no one discovered anything unusual until after the press left and the maintenance department started cleaning off the wagon. That's when they found it."

"*It?* I had been expecting *him or her*."

"It was a he, but *he* was an African Lion," she said with a flourish.

"An African Lion? That's crazy. How did it get there? How long has it been there? Didn't anyone notice they were missing a lion?"

"Wait, it gets better," Karen said. She leaned forward and lowered her voice. "They found the bones of a man's hand tangled in the lion's ribcage."

My eyes must have gleamed purple, my personal indicator of excitement or fear. Karen continued. "But that's not the best part. The wagon had a false bottom and when they managed to open that they found…" Karen paused to draw out the moment.

"What? They found what?"

"The rest of the guy that belonged to the hand," she finished with a cat-that-ate-the-canary smile.

"The rest of the guy. What do you mean *the rest of the guy*?"

"Just that. They found a skeleton in the bottom of the cage. Apparently the chemical make-up of a marsh, plus the fact that the wagon was stuck in the mire closer to the shore and not further out in the marsh, kept most of the bones in the wagon."

"Do they know anything yet about whom he was or what happened?"

"Nope, not a clue. They've shipped everything to the Illinois State Police forensics lab."

"How is the zoo handling the story?" I asked.

"Right now there is no answer. The docents have been told to say they don't know, that they weren't there, which is true. No one knows." Karen motioned for the next round and continued. "Dr. Barr, the director of the zoo, has been careful not to disclose too much or form any opinions until after the tests and reports are completed. That was the word we received at the emergency board meeting last night."

"The zoo will get their fifteen minutes of fame when the media gets wind of this." We both sat silent after my comment. I think we both remembered the media blitz surrounding Karen's family and the solving of a fifty-year-old murder at Regina College.

"What mystery shrouds this murder?" I wondered aloud.

"Murder, who said anything about murder?" Karen's voice was plaintive.

"What, who, I mean who said…?"

"You did, just now. You were sitting there with that look on your face and you said *murder*."

"What look? Karen you're a pain sometimes," I teased.

"What look?" she mimicked. "The look you get when you visit that part of your brain that always causes trouble."

"It doesn't take an astral physicist to figure out there was *foul play*. How's a guy going to get his hand chewed off by a lion, end up hidden in the bottom of a cage, and the entire cage end up in a marsh?"

"Astral? Where did you get your degree…from Woolworths?"

We laughed over my simple synopsis and even simpler grasp of physics. It felt so right to be laughing with Karen and sharing my zany thoughts with her. A dull ache in my heart had been replaced with a warm fuzzy. The third vodka tonic hadn't hurt either. Our reconciliation gave me the sensation of soaring. For one tiny instant,

I remembered the story of Icarus flying too close to the sun. I shrugged off the analogy. After all, his wings were made of wax. I was soaring on wings of friendship. I hate it when I don't expect the crash.

Karen's eyes widened in surprise at something behind my left shoulder. Her gesture gave me a split second of warning before I heard his voice.

"I must say, I'm surprised and happy to see the two of you together again and smiling about it." Karen's incredibly handsome brother, Ric Kramer, smiled down at us from his imposing six-foot, four-inch height. His dark brown hair and even darker eyes set off the camel hued corduroy jacket and cream-colored polo shirt to perfection. I guess I'd never stop marveling at how his appearance (literally and figuratively) caused definite physiological changes in me. Case in point, my palms moistened and my neck and cheeks flushed.

"Can anyone join this party?" came the query and the dazzling smile.

"Ah, sure," Karen said, glancing up at me through a fringe of curly bangs. "Just don't monopolize the conversation," she warned.

"Thought never entered my mind." The waiter appeared at Ric's side. "I'll have a bourbon and water. Ladies?" He paused to let us order. I changed my order to coffee. Karen ordered hot tea.

"*Ah ha.* I see Hannah's influence at work here." I wished I could have bitten back my words as I noticed a tiny flinch in Karen's face and the quickly lowered eyes beneath those curls. Ric's face clouded over for an instant, as his expression seemed to struggle with the reminder that his sister was gay. Harry and his twin sister Hannah were consummate tea drinkers and joked that any other beverage was uncivilized. Hannah and Karen had been in a relationship for several years. I blurted out the first thing I could think of to change the direction of the conversation.

"Ric, has Karen filled you in on the skeleton at the zoo?" Karen's eyes rolled up and Ric fastened his gaze on her.

"No, she hasn't. Do tell, sister dear." We were all smiling again. Karen filled him in with a condensed version and we were all laughing at the end of her description of my pronouncement of *foul play*.

"This is one investigation I'm glad has absolutely no connection whatsoever to my department." Ric smiled. He was a police inspector, not an anthropologist.

"Wouldn't it be fascinating to find out the circumstances of this case? I mean who was he? How did his hand get into the lion and the rest of him elsewhere? When did it happen?" I asked.

"Whoa, Grace. There's no case and it would not be fascinating. Have you already forgotten the last skeleton..." Ric's voice slowed and stopped. None of us had forgotten.

The waiter sidled up to the table to refill my cup and bring Karen a new tea bag. His arrival effectively stopped further conversation. We all sipped at our drinks. My mind raced trying to think of a tactful way to leave. Deliverance came from across the room in the form of a gorgeous, willowy redhead waving to Ric. Her copper tresses swirled around her face with each increasingly broader wave. Her entire body seemed intent on signaling her presence.

"A new friend, Ric?" was Karen's coy question. "You'd better get over there before she knocks something over or sprains something," she added with a smirk.

"If you'll excuse me." Ric stood. His movement stopped the waving. "It's good to see you again, Grace." His eyes held mine for a second too long. I felt the traitorous warmth creep up my neck and settle itself defiantly on my cheeks.

"It is warm in here, isn't it?" A corner of his mouth lifted.

Chapter Two

Karen and I said good-bye and promised to talk again soon. I asked her to keep me up-to-date on the skeleton. My niece and godchild, Jolene Grant, was a docent at the zoo. Jolene was the only child of my eldest brother, Joseph, a priest in Seattle.

He had dated a theology major all through college named Darlene Grant. The family expected wedding bells, but after graduation, Joseph chose the seminary instead of matrimony. Darlene never told him she was pregnant before she moved back home. Ten years later, Joseph received a letter informing him of his fatherhood. Darlene had never married and was dying from cancer. She wanted Joseph to know he had a daughter.

The entire Morelli family descended on the small Ohio town where Jolene lived with her maternal grandparents. We were all there for Darlene's funeral and stayed as long as we could to get to know our new relative. Most ten-year-olds would have been overwhelmed, but I think the Morelli genes kicked in, by the end of the week, Jolene had all of us wrapped around her little finger. She stayed with her grandparents during the school year and spent the summers with our family.

When college loomed on the horizon, we campaigned for a Chicago area school and Jolene chose DePaul University. She stayed in Chicago after college. By day, she is a marketing manager for a hospital consortium and on the weekends, she is a docent at the zoo.

I wondered what she had heard through the grapevine. Jolene had kept the family informed with some inside info a year ago when one of the gorillas gained fame by rescuing a toddler who had fallen into the exhibit. We knew more than the general public. One of the unadvertised perks of volunteerism. I dialed her number, heard her machine pick up, then said, "Hi, sweetie. It's Aunt Grace. I heard a bizarre story about happenings at the zoo. I'm being nosy. Please call. Bye."

The turnoff to Pine Marsh was fifty yards ahead. The only automobile entrance to the complex spanned a single lane bridge. The developers never intended it to be used for high traffic since only six families lived here. There was access to the golf course from the west side close to Route 30. Our homes were not built on the course so most people didn't know we were out here. I pressed the remote and parked my Jeep next to my husband's coveted Jaguar. My personal belief is that a vehicle gets you from point A to point B, has room to carry garage sale treasures and necessary groceries. Harry Marsden would argue the importance of the absolute right vehicle in a person's life. A guy thing, no doubt.

"Darling, over here." I turned toward Harry's voice. He was where I expected him to be in his spare time, the garden. I walked toward him, my eyes absorbing the pleasant picture of my English husband standing amongst his flowers. He stood with his hands on his hips, one hand holding his heavy rubber gloves and pruning shears, the other clasping his garden fedora.

Harry's blond hair reflected streaks of platinum from a recent vacation spent sailing and water skiing. His cornflower blue eyes sparkled as he watched my approach. A spreading smile filled his handsome face and I felt a catch in my throat as I reached his side. He kept his hands on his hips and leaned forward slightly to kiss me. I stepped into the kiss and slipped my arms around his neck.

"*Mmm*," I murmured as our lips parted. I could smell sweat, earth, and peat moss as I lingered close to his body.

"Watch it, love. I'm all dirty," he cautioned as he stepped back from me. "I've been at this for the better part of the afternoon. I saw your note. Must have just missed you. How did it go?"

His voice was cautious with a hint of concern. Harry more than anyone knew how awful I felt about losing Karen's friendship.

"Great. It went great. Let me get us some iced tea and I'll fill you in."

"I like the way you think, but you'll have to forego the tea. I drained the last drop an hour ago. This is thirsty work. I did have the good sense to put some wine to chill." His smile beamed at his domesticity. "Oh, and I bought some of the crusty sourdough bread you like."

"It sounds to me like we're on our way to a cheese and wine interlude. I remember seeing a quarter wheel of Brie and a small chunk of Gouda in the fridge. Why don't you clean up and I'll put together a snack. I'll fill you in then."

"I need to collect my tools and such, but I'll be in shortly."

Actually, it would take Harry longer than *shortly* to put up all of his gardening paraphernalia. He was meticulous about cleaning up and returning each item to the proper hook in the garden shed. On the rare occasion when I gardened, I gathered up everything in the wheelbarrow with the intention of hanging it up. All those pegs were intimidating. Worse than not putting them up on the wall, was putting them all back in the wrong places. I knew Harry would be cleaning and sorting and hanging tools for a while. I reasoned I had enough time to look through the mail. The stack was small, but held two interesting looking envelopes.

One envelope had swirls of black in a zebra pattern on the bottom front and back flap. The zebra theme carried on with the panel invitation enclosed. *The Chicago Zoological Society Invites You to the Seventh Annual "Whirl."* I could see Karen's hand in this. She had mentioned how much fun these *Whirl*s were and how much money they collected for important zoo issues. The dinner dance would be held in Zone Africa, the zoo's newest exhibit. I checked the calendar. Three weeks from tonight and we had the date open.

I heard Harry call from the back stairs. "Darling, we still have some of the dill chicken left in the fridge. Put that out, too. Oh, and get those fancy Greek olives Hannah gave us. You might slice up some of those sun-dried tomatoes too. Chop up some parsley for the olives and tomatoes. Don't forget, use the ones closest to the door."

His last comment was to remind me which herbs planted in a huge stone sarcophagus outside the kitchen door to use. The structure was unearthed in the graveyard of one of the many country churches dotting the English countryside. Hannah had heard about the treasure and had called to see if her brother wanted it. No one was certain if it had ever been occupied or if the former tenant had been rudely evicted. Hannah's office-mate's sister worked for a company tha shipped farm equipment overseas and she arranged for our *planter* t be shipped in a container.

The reason for the reminder was that Harry was writing a boo on poisonous plants that mimic benign ones. He used th sarcophagus to plant his poison and non-poison plants close enoug to study and photograph but far enough apart to avoid misuse. H thought using the stone coffin was appropriate in some macabre way I had encouraged him to start writing about his passion, gardening. didn't realize he had such interest in the *dark* side of flora.

Our wine and cheese snack blossomed into a light buffe Harry's favorite food style. He was the consummate snacker. H could survive on cheese, olives, caviar, and tins of crackers. He neve gained an ounce of fat, but he never ate a balanced meal. Our earl years of dinners together had been disastrous. I would cook as m mother had, for lots of hungry men, four brothers, and dad. Harr picked and pushed at all my *meat and potatoes* meals before I caugh on. I began to concoct unusual salads filled with hearts of palm pickled baby corn, bits of fruit and cheese and pared the meat down t a tidbit. My new style of cooking was an instant success with Harry My parents and brothers thought I was starving him, but each sister in-law grew envious of our picnic style dinners. Harry adore leftovers. He claims chicken and pasta and some salads aren't tast till the second go-around. The Morelli men, on the other hand, abho leftovers.

The joke in our family, when I was growing up was if one of m brothers worked late and had to have his dinner re-heated, he wa eating leftovers. I thought one of my marriage vows pertained t keeping my mate well nourished. I was prepared to follow my mom example: love, honor, and overfeed.

"*Mmm*, looks wonderful. I'm famished," he said as he snatche an olive. Harry picked up the invitation. "This is that event Karen always going on about, isn't it? Looks like fun. Are we going?"

"We have the date open. I'd like to go. Especially since I'm sur the main topic will be the skeleton the zoo raised from Iroquoi Lake." I dropped my little bombshell and enjoyed Harry's reaction A momentary pause in munching and an arched eyebrow betrayed m husband's interest.

"Really? Do tell." He smiled conspiratorially as he poured two glasses of what Harry calls *an especially pouty Riesling* and motioned me over to the window seat. Food forgotten momentarily, I chatted easily about my conversation with Karen. Instinct told me to avoid any mention of Ric Kramer. I hoped that omission wouldn't backfire on me.

I was cleaning up in the kitchen when I remembered the other interesting envelope in the mail. I retrieved the rose colored packet from the counter and opened the length of the heavy stock paper. There was something familiar about the stationery, but I couldn't place it. I read the first few lines. My fingers turned numb and the pages slipped from my hands to the floor. I felt weak. My full weight sagged against the counter and I took several deep breaths. "Harry," I called.

He was on his way back into the kitchen when he heard the quiet summons. His step quickened as he saw my condition. "Grace, what is it? What's wrong?" His eyes searched my face for an answer. I pointed to the floor, at the scattered pages. "What is it?" he repeated.

"She wrote to me…from Hell." I scarcely breathed as I answered. I would have slumped to the tile if not for Harry's quick response and strong arms. He guided me into the living room and settled me on the love seat nearest the fireplace. He had started a fire while I had cleared our dinner things. It blazed steadily now casting a soft glow and warmth from its interior.

He put a gentle hand on my shoulder. "You rest here. I'll make us some tea. I'll be back in two shakes." Tea was Harry's answer to most situations, problems, calamities, etc. Moreover, it would take only *two shakes*. His pride and joy was a chrome electric kettle that heated the water to scalding in no time. I heard him gathering the tea things and within seconds, the kettle whistled its early warning.

The whistle is louder, angry, demanding. *Why doesn't Harry turn off the kettle?* It's not a whistle; it's a howl. A human screech, louder, fierce; the horrible sound fills my head. I clap my hands to my ears to block the screaming.

"Here we are, two shakes. Darling, what's wrong?" Harry

quickly set down the tray causing the china to clink and rattle. He knelt beside me and gently pulled my hands from my ears. "Gracie, look at me," he murmured. The wraith-like sound ceased. Harry's soothing voice and gentle touch had broken its hold. "It's all right," he said while stroking the side of my face with his fingers.

"It was horrible," I stammered. "It was *her,* screaming at me from Hell." Harry moved up to sit next to me. He put his arms around me as I fought a shiver.

"*Shh*, Gracie. *Shh*." He tightened his arms around me and guided my head against his chest. "You've had a nasty shock, Darling. There's nothing here." He freed one of his arms and reached over to pour a cup of tea. The strong cinnamon scent reached my nostrils as soon as the hot liquid flowed from the spout. It was one of my favorite tea flavors. I straightened up on the couch as Harry carefully passed the cup and saucer to me. I leaned back against Harry's arm. It felt reassuring.

"There now. Have your tea and you'll start up right as rain." The concern in his face gave way to a smile.

"Thank you." I lifted my cup from the saucer in a tiny salute to him. Between my husband's English penchant for prescribing hot tea for any emergency and his equally English colloquialisms, I felt I would soon *start up as right as rain.* I sipped my tea, savoring the spicy taste. My mind forced itself back to the letter that had shattered the happy event of my reunion with Karen. The timing of receiving a letter from Sheila Walsh on the same day I reconciled with her niece was eerie. If was as if an occult hand had held the letter until my reconciliation with Karen could give me the strength to handle it.

I placed my teacup on the table and pulled a length of blue yarn from my pocket to start an intricate weave. My thoughts wandered back five months to the events responsible for the rift between Karen and me. Our lives had taken a collision course the day a skeleton was discovered in the walls of the old fireplace at Regina College. During the weeks following the discovery, I became obsessed in pursuing the identity of the skeleton for personal reasons. Karen's brother, Ric Kramer, was brought into the web when someone tried to run me off the road. He was a police inspector and the one man I needed to keep out of my life.

The tortured lengths people would go to in order to hide the truth became fatally apparent the night I followed a hunch and entered the tunnels beneath Regina College. I learned the identity of a murderer and the secret a twisted mind had hidden for fifty years. Karen lost part of her life that night. She blamed me because I wouldn't let go.

At the funeral she received Harry's words of condolence with a weak smile, but when I leaned closer to speak to her, she grabbed my wrist with one hand and waved her other hand toward the ground. Her finger outstretched and pointed downwards, she whispered in a hoarse voice, "You did this. You put them there and I'll never forgive you." Her fingers cinched my wrist like a vise. I could feel her nails piercing the soft skin.

Harry had walked away to give us some privacy. He never saw or heard the exchange. Minutes seemed to pass; it was only seconds. My voice caught in my throat at the wild hatred in her eyes. Then, Hannah stepped close to Karen putting one arm around her shoulders. She gently put her hand over Karen's and slowly pulled her away. "C'mon Karen, let's go," she murmured soothingly to my lost friend and led her away to their car.

That was the last conversation I had with my best friend, until today when we were able to put that shocking and tragic time behind us. Both Harry and his sister had told me that in time Karen would accept the truth and understand that what had happened had been inevitable. Unfortunately, I was the one who'd stumbled onto the key to the murders. It was easy to blame me. Karen was a strong person with a genuine respect for the truth and I had been hoping Harry and Hannah were right in their assessment of her healing ability.

A shift in weight on the couch made me realize Harry had positioned himself closer to the reading lamp. His hand held the two sheets. I shivered looking at them. I picked up the cup and saucer and took a bigger sip of tea. My hair slipped forward across the sides of my face. I stopped my hand from the automatic response of pushing the errant strands back behind my ears. It seemed silly, but I felt more protected with my heavy hair screening my face from the words to come. I focused my eyes on the teacup in front of me. Tiny sprigs of violets on a cream background decorated the dainty cup. The set had belonged to my Aunt Cecilia. One of the nuns at Regina

College had been using the china set all the years since my aunt's disappearance, never knowing the gruesome details of how the lovely treasure came to be left behind.

"Go ahead," I said. Harry had been waiting for my signal. He started speaking; his familiar voice comforted though I knew his words would not.

Chapter Three

My Dear Grace,

As the cliché goes, if you're reading this I must be dead. Actually, I hope you're dead too. I took the precaution or had the foresight to write this letter in the event my attempts to kill you failed. I wanted you to know why I hated you. You've been nothing but trouble, whining and sniveling about your aunt. Your aunt was a tramp, like you.

My startled gasp and the rattle of china stopped Harry for a moment. He reached over, took the cup and saucer out of my hands, and placed his hand over mine. He continued in a smooth tone.

She wasn't the 'good girl,' 'sweet girl' all the nuns raved about. She was sleeping with my Tommy, the whole time pretending to be my best friend. Everyone knew I loved Tommy. After he dated my older sister Elizabeth and slept with her, I knew I'd be next. Then your aunt came to spend two weeks in the summer, she met Tommy and interfered with his love for me. After all, he was only human and there she was throwing herself at him. She used the oldest trick in the book to get him to marry her; got herself pregnant. He didn't love her. Tommy wasn't going to marry her. He was pretending to be in love with her so he could 'screw her silly' every weekend; he was pretending to be in love with a judge's daughter

*so he could get a good job. Once he had that job
and could provide for a wife, I knew he would have
found a way to marry me. He always loved me.
Your aunt spoiled everything. She made him crazy.
He ran off to war, to avoid trouble about her.*

*At last, after the war, everything was perfect
because Tommy realized how much he loved me.
My father gave him a good job in his law firm and
we were married. The only flaw was we could never
have children. That changed when my sister
Elizabeth died. Now indeed my life was complete
raising the daughter I should have had. Then, my
precious Karen met you. You practically kidnapped
her. She ran off to your house every chance she had
to be with your wild family.*

I stopped listening as I thought of that time in Karen's life.
"That was such an awful period in her life. It happened about two
months before we started our freshman year. She was so lost, so sad
after her mom's death. On the first day of school, we had three
classes together. We clicked. It was a few days before she told me
about her mother's death. You know my family. We opened our
hearts and home to her."

"You mean it's not only displaced Englishmen you take in?"

"One so far; we've decided to keep him. We also had decided to
keep Karen. She spent hours at my house, learning my brothers
quirks and meeting all the cousins at family gatherings."

"Oh, no. All the cousins?" Harry asked, feigning horror with a
dramatic hand to his brow. "Cousin Angelo, I-know-a-guy-who-can-
get-it-for-cheaper?" I nodded my head. "Cousin Dominic, you-can-
buy-better-but-you-can't-pay-more?" Harry continued. "Cousin
Claudia, make-him-a-plate-he-looks-hungry, the cousin married to the
fellow with a fifty-two inch waist?"

"Okay, okay. Stop. She didn't see them often. One of my
brothers, Glen, I think, usually ran interference for her. He took to
her. One weekend, after I yelled at him for scratching the side of my

car with his bike, he campaigned for a trade. He had Marty in his corner 'cause I think I yelled at him too. The point is we gave her mega doses of support, love, and pasta. I know we helped her."

"You did, darling. Anyone in her right mind would agree. But we're not dealing with that person here." Harry tapped the pages with his forefinger. I tucked the memory back where it belonged and motioned at him to continue.

> *I couldn't believe my ears the day your mother called to invite Tommy and me to your home for Thanksgiving! Karen chose to celebrate a family holiday with your rabble, rather than flying to Palm Springs with us. Ric spent the holiday with us, as Karen should have done. Ric hadn't succumbed to your shameless brand of coercion. That didn't happen until your husband turned up missing in South America. There you were whining and sniveling. Ric tried to help you and you seduced him.*

This time Harry's voice sounded strained, as he no doubt remembered how his young wife had turned to another man. His voice resumed its normal tone.

> *Did you think you could move into my circles and bring your 'greaseballs' with you? Oh, but weren't you surprised when your husband turned out to be alive. You tossed Ric aside like he was trash. Your kind of evil was just getting started. You turned your eye to Karen and offered her to your lesbian bitch of a sister-in-law.*

"This is drivel. This woman was a lunatic!" Harry tossed the pages on the couch between us. He stood up and walked across the room to the bar cart. He lifted a square, crystal decanter and pulled off the stopper. Amber liquid sloshed around the bottom of a matching crystal rocks glass. He stared down at the whiskey watching the patterns as he swirled the liquid in the glass. "I'm sorry love. Why are we doing this to ourselves? We saw Richard's 'if I'm dead, you must be watching this video' confession. Now we have his delusional wife's version. This is crazy."

"We're doing this because we have to and because this letter doesn't sound like a confession, anything but." I picked up the page and read aloud.

> *Karen was normal until she met Hannah Marsden. There had been some ridiculous rumors about Karen, but she was a normal woman. She was my own flesh and blood. You enjoyed watching Karen become 'sick.' She was confused about life and her role as a woman. She didn't have a man in her life because she was always involved in your life, your problems, and your crude family. She couldn't help herself when that evil woman lured her into that disgusting lifestyle. I blame you for her corruption.*

"Corruption?" I interrupted myself. "Karen has never been happier since she met Hannah." My mind pulled another memory from its spot on the shelf. When Harry was rescued and returned home, his twin Hannah came from England to help with his recovery. In the weeks Hannah was here, she and Karen developed a strong friendship, which eventually flourished into love. I was preoccupied with nursing Harry, but not so much that I didn't notice the change in my friend. She grew more animated and excited about everything she did. Her family noticed the change too, but they wouldn't accept the reason.

"Grace, are you all right?" Harry's quiet voice questioned my silence. I smiled at him and continued.

> *And then you found the skeleton, a bitch who got her 'just desserts.'*
>
> *You had to involve Ric again, trying to lure him back to you. Karen told me how you specifically asked*

*for him. Ric thought he was still in love with you.
He never said it, but I could see it in his eyes when
he talked about you; it was like before. You were
going to destroy him this time. He needed a woman
like me in his life. You certainly weren't right for
him. I knew you were trying to embroil him in your
life. I thought I could frighten you off. You kept
pulling him in, inch by inch like a prize Marlin.
When you actually found those trunks, I knew I had
to stop you. I called a friend, someone who hated
your husband as much as I hated you.*

My fingers tightened on the parchment.

*As I said in my opening line, if this was mailed to
you per my instructions to an attorney, my attempts
have failed. Now it's his turn to try.
Rot in hell, my dear!*

The letter was signed with a flourish, Mrs. Thomason Richard
Walsh. I slumped back against the soft cushion, reeling from the
overwhelming hatred I had read. I started to crumple the sheets in my
hands.

"Grace, no!" He reached my side in three strides and gingerly
lifted the pages from my hands. He held them carefully by the
corners. "We've been fools. As soon as we saw the contents we
should have stopped touching them and brought them to the police. I
don't know where my mind was."

It was my turn to look at my husband as though he was crazy.
"What are you talking about? We know who wrote the letter. She
signed it. She was nuts."

"Yes, we know who wrote it, but who mailed it?"

"She said some attorney, what difference does…"

"What if it wasn't an attorney?" Harry interrupted. "What if it
was the other person she mentions? The person who hates me as
much as she hated you?"

The logic and irony of Harry's point finally hit home. "Derek

Rhodes," I said softly.

Chapter Four

The name loomed between us, conjuring memories from both our subconscious minds. Derek had been kidnapped with Harry seven years ago. I had turned to Karen's uncle, Richard Walsh, for help. He was a retired judge with connections in many areas of law enforcement. I needed those connections to secure Harry's release. I had no idea Derek was with Harry; the information on Harry's whereabouts was sketchy, garnered through Ric's help from an Army buddy who was with the FBI and who owed Ric. So, Harry's release had been arranged, but not Derek's. It wasn't until Harry recovered enough to ask about Derek that we realized the truth. The process began again, but it was more difficult a second time, taking six months to gain Derek's freedom.

"I know Derek blames you for leaving him behind," I started cautiously, "but you told me you were unconscious when they carried you out. I still don't…

Harry's heavy sigh interrupted me. He leaned his head back and stared up at the ceiling as though playing back a film in his head. "A guard slipped a sedative in my food the night they came for me. I didn't know the plan. I was barely conscious. Derek demanded they take him too. I tried to nod my agreement, but my head felt like lead. The last thing I remembered was one of the guards slamming Derek in the face with the butt of his rifle to silence him. Apparently, they were being paid to deliver *one* dead Englishman. There was no money for two.

"Exactly what I mean," I began again. "You told Derek what happened when you met the plane that brought him home."

"What I told him in the light of day isn't what he believed each night as he lay alone in filth and despair. We waited at first, expecting the good guys to liberate us. One month led to two, to three. We started to think that maybe the people who'd sent us into that hell thought it would be politically incorrect to come after us. When we realized no one was coming for us, both of us sank into a morass of despair. After five months, we lost hope. Each of us developed our own way of coping." Harry's eyes closed as he tilted his head back against the firm cushion. He seemed again to be watching film in his head. I watched as he made slow, small circles on the fabric with the tips of his fingers. He didn't seem aware of the motion or me. I could only imagine from what he had told me of that horror which parts he was replaying in his head.

"Do you have to stare at the wall all day?" Derek snarled. "All you ever do is stare at the god-damn wall."

"There's more there than the wall," Harry said. "Through the bricks and the grime I see Gracie. She's there, on the other side. know she's waiting for me."

Derek smacked the wall hard with the flat of his palm. A fine dust drifted toward the floor. "You're loony. There's nothing here but this stinking prison. There's no Grace. There's no hope."

Harry replied the only way he could. "You're wrong, Derek. see her clearly; her gentle smile. The way she…"

Derek kicked the dark stone with his scuffed boot. "You're an idiot," he muttered. He crossed the cell and began running through the routine he repeated ten times a day…when he wasn't in the room with *them*. Starting first with stretches, he flexed his limber body bending impossibly head to knee to ground. Then, reaching high to the window bar above his head, Derek performed a set of thirty pull ups. With an incredible display of arm strength, he maneuvered his body through each repetition so it never once touched the wall. He immediately threw himself at the floor and performed one hundred two-handed push-ups. Turning over he wedged his toes into a crack on the brick wall and did two hundred sit-ups.

Not long after Derek finished his regimen the inquisitors arrived for *their* daily session. Harry was always first. They led him out of the cell, down the long dirty corridor to a dingy, windowless room. In the classic tradition a single light bulb dangled from a frayed cord in the center of the room, hanging above a battered straight-backed wooden chair.

There were two of them, Andres, the one in charge, a skinny man with wire-rimmed glasses and a kindly face; the other, Martin, his physical tormentor, a bull with sneaky eyes who pleasured himself with Harry's pain. Andres self-styled himself as the savior and Harry came to see him that way. When the pain threatened to overwhelm him, Andres would stay Martin's ministrations to comfort Harry. He stroked Harry's face, whispering in his accented English, "Everything will be okay. I will deliver you from this. Tell me what Martin asks of you. Tell it all and the pain will disappear."

Harry couldn't or wouldn't tell. The bruises on his body multiplied under Martin's skillful touch. Harry could only stop himself from screaming by pushing down hard with the tips of his fingers on the solid wood of the chair he was strapped into.

He pushed now against the sofa's plush fabric. Was it soft to his touch or was he still in that hell hole?

Harry sat rigidly on the couch; his eyes flew open. I saw a flash of shame and bewilderment. His face was tense; his breath came in jagged streams.

"Harry, you're safe." I picked up his hand; it was cold. I brought it up to my lips and gently kissed each fingertip. I had seen Harry this way before. "Don't think about it, darling."

Harry's breathing slowed and he placed his other hand over mine, now enclosing mine in both of his. "I kept my sanity by concentrating on your beautiful eyes, wondering if they were purple because you were afraid, on your serious smile, and on the way you tuck your hair behind your ears when too much escapes a headband or clip." He stopped his narrative and leaned forward to guide an errant strand behind my left ear. "I kept my mind here with you and let them have a go at what was there. With Derek, it was different. He was younger, stronger. He fought back with his body, considered the torture a contest, a battle of wills. He survived the physical abuse better than I ever could. Poor bastard. He couldn't keep his mind safe. After I was gone, I can only imagine his horrible reality."

Harry's voice was barely a whisper. I hated to see him relive the pain and despair, remembering how battered he was when rescued. I couldn't imagine how he had survived. The doctors had said there would be permanent damage, a slight limp, and a weakened left arm. Harry's mind had survived the nightmares and dayscapes (moments during waking hours that border on hallucination) that had plagued him. In time those ceased.

Derek's case had been the exact opposite. His body had withstood the abuse in remarkable condition. I remembered how he nearly jogged down the steps from the airplane. I was amazed at his comparative robust figure. Harry stilled used a cane when he met him at the airport. He was pleased to see Derek in such good shape. Harry held out his hand to Derek as he reached the bottom step. Derek looked at the hand leaning on the cane, the other one outstretched to him and took the hand but dropped his hold immediately, as though the touch burned.

It wasn't until later that we started to hear the reports of his odd behavior. His wife, Julia was worried because she suspected Derek wasn't taking the medication the doctors had prescribed to even out his mood swings. She tearfully told us Derek's rage was out of control and the event responsible for her leaving him happened a week earlier. What had started as a tickling contest between Derek and his eight-year-old had escalated to some cruel rite of passage; Derek's tickles turned to mean pinches, making their son cry in pain. Derek taunted his son to *be strong, toughen up, because you can't count on anyone but yourself.* The little boy's howls had seemed to fuel the fire burning inside Derek.

Thoughts swirled in my head about how fragile each of us were and about how many times each day did we choose a word or a thought and inevitably an action which led us closer to or farther from our personal breaking point.

"We have to call the police." Harry's voice interrupted my grim memories. "If this letter is referring to Derek then you're still in danger."

"The letter is dated four months ago. How do we know what she said is true? Nothing else is. If it is Derek, what's he been waiting for all these months?"

"I don't know and I don't care. I'm not taking chances with your life." Harry was firm on that point. His only hesitation was that he'd have to call the one man he never wanted to see again. I knew that inviting Ric Kramer into our lives, under any guise, would put a strain on us.

"We'll call in the police, but it doesn't have to be Ric."

"Yes it does. He knows more about this case than anyone else does. He's even met Derek. I want you safe and he's the best I've met. Kramer is my ace-in-the-hole where you're concerned. He wants you safe too."

Harry's face was in the shadows thrown from the torchiere style lamp next to the couch. I couldn't see his eyes, couldn't read their expression. He crossed the room to the small Queen Anne style desk and lifted the receiver. Harry turned to face me with his hand poised over the dial. I repeated the number with no hesitation, the curse of a photographic memory. I turned my profile to him to hide a rush a color to my face. The length of cord I had left on the table earlier in the day leaped into my hands as I did the obsessive-compulsive drill of ten finger twists before I could face forward again. Harry waited for the call to ring through. I heard his fingers drum a staccato rhythm on the desktop.

"Hullo, Kramer. Harry Marsden. Something has come up concerning your aunt. I thought you'd best know about it. Apparently, she's posted a letter to Grace."

Harry stayed quiet during Ric's response.

"No, I don't suppose it can wait. Grace's life may be in danger." Silence from Harry. "Fine, an hour is fine." Harry replaced the receiver and looked up at me. "He's canceling dinner plans and coming right out. I knew he would." Now I could see the expression in Harry's eyes; I felt the strain.

The phone rang and startled both of us. I hoped it was Ric calling back to cancel his hastily made appointment. Harry's voice sounded cheery. He held the phone out to me as he identified the caller.

"It's for you, 'Aunt Gem,' Jolene returning your call." Harry smiled at my niece's nickname for me. My brothers used the initials from Grace Eileen Morelli, to fashion the name and it had stuck.

I had forgotten about the call I made to my niece earlier. My reason seemed unimportant now. I shook off the gloom, accepted the phone, and smiled. "Hi, sweetie. Thanks for calling back."

"I just walked in. Boy, it doesn't take you long," laughed Jolene. "Not even all the docents know about it. They're trying to keep the lid on this one. We've been told to say *vee know nothhink.*"

I laughed at her impression of Sergeant Schultz. "I happen to know a trustee," I explained. "Anyway, what's the buzz in the docent corps?"

"Slim pickings. Honestly, no one is talking. There were more loose lips when Binti Jua rescued that little boy in Tropic Sphere. I can't tell you how many times I've been asked to point out Binti to her admiring fans. A few people wanted to see the spot where the little boy fell, but most everyone wanted to see *super mom*. That was fun. This is…"

"Bizarre?" I offered.

"Yes, bizarre. Exactly. Anyway, how would you like to see where it all happened? My duty day is tomorrow. Meet me at two o'clock at the South Gate and I'll take you on a tour."

"Sure, sounds like fun. I haven't been to the zoo in years. Oh, that reminds me. We were invited to the *Whirl*. Karen always raves about it. Is it a bore?"

"Absolutely not, Aunt Gem. The *Whirl* is elegant and very *who's who*. It's loads of fun; at least everyone seems to have a good time. Docents, of course, don't attend as guests. We volunteer to work in the exhibits answering questions or staffing the touch carts. Some docents sell raffle tickets at the affair. I hope you come, I'm selling raffle tickets."

I heard *cha ching* as the cash register rang up a sale in her mind as she computed how many tickets Harry would buy. There was probably a prize for top sales; my niece had always been carrot motivated. Through the years, she sold Girl Scout Cookies, wrapping paper, Christmas cards, popcorn, magazine subscriptions, seasonal door wreaths, cookie dough, and pledges for hopping, walking running, biking and roller-blading for various charities and causes. We bought it all.

"You'll have fun if you come," she finished.

"I'm not sure if we're free," I hedged, "but I know I'll be there tomorrow. Where shall I meet you?"

"When you come in the South Gate, the docent office is to your right. It's the middle door between the restrooms. Go up the stairs and the office is on the left."

"It's a date. See you tomorrow."

"Sure thing, Aunt Gem. Bye-bye."

I always felt better after talking to one of the kids in my family. They were all interesting in their own ways. Their friends were good kids too. It had been my experience that older generations took desperate measures to hide their indiscretions and peccadilloes. There wasn't too much being swept under the carpet in the nineties. If it did get out, you took the heat and then wrote a book and ended up on Sixty Minutes or Oprah. How desperate had Sheila Walsh been to try to reach me from beyond the grave? Was Derek desperate to have his revenge?

I cleared the remains of our hurried dinner while Harry placed a few calls to friends who might know of Derek's whereabouts. The people he wanted to talk to were in London, but they would hardly appreciate a call at three o'clock in the morning. Two of his long time London chums lived in the states now. I wished Harry would hurry with those calls. I wanted to tell him about Ric showing up at The Braxton. Harry walked into the kitchen looking puzzled.

"What's wrong?"

"I'm not sure anything is wrong. I rang up Roger. Joanna said he'd left for London on Wednesday, and when I talked to John's son, he said his dad had been in London since last week. It seems odd."

"It wouldn't be odd if they're still working for the House. Are they still involved?" My question hung between us, unanswered for the moment. Harry, Roger Neal, John Bynford, Derek Rhodes, and many other talented Englishmen had all worked in London for the largest government-publishing house in England. They were all experienced and extraordinarily talented researchers, editors, marketing directors, and publishers. As it turned out, at least two of them, Harry and Derek, had used their extraordinary talents for the British government in other ways. Harry still insisted not everyone who worked there also worked for British Intelligence, but I had my doubts. The House provided excellent subterfuge for training and coordinating movements and events. I hadn't known of Harry's involvement when I married him. He had technically retired from active duty shortly after our wedding. We honeymooned in England and Harry spent, what I thought under the circumstances, an excessive amount of time tying up loose ends. Several months later Harry's replacement was injured in a car accident. Harry was the only other agent that had any training on this particular mission. They had to go now or waste two years of preparation. There was no one else to step in and it had to be a two-person drill. It would have been too risky for one person. The assignment that landed him and Derek in a South American prison and nearly cost him his life had been acknowledged and guaranteed as his last.

"Do you think they're still involved?" I asked again.

"Darling, don't ask me questions, I can't answer," was Harry's response. His loyalty to *those* people, who I believed, left him to rot infuriated me. I was about to tell him so when the doorbell rang and stopped our conversation.

Harry opened the door to admit Ric Kramer. The sight of the two of them standing side by side sent shivers rolling the length of my spine. They played a perfect point and counterpoint to each other. Ric stood taller at six feet, four inches to Harry's six-foot height. They both possessed trim physiques. Ric's would be described as more muscular; Harry's as more compact. Harry's sandy blond hair and gray blue eyes contrasted sharply with Ric's dark brown hair and deep brown eyes. Ric was *drop dead* gorgeous, especially now with streaks of gray settled at his temples. Harry was a sophisticated handsome, the Roger Moore type, my friends always said.

"Hullo, Kramer. Thanks for coming so quickly." He motioned him toward the center of the room.

"I'm a little surprised you want me here," Ric said. "I'm more curious about this letter."

"Let's be clear on one thing, Kramer. I called you because you're involved in this to a point and because you are extremely good at what you do. Don't think for a moment you'd be standing here if there were anyone else with those qualifications. Are we clear?"

"Absolutely," Ric assured him with offhanded carelessness. He reached the couch and I stood up. "Hello, Grace. I don't see you for months and then twice in one day." Ric unleashed his dazzling smile.

Dammit! I didn't tell Harry about Ric's appearance at Braxton's. Now he'll think I'm keeping secrets...again. Ric stood smiling while Harry's face wore a puzzled look.

"Some things can't be helped," I responded with more than a touch of coolness.

"Yes, things happen; usually for a reason. Let me see this letter and we'll make this as brief as possible. Can I trouble you for a drink?"

"Yes, of course." I walked to the bar cart and began to automatically lift the bottle I knew he drank. I forced myself to stop the intimate gesture and turned to ask him what he'd like.

"Oh, come now, Gracie," interrupted Harry. "Even I know he's a Bourbon and water man. Pour the drink, darling. He's the only one who enjoys the stuff; the bottle's been here for years." Harry's sarcasm wasn't lost on the room. Ric's shoulders stiffened. I handed him the glass and freshened my own drink. Harry had poured himself another right before Ric's arrival.

Harry and I sat on the couch, leaving Ric the choice of a wing back chair or the love seat. He chose the chair and carefully spread out the two pages from the folder across the coffee table. The silence while Ric read the letter weighed down on me.

I kept wishing he wasn't sitting across from me, no matter how involved he was or how well he did his job. Harry seemed calm; inflappable English genes no doubt. Ric glanced up at me at one point during the reading, somewhere on the second page. His glance held my eyes for the briefest moment, but I couldn't read the darkness in those depths. He sat back against the deep cushion and stared down at the sheets of pink contrasting against the gleaming mahogany of the table.

"I've seen enough of my aunt's writing to know this is legit. Moreover, I think we all heard enough of my uncle's confession to know she was crazy, *mean* crazy. I believe she hired someone. From her words, my guess is Derek Rhodes. I'm sure you thought of him, too." He ended his sentence looking at Harry.

"Of course we did. She could have paid any number of people to kill Grace. Only Derek would have a personal reason for revenge."

The Lion Tamer: A Caged Death

"No one else could have held a grudge all these years? Maybe someone you brought down, someone recently released from prison or a son, all grown up and ready to fulfill an oath made to a dying father?"

"My God, Kramer, how would I know these things? I've been out of that mix for years."

"Some of the men you tracked went to jail for more than ten years. The ones who made it to trial." The barb was not lost on Harry or me. Ric Kramer took every opportunity to remind me my husband's past crept behind us never more than a shadow away. After I thought Harry had been killed, Ric and I started to share our lives. He repeatedly pointed out how much safer I was with him and how much more normal life with him would be. He arrested people and brought them to trial. Harry was never held to that process or code. It seemed ironic that the threat against me came from, in a sense, Ric's side. I wanted to tell him the only person who ever tried to kill me was his aunt, not some vengeance driven psycho from Harry's past. Harry beat me to it.

"Admit it, Kramer," Harry began, "it's the doings of that crazy bitch. Who knows what ideas she planted in Rhodes' sick mind? Isn't it odd Derek never even surfaced near us until *Auntie Dearest* lured him with who knows what twisted bait? We don't need to look any further than your precious family tree." Harry moved toward the coffee table and bent to slide the pages back into the folder.

"Leave those, Marsden. Those pages are evidence in what appears to be part of an earlier crime. I'll take those with me." He put down his drink and took the folder from Harry. "I'll take them to the lab tonight, a few people there owe me a favor. In the meantime I'd contact your rent-a-cops out here and ask for some beefed-up patrols. That sergeant I met, Peterson was his name, seemed better than most. Ric walked to the door during his last statement. Harry opened it and glanced perfunctorily at the densely packed, low growing yews around our front entrance. Ric turned at the threshold. "I'll be in touch, Marsden. Maybe we closed this case too soon," he admitted in a non-committal voice. No handshake passed between them this time. I heard a muffled "Good night, Grace" from behind the closing door.

Harry leaned his back against the door as though to further shut out Ric Kramer. Each time the two men who meant the most to me squared off, we all suffered the consequences. I had made my choice to stay with Harry. I knew at the time the choice meant never seeing Ric again in any way, shape, or form. We both knew. For years, our paths never crossed. Now, in the last five months events caused us to tumble over each other at every turn.

"He'll always be an arrogant SOB, but I know he'll move heaven and earth to keep you safe." Harry put his arm around my shoulders as he spoke. "With this new craziness going on, the last thing we need is a disinterested third party sweeping our paranoia under the carpet. That's why we have to suffer Inspector Kramer."

I turned in his arms and looked up into his face. "I'm exhausted, let's go up."

"You go, darling. It's almost a decent time to call London. I'll be up soon." Harry saw the hesitancy in my face. "I promise, a few quick calls and I'll be right up. Try and stop me," he finished with a grin.

I started up the stairs to our bedroom. Each step filled me with a sense of dread. The ghosts I had laid to rest seemed anxious to accompany me in my thoughts tonight. *Get a grip*, I chided myself. Like my dad always said, "*It's the live ones you have to watch out for.*"

Chapter Five

Those few quick calls lasted half the night. I vaguely remembered tossing and turning for a while and then sleeping fitfully until I felt Harry come to bed. I heard the clock chime three before settling into a deeper sleep curled up in his arms.

It was six-thirty when I carefully slipped out of bed. I needed an eye-opening cup of coffee and a hot shower to soothe my jangled nerves. My head felt stuffed with cotton, as though I hadn't slept at all. I knew I had, but much of it was burdened by snippets of dream filled with harsh voices and shadowy figures. I walked downstairs, careful to hold onto the banister.

Within minutes, I had coffee brewing in my new *Braun* coffeemaker. This machine boasted an internal charcoal filter in the water compartment, which 'cleaned and purified all types of water to insure a delicious cup of coffee each time.' The sales pitch had sounded good to me when I bought it and it lived up to its claim. Everyone, who knows me, knows I am the only one in this family who makes and drinks coffee. Harry is English to his bones and merely tolerates the smell of Columbian or Rain Forest Nut permeating our kitchen. Never mind his Earl Gray or Good Earth Orange Spice can scent heady. A civilized smell he'd tell you.

I'd needed a new coffeemaker because the old one had been rigged to kill me. We assumed it had been someone hired by my new 'pen pal'; someone who did it for money, then disappeared. Now we had to consider someone scarier than a hired assassin. We had to consider a *crazy* with an attitude.

The aroma of Cinnamon Nut Swirl signaled the end of my reverie. I poured a generous amount into a soup-bowl sized mug and carried it upstairs. I settled into the plump pillows on the window

34

eat, one of my favorite spots in the whole house. Bird books, inoculars, sketch pads, pens, charcoals and probably some empty offee cups filled the interior of the seat. My hands found the long ength of cording hooked over a brass knob positioned to hold the eavy drape off the window. My fingers loosened the cord from the nob and I leaned my shoulder against the drape to keep it from liding forward across my view. The cording came to life in my ands as I twisted and knotted one end to the other into an intricate raid. This was my calming pattern since it required total oncentration. I needed to braid ten before I could sit back with my offee. My task completed, I tossed the knotted cord aside and icked up my mug.

The twelve-foot high bay window provided an incredible view f the back forty (as I called it). I had grown up in a house with a big ackyard by city standards, but ranked puny compared to Pine Marsh. he stand of woods separating our property from the Atwater's loomed with tiny white and pink flowers on the dozens of wild rabapple trees. I watched the seasons of my own mini arboretum. rom this vantage point, I could see the small barn that sheltered my ennessee Walker, April Showers. Maybe I'd take her for an early norning ride. She'd like that; so would I. A hard ride always helped ne clear the cobwebs from my brain. I retraced my steps to the itchen and topped off my mug on the way to the mudroom. I kept iding clothes and boots stored in a small locker. The warmth of oose down a fading memory, I quickly dressed and hung my sleep hirt and wrapper on the peg. A worn, black plaid Pendleton wool icket shirt completed my outfit. I glanced at my riding helmet, but ft it on the shelf. After all, I wouldn't be doing anything tricky out nere.

April snorted a friendly greeting before I opened the barn door. could never sneak up on her. I lifted her lead from the peg inside ne doorframe and led her out of her stall. I greeted her with a hug nd the carrot I had taken from the treat larder I kept in the mudroom. he stood quietly while I saddled her. As soon as she felt my weight n the saddle her body quivered with anticipation. I signaled her to egin the smooth gait that sets her breed apart from the rest of orsedom. We left the yard and picked our way across the first bridge leading to the small meadow adjacent to the golf course.

I enjoyed startling golfers as they caught glimpses of us in th narrow band of woods on the east, which separated the course fro the homeowners' properties. There were no foursomes on the tw holes we passed. Only cool, crisp air and early morning bird chatte greeted us on our way. The grassy field beyond the woods was or destination.

April and I had developed a routine where we enjoyed a le stretching walk through the woods, then a glorious gallop across th field until we reached the top of the knoll. From there, th undeveloped marsh, protected by federal law, was in full view; it's good place to think and sort out life. It's where I came when my brai overloaded. A letter from a dead woman could certainly contribute t frazzled feelings.

We were riding into the sun and the warmth felt pleasant on m face. We reached the top, slowed to a walk, and stopped to take i the view. The magic of an early morning ride was already casting it spell of peacefulness and well-being. I inhaled deeply and exhale slowly, enjoying the therapeutic effect the cold air had on my bod and brain. I turned in the saddle to view the field behind me.

A flash of light sparked from the woods. It looked like reflection from the sun bouncing off glass or something shiny. covey of mourning doves burst into the air and scattered in flight. looked away to focus my eyes. When I looked back the light wa gone; perhaps a duffer searching the rough for an errant driv disturbing the doves, the sun catching the clubs. Maybe Barba Atwater, my neighbor and a devoted bird watcher, focused on sighting. Or maybe our newest neighbor, L.L. DeFreest, shootin nature. She was a well-known nature photographer, with sever books and a greeting card, writing papers, and calendar line to h credit. Any of those explanations seemed valid and yet I gre restless up there on top of the hill in full view of what? Or whom?

My mounting paranoia spoiled the mood and I turned April fo the trip home. I thought to go back through the woods to search or my distraction. Instead, I flanked the section of woods and skirte around to the ninth hole where golfers and horses shared a trail at th turn. I crossed the cart path and looked up the fairway. There was r one coming from where I estimated the light had appeared. I nudged April into a faster gait, quickly left the course behind, and headed across the small meadow toward home.

I was anxious. No. Spooked was a better word. I wanted to get home to Harry. April sensed my anxiety as I hurried through her brush down, a ritual I normally never rushed. I usually lingered and took special care with her grooming. I did nothing this morning but the basics and April resented the cursory treatment. She tossed her head and snorted her dislike.

"Sorry, girl, I'm not up to this now. I promise you a good brush real soon." She seemed placated. I scratched her nose and produced another treat. The soft, wet snuffle against my palm said we were still friends. I latched her stall and walked up to the house. The uneasy feeling stayed with me.

Chapter Six

Harry opened the back door as my hand reached the knob.
jumped back in fright. "My God, Harry. You scared the pants off o
me."

His face battled back the tug of a smile at my last comment. He
paused a few extra beats before he spoke and remained stone col
serious. "Grace, I was worried; why didn't you wake me? I woul
have gone with you."

"Were you going to trot next to April?" A sigh and letdown i
his shoulders answered my question. "Anyway, I think better whe
I'm with April. I get too distracted when I'm around you." I wrappe
my arms around Harry in a playful bear hug.

"All right, all right, but I am allowed to worry in view of the
circumstances."

"Were you able to find out anything from your calls?" I aske
more seriously.

"No, nothing. No one has heard from him or even hear
anything about him. It's as though he's gone to ground."

I stepped back from Harry and started removing my ridin
boots. "I've been thinking about those circumstances. It would b
like Shelly to arrange to have that horrible letter sent. That doesn
mean Derek was ever involved. She knew how he felt about you;
think her twisted mind wanted the last word."

I washed up in the mudroom and then walked into the kitchen t
prepare breakfast. I pulled out English muffins, marmalade, an
butter from the fridge. Harry stood silent the whole time.

"I've thought of that too darling, but I also remember how yo
were nearly killed. I'm not taking any chances with your life. Unt
Kramer determines the validity of that threat, you're going to have

lot of company in your daily routine."

I knew better than to argue with Harry when he used that tone. He would probably hound my steps for the next few days. Could be nice, I thought as I buttered both sides of the muffin that had popped up during Harry's announcement. "That would be peachy." I smiled sweetly, after taking a bite. "Want a muffin?"

Harry seemed stunned and then suspicious when I didn't argue with him about accepting a *guardian angel* until further notice. I loved throwing him off base every now and then; made for a lasting and interesting relationship. Harry refused the offer of a muffin and retreated upstairs to shower. He glanced back once, still looking puzzled, as though checking to make sure I didn't dash out the back door.

He was probably thinking my acquiescence was much too easy. I stuffed the last bite of muffin into my mouth careful to eat over the sink so I didn't scatter crumbs on the black and white tiled floor. We have a cleaning lady, but old habits of doing it all myself died hard. I dashed up the back stairs two at a time and arrived on the landing a nanosecond after Harry. I waited until I heard the shower running to tip toe into our bedroom. He had made the bed and even put the deco pillows in the right places. God bless a modern man.

Harry's struggling tenor was forced a note higher by an assist from me. "You said I'd have company during my day," I grinned as he put his soapy arms around me.

"I love it when you get with the program." I could tell how happy he was to see me.

I am always amazed at how life's coincidences seem more contrived than bad fiction. After our shower and after I remade the bed, Harry sat down to plan *our* day. I definitely enjoyed the first part of our togetherness, but I knew the rest of his plan was going to wear thin. The coincidence was Harry's appointment with the author of a book of animal photographs. She happened to be our new neighbor.

"Darling, why don't you come along on my appointment? It won't take more than an hour or so. We can stop for lunch on our way in to meet Jolene at the zoo."

"Sure, sounds fine." My immediate agreement caused a raise eyebrow, but no comment. This plan actually worked with m agenda. I could easily find out now if the reflection I spotted th morning came from her camera lens.

"We've a little less than an hour before the appointment. Seem we've puttered away the entire morning. I'm going to put the kettl on, care for tea?" Harry asked as he pulled a teal colored sweater ove his head. He adjusted the collar on his oxford cloth shirt and tugge at the cuffs under the sweater. "You sounded a bit nasal this mornin; I've a new blend Hannah sent from her last trip to Wales. It's just th thing for a head cold."

My English husband thought everything from flu to heartache t boredom to fallen arches could be cured with a cup of hot tea Although in the case of fallen arches, I'm not sure if you were to drin it or soak in it. He consulted a chart taped on the inside lid of his te box to determine which tea or blend remedied which malady. "*Ah, n thanks, darling. I've already taken an *Alka-Seltzer* cold tablet. I'll b fine." I reached up to kiss his cheek. "Thanks."

I was wearing walking shorts again, navy blue with a matchin cardigan. My turtleneck and tights were teal and I realized Harry an I matched. He was wearing navy blue trousers and teal socks. W both made the connection and began laughing while pointing at eac other. "I told you if we ever started wearing matching shirt sweatshirts or wind breakers, I've left instructions with my brother t shoot us." Since I had more outfits than Harry, I quickly changed t an Icelandic design skirt in shades of cream, gray, and tan and a gra woolen vest.

When I entered the kitchen, Harry's tea was already steeped. H had this whole ritual about timing and pouring. I nuked a cup c coffee from the pot I had started earlier. I brought my cup over to th breakfast nook and sat opposite Harry. Our nook consisted of an oa trestle-type table I discovered in a garage in River Forest and tw high-back benches from the vicarage in Arundel. There had been fire in that building in 1893 and Harry's grandfather had taken som of the less damaged furniture as payment for carpentry work he did rebuild the vicarage. We had spent hours refinishing the table, but th benches had already been done by Harry's granddad. We adde added cushions for creature comfort and *voila*, an authentic turn-of-the-century nook. From this vantage point, we could see Harry's rose and herb gardens. I enjoyed watching the birds flock to the Yankee Droll feeder that hangs from a low branch on the birch tree. The squirrels offered the real entertainment. We left cracked corn and cobs on the ground for them.

"So when did you take on this client?" I asked after my first sip.

"Actually, John Holter signed her about six months ago. She was living in New York then and agreed to a three-book deal over the next two years. He thinks her books could be successful. When John realized she had taken up residency a stone's throw from us, he asked if I would meet her and make nice-nice."

My eyebrows arched at the expression. Harry answered my unspoken question. "You know what I mean, darling. Make sure she's adjusting. Introduce her around to a few good sorts. Get her tickets to the Bulls. You know, nice-nice."

I smiled and Harry stopped sputtering. "Let's go Mr. Nice-Nice, or we'll be late."

I put our mugs in the sink and ran water in each. I lifted my jacket and cap from the hall tree. We decided to walk, as her house was only half a mile on foot. We went out through the mudroom and picked up the path that connected all the homes at the back of their properties. It's sort of a common area used for jogging or walking. It's shorter than walking along the front of the properties. The path covered with crushed pecan shells winds through alternate areas of woods and field. The crunching noise our shoes made sounded as crisp as the air felt. The path was wide enough for us to walk side by side. I followed this route more often than Harry did. Our neighbor, Barb Atwater, and I walked these shells three mornings a week. Our route took us through the backside of half the residential areas, across the ninth hole, back up the barrier woods to the fourth hole and finally across once more to the residential side and my backyard. We usually ended our brisk walk on my patio with coffee and any bakery I had handy. Tomorrow I would ask her if she'd been out bird watching this morning. Harry interrupted my thoughts. "You're so quiet. Penny for your thoughts?"

I wanted to tell Harry about the flash I had seen earlier, the feeling I had riding back. In fact, the spot I estimated seeing the flas was directly across the golf course and into the woods from where w were standing now, between the Atwaters and our new neighbor. bad feeling started to take hold of me again.

"You're not upset about that 'nice-nice' crack, are you old girl Harry asked affectionately. I laughed at his concern. "No, of cours not. Would you bring your wife along if you were intending an illic rendezvous?"

"It would be trickier that way," he conceded with a smirk.

"I was thinking about something I saw this morning with Apri It's probably nothing, but I had this feeling."

"Feeling?" Harry's voice and eyebrow lifted in query.

"Yes, a feeling. You know, when you shiver for no reason an someone says someone walked over your grave? That kind c feeling."

"Go on, darling. You said you saw something."

We stopped on the path and I turned toward Harry. He held m hands; we were facing each other as though plighting our troth. opened my mouth and what started as a simple explanation ended i an ear-splitting scream.

Chapter Seven

"Harry!" My scream intruded on the silence like a boom box at a wake. I jerked my hands from Harry's grasp. One pointed trembling at a place behind him while the other covered my mouth holding in another scream and my breakfast. Harry had turned at my first movement, instinctively blocking me with his body. Two crows pecking at the ground had drawn my initial attention to the body sprawled in the undergrowth off the path, not more than five yards away.

He was stretched out on his right side perpendicular to the path, feet toward the shells, head toward the hill. His left arm rested on his side, but his right arm was twisted up holding the top of his left shoulder, like some rigor mortis *Macarena*. He looked as if he might have laid down for a nap or succumbed to a heart attack except the left side of his head was gone. Something had smashed a human face into a grizzly pulp of bloody tissue and shards of bone.

Harry moved back to me to shield my view, but I had already seen what I'd never forget. I felt Harry's body tense and I looked up at him. He stared up the hill. I turned and caught a glimpse of someone running toward the Bishop's house. Harry turned me by the shoulders and pointed me toward the Atwater's property. "Get to Barbara's and call the police. I'll stay here."

"I'm staying with you. What if whoever did this comes back?"

"No one is coming back. Now go on and get to Atwater's house."

I launched another reason why I should stay. The seesaw conversation continued for a minute at most. We heard the distant wail of a siren. My going for the cops seemed a moot issue.

Harry waved both his arms above his head to direct the police back to the body and us. We both recognized Sergeant Peterson. His long stride placed him in front of us a few paces before the other officer with him. I noticed one officer had stayed atop the hill near the Bishop's house. Harry and the sergeant shook hands. "Hello Sergeant. I can't believe I'm seeing you again so soon." Harry's reference prompted Sergeant Peterson to shake his head slowly.

"I can't believe how trouble seems to find your doorstep." He smiled tightly. He nodded his head to me in recognition. "Why don't you both go up to that officer." His arm indicated the policeman standing up at the house line. "You can wait for me there. I'll be up as soon as the lab arrives."

"Sounds good to me. Thank you." Harry took my hand. By the time we reached the house, two more policemen had arrived. They carried cases of equipment. The officer who had stayed behind directed them to the back of the property.

Barbara Atwater covered the last few yards from her house to where we were standing in a fast walk. "What's going on?" she asked. "I heard sirens." She paused to catch her breath. "And then I saw the two of you. Is something wrong?"

I hesitated briefly. "Definitely wrong, Barb. There's a body back in the woods near the path."

"Near the path?" Barbara squeaked the question. Her face showed the concern I was feeling. It was one thing to hear about dead bodies on the news, but quite another to find one practically in your backyard.

"Who is it? I mean, do they know? Is it someone from Pine Marsh?"

"No, no. He's not one of the marshers," Harry assured her. "At least I'm fairly certain he isn't," he added. Barbara fixed him with a questioning look. "What I mean is the cause of death makes identification a little difficult."

"Oh, I see," Barbara said with a sinking voice, and, I suspected a sinking stomach as well.

An unfamiliar voice broke into our conversation. "Why don't all of you come inside? I've put on the kettle and I can offer you tea or coffee." The invitation came from the new owner of the Bishop's house; the person Harry and I saw running out of the woods earlier. That realization made me uneasy. The next one stunned me.

"Lily?" I heard Harry's questioning voice behind me. "I don't believe it," he continued. "Lily, it *is* you."

While an astounded Barbara and I stood by, Harry closed the gap between him and our new neighbor and engulfed her in a huge hug. This wasn't the proprietary, slight embrace you use to be polite. This was the kind reserved for dear friends whom you haven't seen or family members you liked. The *hug*, as it was now labeled in my mind, lasted a *skosh* longer than I thought necessary. At last, he released her to hold her at arm's length.

"I can't believe it. How long has it been? My God, you look fabulous. Where did you disappear to?"

Harry didn't sputter. At least I never heard him; until now.

Lily smiled sweetly. "Harry, you have all of us standing on the porch with all these questions. Please come inside and warm up. We'll have tea, we'll relax, and you will introduce me to these ladies, who, I believe, are also neighbors."

Harry interrupted Lily, embarrassed at his lapse in social graces. "This is Barbara Atwater your immediate neighbor to the south." Barbara preceded me into the great room. Harry's charm was returning. "And this is Grace, my wife. We live next to Barbara." He slipped his arm around my shoulders during the introduction, not as the *little woman* type of explanation, but rather as a visual aid to expressing the *couple* concept. For the briefest moment, I wondered who needed reminding.

Our hostess smiled and encouraged us to pile our jackets on a chair and to sit and relax. She removed her own outerwear to revel a slim body with enough angles to make her the envy of most models. She stood at least several inches taller than my five foot, four inch stature, the illusion of height enhanced by the long, poker straight blond hair that tumbled free from her cap. She tugged a blue scarf from around her slender Hepburn neck. The wheat colored hair blended with her Nordic coloring, pale eyebrows, barely visible lashes, and a complexion of cream sans peaches. Her eyes, the one feature that prevented her from slipping into color obscurity glanced at us now as she asked our beverage preference. They gleamed like two perfect tourmaline jewels in a custom setting. The effect gave sparkle and life to an otherwise technically perfect but boring face.

"I can brew coffee or tea," our hostess was saying. "I'm more of a tea drinker myself, but I do have some French roasted beans or a Colombian blend."

"Tea would be fine for me. Whatever you choose, I'm sure." Harry smiled broadly. Those lovely green eyes now stopped on Barbara. My neighbor is an Anglophile. I'm convinced our friendship is three-quarters common interests and one quarter a specific interest…my husband. I say that in the nicest way. Barb adores *anything* English. She would never drink coffee, how colonial. "Oh, yes. Tea, please," came Barb's nodding assent.

I faced her verdant gaze. "Tea would be lovely." Had Barb and Harry already been sipping their English 'chicken soup', they would have spit tea through their noses. Instead, two pairs of eyes fixed me with a puzzled look our hostess missed. Harry recovered first. "Let me help you with the tea things and we can catch up on the last ten years."

Ten years. Suddenly, I knew why she looked familiar to me. I assumed I had seen her book jacket or her photo in a magazine. My memory re-played the day I met Harry ten years ago and she was there. In fact, she had been Harry's date for the event held at Regina College. At the time, I thought she looked beautiful. Now? Now, I thought I should offer to help in the kitchen. I didn't know beans about tea leaves, but I did know when a woman was interested in my husband. Barb was interested because he was English. Lily was because he was Harry.

When I entered the hall to the kitchen, I could hear Harry and Lily reliving the seventies. "When did Lily Jackson become L.L DeFreest?" Harry asked.

I had moved down the hall and paused in the doorway. I hadn't actually moved into the room but they wouldn't have noticed me anyway. Lily smiled at Harry as she measured loose-leaf tea into the chrome infuser. "I always thought it would be a statement to use only my first name on my photographs. Back in the sixties and seventies everyone was trying to make a statement. Jackson was my married name." Lily hurried to answer the question forming on Harry's face

When you and I met I was already estranged from my husband. Ben and I hadn't been married long and, it hadn't worked out. We were two headstrong kids with opposing dreams. I wanted to travel and photograph wildlife throughout the world. Ben wanted to put down roots and be a master chef in his own 5-star restaurant. 'B' movie stuff at best. I didn't see any reason to mention that part of my life. After the divorce, I reclaimed my maiden name." Lily finished her explanation about the same time she completed her tea preparations.

"Hullo darling," Harry greeted me as I stepped into the room. *Did I see a tiny frown cross Lily's face at my husband's use of darling'?* "Come to change your order have you?"

"Um, no. Actually, I came to get some water, cold water."

"There's Evian in the fridge and glasses upper left cabinet." Lily pointed the direction with a toss of her head. She carried a tray holding the teapot, sugar bowl, and creamer. Harry followed with a larger tray filled with teacups, saucers, spoons, lemon wedges, and napkins.

"Pour a glass for me, too," Harry called over his shoulder as he left the room. I opened the cabinet and took out two heavy water glasses. Harry would opt for Evian, but I preferred tap water. I pushed the lever to cold and let the water run.

The view from Lily's kitchen window reminded me of why we were about to sit down to tea. I could see the yellow tape stretched out around the trees. It intruded on the natural order of things…but then, so did murder. I filled my glass, poured the bottled water for Harry, and carried them into the great room. I had been in this room before, when the Bishop's lived here.

An entire wall of windows faced north. Arlene and Bill Bishop had always centered their furniture and lifestyle around the huge pool table and bar that had stood ready to entertain and serve them and their friends most weekends. Arlene had installed floor to ceiling green velvet drapes that covered the expanse of windows and light. She thought the drapes complimented the green felt of the table and the green hanging lamps over the table and bar. Fortunately, Arlene never did anything green to the beautiful oak floor.

Lily embraced those windows as the focal point of the room. No drapery muted their grandeur. A series of stained glass sun-catchers

of varied shapes and sizes hung from thin strings. The effect wa
stunning. A round, heavy oak table surrounded by straight bac
chairs held a position of prominence near those windows. The rest o
the room was sparsely furnished compared to its previous load. I
this case, less was definitely more.

Harry and Lily's blond heads almost touched as they both bent t
their task of pouring and passing teacups around the table. I sat dow
next to Barb and put Harry's glass at the place to my left. Lil
quickly passed the glass to Harry where he stood, and she sat dow
next to me. That left the chair between Barb and Lily for hin
Seemed petty, but I usually liked to sit next to Harry. Apparently, s
did Lily. The conversation was all about Lily when I had joine
them. Barb was curious about Lily's use of initials. Lily repeated he
thought on using a single name then, but this was now and in th
nineties initials obscuring the artist's gender seemed to be politicall
correct.

"Using 'Lily' seemed fluffy and using 'Lily Louise' seeme
formal." She continued. "It's such an old-fashioned sounding name
When my father was a young man in Johannesburg, he attended
concert of a popular chanteuse. He became smitten with her; wrot
her poems and sent her flowers. She was flattered by the youn
man's attention and was sweet to him. Soon the tour moved on t
Australia and my father was left with an autographed playbill, a
inscribed photo, "To Leonard, Fondly, Lily Louise" and pangs of
first love. Years later when I was born, he named me after his elusiv
songbird. He always teased that I *sang* so lovely when the docto
slapped me on the arse." Lily laughed at the telling of the story. W
all did. I realized two things about her. She was truly charming an
maybe I could like her. "And that's where L.L. came from," sh
finished with a flourish.

The doorbell rang and we realized in the same moment that w
had all but forgotten the reason we were sitting down to tea. Th
frivolity of the last few minutes fell away from the table like a pape
napkin at a picnic. Lily answered the door and escorted the local, an
not so local, *gendarmes* into the room.

"Well, well, well," came Ric's mocking tone as he crossed th
room. "The Marsdens come to tea and bring a body. Charming."

"What are you doing here, Kramer?" Harry stood up.

Sergeant Peterson stepped forward to answer. "My office called him. We still had a flag on your file from the *uh,* last time and dispatch called him."

"The *last* time?" Lily asked looking at Harry.

"Oh, sure," said Ric. "You've invited the Marsdens, *Murder & Mayhem, Inc.* to your tea party. They specialize in discovering bodies, especially that one," Ric finished, tilting his head toward me. "It's what they do."

Barb had been through the previous police investigation at Pine Marsh that involved us, but Lily stared at us wide-eyed.

"That's enough, Kramer. I had an appointment with Ms. DeFreest today. Grace and I walked over through the woods. That body hasn't anything to do with us," Harry said in our defense.

"I wouldn't be too sure of that. His papers ID him as Derek Rhodes." Ric dropped that bombshell with perfect aplomb. He knew how shaken Harry and I would be, and I think he enjoyed watching the effect. Questions exploded from everyone.

"Who's Derek Rhodes?" came from Lily.

From Peterson, "Wasn't he the one we were watching for last time?"

"Why was he in our woods?" asked a worried looking Barb Atwater.

Only Ric, Harry, and I remained silent. We knew that Derek's murder would draw us into another painful encounter.

"Those questions can wait. I have some other questions." Sergeant Peterson reestablished control. "Let's sit down please. I'd like to ask each of you if you saw or heard anything out of the ordinary this morning. Your properties," he indicated Barb and Lily, "are the closest. If there was anything to hear or see it would have been from your vantage points."

Barb volunteered her thoughts first. "I didn't hear or see anything, Sergeant. I'm sorry. I was out early scanning for birds, about six-fifteen."

"Were you using your field glasses?" I asked.

"Yes, I was."

"Which side of the course woods were you in?"

"Our side. Why?"

"Yes, Mrs. Marsden, why?" Sergeant Peterson asked.

"I went out riding this morning, about six o'clock. I saw something in the east woods." Harry stirred next to me. I turned to him. "That's what I started to tell you earlier before we found the, *um*, Derek's body." I faced Peterson again. "When I stopped at the top of the hill, I turned to take in the view behind me. That's when I saw a reflection in the woods."

"What kind?" It was Peterson, who interrupted me.

"I'm not sure. Not a steady blinking, more like a flash, a reflection. I thought it could be the sun reflecting off metal or glass. At first, I thought maybe it was reflecting off metal clubs. It was off the sixth fairway. That early in the morning, I don't think anyone could have teed off at first light and played that far."

"Maybe he was concentrating on his long irons and picking up on the greens," Harry offered.

"Maybe, but why would he search for a ball he'd sliced? Seems he'd drop another and continue," I countered. "Anyway, when I rode down and came through the trail that cuts across the ninth hole I didn't see anyone, and from that point you can see the seventh fairway, the eighth green and part of the ninth fairway. That's why I thought it more likely that it could be a reflection from Barb's field glasses or even the lens of a camera."

I looked directly at Lily when I said that. She seemed to stiffen at the abrupt shift in attention.

"Were you out this morning, Ms. DeFreest?"

Lily looked at Sergeant Peterson and nodded. "Yes. I was out early to set up some equipment. While I was there I took some shots of the sunrise."

"So, all three of you ladies were out in the woods this morning at the approximate time that a man was bludgeoned to death, but no one saw or heard anything?"

I think we all assumed the Sergeant's question was rhetorical since none of us commented. Sergeant Peterson stood up. "I'll check with the pro shop on any early tee times. In the meantime, please call me if you think of anything else." Peterson handed each of us a card. He turned to address Ric. "I'll let you know the results when we run the dental records and prints."

"Thanks, Sergeant." Ric stood up to shake hands with him and walk him to the door. When he came back Barb had already retrieved her coat and was saying her good-byes. "Thank you for tea. I admire the pictures you take of the birds I can only glimpse. I hope we get together again under different circumstances."

"I'd like that," replied Lily, her warm smile reached across the room to her departing guest.

The door had barely closed when Ric turned to face me. "I can't believe you went for a ride this morning to clear *the cobwebs*," Ric said through clenched teeth. "Those cobwebs could have been *blown away* along with your thick head," he finished in exasperation. His left hand pushed the lock of dark hair that had slipped across his forehead. "We found field glasses, a rifle and scope and a sleeping bag in the pack next to his body. He's probably been out there a couple of nights stalking you."

During this fifteen-second diatribe Harry and Lily stood as observers held in check by some off-stage director. The word 'stalking' and the drain of color from my face prompted their action.

"Stalking?" Lily questioned. "He was out there all night?" She motioned toward the expanse of windows that up until that moment had held no terror for her.

Harry moved to my side stepping between Ric and me. "That's enough, Kramer. You didn't need to do that." Harry's voice sounded harsh. Ric wasn't having any of it.

"Someone has to get through to her. Apparently, you can't. You must have known she'd go riding. Even I know that's how she unwinds and sorts out."

"Stop it, Kramer. You've made your point. Lily was kind enough to make us comfortable while we waited for the sergeant. I hardly think she wants to hear your lecture. Peterson took our statements, so from an official standpoint we're finished. We're leaving." Harry punctuated his comment by swinging into his jacket and holding mine out for me. I murmured something in the way of good-bye and thanked our hostess as Harry moved us toward the door.

"I'll call you later, Lily," he said over his shoulder. "We'll set up another meeting. It's been wonderful seeing you again."

Lily had looked a little stunned during Ric's earlier comments but her recovery was complete now. Her jewel green eyes flickered briefly across my face, and then held fast to Harry's. "Yes, it has. I'll wait for your call."

"Let's hold on a moment." Ric moved to block the front door. "I could call Peterson, but I'm sure one of you knows the answer. Who called 9-1-1?" The question came as a surprise. I hadn't given it any thought since we'd heard the sirens two hours earlier. Harry and I looked at each other.

Lily's voice broke the silence. "I did."

Ric focused his dark eyes on her pale face. "How did you know to call? You told Peterson you were out early this morning. Were you in the woods when they discovered the body?"

"No, I was outside, out back, but not down there," Lily said.

"But we saw you running toward the house," I interrupted.

"When was this?" Ric asked.

"Right after we found the body. I saw it and screamed. I had my back to the house, but Harry saw her running first. I turned around and she was up to the back, the side near the tool shed. Isn't that right?" I turned to Harry for confirmation of my timeline.

"Yes, there was someone sprinting through the yard at a right angle from the thicker woods. I lost sight of him behind those pines at the property line."

"Him? It was a man you saw?" asked Ric.

"Just a figure of speech. Him, her, I caught only a glimpse."

"What did you see, Grace? You seemed certain it was Ms DeFreest." I looked quickly between Lily and my husband. Had I jumped to conclusions about the identity of the runner? I didn't think so. I cleared my mind and tried to bring up the few seconds in which I had seen the figure run toward the shed. I replayed the footage in slow motion. The figure was tall and dressed in black or dark navy. The jacket was open. It seemed to billow at the sides, disguising the size of the person wearing it. The stride was long but not the ground-churning gait of a heavy man. Then my mind's eye saw it. I looked at Lily abruptly. "Is your scarf a turquoise teal sort of color?"

Ric immediately looked at the hall tree where Lily's navy blue oat perched next to his. "*Ah,* yes it is." She stammered as Ric lifted he jacket to expose the colorful wool.

"That's the flash of color I saw when you made the turn."

"I wasn't in the woods," Lily denied. "I was out back near the eeders. I ran that way because it was the shortest way to the house. You saw me running up to the side door by the shed to call 9-1-1."

"How did you know to call 9-1-1? If you weren't in the woods, how would you know there was a body?"

"I heard you scream."

"Fine, you heard her scream. But why call 9-1-1?" Ric asked. "She could have been startled by an animal or been arguing with her husband."

"No, no. When Mrs. Marsden saw that awful crushed head and screamed, believe me Inspector, I knew to call." Lily seemed pleased with her explanation. She closed her eyes perhaps to banish the visceral description she offered.

"And how did you know Mrs. Marsden had seen that 'awful crushed head'? From where you said you were standing, you couldn't see the body."

Lily's eyes flew open at the trap she had talked herself into. "My father would be impressed, Inspector," Lily said quietly.

I didn't understand the reference, but I knew better than to interrupt Ric at this point.

"Listen, Ms. DeFreest. You can answer this question here or I can take you to Sergeant Peterson's office."

"I didn't know police officers really said that." She smiled meekly. "I knew it was a body because I was watching the Marsdens come through the woods. I told you that I had set up some equipment the night before. I had my 1200mm telephoto lens on the tripod. I was scanning when I first saw them. Of course, I recognized Harry. I kept watching as they walked along. They stopped for a moment and then I heard his wife scream. She was pointing at the ground, so I panned the underbrush, and that's how I saw the body from here. I wasn't down there, Inspector."

"Why didn't you explain this the first time?" Ric asked.

"I felt awkward about watching them for as long as I did," Lily said. Ric shook his head.

"Where's the camera now?" he asked.

"Still on the tripod, I expect. Why?"

"I like to check out what I'm told."

"Are you finished *now*, Inspector?" Harry's tight-lipped tone surprised me.

"With you and Grace, yes. Thank you for your keen observation." That comment was directed at me. Both Harry and Lily seemed to regard that statement with an icy view. I mean, wasn't glowing with civic pride, but I felt that my observation helped to clear up some facts. I waited until we were down the walkway and on the road before I commented.

"Lily seemed upset that I called her on her version of the events I'm surprised she didn't fess up sooner. You wouldn't think there'd be any hesitation choosing between being a suspect in murder or a voyeur."

"She's not a voyeur, dammit." Harry's burst startled me. "She's a professional photographer and a private person. Now Ric Kramer is sniffing around her for motive and means."

I was stunned and hurt by his tone. "Harry, I only meant to…"

"I know exactly what you meant to do," interrupted Harry "Grace Marsden Drew, girl detective. You couldn't wait to join forces with the good Inspector to solve another crime. Are you drawn to the drama of crime or are you drawn to the detective?" Harry's comment scored a partial bull's eye. In the past, it did seem as though I sought out Ric for help, but calling him, last night had been Harry's idea, entirely. I rushed to tell him so. Before I could, he continued to extol the virtues of Ms. DeFreest.

"She's a talented, gentle person and she deserves our support Kramer will badger her with questions. The tables will be turned in there, a DeFreest being stalked by a beast. Definitely not her father's daughter."

"What does that mean? I didn't understand what she mean about her father."

"Her father is Leonard 'Leo' DeFreest," Harry explained. "He became famous and rich during the 1940's and 1950's by live trapping exotic game for zoos and private collectors. He shipped his captives to every part of the world. He had an excellent reputation for delivering his animals alive and healthy. I've read quite a bit about

im, even met him once at a house party in up state New York. I
didn't make the connection with Lily, of course, until today. Now the
inspector has his panties in a bunch over her alibi...thanks to you."
Harry's voice sounded harsh again; a quality I wasn't accustomed to
with my husband. I wanted to smile at Harry's description of Ric to
ease the tension, but I remembered his earlier sting.

"What did you want me to do?" I asked. "Did you want me to
forget what I saw?"

"I wanted you to give her the benefit of the doubt. We could
have talked about it later, decided what to do. I didn't want you to
throw her to Kramer."

"If she has nothing to hide, she has nothing to worry about."

"Grace, I know her. I mean I knew her before. She's a
wonderful person who didn't deserve to be treated so coldly."

My temper overrode rational thought and grammar. "Excuse
me. I didn't know you wanted to treat her so *hotly.*"

We passed the Atwater house. I veered off the road onto the
trail that would take me home the back way. I could hear Harry
calling me as the pecan shells flew out like tiny wooden missiles from
beneath my running feet. He didn't follow. Fine! I arrived home
first and left before he made it back.

Chapter Eight

Part of me understood the anger I felt toward Harry. Most of me recognized the anger I felt at myself for wanting to impress Ric. When would he ever go away? I pushed thoughts of Ric out of my head and tried to think of the fun afternoon I'd have with my niece at the zoo.

She was planning the deluxe docent tour of Zone Africa. Maybe I'd see a descendant of one of Leonard DeFreest's captives. I spotted Jolene talking with three other women. She waved me over when she saw me and greeted me with a hug and a kiss. "Hi, Aunt Grace. I'm glad you could make it today."

"Are you kidding? Miss a chance at my own private deluxe docent tour?" Everyone laughed. Jolene made quick introduction and we left the other docents as they scattered to their last assignments for the day.

"I have house stationing. I can choose where I want to be from two o'clock to three o'clock. This works out even better. We can spend more time in Zone Africa. Susan, the docent you met, might join us at three. She's doing giraffe observations."

We walked in the general direction of Pachyderm. I realized that I hadn't been in the zoo in years. I used to visit on a regular basis when I wrote my first children's book. I would watch kids walk and talk and interact with other kids and with the animals, especially at Children's Zoo. I spent hours watching reactions, facial expressions and catching snippets of speech. Jolene had been along many times when I was researching a new book. Now she was returning the favor. Jolene's favorite had been the elephant show. She would sit in the small outdoor arena and clap her hands at all the amazing tricks the elephants could do under expert guidance from their handler. The

eepers would stretch out two thick ropes from Pachyderm to the
rena creating a wide aisle and walk the elephant across the road. It
vas exciting for me to have such a large animal walking a few feet
way. Imagine the thrill for a child no higher than the animal's leg.

We walked passed the elephants' yard and paused to view the
black rhinos that were outside in their yard. Jolene explained that
hey were part of the Species Survival Plan that Brookfield Zoo and
ther zoos throughout the country support. There were already some
pecies that existed only in zoos. The *Whirl*, the fundraising event
oming up, was one way that the zoo raised the funds needed to
rovide good stewardship to these animals.

A short walk and we arrived in Africa. Our first stop, a
raveler's rest stop. *Makundi Boma*–welcome traveler–in Swahili.
Ve sat on the benches in this circular room and watched the African
vild dogs playing chase and tumble on the other side of a ceiling to
loor glass window.

"There is a warmed rock outside this window here," Jolene
ointed, "that lures them over during the cold weather. Otherwise,
isitors might not see them."

I smiled at the incongruity zoos are forced to accept. Provide a
aturalistic setting for the animals so that they feel secure enough to
isplay natural behavior, but design it so the public can see them up
lose and personal. Our next stop, the *Kopje*; translation, *rocky
utcropping*. This outcrop provided homes for several beautiful and
xotic birds and animals. Jolene pointed out a colorful Bishop's
Veaver while an inquisitive Kingfisher eyed us from his lofty perch.
urry little rock hyraxes peeked from nooks in their artificial outcrop
nd then boldly stepped out to have a better look. The tiny antelope
hat stood atop the highest point on this man-made mountain stole my
eart. I read the signage about the Klipspringer, a small, agile
ountain antelope. I stared at the creature with the moppet eyes and
weet face and wished for the umpteenth time, I had remembered to
ring my camera.

"C'mon, Aunt. There's more to see. Look at these little guys."
Iy niece guided me to the next enclosure. Small animals with
ointed muzzles and striking patterns on their furry bodies stood up
n their hind legs and looked amiably at us. "They're in the

mongoose family. These days it's easier to describe a meerkat b
explaining it's like Timon in *The Lion King*."

I enjoyed observing Jolene move in and out of her docent spie
I wondered if she was even aware of doing it. We walked outside t
view the giraffes. They were one of my favorite animals. A lot c
visitors felt the same apparently since the railing was crowded wit
zoo goers enjoying the sight of those graceful creatures who have th
distinction of being the tallest living animals. It was warm enough i
our late spring for them to relish their spacious yard. They appeare
to be enjoying their release from the indoor exhibit that th
temperatures of a Chicago winter forced on them.

We moved away from the railing, our vacated spots filled i
immediately, like water rushing into a sandpit. Jolene pointed out
bleached animal skull at the base of a sign that read, "Thirsty Anim
Trail." The tag line continued with, "Can you survive the search fc
water?"

"Let's do the trail," Jolene suggested.

"Sure." I started down the path, moving toward a display boar
attached on a three-foot high post. Before I reached the board,
heard a loud snarl in the underbrush. My knee jerk reaction was
jump back much to the amusement of my niece.

"Gotcha," she laughed. "I love to watch visitors react. Yo
know, the kids don't react the same way. They just look around. Th
adults are usually the jumpy ones."

"That's because adults usually have a reason to be jumpy. Gla
you enjoyed that. I didn't know docents were so desperate for kicks
I smiled as Jolene's steps tripped the electric eye and set off th
snorting wild boar. We continued along the path and heard lion
hyenas and birds. Each display board asked the question, *Run c
Stay?* By lifting the wooden plaque under the sign, you discovered
your response was right or wrong. Grunts, snorts, and growls don
always signal danger.

I smiled to myself as I remembered all the grunts, snorts, an
growls I'd heard growing up with four brothers that hadn't signale
danger, maybe a few of the deadly sins, sloth and gluttony came t
mind.

We made it to the water hole, a set of three fountains, an

urped our cool reward.

"What other docent amusements do you have in store for me?"

"I could take you to the lower level of Jungle World and we ould look for Terrance."

"Something tells me looking in a basement for some guy named errance is not the entire picture here. After that last stunt, what akes you think I'd follow you?"

Jolene laughed at my exaggerated skepticism. "Cause I know ou, Aunt. If I were to tell you that Terrance is the ghost of an frican Lion that lived at the zoo fifty years ago, you'd follow me. If were to tell you how late at night keepers hear stealthy footsteps, d a clicking sound like an animal's nails on the cement floors in the allways, you'd follow me. If I then told you that these same keepers d even an occasional docent working on a project in the building ter hours have heard the low roar of a big cat, you'd follow me. ne keeper described it like a 'rumble from a distance that never me closer'."

"Okay, okay. I'd say you know your aunt pretty well. "Is that here we're going?" I tried to keep the high pitch of excitement out f my voice. My niece smiled at me and leaned forward with a ontaneous hug.

"You're such a kid for an adult. That's why you're my favorite lative," she said. I'm not authorized to go below levels. I'll sign ou up for the next Behind the Scenes Breakfast for Jungle World. l sign up to work it. The keeper won't talk about Terrance, but u'll get to see the area where they hear him."

"Great. I'd love to go on one of those tours. About the owling, couldn't the keepers be hearing one of the other animals in e exhibit?"

"No way. Jungle World doesn't have big cats in the exhibit; onkeys, primates, otter, and birds, but no cats."

"Maybe a gorilla's roar echoing through the ductwork?"

"Nope; two entirely different vocalizations. Besides, a keeper ould know a lion's roar."

"How about that low rumble description? Maybe they hear a stant freight train and the underground area distorts the sound and ey can hear it the best in that one particular hallway." I thought that explanation was brilliant.

"Someone thought of that and checked the times that Terrance had been heard against trains moving through here at night. No matches." Jolene shrugged her shoulders. "He's a bona-fide ghost."

I was still skeptical. "How do the live animals react when Terrance is in the building; I mean, do they get anxious? Do they sense him?"

"That part is really strange," Jolene answered.

I thought the entire conversation was strange.

"Terrance seems to only stalk the hallway closest to the kitchen an area furthest from the animal collection and their enclosures. Jean the docent you met earlier, has a theory on that. She thinks the lion stays near the kitchen hallway because it is a high traffic zone with keepers passing through to and from the animals. Someone is usually in that area. Anyway, Jean's theory is that this lion was accustomed to being around people and lingers near them now."

An unexplained chill skittered down my spine and jolted my shoulders back in response. Involuntarily I thought of the movie, *The Ghost and the Darkness*, a suspense story about two rogue male lions that stalked the camp of an expedition attempting to build a bridge in India. The story was true and the remains of those lions were stuffed and given to the Field Museum of Natural History. They had wanted to be around people–to eat them! What reason could Terrance have for staying earthbound?

"Aunt? Aunt Grace?"

"*Ah,* lost in thought. Sorry. Say, let's move on from all things ethereal for now. What else have you planned for me?"

"I thought we might go around Iroquois Lake and see where the bones were discovered. Unless you'd rather not?'

"No, I'd like to see that."

We walked along in comfortable silence broken occasionally by Jolene explaining or announcing an animal fact. She finally turned to me after a particularly long silence. "You don't seem yourself, something bothering you?"

I put my arm around her shoulders and pulled her close. "That obvious, *eh*?" I released her and walked a few more steps in silence.

"Yes, that obvious, *A*" Jolene had segued my grammatical

idiosyncrasy to an inside joke. When I first learned of her existence, I didn't want her to feel obligated to call me Aunt if she wasn't comfortable with that title. I always signed cards and letters to her with 'A. Grace.' We both enjoyed the abbreviation and had fun with it. Even now she leaves messages on the machine for me or addresses cards to me using the initial.

"Doing some heavy thinking." I didn't want my mood to spoil Jolene's plans. I took a chance that her interest in animals would make her appreciative of my newest neighbor.

"We have a new neighbor in Pine Marsh," I started. "You may have seen some of her work. She's a nature photographer, quite good Harry says. Her name is L.L. DeFreest." My hunch was correct.

"L.L. DeFreest is your neighbor?" Jolene nearly squeaked with excitement. "Oh, I love her work. I can't believe some of the pictures she's been able to get. She has an entire series of animal babies on stationery and calendars called 'Wild Wee'uns.' In fact, you gave me the collections for Christmas last year. Those were DeFreest. Remember?"

I remembered the gift. I knew she'd like it, but I didn't pay attention to the artist.

"Do you think you could get her autograph on my calendar?"

"Sure. I'm sure I can, or at least your uncle can. They go way back, before I met him." I hoped my attempt at a casual tone worked. Apparently it did. Jolene's response was a grin and "Thanks, A."

That exchange brought us to Iroquois Lake. The path stretched a quarter mile around the marsh and exited close to the wolves' exhibit. We couldn't go down to the water. We had to stay on a path a good fifty yards up the embankment.

"The hoopla didn't start until after maintenance people started hosing down the wagon. The plan was to clean up the wagon, restore it to its original state, and use it as a display of an old time zoo. They never used those types of displays. One of the trustees thought it looked more like a circus wagon than a zoo exhibit. How would a wagon get into the zoo? Anyway, all that speculation stopped as soon as the water washed off years of muck."

"I bet they freaked when they found the other skeleton." I said this more to myself than to Jolene. Her response startled me.

"What other skeleton?" She stared at me her mouth agape.

"Oops. I thought you, that is, I thought everyone knew. Karen didn't tell me that not everyone knew."

"Karen Kramer? She's a trustee here, right? What other skeleton? What's going on?"

I waved my hand in front of Jolene's face to stop the flow of questions.

"All right, Jo. I'll tell you, but do not tell anyone else, especially other docents." I cautioned. I waited for her to agree before I filled in the rest of the story.

"Wow, that is too bizarre." Her dark eyes gleamed as she looked back to the *scene of the crime.* "Please keep me up to date," those same eyes implored me to agree.

"I'll do my best, honey, but Karen may not find out anymore. The zoo might put a real lid on the whole thing."

"You have a better source than Karen. Use that." Jolene continued when I looked puzzled. "Your new neighbor. Her father is Leonard DeFreest. He's some big shot honcho in the World Zoological Association."

It seemed as though everyone knew my neighbor's background except me; an oversight I would soon address.

Chapter Nine

I maneuvered around an unfamiliar car parked in our driveway and parked my Jeep next to Harry's car in the garage. My curiosity was satisfied moments later when I entered our kitchen and found Harry and Lily seated in the breakfast nook, both blonde heads close together in earnest conversation over a piece of paper spread out on the table.

"Hullo, Grace. Didn't expect you so soon. Thought you and Jo would be zooing much longer."

Does he seem a tad uneasy about my early return, or am I the one who's uneasy in my own home? "Jolene is meeting some friends. You know, girls' night out and all." I answered in what I hoped was an offhand casualness. My eyes inventoried Lily in that guardedly intense way women do. She had exchanged her earlier monochromatic outfit for a turquoise and black sheath that ended several revealing inches above her knees. Her hair was swept back and coiled into a smooth French braid. The effect highlighted already lofty cheekbones and deepened the green of her eyes.

"Lily rang me up a little while ago and suggested we tackle this paperwork. Seems her father is flying in this evening." Harry shuffled the papers on the table as if to confirm his statement.

"I know my father. Once he arrives, he's as likely to want to stay put and relax, as he is to want to fill each hour with an event. I never know his moods. He has never seen Pine Marsh, so I hope he'll want to relax here." Lily looked at her watch. "I'll know his mood in about an hour. I better get going." She stood and Harry hurried to place a lightweight woolen cape around her slim shoulders. The cape was the same deep turquoise. The material draped her body to right at the knees, leaving enough shapely leg to divert and distract most

63

men.

"Thank you for your time," she said pointing to the papers. "When I know my father's schedule, I'll call you and we can finish the job."

"There's no rush, Lily. Unlike your father, I am a creature of habit. Most of which involves staying in Pine Marsh as much as possible."

"You've certainly changed from the Harry Marsden I remember." A strange expression crossed Lily's face and in that moment, I felt like the outsider. She was in *my house*, cozying up to *my husband* and I felt like *I* was the intruder. They had a history together and the undercurrent of that old relationship grew stronger each time they talked. I could see the visible struggle in Lily's face to not ask the questions she was probably dying to ask.

Harry sensed it too because he finally broke the uncomfortable silence. "Which carrier is your father coming in on? International arrivals can take forever."

"He's flying United from New York. His cable gave me his flight number and arrival time. My father never offers more information than necessary. Sort of like–" Lily stopped.

I have no doubt the end of the sentence would have been 'you.' Another awkward pause. I jumped in to assert myself as mistress of the house and general know-it-all. "There's some construction on 294, *there's always construction somewhere in Chicago,* and domestic flights have been touting on time arrival records, so your father will probably be on the ground before you get there." I ended my statement with a slight shrug of my shoulders. "Harry," I added for good measure, "Barbara and Jack are stopping by around six thirty."

His quick glance delivered over his shoulder as he walked Lily to the door promised a discussion later. His outburst and the door closing must have been a photo finish.

"Good grief. I can't believe you're so incredibly jealous of Lily. That was the most sophomoric display of school girl pettiness I've seen since, since, Little Women," he sputtered.

"Petty? Who had their heads together whispering in our nook? You have an office for business. You said you'd call her tomorrow.

ouldn't you wait?"

"God's sake, Grace. Stop it. You're being silly. I purposely sat s in the kitchen so it would be less private. I didn't call her. She ook a chance that I'd be home. She wanted to drop off some samples f her work for possible displays for her book tour." Harry waved his and in the direction of the mudroom. "If the third degree is over, et's talk about 'Barbara and Jack coming over at six-thirty'," he nimicked.

"Okay, okay. I guess I overreacted. I felt like the college girl ou met all those years ago. Lily was beautiful and sophisticated and felt plain compared to her. Now, she's still all of those things. I still eel plain next to her."

"Grace. You are anything but plain." Harry's entire mood hifted. He put his hands on each side of my face, pushing my thick air behind my ears and lifting the corners of my sternly set mouth vith his thumbs. He tipped my chin up and stared into my eyes. When your eyes turn that intriguing shade of purple you're either xcited or frightened. Now, what is your adrenaline up to?"

My quirky physiology prevented me from ever being able to lie r even bluff successfully. Harry's closeness set off another part of ny physiology, this one not so quirky. A slow smile spread across larry's face as he read the answer in my pansy-purple eyes.

"Too bad about Barbara and Jack coming over," Harry said as he lipped the cardigan off my shoulders and began undoing the buttons n my blouse. "Not much time," he murmured as his hands reached nside my open blouse. "Too bad." He started to remove his hands.

"I lied." I pulled his hands back to their business.

"I know." Harry lifted me easily and carried me to the thick ushions in the nook.

My focus was on Harry and the direction this afternoon was aking. A niggling thought tried to push through my impending bliss. Vhy did Harry feel he had to keep his meeting with Lily in a less rivate venue? Which one could not be trusted behind closed doors? n ardent caress drew me back. Harry's touch pushed thoughts of ily off the surface of my mind, like crumbs being swept from a able.

Chapter Ten

The face at the window leered at me through the glass. couldn't scream, I couldn't move. My breath felt trapped in my lungs. Where was Harry? Didn't he see? Didn't he hear the shrill laughter from the shattered mouth in that hideous face?

Slowly, the face began to fade as the shrill sound registered a the ringing of the telephone and my subconscious released me from horrible nightmare. I sat up in bed and rubbed my eyes in an effort t orient myself. The *Betty Boop* clock, with the timepiece placed in he midsection, showed me 6:40 a.m. Who would call this early? Th sound of the telephone had stopped so Harry must have picked u downstairs. The entire upstairs floor had only one telephone. Th three-line ceramic and plastic statuette of the forties' lady stoo quietly in her trademarked pose. The light under the second butto blinked sedately. I leaned over and pressed the tiny square.

"Good morning. It's early, but I'm up. I had to get up to answe the phone," I quipped. In the brief silence that followed, I realize that my assumption that this was a friend calling was wrong. "Uh this is Grace, who's this?" I amended my greeting.

"Oh, good morning. It's Lily. I'm sorry to be calling so early. think Harry put me on hold. I'm leaving the house rather soon thi morning and I've forgotten to get an address I need."

Harry's voice on the line stopped further conversation. "I hav it, Grace." No one spoke. The silence lingered for several second until I understood that they were both waiting for me to hang up th receiver. Memories of a similar silence as my older brother and h girlfriend waited in exasperation for the little, pesky sister to hang u the extension leaped to my mind. I didn't like the feeling then and surely didn't like it now. How could this woman make me feel like third wheel in my own home?

Harry entered the room and greeted me with what seemed like forced cheerfulness. "Good morning. Sorry the phone woke you." Harry walked toward the bathroom, stopping only long enough at my bedside to squeeze my shoulder as a greeting. I reached up to his wrist to stop his forward progress.

"I'm glad it did. I was having an awful dream. Curious though, why did she call on the second line? Only friends and family have that number."

"Second line? Don't think it was the second line. Didn't look."

His denial infuriated me. "Of course it was the second line. Do I normally answer the phone with a Henny Youngman gag unless I think the caller is family or a friend?" The question was rhetorical; Harry knew I was furious.

"I must have given it to her without thinking. What's the difference? Why the third degree? For heaven's sake, Gracie, you're not going to start up on that again?"

We were headed for a full-blown battle when the second line interrupted with a shrill demand. "You get it. It could be your mother or it could be Ed McMahon telling you you're a winner." I said that with as much righteously indignant smugness as I could muster.

Harry scowled at me as he lifted the receiver. "Hullo?" Harry's voice took on a smugness of its own. "Good morning, Inspector. No, it's not too early. Hold on." He passed the receiver to me. The arched eyebrow and smile on his lips was anything but cheery. As I took the telephone, I silently cursed myself for giving Ric this number. Harry stood expectantly as I said hello.

"No, I was up. Really." I knew that Ric Kramer had to have a good reason to be calling this early. Harry knew that too. He hadn't budged. I listened carefully, nodded once, and then froze. I tried to keep my expression neutral, but Harry had already seen the shock register on my face.

"What is it?" Harry's voice was low. I had carefully replaced the receiver and now turned my full attention to my husband.

"Ric wants us to be available for more questions. A squad is already on its way to Lily's house. They found the murder weapon.

The Lion Tamer: A Caged Death

It's her tripod." I delivered the information in a rather low, monoton(
The room was so still I didn't expect Harry's outburst and jumpe
when he shouted.

"That's ridiculous! Damn him. I knew he'd go after her. Dam
him." Harry punctuated his tirade with a fist slammed down har
next to the phone. Items on the nightstand were lifted an
repositioned as he brought his clenched fist down again.

"Harry, stop it. He said he needed to question her, not arre
her." My plea seemed to calm him a little. He continued to pace th
floor, but at a slower pace.

"I know Kramer. He has an idea that it's her and the next ste
will be to arrest her." He broke off pacing and opened the door of h
armoire.

"What are you doing?"

"Getting dressed. I'm going over to Lily's house before th
Gestapo arrives." He threw on a pair of jeans and a navy blue cre
neck sweater and slipped bare feet into a pair of deck shoes.

"Harry, think. What are you going to do over there? You'll on
cause more commotion. Her father is with her now. She doesn't nee
you too. Or, does she?" That last bit was a cheap shot but I wa
getting more confused and hurt by his reactions.

"Grace, she's a friend. You don't get it, do you?" He turne
abruptly and left the room. I sat stunned for a few moments and the
a familiar regimen began to load my brain. *Not now, I thoug*
desperately. I need to get over there. No use. The obsessiv
behavior I struggled with was taking an upper hand. I had to fing
braid before I could get out of bed. *100! No! I pleaded with m*
brain to accept 10. No use. Please, please 50? No good. A chai
Yes. A chain is a row. 100.

I lurched sideways across the bed to reach underneath and pull
up a cardboard box filled with yarn. I yanked a piece from the tang
and began a practiced braid that I had been using since childhoo
The pink chain grew under my flying fingers. My thoughts flew
quickly as my nimble digits. *What stunt was Harry going to pul*
He's right of course. I know how pigheaded Ric could be. A fe
months ago, Ric was convinced that Harry was trying to kill me. M
count came forward in my mind. *Ninety-seven, ninety-eight, ninet*

ine, one hundred!

"Yes," I shouted and jumped out of bed and into action. I pulled on old jeans and the first shirt my frantic hands touched and ran down he back staircase. I knew it was hopeless to try to stop him. I'd wasted too much time. He must have left in a hurry; the garage door was still up. I pressed the button to close the door. I stood in the arkening garage shaking with anger and fear. What was happening) our relationship? How much did Lily mean to him? I had no nswers, but I did have a plan. I retraced my steps to our bedroom nd dressed as quickly as my husband had minutes earlier. I wanted) watch Harry 'swing into action' for this other woman. I did and I idn't. I knew I had to be there.

Twenty minutes behind Harry, I drove my Jeep out of the arage. Minutes later I pulled up in front of the DeFreest home. A ounty Sheriff's squad car was in the driveway and Rick's car was arked on the street. He must have called me from his cell phone; he ouldn't have made it here that fast. Before I could put my vehicle in ark, Ric's faced loomed at my window.

"Where are they, Grace? Where did he take her?"

Chapter Eleven

"Where are…? You mean they're not here?" My turn to ┃
stunned for the second or third time this morning. Ric realized m┃
confusion was genuine and opened the door. He took my arm a┃
guided me toward the house.

"I'm sorry, Grace. I didn't mean to jump down your throat. ┃
knew you'd tell him our conversation and I thought you were part ┃
this. What are you doing here?"

My half-formed answer swirled through my brain. *Should I t┃
Ric the total truth of Harry's erratic behavior this morning, or shou┃
I tell him a partial truth that Harry wanted to be here for mor┃
support?* Before I could answer, the front door opened and an old┃
gentleman stood in the doorway inviting me in. He was as tall as R┃
but a stockier build. His hair was thick and shot with more gray tha┃
the original shade of light brown. His eyes, tourmaline green, ma┃
the introduction unnecessary.

"Mr. DeFreest, this is Grace Marsden. Grace, this is L┃
DeFreest." I shook his hand, but didn't know what to say. I st┃
didn't even know what to think. Part of my confusion was that ┃
extended his left hand. I noticed that his right hand, covered by┃
glove, hung at his side. He deftly stepped into the breach.

"I'm happy to meet you Mrs. Marsden, though the circumstanc┃
of this meeting are a little unclear to me." He nodded graciously a┃
indicated I should take a seat at the table where a cup of coffee a┃
folded newspaper occupied one place mat.

"*Uh*, thank you. I'm not sure of too much either."

He turned to Ric and indicated the other seat. "Perhaps we┃
learn together."

"Excuse me, Mr. DeFreest. I need to speak with the sherif┃

eputy. I'll be right back. Ric retrieved his jacket from the coat tree
nd hurried outside.

"Mrs. Marsden, can I get you some coffee or tea?"

He seemed too calm for someone whose morning solitude had
een invaded by police and strangers. The jury was out on whether I
ked this DeFreest any better than the other one. I did accept a hot
p of Rain Forest Nut coffee.

"Perhaps when Inspector Kramer returns he can explain his visit.
arrived here last night. I'm in the dark about his concern." He
niled politely enough, but his eye movement didn't match his serene
anner. He repeatedly glanced out the window to the two men and
anned the room as though looking for an escape route.

"Come now, Mr. DeFreest. You've been in town since six
clock last night and I'm sure your daughter mentioned the fact that a
an, bludgeoned to death, was found in her backyard." I was tiring
his condescending attitude. I wanted to shake him up. "I know
spector Kramer must have at least explained the reason he came
lling since he'd been in the house with you already."

A more genuine smile appeared on his face and his eyes stopped
king the room and settled on my face. "I apologize, Mrs. Marsden
r my attitude. I wasn't sure with whom I was dealing. I'm still not,
t I do realize now that you are a player in this scenario."

"What exactly *is* this scenario?" It was Ric's voice behind me
at spoke my thought. "I am close to issuing an all points bulletin on
ur daughter and your husband." He turned slightly to include me in
s statement. "The only reason I haven't, is because I'm hoping there
a logical and acceptable explanation that will convince me that they
ve not taken flight."

"Inspector, that is ridiculous."

"Ric, that's so wrong."

Both statements must have rang in his ears as one. He put up his
nds to silence us. "Wrong? Ridiculous? Then where are they?"

That took the wind out of my sails. Leo DeFreest tried a
fferent tack. "Of course there is an explanation. My daughter had
early morning appointment in the city and Mr. Marsden was kind
ough to drive her. I'm sure they would have waited for you had
u called ahead." His smile seemed to reproach Ric for his early

morning raid.

"Forgive me for not making an appointment to question you daughter about a murder committed with her tripod. Your stor doesn't wash, since Marsden knew about the questioning." H finished his comment with a penetrating look toward me. He hadn said *not* to tell Harry.

I was starting to squirm under his baleful gaze and about t speak up in my defense. The front door opened and slammed again the wall as Harry and Lily raced in closely followed by the Sheriff deputy. Lily was at her father's side in a flash of color as she tumble out of a multicolored jacket, hat, scarf, and gloves. The discarde outerwear brightened the corner of the beige carpeting like a falle rainbow. Harry stopped inside the door watching the reunion. R had moved closer to Harry, it seemed to block his path to the doo They exchanged words. I couldn't hear them, but the look on Ric face wasn't friendly. I tried to listen harder but Lily's voice wa raised.

"I came back as soon as Harry explained why he insisted o driving me. I can't believe it. Dad, I'm sorry about this mess." Li stopped speaking and looked expectantly at her father. Ric's voic filled the silence.

"'Sorry about this mess.' Is that a confession of sorts?" R didn't seem serious, but then I hadn't been right about anything yet.

"Confession!" Lily sputtered. "Are you insane, Inspector?"

My sidelong glance at Harry revealed a tiny smile hurried wiped from his mouth. He was enjoying this repartee. He moved few feet closer to the huge window. He appeared to be trying to sta out of the fray. He picked up one of Lily's cameras and was holdin it up to his eyes, fiddling with the dials.

"Give me that. I have the settings all in place for an afterno shot." Lily walked up to Harry and took hold of both straps firmly close to the camera as she could reach. She pulled it away fro Harry and took the extra minute to set it outside the patio door on set-up table.

Lily continued in an exasperated tone that seemed to inclu both Harry and Ric. "I'm apologizing, Inspector, because my fatl came here to relax before a conference he is running in two weeks.

romised him quiet solitude and fresh air. His first morning here and
ou descend on him."

The mental image of Ric as a raptor with talons extended ready
o snatch at prey flashed through my mind at Lily's last words. I
vould not want Ric Kramer on my proverbial tail. Joliet State Prison
vas probably filled with thugs who felt the same way.

"Lily, stop. Inspector Kramer is doing his job." Leo DeFreest's
alm voice drew everyone's attention. "Please, gentlemen, Mrs.
Aarsden. Please be seated. Lily, have you misplaced your manners?
As mistress of this house, won't you offer your guests a beverage?"

"Guests?" She fixed a look on Harry. "He whisked me away
vith no explanation and apparently no belief in my innocence, and
e," turning her head to impale Ric with her glacial gaze, "rushed out
ere, with back up," inclining her head toward the deputy, "to arrest
ie. Guests? I'd sooner serve piranha!" Lily turned her back on us
nd started toward the door.

"Lily Louise."

She stopped in her tracks at her father's voice. Instant reaction.
he turned to face her father. The anger that had flared on her face a
noment before was replaced with a calm detachment, as though a
witch had been thrown. She returned to his side.

He slipped an arm around her shoulders and again asked that we
e seated. His voice sounded so smooth, so stress free compared to
iy jangled squeak when I thanked him and sat down.

Even Ric allowed DeFreest to run the show for now. He sat
own next to me. The deputy, whose name I still didn't know, sat
ext to Ric. Harry moved two seats over which put him next to
)eFreest, who was next to me. Lily brought in a tray with mugs,
ugar, creamer, tea bags, and spoons. She left us to sort out settings
nd returned with a large chrome butler filled with coffee and a
maller pot of hot water. We settled ourselves as amiably as possible
nd began the innocuous task of passing cream and sugar. DeFreest's
loy had worked to some degree. It's difficult to stay angry when
rced to observe basic amenities. Ric was the first to break the
rained silence.

"I didn't come here to arrest you," he said quietly to our hostess.
needed to ask you some questions. Your tripod has blood from the

victim on it. We found where Rhodes was killed before he wa dumped on your property."

Everyone at the table leaned forward. No one seemed to eve swallow while we waited for Ric to continue.

"The police searched a small structure at the apex of thi property and the adjoining lot."

"The Rowe's sauna?" The question blurted out of my mout Our friends had built their spa in the woods two years ago. Harry an I had attended their first *open house*. It had been after a Februar snow when we joined in the traditional Scandinavian custom (enjoying the intense heat and then dashing outside to roll in the snov They had arranged for the guests to wrap up in faux fur throws an snow boots for the walk up to the house. I couldn't imagine a murd(taking place there. "My God, do they know? Are they back yet?"

Ric looked annoyed at my interruption. "They know. They'i not home yet." His short answer signaled everyone to keep quiet.

"We know the murder was committed there. In fact, tha appears to be where Rhodes was holed up. I need to ask all of you few more questions based on this new information. My *back up* : here because I have no jurisdiction in Pine Marsh. I thought th questions might be easier from someone you'd already met."

"But I thought you were convinced..." slipped out before Lil glanced at Harry and stopped talking. She picked up her cup an sipped carefully at the hot liquid.

"What exactly did Marsden tell you when he rushed over th morning? Weren't you surprised to see him? Or were you expectin him?"

Lily's hand shook as she lowered her cup. Some of the h(liquid splashed over the rim, missing her fingers, but spreading acros the oak table. She automatically mopped at the tea with her napkin.

"That's enough, Kramer," burst from Harry's mouth. "Leave h(alone. You've some sort of lunatic Clue game accusation of Lily wit the tripod in the sauna." Harry's sarcasm infuriated Ric.

"You're right, Marsden. That is enough...out of you. You'v interfered with an ongoing investigation and I've had it." Ric stoo and motioned to the officer to do likewise. "Deputy Jordan place M Marsden under arrest for obstructing a police officer in th erformance of his duty."

Harry stood abruptly and looked ready to come across the table
t Ric. Deputy Jordan placed his hand lightly on Harry's shoulder.
Ie shrugged it off but made no move.

"You're crazy, Kramer. You can't hold me on that ridiculous
harge."

"Maybe not for long, but long enough. Jordan, make sure you
ead him his rights." Ric looked directly at my husband. "I'll cuff
im, Jordan." Ric pulled handcuffs from his back pocket and walked
oward Harry.

"Inspector Kramer."

"Ric."

Two voices uttered as one. Ric shook his head slowly from side
o side. "Now you have *two* women pleading your case. What
harms." Ric saw Harry's fist but couldn't block the full force.
Iarry's punch, deflected to the jaw rather than the nose, still caught
ic off balance enough to topple a chair and send some of the
rockery to the floor. I think I screamed. I know Lily did. In that
uick second, my subconscious noted that only Leo DeFreest seemed
bove the fray. He actually sipped at his coffee with what my
renzied brain registered as a bemused smile.

The position of Deputy Jordan became apparent in the next
istant. "Stop, right there, Mr. Marsden." His stern command was
unctuated by the appearance of his service revolver in his hand.
veryone stopped. Harry immediately lowered his hand to his side
nd stood quietly, not even turning to face the deputy. He continued
o stand meekly as Jordan ordered him to put his hands behind his
ack. The click of the handcuffs and the catch in my voice as I called
Iarry's name sounded simultaneously. He turned his head and stared
t me.

"I'll call David. He'll get there as soon as he can. I'll follow
ou."

"No." Nothing more. He turned toward the door and started
oving without further direction from the deputy.

I felt helpless and astonished. I didn't know if I was in shock or
' Harry was with the realization of what he had done. I watched my
andcuffed husband being loaded into the backseat of a squad car and

never said a word.

"If David is your attorney, Mrs. Marsden, I suggest that you c call him immediately." Mr. DeFreest's voice brought a modicum reasoning to my mind.

I shook myself mentally and turned to face him. My line vision took in Lily, white faced and staring at the door, Leo DeFree calmly surveying his daughter, and Ric now sitting on the righte chair. I saw it then–the blood streaming from his left hand. "Ri My God, you're hurt."

He was holding his wrist trying to stop the bleeding. I thought first that his wrist was cut but when he repositioned the blooc napkin, I could see that the gash was directly under his thumb in th meaty part of his palm. I started to kneel next to him, but he warne me off pointing to the floor. The heavy dishes had shattered int lethal shards, the longest one covered with blood. I shuddered as thought of kneeling on one of those. Ric must have put his hand o to break his fall and jammed it into the razor sharp fragment.

Lily and her father had drawn closer to Ric. "I'll get som bandages and salve," offered Lily.

"Wait," her father commanded. "This wound needs immedia attention. It's too deep to heal without stitches or possibly surger Don't move your thumb too much until someone can check it fo possible damage to the tendon." He had delivered his diagnosis aft a cursory exam of Ric's hand.

Ric asked the question I was thinking. "How do you know s much about wounds?" Ric's voice was softer than usual. I wa worried about shock.

Leo DeFreest raised his gloved hand and lifted his shoulders an eloquent gesture. "I learned more than I wanted to during th war." He looked at his cosmetic hand as though he had just noticed on the end of his arm.

I looked down at Ric's still bleeding hand and gulped back feeling of nausea. My fingers were groping for the length of yarn ti to my belt loop. I needed to braid. I could hear the mantra forming my head–*braid ten and you won't throw up*. I clasped my han together to fight off the temptation. I had to refocus. I needed think of Ric.

"I'll call an ambulance. Where's the phone?"

"No ambulance. Drive me to the hospital." Ric's face looked armingly pale. DeFreest had directed Ric to lower his head between s knees with a gentle push on his head.

Anxious to do something, I put on my jacket and lifted Ric's om its peg. "I'll drive him to the hospital. Help me get him into my r."

"No, I'll drive him." Lily moved to retrieve her jacket from the oor. "I feel responsible."

"I'm responsible for this mess. I repeated Ric's conversation this orning."

Lily turned and spoke to Ric's bowed head. "You called *her* to ll her you were coming here?" Lily's voice was a higher pitch than er normal tone.

Ric raised his head. He looked awful. I moved quickly to his de. "Look, it doesn't matter. Now help me get him to my car. You n't even know there the hospital is, do you?" I had Ric on his feet d his jacket around his shoulders. The gash was still bleeding. I uldn't believe all the blood on his clothes, the carpet, and now my othes.

DeFreest opened the front door and helped Ric down the steps. ly gave one last try. "What about Harry? You have to call for m."

My God, Harry. I had all but forgotten about him. No time to rate myself. It was his rash behavior that caused this mess. I pped a mental coin and then did what I was going to do anyway. avid Katernak, K-a-t-e-r-n-a-k, he's in the book." I closed the ssenger door and hurried to my side. A quick glance showed me a hug Lily. I had turned over my husband's rescue to his beautiful ex- ver.

Ric must have read my mind. "He'd be even crazier than I ready think he is."

"Shut up," I growled. "You're both crazy and I should strangle *th* of you." My tone invited no argument.

"Thanks, Gracie," Ric mumbled as he closed his eyes.

Chapter Twelve

The emergency room personnel helped Ric from the car and int[o] a wheelchair. The triage nurse asked questions to make h[er] determination. She also noted his badge number on her papers. [I] wondered if his occupation would give him preferential treatment [or] more red tape than most accidents.

I left Ric in good hands and walked toward the bank [of] telephones and vending machines at the other end of the lobby. M[y] journey to buy a cup of coffee and call Karen to come fetch h[er] brother home was interrupted by a heavily accented voice.

"Mrs. Grace, Mrs. Grace. Over here I am standing. Over here.["]

I turned to trace the caller and spotted Gertrude Klops inde[ed] standing *over here*. Gertrude is the lady friend of Harry's masseu[se] handyman, and friend, Walter Stahl. Harry and Walter have [an] unusual employer-friend relationship that started long before I m[et] Harry. Gertrude met Walter during the trouble at Regina Colleg[e.] Her Oak Park residence had been set afire in an attempt to destr[oy] evidence of a crime. Walter had been helping her renovate her hom[e.] In the course of the last few months love had flourished. It was swe[et] to see them holding hands and fussing over each other. Walter wou[ld] turn seventy next month and she was an easy sixty-something.

Gertrude was barely two yards behind me. I must have walk[ed] right past her in my quest for coffee. In silence she would be easy [to] miss. Gertrude is a tiny, small boned woman with lively blue ey[es] and light brown hair captured in a never neat bun. The eyes belie h[er] exuberance. Once her mouth opens, her entire body springs in[to] action.

"Good morning, Gertrude. Are you okay?" Call it a bias [of] youth, but with the over sixty bunch I assume the worse ca[se] enario.

"Oh, ja. I am *sehr gut*. I *vas tinking* the same to you." Gertrude ad been in this country for forty years but her accent still astounded e. With that sentence, she had taken four birdlike steps, head obbing, and hands fluttering and moved directly next to me. In ivate I called her the *German Canary*. Before I could answer, she ootted the stain on my clothes from Ric's blood.

"*Mein Gott*, Mrs., *du bist* hurt!" Her hands were flying now.

"No, Gertrude. I'm fine. I seized one of her hands and she ought the other one in for a landing over mine. "I'm fine," I peated. "A friend of mine cut his hand badly and I drove him here." nodded my head toward where I had left Ric.

Gertrude appeared to recognize him and looked at me with a estion that she was too polite to ask. She patted my hand and umbled something about being happy that I was fine. It was my rn to ask the question. "Why are you here?"

Her face beamed as she fingered the button on her sweater. OLUNTEER. I am helping peoples *mit vat* is needed. I am inging coffee *und* newspaper."

She was the oldest candy striper I'd ever seen, but then everyone living longer; I guess mature candy stripers are the order of the day. y usually not chauvinistic husband still laments the changes in the ight attendant requirements. He is gracious, but resents being rved in flight by someone older than his mum.

Assuming her duties, Gertrude offered to get me a cup of coffee. accepted gratefully and continued my route to the telephones. After veral assurances to Karen that Ric was fine, but needed a lift home, nung up and accepted my coffee.

I intended to finish my coffee, check on Ric, go home, and try to nd news on Harry. Maybe he would already be home and waiting to nd out where I'd been. Maybe he wouldn't care. Yet another cented voice interrupted my thoughts.

"*Gut Morgan*, Mrs. Grace. I come to get Gertrude and I find o pretty *Fraus*." Walter's flirting sent Gertrude fluttering. A rfect description of Walter would be a fireplug or brick outhouse. e was about 5'10" and solid. He had huge forearms and a deep rrel chest. I know one of his previous occupations in the *old*

country was that of a carpenter. It showed in his strength–even at h
age. His blue eyes focused on me.

"Good morning, Walter. I'm fine," I hurried to explain before I
spotted the blood on my clothes. "Are you a volunteer too?" I teased

"*Nein, nein*. I am volunteer chauffeur." He laughed at his jok
Gertrude's soft chirp-like chuckle encouraged Walter. "Ja, *Ich bin c
volunteer's volunteer*." More laughter and then Walter stopp
smiling. "You are fine. Where is Mr. Harry?" He looked at the sta
on my clothes with renewed interest. I didn't want to explain abo
Ric. "Mr. Harry, I mean Harry is fine. Really. He's not here. He's
he's in jail."

Chapter Thirteen

Walter's reaction was expected. He seemed to snap to attention and his eyes pierced mine with a disturbing intensity. "Jail. *Vas ist* *s*? Why Mr. Harry is in jail?"

I stared at Walter, returning his beseeching look with silence. My mind wondered at the possibilities going through his mind; this long time friend, personal trainer and confidant of my currently jailed husband.

"*Gott in Himmel*, Mrs. Grace, *vas ist los*?"

What is happening?   Good question.   What the hell is happening?

"It's a long story. Harry argued with Inspector Kramer, there was a fight and he was arrested. Ric is in there somewhere," I motioned behind me, "receiving care for a deep cut he received when Harry punched him. I drove Ric here, Lily called our attorney for Harry, and that's about what's happening." The result of my one breath explanation was an expected outburst of questions, exclamations, and more questions. The words blended, the faces blurred and I realized how dogged tired I was. I knew they wanted more than the *Reader's Digest* version, but I was tired, hungry, and a much cranky.

Gertrude had stretched up on her tiptoes to whisper to Walter. He had turned his head toward the area where Ric had been seated. I could imagine what the *German Canary* had sung in his ear. Walter's look was still intense, but with a little confusion and concern mixed

"*Vat* did the lawyer, Mr. Katernak say? Can we go get Mr. Harry from jail?" Walter waited for my answer.

I hesitated; I hadn't formed an easy explanation for the turn of

events since six o'clock this morning. My hand sidled down to m
yearned for yarn and Walter followed the motion. He knew I wa
OCD. Harry had explained my quirk and instructed Walter to ignor
it as per my wishes. He was torn now. Should he back off and no
upset *Mr. Harry's* missus or should he persist on behalf of his frienc
I could envision the scales tipping to and fro. Walter was too good
person to be left twisting in the wind.

"Walter, I needed to get Inspector Kramer here as quickly a
possible because we couldn't stop the bleeding. So, Ms. DeFreest an
her father were going to call our attorney for Harry." I threw in *an
her father* to give my decision to choose helping Ric over helpin
Harry more credibility. Walter wasn't buying those apples.

"You let Miss Lily call lawyer for Mr. Harry?" His tone was s
incredulous I knew I had lost favor with Walter. Before I could sa
anything more, Karen called my name as she walked toward us.

"Grace. What's happened?"

"Not good things." Walter answered with his two cents before
could. "I go to your house and get things for Mr. Harry if he n
home from jail."

"Jail?" interrupted Karen.

"*Ja.* Your brother put Mr. Harry in jail."

"Walter, wait. Karen, I'll explain everything in a minut
Walter, you don't need to get Harry's things. I can do that. I'll ta
care of it."

"Sorry, Missus, but so far you not take good care of Mr. Harr
I go."

Walter took Gertrude by the hand and they both turned a
walked toward the exit. I didn't know if I was furious with him
grateful that somebody other than Lily would be helping Harry.
turned my attention to Karen.

"I will explain all, but could you please get more coffee." Whi
Karen went off in search of caffeine, I untied the length of yarn fro
my belt loop and began a braiding pattern in earnest. When Kar
returned with the coffee she knew to sit quietly while I finished n
loops and crossovers.

"Grace, I'm going to check on Ric and let him know I'm he
I'll be back soon."

I smiled up at her and nodded. A few more minutes would be all needed to calm my *jitters*. That was the name my mom had given y particular idiosyncrasy when I was a child. She was the one who d taught me to braid and knot yarn after I had worn bald patches on y head from constantly twirling my hair around my finger. My others were all Boy Scouts. They had taught me all the knots they d to learn. *Fifteen bowlines*. Finished.

"Grace, Ric's not ready to leave. They need to do surgery on his nd." Karen looked paler than she had ten minutes ago.

"Oh no. Is he going to be all right?" I probably looked paler an I had one minute ago.

"The doctor doesn't think Ric will lose mobility of his thumb. ae tendon is partially cut and they want to suture it and place some pe of membrane over the area to promote healing and strengthen it. aey'll probably release him later today."

"Thank goodness he'll be okay. I suppose you're wondering…"

"No, actually I'm not. Ric filled me in."

Did her voice seem tight, a little accusatory perhaps? I didn't ow if I was hearing between the lines or feeling guilty about erything.

"I'm going to head back."

"Since you're all the way out here, I thought we'd grab a bite. e can go to…"

"Grace, shouldn't you be doing something about Harry?" she ked.

Dammit, what was wrong with me? So far, everyone except me is doing something about Harry. "Sure, I thought since you were re."

"Another time, Grace. I have a meeting for the *Whirl* at my ace at one o'clock. I should get prepared for that. I'll talk to you norrow." She leaned toward me with a half body hug and then left.

I was alienating my friends left and right. I finished my coffee d bought a muffin for the ride home. What would I find at home? y husband? Walter? I pulled out of the parking lot and headed for ne Marsh. I dialed my number hoping Harry would answer and tell ι that he understood why I chose as I did. I didn't understand, why uld he? The machine picked up the call and I hit the end button. I

developed a plan as I drove west on Ogden Avenue toward the ram
to I-355. I would go home, change clothes, call David Katernak, a
start setting things right with everyone. As I crossed the bridge
enter the compound I remembered that Harry's car was still parked
front of Lily's house. I turned the opposite way and drove to h
house. Harry's Jaguar was gone. Maybe Walter had come b
Maybe Harry was home. That thought brought a smile to my hea
and I pulled into the driveway to turn around. The front door open
and Leo DeFreest stepped out onto the porch. He motioned at me
come inside. Maybe he had information on Harry. I parked my c
and walked toward the door. I stepped up the three brick stairs.

"Mrs. Marsden, please come in. I was hoping you'd stop ba
with news of the Inspector.

Ric, again. Always.

He led me through the hall and back to the great room and t
sturdy oak table that had survived this morning's fracas. The brok
crockery had been swept away and all the spills wiped up. Even t
bloodstains I assumed would be everywhere around the table we
absent. I sat in the chair he indicated and accepted his offer of coff
While he prepared the brew in the kitchen, I unzipped my jacket
remove it. I realized I was still wearing the shirt spattered with Ri
blood. The brown stains looked grisly and I briefly flashed back
the scene of Derek's body, the blood on his jacket from the wou
that had once been his face. I quickly zipped up the jacket as I hea
my host enter the room. He placed a steaming mug of coffee in fr
of me and took the seat to my left. He made no comment about m
jacket and I wondered if the rest of me looked as bad and
explanation was necessary.

"I'm assuming you haven't stopped home yet," he bega
"Would you like to freshen up a bit here?"

*Boy, he was smooth. He made it sound like my nose was shi
and needed a touch of powder.* "*Ah,* no thank you. I want to g
news of Harry and go home. Thank you for the offer. The coffee
enough. Really." I took a sip to assure him that his hospitality w
impeccable and appreciated. The coffee was excellent.

He didn't seem reassured. In fact, he seemed upset; as upset
his cool, detached demeanor could appear. Then it hit me. L

asn't home. *She* was probably arranging Harry's release at this very moment. *Dammit!*

"Has Lily gone to res–pick-up Harry? Is that why you looked so preoccupied?

"No, Lily is upstairs. I thought she would have come down at our arrival. Perhaps she has fallen asleep. She did tell me that the ttorney said your husband's arraignment wouldn't be until Monday."

"That's not possible. He didn't mean it. They don't understand."

"What they understand is that your husband assaulted a police fficer. He meant it Mrs. Marsden. I saw the look of satisfaction on is face. He knew he would be arrested. At that moment, I don't ink he cared. Those two must have some history together to evoke ose emotions."

I wasn't going to enlighten him. I stood up feeling numb. Thank you again for the coffee. You've been kind considering day's events. I need to go home and pack some things for Harry." I irned toward the door.

"Mrs. Marsden?"

It was one cup of coffee. How much did he expect in return? I irned back to catch that look again. "I'm sorry, Mr. DeFreest, but m tired. What is it now?"

"I believe whatever Lily has done today was in your husband's est interest; they were close at one time. She spent an hour with our attorney."

"Damn," exploded from my mouth. "Let me guess. Princess ily is rescuing her white knight. Is that the playbill here?" I didn't ait for his response. I exited the house in an ungracious and irnyard mode leaving the oak door banging open on its hinges.

I hadn't moved but three yards across the lawn when I heard ily's voice behind me. I knew I should keep moving toward my car it my feet stopped and I turned to face her.

Lily swept down the steps as gracefully as any person I had ever en. I felt a lurch in my chest as I realized her poise and movement minded me of Grace Kelly, my dad's all-time favorite actress and e person for whom I was named. She glided toward me holding arry's jacket in one hand and a camera, with the strap trailing down, her other hand. She slipped the strap over her arm and head in one fluid motion as she approached me.

"Grace, I guess you came for this." Lily extended the jacket in front of her as she met me on the lawn. "I could have saved you the trip, but I forgot it here when I brought Harry's Jaguar home."

My hand stopped in mid-air inches from the jacket she was offering. "You brought Harry's car home?"

"Yes. David called me after he spoke with Harry. He said Harry had asked for some things and since we didn't know when you'd be back, I ran the car over and collected the items for David to bring to Harry."

By this time, my temper was so close to exploding through the top of my head that I felt my scalp bubbling. This was too much. "How did you get into my house?" I already knew the answer but couldn't stop the painful query. At least she had the decency to turn deep shade of pink.

"*Ah*, when I was in your house the other night it came up in conversation. About how much easier it was to hide a key rather than have to run to the neighbor's house, especially in this compound."

Her weak narrative wound down as mine shot up. "How dare you enter my house and sneak through *our* bedroom to help yourself to Harry's things. Have you done your good deed for the day?" dripped sarcastically from my mouth. "Did you enjoy *gathering* Harry's things and *snooping* through our bedroom?"

"Actually, I didn't need to enter the bedroom. Walter was there with much the same idea. He collected the items and drove me back to my house to wait for David."

Her calm, smug answer angered me even more. In contrast to my molten temper, she was a regular ice queen. I was certain that if I touched her, steam would result from the contact. I reached for the jacket she had been holding and jerked it from her hands. "He didn't choose you then and there's no contest now. You're on notice, Lily. Stop trying to weasel your way back into Harry's life." I turned toward my car. She followed me with her parting shot. "He certainly needed someone in his life this morning. You were nowhere to be found.

Genes. I blame it on the genes. The instinct of generations of Italian women fighting for their men surged through me and I leaped

ack at her and filled my right hand with as much of her long, blonde
air as I could grab before she reacted.

I didn't see the hand come up from her side until it was inches
om my face. I felt the smarting sting and heard the loud smack
gainst my cheek in one of those slow motion seconds everyone talks
bout. She pulled her hand back for another slap. I dropped the
cket and reached up to her hair with my other hand. I dug into her
ale hair and turned my fingers as though holding the reins on a
ubborn mount. My right knee came up into her abdomen and I
eard a satisfying thump. My nonna taught me that move when we
ved in the city on Taylor Street. I had used it only once on a boy
amed Gregory Lewis when we were kids and he made fun of Nonna
anta's broken English.

Triumph was short-lived as Lily leaned into me, grabbed my
rists, and pressed hard with powerful thumbs against the base of my
and. That move loosened my grip on her hair long enough for her to
eave me over her hip and onto my back with a loud thud. She was
n top of me with a *whoosh* as the breath escaped from my lungs.
he camera that had hung at her side now swung forward narrowly
issing my left ear. I felt the breeze as it ruffled my hair. I didn't
emember much about physics, but I knew what swung one way
robably would swing back. I moved my head to the right and felt
e camera smack against my shoulder on its return path. One of my
nds managed to stop one of hers from its intended target, my face,
t my other hand was pinned under her right knee. She could still
serious damage. I tried to pull my leg up far enough to push her
f. I wasn't that flexible so all I could manage was to flail my leg
ound hoping to hit her. I must have looked like a turtle with a
arlie-horse. If I weren't about to be pummeled, I would be
ughing.

"Lily Louise," boomed from somewhere above me. I thought
e Almighty had weighed in on my side. I thought of Bill Cosby's
oah skit and started to smile in spite of my imminent peril. Relief
ashed over me. Lily's fist was stayed in its forward motion toward
y face by the owner of the voice. Leo DeFreest was holding his
ughter's forearm and pulling her off me. He sternly motioned her
ck to the house and turned to help me stand. "Mrs. Marsden, are

you all right. Please come and sit down and catch your breath."

I gulped some deep breaths to fill the void. "I'll stand. I'm fine" I was finally able to say.

"Mrs. Marsden, I won't speak for my daughter. I wish to conve *my* sincere apology for all the problems my daughter's arrival here Pine Marsh has caused."

I murmured something appropriate and walked to my car. I w too tired to worry about his concerns. He attempted to follow me the car. My arched eyebrow with an expression of annoyan stopped him in his tracks.

The short drive home barely gave me time to register the reali of what had happened. Brawling on the beautifully manicured law of a six-figure home in an exclusive, upscale suburb. Was Jer Springer next? *Wealthy, winsome women who wallop weekly!*

The teaser line brought a smile to my lips. What would my da think? Hardly the behavior he'd expect from his *Grace Kel* daughter. How could so much have gone so wrong in so little tim My question sounded like the title to a country and western tun Three days ago, I reestablished my friendship with a dear friend; high water mark that had been drained by being threatened by a de woman, stalked by a hired assassin, and involved in a *cat fight* wi my husband's ex-lover. Oh, and my husband? Him I left rotting jail while I played Florence Nightingale to *my* ex-lover. *Gee, Grac even Dynasty and Dallas didn't top this. Maybe the dream season (Dallas. This was a nightmare!*

I turned my car into our driveway and pressed the remote. T overhead door rode up smoothly on its tracks and I pulled up on n side of the garage and nearly rammed Harry's Jag, so accustomed a was to parking on the right side. Lily had pulled Harry's car into n spot. A momentary flare of pique enveloped me as I thought again her in my house. I backed up and repositioned my entry into t garage. It's not as though I never parked on this side, but my routi was to park right and walk around the front of my car to enter t house. On my way around the Jag's front end, I noticed that t boxes of *jumble* donations had been moved around a bit. Odd, bu didn't remember Harry having any more items or any more interest the upcoming church bazaar. Odder still, there were items in a b hich contents I knew by heart that weren't there yesterday. I ached in and pulled up a wide colorful strap connected to a 35mm mera. It looked to be in excellent condition. The strap was a inbow of jewel tones. Another search yielded a nicked and battered *ppo* lighter and a long, narrow C.D. Peacock box. I started to open e box, anticipating a bracelet or watch. Inside the box was a irrow, turquoise colored velvet case. It looked older than the box. [y level of excitement crept up as I lifted the hinged lid. The ntents snapped my eyes to *dinner plate* size.

The sound of the overhead door on its return journey to the irage floor gained my complete attention. I hadn't pressed the itton. I snapped shut the case and moved toward the door into the use. A dark garage brought back unpleasant memories. My hand as reaching for the doorknob. I realized the knob was turning.

Chapter Fourteen

I stood like a deer in headlights only there weren't ar headlights. In fact, the overhead light activated by the garage do had gone out. There was ambient light in the garage to be able to se my way, but I couldn't move. I'm certain my brain was sending figh flight signals. My body was responding with ostrich syndrome sinc I squeezed my eyes shut to the tiniest possible slit.

Relief and Walter's words reached me at the same tim "Missus. Are you all right? Your face, you look in pain. You g pain?"

I almost laughed at his question. Instead I rushed him and thre my arms around his neck. The sobs started and for the next thir seconds I hung on to Walter as though I would be tossed overboar on the next high roller. I had felt unsteady and adrift from famili routine all day. The sensation of swaying didn't stop; in fact, heightened. Walter lifted me off the ground easily and carried n inside to the loveseat in the living room. A surge of embarrassme colored my neck and face if the increased heat in that part of my boc was any indication and I immediately tried to sit up. Walter's p roast sized hand gently stayed my attempt.

"You stay lay down. I am sorry I scare you now. I am sorry not help you today at hospital. I think only of Mr. Harry. He wou not be pleased I not think of you first."

Walter's self-recrimination summoned the tears again. I looked aghast at what he had wrought with his touching speech. forced myself to gulp and stem the flow of tears. In a sweet gestur which threatened to continue the waterworks, Walter handed me h crisp, white handkerchief. Gertrude had probably ironed into tl perfect square for his back pocket. I used it several times to stop tl ears and clear the way for normal breathing.

"Thank you, Walter. Please don't be so hard on yourself. This has been a crazy day and you don't know the half of it." Walter's face looked confused at my last comment. I started to fill him in on my encounter with Lily. Before I recounted round one he interrupted me.

"Missus. I must tell you, that lady Lily *vas* here in your house. I was here too but she come in with the key from the back porch. I tell her she doesn't must be here, but she tell she has permission from Mr. Harry to come in and get his things. I don't like *dis* permission. I tell her I get his things. She don't like I tell her wait."

A new stream of tears threatened to flow as I listened to Walter. His loyalty to Harry filled me with pride for a man who could engender such friendship. I realized Walter was loyal to me too. "Walter. I know you did your best. Thank you." I decided not to continue my story. He seemed upset enough. I didn't want him to feel he'd somehow let me down.

"I make you English tea to feel better. Or will you like *eine bier*?" He waited for my answer sincerely thinking both choices were equally viable.

"*Ah*, actually Walter, I'd like some water. I haven't eaten all day and I don't…"

"*Ach*! *Das ist vas* is wrong *mit* you. You are hungry. I will make big dinner for you." Walter beamed at me. He made a move toward the kitchen. I couldn't imagine what *big dinner* he would make, but I knew I couldn't eat anything *wiener* or *schnitzel* at this point.

"Wait. I'm not hungry. I was going to reheat some of the split pea soup Harry made and maybe have a ham sandwich and some potato salad…" I stopped reviewing my *menu* when I noticed Walter's smile.

"*Das ist gut*. I know now *vas* you want." Walter motioned me to stay put while he marched into the kitchen. I felt guilty sitting on my behind while he puttered in my kitchen, but I reasoned Walter felt the need to do this for *Mr. Harry*. I leaned back against the firm pillow and tried to sort out the day's events, my feelings, my actions, and my motives. Why was everything connected with Ric always so complicated? I knew we shouldn't have called him.

The Lion Tamer: A Caged Death

Twenty minutes of self-recrimination and self-evaluation netted me nothing except a renewed throbbing at my left temple and the realization I was surely getting weak from lack of food. I was dramatic about meals. When we vacationed, Harry could always recognize the signs of my decline if he didn't stop and feed me three squares a day. The most beautiful scenery would wane as my stomach took charge of my brain. I hadn't eaten even one proper meal today. I was seconds away from hauling myself off the loveseat to check on my dinner, when I heard Walter's voice announcing his return.

"I *tink* you sleep a little bit, *ja?"* Walter beamed at me as he placed a tray on the coffee table in front of the loveseat. "I put here so you can be comfortable when you eat."

"Walter, thank you for your kindness. Did you make some dinner for yourself? Please join me?"

"Oh, no. I go to Gertrude house for supper. She is very excellent cook." He patted his stomach and smiled.

I hadn't noticed, but his middle section did seem a little more rotund. I started to stand, but he motioned me to stay put. I knew he could show himself out. "Good night, Walter. Say hello to Gertrude for me."

"*Ja*. You sleep after eating. I *vill* call in morning." Walter went out the front door and closed it carefully behind him.

I stuffed another pillow behind me and approached my food. I am obsessive-compulsive about some things and food placement is one of them. This compulsion makes me a royal pain when dining out. I never made it to second dates when I was a teenager if the first date was dinner. My potato salad should have been at three o'clock and my ham sandwich was a little off mark, but the piping hot bowl of split pea soup was exactly centered. A bit of rearranging and made fast and easy work of devouring my breakfast, lunch, and dinner meal.

Finally sated, I stretched my arms over my head and rolled my neck from side to side, wishing I would have requested a massage from Walter instead of a meal. Well, maybe both. I stood up to bring my tray to the kitchen. The jewelry box I had apparently held onto and then released when Walter tucked me onto to the loveseat fell to he floor. Good grief, how could I have forgotten the contents? I eached down to retrieve the box.

A noise from the garage stopped me. Had Walter returned? He vouldn't use the garage. He knew I was home. He'd ring the bell. Maybe not. He might think I followed his advice and went to bed. Vhy would he come back?

This thought process was getting me nowhere. Darkness had settled slowly in the room over the last few minutes. I strained my eyes toward the kitchen. Either check it out or call the police. Decision made I moved toward the phone. My toe bumped the box and pushed it under the loveseat. I reached the phone and lifted the eceiver about the same time I heard a loud thump. It sounded like someone was in the kitchen. I pushed 9-1-1.

Oh, God, not again. "This is Grace Marsden at Six Pine Road in he Pine Marsh compound," I blurted as soon as the operator came on he line. "Someone is in my house. Please help me."

"Mrs. Marsden we're sending a unit. Can you leave your house and get to a neighbor?"

"No. I'm afraid to leave. I'm going to hide in the house." I dropped the phone and ran into the adjoining room. Our library's unique feature saved my life once before. I reached the fireplace and wisted a triangularly shaped stone. A panel in the wall slid open noiselessly and I quickly slipped into its interior. A touch of a knob and the panel was in place again.

This was *de ja vu* all over again. Less than a year ago, I stood in his darkened priest's hole hiding from a hired killer. Who was out here now? The man who had been hired to kill me had met his own brutal death. My heart thumped like a jackhammer and the dinner I relished moments before threatened to explode from my throat. My thoughts churned as quickly as my stomach. *Was anyone out there? Did I imagine noises? Am I hiding in the dark from no one?*

The sound of a siren grew louder and I felt relief replace nausea as I calmed myself with the knowledge that I was safe. I heard pounding on the door and shouts of, "Police, open the door." I knew from the last time if I didn't open the door they'd break it down. I pressed the release believing if anyone had been in the house they'd have fled by now. I was wrong.

Chapter Fifteen

I rushed into the room. Halfway across, almost to the center, heard a soft gasp from my left. I froze in my steps, literally as m body temperature dropped due to the shock and fright. Whoever wa in the room stood between me the hallway. My eyes were alread accustomed to the dark. I couldn't see anyone but there was a larg *armoire* positioned at the entrance to the living room. He could b there. The pounding at the door stopped; my heart picked up the lou staccato beat. Only seconds passed as my mind struggled with course of action.

I could return to the priest's hole. I could run screaming like crazy lady toward the hallway and hope I startled the intruder lon enough to reach the front door. I could pick up the fireplace poke and charge whoever was there.

A faint sound registered. A stealthy *whoosh*, the tinie movement of air behind me propelled me forward across the roon through the door, down the hallway, skidding to a stop at th oversized oak door. A quick flip of the deadbolt and the door jumpe back in my hand, seemingly aware of how close it came to b splintered.

The officer wielding a battering ram contorted and stumbled t keep from delivering the blow meant to gain access and save me as rushed forward to escape the house. The pool of light from ou security system illuminated three surprised expressions. Two officer rushed into the house.

"Holy crap! I almost broke you in two." The officer tremble with that realization. I wasn't holding up well either. My knees fe like stretched out rubber bands. He noticed my wobbly movemer and reached out his arm to support me. "Here, sit down," he ordered

He guided me to the top step and held on to my arm until I was seated. "You might want to put your head between your legs for a few minutes. You look too pale," he said as he followed his suggestion with a gentle push on the top of my head.

"Are you ill? Do you want me to call an ambulance?"

"I'm fine. No ambulance please." I wasn't fine. I was scared to death. A trip to Good Sam wouldn't fix that. I sat on the top step of my beautiful home wishing I were back home in my parents' bungalow surrounded by brothers, pets, parents, and a time before now.

I don't know how much time passed before I became aware of the other officers outside again. "Mrs. Marsden, we've checked the house. There's no one in there. Let's move inside."

I hesitated at the door. "No one is in the house Mrs. Marsden. You can go in." He spoke with a reassuring and familiar voice. It was then I recognized Sergeant Peterson. This must have been *de ja vu* for him since he had taken the call the last time.

We moved into the kitchen. I flipped all the toggles flooding every nook and cranny with Bogeyman vanquishing light.

"Can I make you some coffee?" I asked, automatically reverting to hostess manners.

"Only if you'd like some, Mrs. Marsden," was the polite reply. I busied myself brewing a fresh pot of *Kona Blue*. I plucked a length of purple yarn from a book lying on the counter thinking that I might need it more than the book. Sergeant Peterson seemed to understand the therapeutic effects of routine and putter since he didn't speak until I had placed a mug of piping hot coffee in front of him and pushed the cake plate closer to him. Along with the mug I had set some dessert plates and forks on the table. I lifted the top off the plate to reveal Danish from Lindstrom's, a local and yummy bakery in downtown Lisle.

"Where are the other officers?" I looked around not aware they had gone.

"They're doing a search of the grounds and then they'll be going back to the station. I came in a separate squad when I heard the call come in. Actually, I brought the ram. I thought they might need it." His tone had shifted from informational to a little sheepish at his mention of his foresight.

"Please, help yourself," I said trying to hold on to som
semblance of normalcy. I knew the questions he would ask. I wa
surprised by the first one.

"Mrs. Marsden, I didn't notice in the light outside, but you
cheek looks swollen. Are you all right? Did you hurt yourself gettin
out?"

I had forgotten about the slugfest earlier. *Damn!* Now wha
could I say. He was waiting for some response. "*Ah,* I tripped ove
some boxes in the garage earlier. Caught the edge of the workbench
I lied. I mumbled something about putting ice on it. He seeme
satisfied with my answer.

"That answers another question I had. We checked the garag
and are confident the intruder entered through the side door. It wa
unlocked. There was no forced entry and your alarm was off."

"I know the door was locked. No one's been home all day
Then I thought about Lily being here and Walter coming in and th
strange boxes on the workbench. My face must have reflected m
thoughts.

"Have you thought of something, Mrs. Marsden?"

"Oh, something and probably nothing." I told him about th
people traffic I knew about. The news that Lily knew where we kep
the key seemed to interest him. His eyebrow moved up the tiniest b
when he jotted a note in his notebook. I took some perverse teenag
type hormonal joy in thinking I may have caused her a little trouble.

"Back to those boxes. We found them upended with th
contents on the bench and floor. Did you do that?"

"No, I noticed them when I came home and looked inside.
picked up a few things, but put them back before I came inside."

"*Hmm.* Before or after you tripped over them?"

I felt my face blush hot with embarrassment at being caught in
lie. My right hand found the yarn I had looped once around my le
wrist. I *had* to braid five knots before I could look up. Sergea
Peterson seemed to understand I was working my way to an answe
He saved me further guilt pangs when he continued his questionin
Now it seemed to be *off the record* as he had closed the notebook
had been writing in, clicked off his pen, and placed it neatly next

ne notebook.

"Mrs. Marsden, I know Mr. Marsden isn't home and you haven't mentioned him once during this entire ordeal. Should we be moving on a specific issue? There are people you could talk to about any personal concerns."

Several seconds of silence followed as the meaning of his words reached my brain. *He thinks Harry hit me! Oh my God!* Another wave of crimson washed across my neck and face if the heat I felt and the widening of his eyes were any indication. "Harry didn't do this." I touched my cheek. I gave him the Reader's Digest condensed version of my day. I give him credit for not choking on his Danish when I described the scene on the lawn.

"All right then," he said briskly as he opened his notebook, clicked his *Bic,* and poised to take notes. "How long after Mr. Stahl left did you hear the noise?"

I answered a few more questions on timeline. He wanted me to go out to the garage with him to determine if anything was missing.

The boxes I had left stacked on the workbench were on the floor in front of my car, their contents carelessly strewn across the concrete. I explained most of the items were known to me and they were being donated to the church bazaar. "There were a couple of items I didn't recognize. Maybe a neighbor brought them over yesterday and Harry didn't tell me. There was a 35mm camera, an old *ippo* lighter and a*, ah* box, a small box."

The little voice that questions our motives now spoke up in my head wondering why I didn't *come clean* about the jewelry box.

He lifted the boxes onto the bench looking at the contents as I described the foreign objects. "Nothing like that is in here now."

"What? Are you sure? Someone donates to a jumble and then breaks in to take back their donation? Is that some form of *donator's remorse?*"

Sergeant Peterson offered the tiniest smile at my confusion. "Maybe someone knew you were the collection point for Pine Marsh residents and they thought there might be items of value in here. Since the developers have opened three more bridges into the compound, access is harder to monitor."

"Oh, the one man's trash another's treasure explanation?" I

sounded bitchy and knew it. I brushed a lock of hair back behind m ear. My arm felt like lead. Sergeant Peterson must have noticed th movement and recognized my extreme fatigue.

"Mrs. Marsden, you're exhausted. We can continue th tomorrow. The house is secure; you should get some rest. I can b back here in the morning. I'll call you to arrange an appointment."

We had walked back into the kitchen during the last fe minutes. He walked to the back door and made sure the deadbolt wa turned. I followed him as he walked to front door preparing to leave "Lock this after me," he ordered.

"Thank you."

"Your welcome, Mrs. Marsden. If you hear or see anything o of the ordinary, call me immediately. He handed me a business car and pointed to a second number. "My home phone. Use it if yo need too. Good night."

"Good night," I responded automatically. I closed the heav door and flipped the deadbolt into place. He hadn't given us his car the last time he was called out. I tossed the card on the hall table an dragged myself upstairs. The landing outside the master bedroo was decorated with an attorney's bookcase, an old student desk fro my days at Regina, and a hat tree filled with seasonal hats. Ever now and then when I'm approaching the bedroom, I catch the hat tre out of the corner of my eye and for one split second it looks lik someone is standing beyond the corner. I've thought about moving i Tonight, I thought about shooting it. I'd move it in the morning.

The bedroom felt cool and inviting after the frantic even downstairs. I thought I'd be nervous about staying alone in the hous but the police had been thorough and now I wasn't sure I had hear anything beyond the noises from the garage. As Sergeant Peterso had pointed out, the small sounds I heard in the darkness could hav been normal noises gone unnoticed during the bustle of activity. H never actually said that I imagined it, but the suggestion wa definitely on the table.

I pulled off my clothes and glanced at our one-of-a-kind *Bet Boop* clock. She was pointing her hand at nine p.m. It felt like thre in the morning! I pulled back the covers deciding to skip my usu regime of cleansing and moisturizing. I could hear Bonnie, my *Mar

Kay consultant, chastising me; "*Do you want to age thirteen days every time you leave your makeup on overnight?*"   *I could hardly afford that timeline.   Why didn't I know this when I was fifteen and wanted to look older?*

Cleansed, hydrated, and moisturized I climbed into bed with no thought but immediate sleep. Not exactly true. I did think of Harry; how he was feeling tonight. Was he stretched out on a prison cot staring up at the ceiling thinking of me? Was he pacing the small perimeter of his cell remembering another time? My eyes filled with tears that slid down the sides of my face rolling past my earlobes to pool in the hollow of my collarbone. My mind ached at all the snippets of sight and sound I replayed in my head. After some minutes, I realized the images were slowing, white space was flowing between flashes. The motion in my head ebbed and flowed until only a calm pool of memories lingered.

The ringing phone shattered the calm. *Damn.* I rolled over to Harry's side and reached for the annoying instrument. "Hello," I said.

"Hello, Grace. It's David Katernak. I apologize for not calling sooner; I had a dinner function tonight. This is the first time I could get away to call. I'm sure you're worried about Harry."

"Yes, I am. How is he? Did you see him? When can he come home?" My questions tumbled over each other in their rush from my mind.

"I did see him. He's doing as well as can be expected. He should be home after his arraignment day after tomorrow," was his quick professional response.

"Day after tomorrow? Why? Why not tomorrow? Can't you speed up the arraignment? He's not a criminal."

"After the punch he threw and the ensuing injury to Inspector Kramer, the police think he's a criminal. I did what I could, but Harry is no help to himself. You can see him before Monday. I'm going out there tomorrow. I'll pick you up at ten o'clock."

"Thanks, David. *Ah*, how much trouble is he in exactly? I mean he couldn't be sent to jail, could he?"

"Oh, he's in trouble, Grace. Don't doubt that for a minute. The police filed the complaint and booked Harry based on the eyewitness account of the officer at the scene. They couldn't talk to Ric Kramer because he was in surgery. Harry's best hope is that Inspector Kramer drops the charges. If he did, we could spring Harry tomorrow. Grace, I know you have a lot questions. Let's leave them until tomorrow and hopefully get them all answered.

I was totally awake, I wanted answers now, but I knew his plan made more sense. "Sure, David. I'll see you at ten." I replaced the phone and started to roll back to my side when it ranged again. David probably forgot something. "Hello," I said expecting his voice.

"Hi, Grace, it's Karen.

"Hi."

"Grace, you sound funny."

"I'm fine. I'm in bed is all."

"Bed, at 9:15. Are you sick?"

"No, I'm fine. Can't a person be tired?" I sounded more snappish than I had intended.

"Sorry, Grace. I didn't think about the day you've had. How's Harry? Have you had a chance to see him?"

"No, I haven't seen him. I don't know anything more than this morning except Walter took him some things. David Katernak is picking me up tomorrow and we're going to see Harry. How's Ric feeling? Did you get him home?"

"Not exactly," answered Karen. "The doctor didn't like the way he came out of the anesthesia, so they're keeping him overnight for observation. The surgery went fine. No nerve damage. It was close, a matter of a few millimeters and Ric would have lost movement of the thumb and forefinger."

Oh, great. Fat chance he'll drop the charges now. Harry damn near maimed him.

"Grace? Are you there? I said I need a favor."

"Sorry, Karen, I zoned out for a minute. What favor? What do you need?"

"I hate to ask, but I'm flying to Toronto tomorrow morning and thought I'd be taking Ric home this afternoon."

"Karen," I interrupted. "You're not asking me to do what sounds like you're asking me to do, are you?" *I don't believe it! She wants me to pick up Ric.* "Karen, I can't. First of all I'm going to see Harry in the morning. Anyway, I don't want to see Ric."

"Grace, there's no one else."

"What do you mean there's no one else? Ric has tons of friends. What about that redhead we saw at the restaurant? Call her."

"I don't even know who she is. C'mon, Grace? I wouldn't ask if I could reach one of his good friends. My flight leaves at six a.m.; I can't leave this on someone's voice mail."

"It's still early, you said so yourself. Surely you can reach somebody else."

"I tried, I can't and don't call me *Shirley*." Her attempt at humor fell flat like an anvil through a wet paper towel. "I'm sorry, Grace. Please?"

"Oh, hell. Yeah, sure."

"Thanks, Gracie. I owe you big time." She said a quick good bye and hung up before I could change my mind. I glared at the receiver this time as I cradled it daring it to ring again. It did!

I snatched up the receiver and grumbled, "Now what?" Of course, I thought it was Karen with an addendum to her favor. It was my neighbor, Barb Atwater.

"Barb, I'm sorry. I thought you were someone else."

"I'm glad I'm not them." She laughed. "I missed you this morning. I thought we were walking. Is everything okay?"

I had totally forgotten about Barb and our walk. *Was everything okay? Boy, tough to answer in twenty-five words or less.*

"I'm sorry. Something came up and I've been out all day. I know we don't normally walk on Sundays, but I could use the workout."

"Sure. Those slugs at my house never get up until noon on Sundays anyway. I could be out of the country before they knew it."

I laughed at her description of her husband and son. She adored them both. "I'll see you at seven."

I returned to my side of the bed and punched up my pillows, more from frustration than for comfort. Barb's call had relaxed me a little, but I was still keyed up. I began a breathing exercise designed to help you relax individual parts of the body until you felt total relaxation. I had been successfully using this technique for years. Ric had taught it to me...*Damn! Everything betrays me with him.* I pushed my pillows up against the headboard and grabbed the remote from under Harry's pillow. It was noise, I didn't have to think, and eventually I would fall asleep.

Chapter Sixteen

The Sunday morning temperature was barely above fifty degrees hen I greeted Barb Atwater at our usual meeting point, the apex of ur back lots at the pecan shell walking path. By unspoken greement, we took the direction away from Barb's house. After a w yards of adjusted paces and positions, Barb spoke first.

"Grace, I don't mean to be nosey, but I'm so curious I'll burst if ou don't explain yesterday."

I smiled at her tone of voice and began a brief explanation. I hit e high points and the low one on the lawn; delivered with my eyes raight ahead and arms pumping at my side. I sneaked a peek at arb's profile.

"I would have paid money to see you scrambling on the lawn," e laughed. "I'm sorry, that wasn't nice. It's so unlike you. Though don't know Lily at all, she seems so poised and unflappable. "How n they keep Harry in jail?" she shifted her focus to the serious issue. ow awful for him. I can't imagine how he must feel."

Another woman with an interest in my husband. My thoughts ere nicer concerning Barb. I'd always known she had a kind of ush on Harry's "Englishness." I wasn't in the mood to be amused by as I usually am. "No one is behaving normally. It's not exactly in arry's nature to punch out policemen," I said with more sarcasm an I had intended. Barb looked upset.

"Barb, I promise to keep you up to speed on everything. Right w, I'd like to walk and pretend it was a bad dream."

We agreed to enjoy the morning. Our route took us down the le of several holes on the east side of the golf course. The path was the other side bordering the rough. We didn't normally talk on our cursions; conversation was served up later with the bakery. I usually wore an earpiece and listened to music on my Walkm[an] strapped to my waist. Barb always carried a small tape recorder [to] pinpoint the location of lost balls.

Her son, Devin comes by at his leisure and collects them. M[ost] of them are one-shot balls, lost immediately off the tee. He mak[es] money for all the extras teen-aged boys need by selling the balls [to] local offices, his father's mainly. Barb sews bags from mate[rial] printed with golf motifs to hold six or twelve balls. The bags hav[e a] drawstring closure and Devin makes computer-generated tags wit[h a] picture of a golf ball with eyes peeking out from the undergrow[th.] The caption reads, "Over Here!" Their search and recovery team h[as] turned into a clever cottage industry.

Barb recorded a *find* as we briskly paced down the 7th hole. S[he] never broke stride as she documented locations.

"How many this week?" I asked.

"Close to seventy. They had a particularly bad group of duff[ers] at an outing on Thursday. The Chicago Orthopedic Association h[ad] their fundraiser here."

"Didn't you belong to that group?"

"No, no. I worked for an orthopedic surgeon after I gradua[ted] nursing school, before Devin was born. Andrew was on the C.O.A[.] board two years ago and we've remained friends with a few coupl[es.] Andrew suggested they have their outing at Pine Marsh Coun[try] Club. I wish more women had played," she continued in a wist[ful] tone. "There's a market for gently used *Flying Ladies* and *Gol[d] Girls*."

I laughed at Barb's insightful comment. "I lose most of mine [in] the water. Maybe Devin should harvest the ponds."

We laughed together at the thought of her son in scuba ge[ar.] Their method was actually quite scientific. They had mapped the [out] the bounds and rough areas of the course and created a grid Ba[rb] referred to as she recorded the location. The grid was on [a] computer and could track where the balls went astray. Barb and I h[ad] joked about what people would think if they spotted us in the wo[ods] reconnoitering and talking into a recorder. No one could see us fr[om] the course and we seldom found golfers hunting down their golf ba[lls] this far out of bounds. If you could afford to play *Broken Feath[er*] u could afford to forego a search party for a few lost balls.

Since our route was an oval, we had to pass behind Lily's house d the taped off scene of the crime to get back to my house. I tried keep moving, but couldn't stop myself from slowing down as we proached the spot where I had seen Derek's body.

Barb sensed my change in pace. "Is this where the body was?" e seemed nervous and thrilled at the same time. She shivered a tle and handed me the recorder so she could pull down the sleeves her sweatshirt.

"Yes," I answered simply. We had stopped and were staring at e area off the path up to Lily's yard. Bits of yellow police tape, agged on the trees, moved in the breeze. Not much else advertised at someone had died here. No struggle, no trampled ground, no ood, no broken brush.

Suddenly, my brain hit replay and I forced myself to review hat I had seen last week. My memory skirted around the mangled ce and remembered how neat the area was and how intrusive the dy appeared, as though it had been dropped into the scene. ithout thinking, I pressed the button on the recorder and transferred y thoughts to the tape. I moved closer and added some other servations.

Barb's eyes gleamed with anticipation. "Why did you say that? hat did you find?"

"The body was dumped here afterwards. The police know here he was killed." I hadn't told Barb when we passed the Rowe's t that their sauna had been Derek's hiding place.

"Why didn't they tell us? It seems safer if he were left here and t killed here."

Suddenly, I had that creepy feeling when someone's watching u. *Nerves. Get a grip.* "Let's go. I'm getting spooked standing re." I turned and started back to the path that would lead home. arb moved as quickly as I did. Maybe she felt the same uneasiness.

Ten minutes later, settled on my patio with fresh coffee and stries, the feeling of being watched seemed far removed and diculous. We chatted easily about other things until I realized I eded to get ready to go see Harry. I reiterated my promise to Barb keep her informed. She waved a final goodbye when she reached the back of the yard and turned toward her property.

I realized I still had her recorder when I hung up my black a white plaid wool, walking jacket on its peg. I had slipped t recorder into the pocket along with a pretty rock I had spotted and empty, plastic film container from the path. People were messy. was in the habit of picking up litter and rocks, and seedpods and suc on my walks. If I didn't empty my pockets on a daily basis the dang was I'd be carrying extra weight or worse yet would have no room the new treasure.

I walked up the back stairs to my bedroom and turned on t shower while I chose an outfit. *What does one where to visit on husband in the slammer?* Emily Post never covered this dilemma. knew I had to keep joking or I would dissolve into tears. I wanted see Harry, but I had a bad feeling about today. Maybe a steamin hot shower would calm my jitters. I carried a piece of nyl clothesline into the shower with me just in case.

Chapter Seventeen

David Katernak arrived at ten o'clock and we left for the county ck-up within minutes. I had not offered him the coffee I had ewed earlier. I had merely taken a moment to get a jacket after I ened the door to him. We took David's car.

"Grace, I want to let you know seeing Harry might be awkward. ople react differently in these circumstances. Harry is accustomed being on the other side of the bars. His demeanor might not be at you expect."

"He's my husband for heaven's sake. You're talking about rry. He'll be fine with me. We've been through worse than this," I sured David.

The drive was shorter than I expected and soon we were signing register, pinning on I.D. passes, walking down a short corridor to a sitor's room. The room was an unhealthy shade of green with small uares of Plexiglas lighting flush to the ceiling, no windows, and nimal décor consisting of square top picnic table type furniture th attached seats bolted to the floor. David had explained the room uld look bleak.

In spite of my assurances, now that I was seated in this pressing venue, my palms were sweaty and a lump formed in my oat.

The door on the opposite wall from where we were seated ened and Harry walked in and stopped barely inside the room. He s dressed in an orange jumpsuit; the one size fits most type. He ked as tired as I had seen him in years. "Harry," burst from my s as I rushed to him. My mind was a whirlwind of fragmented ughts, one, noticing he hadn't taken another step toward me. I ng my arms around his neck and sobbed his name into his chest.

The Lion Tamer: A Caged Death

Seeing him incarcerated affected me more than I thought it would. Yet, he didn't seem upset or even particularly concerned. The fact that his arms hung loosely around me registered in my brain and choked back my next sob, released my grip, and stepped back to look up at his face. There had been no resistance when I moved away from him. His arms fell quickly to his sides.

My God, is he drugged? Is he in shock? I had to mentally shake myself to stop the thoughts. He was in an U.S. county jail and not a South American prison. No one had hurt him. No one had drugged him. I stared into his eyes as he looked directly at me. They were clear, calm. He must have read the panic in mine because he gently touched the side of my face and carefully tucked a wisp of hair behind my ear. The familiar gesture pushed me toward a crying jag but I swallowed hard realizing I had to keep calm.

Harry seemed to understand my effort and he lowered his hand from my face. "Hello, Grace. Sorry about all this. Couldn't be helped."

"Oh, Harry." I was struggling not to cry. "I'm sorry too. Don't worry. I know you didn't mean it. I mean you didn't mean to hurt Ric. The judge will see, he'll understand." I was babbling. I felt if I stopped talking I would start crying. My mouth was out of control. "David will tell them. Maybe you could come home today. It must be awful for you to be in here. I know you didn't mean it. Ric knows too. I'll talk to him when I take him home."

The smile tugging at the corners of his mouth throughout my Laura Petrie soliloquy instantly vanished and was replaced with a sneer.

"Don't you dare speak to Kramer on my behalf." His words were measured and precise. He turned around and rapped on the door. It opened and he walked back through the door he had never moved more than a foot from during our entire conversation.

Stupid. Stupid of me. How could I say that? Am I an idiot?

"Harry, wait." My voice squeaked with shock. "I only want to help." He was gone. I turned to David.

He turned his hands palms up and shrugged. "I can't make him come back, Grace. Let's go, I'll take you home."

"No. I want to talk to him. I only wanted to help. He has

now. Please, David. Bring him back. Please." The tears came and was helpless to stop them.

"I can't make him. C'mon, let's go. You can't do anymore here. Let me buy you a cup of coffee away from here and I can fill you in on what will happen tomorrow at his arraignment. Please, Grace. That's all I can do."

We stopped at a Starbucks on Roosevelt Road. David filled me with more than I wanted to know or needed to know. I think he kept talking to avoid discussing Harry's behavior. I listened, not interrupting with questions, while David gave me the timetable for tomorrow morning. I actually had no questions, at least none he could answer. He continued to talk. I watched his lips move, his eyebrows lift for affirmation from me, his shoulders shrug in a gesture of wait and see; all this with the sound turned down in my head, like television with the remote on mute.

Two hours later, I headed east on I-88 to exit at Highland Avenue to pick up Ric from Good Samaritan Hospital. Questions without answers paraded through my head, some running to the back of the line to come at me a second time. *Why had Harry been so brutally cold to me? Why had I mentioned Ric? Why am I picking up Ric? Surely, Ric knows other people happy to cart him home? Who is Shirley?* I knew my mind was on overdrive when I started doing stand up comedy routines in my head. I blamed Karen for putting that old word gag in my head last night. That last vaudeville thought snapped me back to the here and now and the problem of finding a parking spot. The first three rows were reserved for clergy and physicians. Sick people and visitors had to park further out. I squeezed into the last space on the ground level.

According to the pimply-faced teenager at the reception desk, Ric was in room 3025. She didn't tell me the North Elevator didn't go there. When I finally found the room, Ric was pacing the perimeter. He stopped, swaying slightly forward on the balls of his feet, like his toes had stuck to flypaper, and stopped his forward motion. I thought he was going to take a step backwards, but he stood his ground.

"What are you doing here? Where's Karen? Why you?" He

finally stopped. He brushed his right hand through his hair. Th gesture was classic Ric, but he always used his left hand, which at th moment, was wrapped in what appeared to be yards of gauze an cradled in a sling. His hair was at odds with his head, being rubbe the wrong way as it were.

"Karen's in Toronto." My reply was brusque. I moved to th chair next to the bed to pick up the small, blue duffel bag on the sea "I don't have a lot of time so let's get going. We can stop by Aldi's you need some groceries, but Karen said she put a few meals togeth for you in the fridge before she left. Is this ready to go?" I aske indicating the bag.

"*Uh*, yes." Ric's confusion was as apparent on his face as if boldly lettered 'HUH?' had materialized on his forehead. The han swiped at the hair again.

I slipped the long strap over my left shoulder. The attenda arrived with the wheelchair. Ric climbed aboard and I followed th pair down to the lobby level. At the doors, Ric lost his ride an walked in silence across the parking lot to his new one. I walke around to the passenger side to open the door. Ric put his hand o mine as I reached for the handle. I turned to face him. "What?"

"You know what. Why are you here?"

"Karen called late last night. She was flying out early. Sh didn't know who else to call. You two don't exactly run in the san circle. I'm pick up and delivery. That's it. That's all. *God, I hop that was all.*

Chapter Eighteen

Ric seemed tired and I certainly didn't feel like talking. We rode
silence for nearly fifteen minutes and then I suppose Ric felt he
eded to make conversation.

"Did you call Dave Katernak? I know he's your attorney."

"*Uh*, no. I didn't call him. Lily called him since I was driving
u." I lifted my shoulders in a small shrug.

"Oh, yeah. I was out of it. If I didn't say thank you then, I'll say
now. I didn't mean to be rude earlier. I was surprised to see you. I
ought you'd be home with Harry." Ric squared his shoulders and
emed to sit up a little straighter in his seat. He seemed to shake off
s sickbed lethargy. "I told the officer who questioned me yesterday
was an accident. I didn't press charges."

Now I sat up straighter and gripped the wheel harder. "You
dn't press charges?" My mind raced through the entire conversation
ith Dave Katernak. I was positive he had said the officer on the
ene had registered the complaint because they couldn't talk to Ric.
as Harry's continued incarceration the result of miscommunication
tween two police departments?

"When did you speak with that policeman? What time?" Ric
oked surprised. My tone was sharp.

"I'm not sure. Right after Karen left, I think. Why?"

"Which time, in the morning before your surgery or later when
u were in recovery?"

"*Ah,* later. I was groggy but I told him. What's with the third
gree?"

Either he didn't know, or he was one damn fine actor. There was
reason for him to pretend. There should have been enough time to
cure Harry's release. I didn't understand. If the victim didn't press

charges there'd be no case. Why hadn't he been released? Not again My brain was stalling, mixing up place and time. Ric was talking, hi voice lifting in question.

"Grace. Grace. Are you in there? Don't think that hard whil you're driving. It's scary from a passenger's point of view." Ri looked concerned as he leaned forward to peer at my face.

I relaxed my grip on the wheel and realized I had driven the las few minutes on *autopilot* to within three blocks of Ric's brownston I pulled up in front of his house, put the car in park but didn't cut th engine.

"All delivered. Can you get the door and everything b yourself? I remembered something I have to do." I knew tha sounded like a brush-off and it was. I had to get away and think an maybe call Dave. A murky, half-formed thought niggled at me an warned me off talking any further to Ric about Harry.

Ric's response was predictable. "Of course I can, but I thoug I'd invite you in for a cup of coffee. It's the least I can do for th trouble you've taken."

"Oh, no trouble. I'm heading over to Regina; had to come rig by here." I hoped my nonchalant attitude struck the appropria chord. Ric had the ability to see right through me sometimes. thanked the sunny day for the need for sunglasses. My eye col change from lavender to purple when I'm excited or scared thwar most of my lies. Maybe the combination of fatigue, drugs, and pa that I saw in his eyes would blur his intuition.

"I won't keep you then." He opened the car door with his rig hand and slid out. He leaned back in to lift the duffel off the sea "Thanks again, Gracie. Maybe a rain-check on the coffee?"

I murmured a vague, "We'll see." I felt guilty about dumpi him on his doorstep. I knew I couldn't let him find his balance. I d want to go to Regina. That's exactly where I could think this out. R must have sensed there was no changing my mind. He straighten up and shrugged his shoulders.

"Yeah, we'll see."

I did have the decency to wait until he entered his building. pulled back into traffic on Franklin and took the familiar route Regina College. My refuge at school had been the south end of t

om in the library that housed the periodicals. The room referred to
the *stacks* had nooks, crannies, and dead-end aisles that provided
clusion. I selected a worn, but comfortable-looking chair and
ttled in for a long think. The only thing missing was a hot cup of
ffee. I didn't feel like walking down to the grill to buy one.

I turned my thoughts away from food and in the direction of why
arry was still in jail when according to Ric he should have been
leased. Was Ric confused? Did the police not tell the district
torney? Why didn't Harry's lawyer know this? Finally, the question
kept skirting until I was getting dizzy from circling: Was Harry in
it? That last one intrigued me the most.

My thoughts were disrupted by a scraping sound down the aisle
my right. I had chosen to sit in one of the dead-end aisles; nowhere
go except over the top of an eight-foot high bookshelf. Less than a
ar ago, I would have jumped through my skin fearful, the legend of
he *Rosary Bride*, a ghost who haunted the old library, was true. On
is April afternoon, I knew *she* was at peace.

Something solid seemed to be bumping into shelves and
rniture as it moved closer to my aisle. *Had someone followed me?*
ad Shelley Walsh hired more than one person to kill me? Thoughts
ere flying through my head faster than the morning express pulling
it when you're a half block from the station.

Fight or flight? The body pumps up adrenaline levels to enable
to act according to the brain's cue. My adrenaline kicked into high;
y brain raced to catch up. The shelving unit three segments down
vayed under the impact of something heavy on the opposite side.

It's fight! I looked around for a weapon. I unsnapped the
oulder strap from my tote and wrapped one end around my hand. I
uld do some damage with the brass swivel clip at the other end.

No, not now. The demon beneath the surface rippled and started
take control as I felt the long length of leather in my hand. *No, I
n't make it shorter! I need it long!* No use. *Five, only five.* Maybe
I still have enough to swing.

Chapter Nineteen

Four, five. I pulled the knot tight and brandished my lum[p]
lanyard in front of me. I'd have to get within six inches of someo[ne]
for this to work. I repositioned my fingers, thinking to use it li[ke]
brass knuckles. The movement swung the clip against the met[al]
shelf. *Damn.*

The noise and movement stopped abruptly. "Hello, is someo[ne]
there?" a shaky voice directly across from me asked softly.

My relief was so complete I couldn't answer for a moment. T[he]
voice floated over the periodical barrier again, "Hello, someone?"

"Hello to you." My voice was strong and loud by comparison. [It]
must have startled her. I heard an *ouch* as the shelf moved slightly. [I]
walked the length of the aisle and turned back up the adjacent on[e.]
"Janet. It's you. I couldn't imagine what or who was making all th[e]
noise coming up the aisle. You scared me half to death."

Janet Henry, the director of alumni relations, stood on the f[ar]
side of an extra-wide cart overflowing with stacks of periodicals, ro[lls]
of paper, and slim volumes that looked like yearbooks. Janet w[as]
rubbing her left elbow. She was short, even compared to my 5'[3"]
stature. Like me, she wore her light brown hair shoulder length. H[er]
clear, gray eyes seemed relieved to see me.

"I thought I was alone in here. I've been trying to reshelve th[is]
stuff since yesterday. Every time I started, something else to[ok]
precedence. I figured this was the best time to try to get this done. [I]
started to feel a chill a few minutes ago and I guess I wasn't bei[ng]
careful about how I maneuvered this thing through the aisle. I had t[he]
oddest feeling I was being watched; guess I was thinking about, y[ou]
know, *her.*" Janet flushed pink as she voiced her fear abo[ut]
encountering the campus spirit.

"Trust me, Janet. She's at peace. It's the live ones we should worry about." I smiled to myself as I repeated my dad's view about ghosts.

Janet smiled at the comment. "I guess you're right. What are you doing in here?"

"Just passing through. Listen, can I help you, as long as I'm here? I worked with Sister Jeanne on her archiving project last summer. I know where some things belong. The yearbooks," I pointed to the slim volumes, "are stored in the room at the end of the last aisle. Blueprints," gesturing to the top shelf, "also get locked up."

"Thanks, Grace. I volunteered to put these away since Sister is in Sinsinawa for the summer, but honestly, I wasn't sure where they went. I made copies of the blueprints and bundled them up to send to your husband. I didn't forget his offer to recreate floor plans of the old dorms for the participating classes in this year's reunion. You can give me the bulk rate and take it with you."

Janet smiled and then her high wattage grin faded. "I don't have a key to the archivist's room. I'll have to wheel this behemoth back to my office until I can call Sister and find out where she keeps it."

"I'll help you. I can pick up the package at the same time." I retrieved my tote and unknotted my shoulder strap. Janet raised an eyebrow in query. "Don't ask."

Since both of us were on the same end of the cart, all I could do was guide her as she backed up pulling the cart. Janet steered the cart down three-quarters of the aisle before she rammed the left side. Several yearbooks tumbled from their unsteady perch.

"Don't worry, Janet. Pull all the way out of the aisle and I'll move up and get them."

I waited for the cart to clear the last upright bookshelf then walked toward the fallen books. I picked up the five volumes; thankful a small college never produced huge social annals. '62, '67, '72, '77, '82. I realized this June was my reunion year. I hadn't given it much thought with all that had happened these last months. My pace slowed as I shifted four books to under my left arm so I could open the fifth–my year. An easy smile stretched my lips as I looked at pictures of friends from all those years ago. Several pages were marked with sticky notes. The notes indicated information about someone on that page. I saw a yellow Post-It with *writes childr* *books* and felt confident that was about me. It was. The note w affixed to the page containing my senior picture. I found interesting note on Mary Kate Collins Nowinsky–she had be appointed to the Minnesota appellate court. *You go, girl,* I thought I remembered a not so serious minded redhead who seemed to m curfew more than most of us. Suellen Rowe, a Pine Marsh neighb (we *beads* were everywhere) had attended Regina years before me. shifted books and opened the one dated ten years before graduation looking for her. Those styles were hilarious. I fleeting wondered what this year's rose recipients would think of my e Another yellow flag caught my eye; *illustrates children books*. *Ah kindred spirit*. I slipped my thumb under the Post-It to open the bo at that page. Four hardbound books slid from my slack arm and the floor. The remaining book gripped so tightly by my hands, knuckles blanched.

A much younger, but even then classically beautiful Lily star up at me from the left-hand page of her yearbook. I knew I h stopped walking. I think I was still standing. I felt as though I shou sit down.

"Grace. I heard a noise." Janet's voice preceded her into t aisle. "Oh," she said as she avoided stepping on the books at her fe She stooped to pick them up. When she straightened, she notice hadn't moved. Janet stepped behind me to see the page I was stari at.

"Lily DeFreest. It's no surprise to me so many of our alums on to such wonderful careers," Janet gushed.

Another famous *bead*; what had started out decades ago as nickname for women from Regina College was now an insider te of endearment. I mumbled agreement and closed the book. followed Janet back to her office where she gave me the packa intended for Harry. I intended to scrutinize it first.

Chapter Twenty

Once I got home, the first thing on my agenda was a call to avid Katernak. I had no doubt I'd reach him. At the fees he harged, he should always available. I dialed his cell phone.

"Hello, David Katernak."

"David, it's Grace. I found out from Ric he didn't press harges."

"How?"

"It's a long story. Not important. The point is, if Ric didn't press harges why is Harry still in jail?"

"Grace, you have to understand something. Harry hit a liceman in front of another cop. He was arrested on the spot. They dn't wait to find out if Ric was going to press charges."

David's explanation did nothing to improve my attitude. I knew was right, that we'd have to wait until tomorrow to secure Harry's lease. I couldn't stand the thought of his being in jail another night.

"I guess I was hoping. Thanks, I'll see you tomorrow."

"Shall I pick you up again?"

"No, I'm fine. I'll meet you there." I wasn't fine. I was worried out Harry, surprised by Lily's connection to Regina, and nervous out being alone in the house. The last problem I could easily solve.

I could call my dad; he'd be on my doorstep with half the orelli cousins and three of my four brothers. A few of their wives uld come along to keep me company and cook for the men. Of urse, some would have to bring their kids. Suddenly that option asn't appealing. I loved my family but I was already overwhelmed.

I could call Walter. He would be here as quickly and his lack of mily would suit me to a tee right now. There was a time I would ve called Ric. Part of me wanted to because he understood me so

well.   The stronger part of me would never call *because* h
understood me so well. Walter won the mental coin toss. I dialed hi
home number and waited through the recording.   I'd never eve
thought he wouldn't be home. He was always home. Always ther
for Harry. I hung up without leaving a message. He was probabl
out with Gertrude. I stopped short of whining and kicking the couch
   The couch. I had kicked the box under the couch last night.
dropped to all fours and pushed my hand under the front end. M
fingertips made contact with the box and I slowly drew it forwar
from its hiding place. I straightened up and sat down on the couc
anticipating a longer look at what I had only glimpsed last night.
discarded the newer outside box and opened the older, perhaj
original box.

A stunning jewel sparkled in a nest of pewter colored foam. Th
hexagon shape was unusual, but it was the color that was s
remarkable. Shafts of blood-red color burst from the center of tl
stone as I moved the box in my hand. I had never seen anything lil
it and walked to the window to hold the box on an angle to the ligh
The stone seemed to explode from its cushion. I expected to see tl
space empty and the jewel splattered against the draperies framing tl
window. I shifted the box and heard a soft scraping sound.
second, identical nest was unoccupied. Maybe the jewel had slipp
under the foam. I eagerly lifted one side. The search revealed a go
setting, slightly twisted and misshapen and a delicate chain. The fir
gold was shaped in the pattern of delicate branches. I felt certain
had held the blood-red jewel at one time. Why would anyone dama
such a lovely piece? Where was the other stone? Most importantl
how did this one end up in my garage?

I had more questions than answers. I knew who to ask about tl
jewel. Kurt Hill owned Cottage Hill Diamonds, a jewelry store
downtown Elmhurst.   The Morelli family had been buying the
baubles and bangles there since my older brother Mike picked c
Carolyn's engagement ring. Cottage Hill had been a wonderf
choice for the quality, originality, and price. Karen and I had pick
out matching circle pins for each other the first Christmas we m
She loved jewelry. When she had inherited her aunt's jewelry she n
with Kurt and had several pieces redone; one of which, a stunni

al ring, graced Hannah Marsden's third finger.

I had been at the store two weeks ago to purchase a gold charm
r Jolene's birthday. Harry and I started the bracelet for her when
e turned sixteen. The recently purchased giraffe charm represented
r Docent status. Her birthday wasn't until May; I hoped I'd
member where I'd put it for safekeeping. Once I found an entire
itchen Scientist Set, purchased for Mike's boys, festively wrapped
behind some coats in the hall closet, six weeks after Christmas. I
-wrapped it and waited for the next Morelli child.

The Cottage Hill business card was upstairs in my address box.
s I climbed the stairs I realized how tired I was despite the lack of
ysical exertion. Emotional turmoil always extracted a toll on me.

I reached the landing and turned toward my bedroom. A shadow
emed to pull back from the hall. I froze to the spot; my heart
mmered against my ribcage. "Damn," exploded from my mouth
ter the split second it took for my brain to recognize the hat tree. I
arched over and grabbed the center pole abruptly uprooting it from
e carpet. The harsh treatment sent hats swinging on their perches
e so many oddly billed birds clutching branches in a windstorm.
y green cap lost its grip, flew off the tree, and landed upside down
the carpet. I carried the hat tree into the guest room and plunked it
wn in the middle of the chintz and ruffles. I closed the door behind
e and stopped short of brushing my hands together in the universal
sture of a job finished.

At the desk I pulled an old wooden box toward me. Its hinged
d made a satisfying s*mack* when you let it drop. Must have been
noying for the librarian at the Gunnerville Library. Harry and I had
ken the scenic route on a trip to New York and stopped for lunch in
unnerville. The Friends of the Library were having a sale to raise
nds. The card catalog boxes were selling for a quarter a piece. I
ught them all and crammed 102 boxes into my jeep. Harry
mplained about the musty smell of old wood and old paper. I
haled deeply and smiled with each breath.

I found uses for the boxes throughout the house. Each room had
least two holding everything from decks of cards and dice to
tpourri in the downstairs powder room. I refinished some and used
em as elaborate gift boxes. Harry used several in his potting shed

for seed packets.

As I opened my address box my fingers stopped. *Oh, here comes. Ten taps and it can stay open for the count of ten. How mu[c] time do I need? Is it under Hill or Cottage Hill? Go ten. 'Smack' t*[e] first of ten.

My obsessive-compulsive quirk had many expressions, ma[ny] outlets. I never bought clothing or purses with snaps. I have driv[e] myself to distraction trying not to snap and unsnap a purse whi[le] attending a wedding, a funeral, a mass; any ceremony. The age-o[ld] question of *What am I going to wear?* isn't as critical for me as, *Wh[at] doesn't make noise? Smack,* nine, s*mack,* ten. *Calvin, Cabba[ge] Patch, Cottage, got it!*

It was after five on a Sunday afternoon. The store would [be] closed. I left the card out on the desk, no sense messing with the b[ox] again. I'd call tomorrow. The phone rang as though prompting me [to] call anyway. It was Walter.

"Hello, Missus. I see your number on my phone. *Ist gut m[it]* you?"

"Not exactly." I filled in the events of last night. As I expecte[d] he berated himself for not staying with me. "Walter, you had no w[ay] of knowing there would be a burglar in the garage. Stop blami[ng] yourself."

"I will be there in few minutes, Missus. Don't open door. Do[n't] go outside."

Walter hung up before I could tell him I was actually feeling le[ss] jittery about staying alone. I knew Walter lived at least ten minut[es] away. The phone rang again. *Probably Walter with mo[re] instructions.* I was wrong.

"Grace, I found out about last night. Why didn't you tell me[?]" Ric's voice was soft and probing.

"Why? Would you have offered double duty of convalesci[ng] and guarding at my house?" I knew I sounded bitchy, but I was tir[ed] of my life popping up in his files.

"Yes, as a matter of fact that's exactly what I would have don[e,] only I wouldn't have offered, I would have insisted. Until we kn[ow] why Rhodes was killed, I'm not convinced you're not in danger."

His words spoken calmly and with conviction chilled me mo[re] an any shouting could have done. "Walter is on his way over to pend the night. I'll be fine."

"I'm glad to hear that. Walter's a good man. I know how he els about me, but tell him to call me if he thinks anything is wrong. race?"

"I'm here. Thank you; I mean for the call and concern."

"I'm always here for you. Goodnight, Grace."

He hung up before I could dispute his last remark. My face felt ushed and my thoughts jumbled with past images that refused to ay behind the curtain. The doorbell saved me from further ontemplation.

I pulled open the door fully expecting Walter. Leo DeFreest ood there instead.

"Mrs. Marsden, I hope I'm not intruding?"

"No, not at all." I looked beyond him toward the driveway. He emed to guess my question.

"Lily is not with me. I thought I would return this," he held up arry's jacket, which had been left behind in the *melee,* "and attempt get started on the right foot with my neighbors."

I must have looked surprised because he continued. "I have ecided to make Pine Marsh my home. Lily cut back her business avels quite a bit. She wanted to return to this area for personal asons and I am at the age where I should call someplace home. We ink it will work out splendidly."

Oh, great, no, splendid. Lily a mere two doors down, forever. ly heart slipped to my waistline and I felt sick. I realized we were ill standing in the doorway. I had better manners, but my body was eling from his one-two punch. Walter, bless his soul, came to the scue. He bounded up the steps and lodged himself between me and y new neighbor. I managed a quick introduction. I noticed the vkward shift when Walter realized he was being offered DeFreest's ft hand. I wondered how many hundreds or thousands of times that d happened. My mind softened a little toward the father of my emesis, who left immediately after the introduction promising to call me at a better time.

"*Ja*, like when Mr. Harry *ist* home," Walter growled under his eath as he stepped inside. "Already, I am not liking him."

"Walter, he hasn't done anything wrong. It's h
daughter…never mind." I closed the heavy door and flipped tl
deadbolt. "Walter, I have some leftover macaroni and braciol
Interested?"

"Oh, *ja*. Sounds *wundebar*."

I knew he'd be interested; Walter loved Italian food. At h
prompting, Gertrude had asked for grandmother Morelli's recipes f
eggplant Parmesan and Melrose peppers. I smiled at his respons
"This won't take long. I'll get this going and then make a salad f
us."

"I *vil* chop for you."

"Thank you, Walter." This new domesticity was no doul
Gertrude's influence. "Everything you need is in the crisper. If yc
want parsley it's outside the door. Take it from the plant closest to tl
door. Scissors are on a hook right there." I nodded my head to tl
wall plaque that held a visor, set of keys, and small trimming scissor

Both Harry and Walter actually ate the parsley used for garnis
They chewed it after a meal to freshen their breath. Must be
European thing; like lemon slices in water. I used parsley sparing
in my gravy, a little sprig while it was simmering. I usually fished
out once the gravy was ready.

Within thirty minutes we were sitting down to a deliciou
dinner. I set a beer next to Walter's plate; I would finish the *pou
Riesling* Harry and I had opened earlier in the week. Had it been on
last week when all this angst was set in motion?

I held up my glass to Walter. "Thank you for coming over. Yc
are a true friend to Harry."

Walter countered with his bottle of Beck. "I am friend of yo
too." He followed his sweet declaration with a healthy swallow.
should have put out two bottles.

Our dinner conversation was unremarkable. We both seemed
steer toward safe subjects like weather and restaurants. Walter ha
unobtrusively glanced at his watch twice since we had sat down
dinner; I wondered if maybe he had broken a date with Gertrude to l
with me. I started to twist a pattern of knots in a piece of raffia on
part of the napkin holder.

I would twist five and then ask him point blank if I was messir

p his love life. I smiled at my plan. *One, cross, cross, loop under*
ross; two, cross, cross…

Walter grunted and grabbed at his chest with his left hand. I
nocked my chair over backward trying to leap up to help him.
Walter, are you choking? What's wrong?" I knew the Heimlich
aaneuver but wasn't certain if I could get my arms around Walter's
irth. He tried to drink some water but immediately vomited. He
rabbed his chest again.

My God. His heart. I ran to the hall table, dialed 9-1-1 and gave
ae pertinent facts, then ran back to Walter who was slumped in his
aair. His breath was ragged. "Oh, God. Please don't let him die," I
rayed. I didn't know what to do. *The door. I should open the door.*

I retraced my steps through the hall into the foyer and slid in my
ocking feet across the tile to the door. I could hear movement on
ae other side as I undid the deadbolt. As the door swung open, I
:alized two things in that many seconds. I hadn't heard any sirens
ad I hadn't turned the knob on the door.

Chapter Twenty-One

There was no time to hide; no way to push the door closed. reached for a walking stick in the umbrella stand behind the fro door. Maybe I could hold them off until the paramedics arrived.

"Grace."

One word; my prayers answered. I turned and threw myself in my startled husband's arms. This time there was no doubt he wante the embrace.

"Harry." My voice choked with emotion. "God, Harry, i Walter. He's in the dining room. I think he's had a heart attac Hurry!" My words ended as the sound of the sirens reached me.

"Stay here and direct them." Harry rushed to Walter's side.

The ambulance pulled up; one medic ran across the lawn a mounted the steps two at a time. A second one followed wi equipment. I motioned them down the hall toward the inner roo and followed them.

Harry had made fast work of getting Walter off the chair and f on his back. He had loosened Walter's clothing and w administering CPR when the first medic knelt next to him, ripp open a mouthpiece, and took over Harry's position. Harry mov back out of the way as the other medic continued the che compressions. This one asked the questions.

"How long has he been unresponsive?"

Harry and I looked at each other. I answered. "He w breathing in a ragged slow way when I left him to open the door."

"Less then three minutes," Harry said.

"Good," the paramedic said to himself more than to anyone els

I heard the scrape of boots on the front steps. More emergen personnel were on the scene. Harry and I moved out of their way a

ito the kitchen. He guided me to a chair. I didn't want to sit; I
ghtened my arms around him. He understood my preference and
ept his hold on me. Tears slipped down my cheeks, blending into
ie absorbent material of Harry's shirt.

"It's okay, Gracie. Walter will be fine." Harry stroked the side
f my face and tried to lift my chin. I relaxed my grip on him and
ooked up into his face. I saw all the love and tenderness I had
oubted. More tears pooled, preparing for a second and more
owerful rush.

Before the first sob could signal the release, I tensed and stepped
ack out of his arms. "How? When?" I realized I sputtered like a
ookie journalist asking the basics. I took a deep breath and started
gain. "How did you get out of jail?"

Harry looked uncomfortable. He stared at me. *Oh, my God.
id he break out?* My heart slammed against my chest. "Harry,
ou're scaring me. How did you get out of jail?" My arms were
olded tight across my chest.

The paramedics interrupted our conversation as they prepared to
ave.

"I'm riding in with him," Harry announced. He put his arms
round me and kissed the top of my head. "I will explain everything
iter."

I started to ask another question.

"*Shh*, not now. I promise you everything is fine. I'll be back as
oon as I can. Call Gertrude. I think she should be there."

He moved quickly following the paramedics and their patient
ut the door. Harry stopped in the doorway.

"I didn't get chance to tell you. Max is outside. He'll stay with
ou until I return."

"Max? Why is he…?"

"Gracie, I'll explain later. Do it." His voice was anxious for me
 agree to cooperate. I knew he was frantic over Walter and
oparently worried about me too. I nodded my head.

A smile of relief flooded the bottom half of his face. "That's my
rl." He sprinted across the lawn to climb into the back of the
nbulance. Doors slammed, sirens started up and they were off. I
ood in the doorway straining to follow their progress across the

bridge first with my eyes and then my ears as the ambulanc
disappeared into the heavy darkness. Within minutes, quiet reclaime
the compound.

"Mrs. Marsden?" A low voice from the driveway broke th
stillness. Instinctively, I stepped back into the house. In the ne:
second, I remembered Max and looked toward the driveway. Hi
over six-foot, frame stood next to a square, bulky sort of SUV. Than
God, he announced himself. I would have wet my pants if he ha
glided up and appeared at the edge of the circle of light. As it wa
my stomach lurched when he stepped across the light and move
toward me.

"Good evening, Mrs. Marsden. Mr. Marsden wants me to sta
with you. Let's go inside." He touched the bill of the cap he wa
wearing. His hand was the size of a catcher's mitt.

I met Max a few months ago when I attracted trouble to m
doorstep. As he followed me into the house, he pulled the cap from
his head revealing short, buzzed hair. I also noticed how easily h
moved for someone his size; each step was effortless.

"Max, can I offer you something to drink?"

"If you have coffee, I do enjoy a good cup of coffee."

If I have coffee? Max scored one in my book. "Coming rigl
up. Kona, Jamaican Blue, Foglifter, Jamestown?"

Max lifted his hand to stop the litany of available bean
"Instant, like Folgers is fine."

*Instant! Like Folgers? Lord save me from pseudo coffe
aficionados.*

"Sorry, no instant." My tone was sharp. Max must hav
realized his faux pas because he mumbled, "*Ah,* blue sounds good."

"Good choice." I smiled and lifted the lid from one of the man
colored glass containers. I scooped the precise amount of beans int
a small grinder, touched the on button, and released the deliciou
smell of Jamaican Blue. Max sniffed the air appreciatively.

Be nice he's trying to make amends. Within three minutes, tl
strong earthy aroma of this lush island coffee swirled around ou
heads as I poured us each a mug. We sat across from each other
the oak expanse of the kitchen table. Max took a tentative first sip.
waited for a response. He knew he had better say something.

"It's good. I like it." He looked at me for approval.

I smiled. Enough with the amenities. My guest had a beverage
d a chair. "So, Max. When did Harry call you? How did he get
t of jail? Why are you here? What…"

His ham hock size hand came up to signal a halt. "Mr. Marsden
ked me to drive him home. When he left I knew he'd want me to
y with you until he got back."

"Why? What's going on? He must have told you something." I
eady knew there would be no answers forthcoming. Harry had a
opensity for attracting loyal, staunch friends who would do most
ything, no, I think, anything for him. I teased him once about being
bin Hood with his band of merry men, Friar Tuck, Little John, and
o knows who else.

Little John spoke. "Mr. Marsden will explain when he gets
ck."

"Don't you think he'd want you to put my mind at ease by
swering a few questions now?"

"No. Ma'am."

So, this is going nowhere. I stood to clear and wash up the
nner dishes. Max stood up. "Stay." I motioned at him to sit down.
m going to clear up the dining room. Something to do since useful
nversation is out of the question." I didn't mean to sound so
meaning. I quickly looked at Max, ready to apologize. He was
iling.

"Mr. Marsden said you *shoot from the hip.*"

"Really. What else did Mr. Marsden say?"

"You know, ma'am *useful* conversation is out of the question."
s slow smile put me in my place.

I laughed and shook my head. "Okay, okay. I'll wait." Please
y here and enjoy your coffee. I'll only be a few minutes."

The phone rang as I walked into the dining room. The kitchen
one was closer but I chose the hall phone. "Hello."

"Grace, it's me. Walter is stable now. He's been admitted."

I heard the worry in his voice. "Gertrude is here. I wanted to
l and ease your mind. I'll be home soon."

"Harry, what's going on? How on earth did you get out of jail?
on't need to call Katernak, do I?"

Harry's laugh sounded genuine. "No, darling, don't call Dav He's quite aware of the situation. I'll explain it all."

He sounded positively buoyant for someone who had spent t days in jail. In the next moment, his statement sounded a t guarded.

"Gracie, don't clear anything from the dining table. Leave it be."

"I was on my way in there to do exactly that. Why shouldn't I

"Go with me on this alright? I'll be there in twenty minute Harry hung up. I walked back to the kitchen.

"Mr. Marsden is on his way home. You don't need to sit w me any longer."

Max smiled ruefully. "Oh, no. Not this time." He folded I arms across his chest as a form of punctuation. "I stay 'til he g here."

Max was referring to the last time he'd been called in to prot me. Max, Ric, and Harry had all been involved in t miscommunication that had left me alone with a killer.

We didn't have long to wait. The key in the front lo announced Harry. Max, being the careful person he was hired to I strode past me and opened the front door. My husband a bodyguard exchanged a few words at the door. Max turned to me a touched the bill on his cap.

"Goodnight, Mrs. Marsden." He turned and moved quicl down the steps and across the lawn to his car. I said goodnight a moved to stand next to Harry in the doorway.

A strange car was parked in our driveway next to Walter's La Rover. I didn't care how Harry had commandeered that vehicle. was thrilled he was home.

Harry closed the door and slid the bolt home. He turned to n His face showed fatigue and concern. "*Shh, Shh*," he cautioned t open mouth. Harry pulled me into his arms and clamped hungry l over mine successfully squelching any thought of speech. My bo pushed into his; the fears, worries, paranoia of the last two da melted from my frame as I greedily kissed at his mouth. A sm moan escaped my lips, a satisfied sigh.

The contact was broken abruptly. Harry stepped back and h

e at arm's length. "Enough now, old girl. We've lots of talking to
 and I won't be able to keep my hands off you unless we get a big
ble and a couple of hot mugs of tea between us." His hand gently
roked the side of my face, tracing a line with his thumb from my
rehead to my lips. I tried to draw his thumb between my lips but he
wered his hand to his side.

As much as I wanted to leap into his arms again, I also wanted
y questions answered. I smiled and slipped past him to the kitchen
here I put on the kettle. Harry walked the other way into the dining
om. I heard him moving plates and cutlery. I thought at first he
as stacking things to bring them in to me. He showed up in the
tchen empty handed, walked quickly through the room, flipped on
e outside light, and opened the door. He spent a few minutes
specting the sarcophagus and its contents.

I moved closer to the door to watch his progress. Harry looked
 as my movement blocked some of the light.

"Grace, please fetch me a torch from the drawer."

I rummaged in the kitchen junk drawer for the neon pink
shlight. He took the light from my hand and began sweeping the
am across the dirt at the base of the parsley plant. He quickly
apped off the beam and stepped back inside bringing me with him.

He took a small baggie from another drawer and walked back
o the dining room. I turned to follow, but the kettle started to
istle then and I lifted it off the burner and filled his mug. The tea
s steeping when Harry came in and sat down at the oak table. He
lled the sugar and creamer toward him. I opened the fridge to get
 ceramic container of lemon wedges.

Harry was staring at the table apparently lost in thought. I
rried a fresh mug of coffee to the table and curled one leg under the
er as I sat down in the chair opposite my quiet husband.

"Grace, tell me about dinner and what you made. Don't leave
 anything."

"Harry, you're scaring me. What's wrong? Why are you fixated
 dinner?" I felt the mounting panic. I think I knew the answer.

"The preliminary examination of Walter's condition points to
veral possibilities. One of which is poison."

"Poison! Oh, my God." My voice caught in my throat. "Will

he live?"

"Yes, the doctor is certain he'll be fine. The type of poison the suspect is one of the alkaloids, a cynopine. Walter ingested enoug of this poison to bring on tachycardia. They were able to lower h runaway heart rate and he's stable now. Like I said he will be fine."

"How did he eat the poison, we ate the same thing?" I paused t picture the two plates filled with ziti pasta and braciole, the exa same food. My eye spotted the baggie on the table.

"Oh, no. You don't think he ate the poison parsley? This is a my fault."

Harry sat quietly waiting for me to continue.

"I told him to cut the parsley from the plant closest to the doo Maybe he didn't hear me or didn't realize why I restricted him to on one plant. He must have thought the other plant looked better. should have cut the parsley myself."

"Grace, stop. It wouldn't have mattered if you had cut t parsley. The plants had been switched."

"What? Switched. How? Why?" My head filled with though pushing against my brain and flashing patterns before my eyes. reached for the length of thin rope tied to the belt loop on my pants. braided a simple crossover pattern while Harry's voice replaced n thoughts.

"Someone has transplanted the Fool's Parsley with the Parsle The last time I recall taking any note of the plants was the night L stopped by on her way to collect her dad at the airport; three da ago."

"Why would anyone do that? Is this some kind of stur prank?"

"I don't know, Darling. I do know I owe you an explanation a an apology. I'll deal with this," holding up the baggie, "in due time need to *come clean* with you."

In spite of his serious tone, I laughed at Harry's use of Americ clichés. The corny words sounded strange when spoken by English tongue.

He smiled at me. "Alright. Let me start at the beginnin Saturday morning when Lily and I returned to her home, I took opportunity to speak with Kramer for a few moments. He didn't l

e idea, but agreed to go with it." Harry held up his hand to silence
e question he saw leaping from my eyes to my mouth. "Darling, if
ou jump in every two minutes, we'll be here all night; I have better
ans for all night." He grinned. I leaned back against the chair,
termined not to interrupt. *All night* couldn't come soon enough for
e.

"The *plan* was for me and Kramer to get into a shoving match so
· would be forced to arrest me. Since we were in Pine Marsh,
eputy Jordan would do the honors and take me to the county lock-
· where I would cause more trouble at my arraignment, which
ould insure me a short stint at the county jail where I hoped to find
en Jackson who has been Derek's cellmate for the last three months.
ramer and I found the same information through different sources.

He was never supposed to get hurt. Jordan wasn't in on the plan.
hought he was going to hand me my head when he put me in the
uad. He was only too happy to forget to loosen the cuffs."

I looked at Harry's wrists as he unconsciously rubbed them
ring his narrative. Red welts were visible under the cuffs of his
ford shirt. One welt appeared to be moist. I bit my tongue to keep
om commenting.

"I explained everything to David. He told me I was crazy and
reatened to expose the plan. He wouldn't cooperate until I
plained about needing to find out if Jackson knew anything about
e letter, the contract on your life, if Derek had an accomplice,
ything."

At this point, Harry's voice sounded heavy with emotion. He
ok a long swallow of his tea. My own throat tightened as I thought
 what he had done to insure my safety. I followed his lead and
pped at my Jamaican Blue.

"Gracie, the most difficult part of this whole plan was having to
t so atrociously to you when you visited. I knew if I held you I
uldn't be able to stay the course. I couldn't look you in the eyes
d see the hurt I was causing you. I'm so sorry. Please forgive me.
new I couldn't tell you what I was doing; you would have spoiled
e plan." He reached across the table and put his hands over mine.

I was angry, furious with him for putting me through hell. I
lled my hand out from under his.

"I thought we were a team, life partners. What happened t honesty? You're damn right I would have *spoiled* the plan! Do yo hear yourself? You sound like an adolescent; you and that othe *Hardy Boy*. He should know better. Why would he agree to you crazy plan?"

Harry interrupted softly, "Because he doesn't think clearly eithe when it comes to you."

The head of steam I had been building escaped in short, angr wisps as I stuttered in confusion. "Is that why Ric lied to me abou dropping the charges when I drove him home?"

"You drove Kramer home?" Harry's eyebrow shot up wha would have been an octave had his forehead been a keyboard.

"Yes. But we're not talking about that."

"Alright for now, but we will be talking about that. Actually, had a moment of panic when I found out about Kramer's surgery. hadn't planned on him not being able to verify our intent to the fe people who had to know. One cheerful chap assured me if Krame lost his hand, I wouldn't be playing the piano anymore."

My gasped stopped him. I reached across the table for h hands. Harry lifted both of mine to his lips and kissed each palm. I closed my palms together like in prayer and held on to them as I continued.

"Plans changed when Walter contacted me through David abou the break-in. I realized how stupid I'd been to leave you alone unti knew if Derek had an accomplice. Kramer refused to sign t complaint and talked with the Captain at the lock-up. I instruct David to call Max to pick me up and bring me to you."

I didn't know what to say. He did what he did because he lov me. He sensed my mood because he stood up, walked behind m and placed his hands on my shoulders, kneading all the tense spo Out of the corner of my eye I could see his mangled wrist on n shoulder. I closed my eyes. He leaned down and whispered.

"Grace, I need to call the police. Sergeant Peterson will be he again, asking questions. Are you up to it?"

"Do I have a choice?"

"Sorry, no."

"Let's get it over with."

Chapter Twenty-Two

The police followed procedure. They collected samples of the food and beverages and questioned me about preparation. They followed Harry outside as he showed them how the earth in the sarcophagus had been disturbed and how some of the leaves on the lower part of the plant had been bent during the process of transplanting.

They accepted coffee and bakery from me though they were investigating a poisoning. I felt better. I knew no one could think I would poison Walter. The question Sergeant Peterson asked was who would want to poison Harry or me.

Harry assured them the transplantation had to have taken place over the weekend since he had picked some parsley Friday night. With Derek Rhodes out of the picture three days before, we couldn't even hazard a guess.

Betty Boop's lacquered hands pointed to 1:30 before Harry and I were alone. I turned off the alarm on our retro clock, a wedding gift from some weirdo on Harry's side. Sleep would be elusive for me in my keyed-up frame of mind. I hurriedly completed my bedtime prep, splashing some toner on my face and smearing Oil of Olay into my crow's-feet, make that laugh lines. I wasn't laughing now. I wasn't sleepy either. I walked out of the bathroom in record time, a skosh under seven minutes.

"Harry, I'm going to heat some milk to help me sleep. Do you want a cup of tea? Harry?"

I moved closer to our bed and realized my husband was fast asleep, fully clothed, on top of the comforter; so much for conversation or anything else. I guess even one night on a prison cot could exhaust you. I leaned over and kissed him lightly on the lips.

He stretched his neck and moved his lips then settled deeper into t
pillow.

Leave him be Gracie girl; time enough tomorrow. My lit
voice instructed me to let my sleeping husband lie and directed r
downstairs to the warm milk.

Sounds of splashing water and a pleasant tenor voice greeted r
as I struggled to climb the tower of total wakefulness. Normally
morning person, I hated being groggy when I woke up. A delicio
aroma filled my nostrils. I sniffed the air like my childhood r
Beagle, Sadie Jane, and found the source to be Cinnamon Nut Swir.

Harry had set out a small carafe and my *attitude* mug. It sport
two words in bold letters, "BREW THIS!"

"Good morning, Love. I actually waved the carafe under yc
nose before I set it down."

I hadn't realized the shower or singing had stopped. Har
stooped down and kissed my forehead. He smelled of Zest and C
Spice. "*Mmm*," I murmured. "You smell lovely." I smiled and
up.

"Lovely? I shall immediately desist from further showers unt
smell manly." Harry laughed as he filled my mug and brought it
me. I sat back against the headboard and crossed my legs Indian st
to give him room to sit.

"Thank you." I took a sip. "It's perfect."

Harry seemed relieved he'd managed the coffee. He picked
his covered mug and sat down next to me.

"Now that your eyes are open and caffeine is coursing throu
your veins, I want a minute by minute account of what happen
First, let's start with a minor point. I damn near put out my eye wh
I went into the guest room to fetch an extra blanket and collided w
the hat rack."

"*Oops.* I came upstairs yesterday evening and out of the corr
of my eye the hat rack looked like someone standing on the landir
It scared me to death so I banished it the guest room. I guess I lef
in the way. Sorry."

Harry smiled at my explanation and topped off my coffee mι
"Mystery solved. Let's move on to what I'm certain does not have

imple an explanation." His tone turned serious. He placed his free and over mine. "I thought with Derek dead you were in no danger ny longer. Stupid of me. Can you forgive me?" His cornflower lue gaze, filled with a look of anguish, held steadfast to my eyes ntil I looked away.

I was still upset over the stunt he pulled, but even more upset he idn't trust me to be part of it. A thought came to my mind, the nswer to which would determine how this day and many more ould proceed. Harry sat waiting for me to respond still holding my and.

I cleared my suddenly dry throat and pulled my hand from arry's grip ostensibly, to steady my mug. Depending on the answer didn't want my hand out of reach, so to speak.

"Did Lily know about the plan?" The proverbial pin would have unded like a firecracker in a metal can if it dropped now.

"Grace. Is it always about Lily? What is this obsession with :r?"

Harry stood up and moved away from the bed. Did he anticipate ojectile coffee?

"Obsession or not, did Lily know?"

"Of course she didn't know. My God, Grace. Kramer only reed minutes before it all took place. No, I didn't get word to her rough David. Only Kramer, David, Walter, and Captain Williams ew. It was a *need to know* basis."

"Great. Walter needed to know but I didn't?" I was thrilled Lily isn't in on the deal, but I still wasn't letting him off the hook too sily. Harry's look was one of frustration. I noticed the slight mor in his left hand as he put down his tea mug. I immediately felt tten for acting so badly.

He turned toward me holding out both hands palms up.

"What would you have me do, Grace? What will make this itude change?"

"Bring me a different mug?" My answer brought a nanosecond confusion and then laughter from Harry. I felt the grin forming on ' face and it felt good to be laughing with Harry. I stood up and lked into his outstretched arms. He closed his arms around me and lipped mine under his and around his back. Now we had *closure*.

The Lion Tamer: A Caged Death

The day would be a good one after all.

Harry offered to cook an American breakfast for me while showered and dressed. His idea of a normal breakfast was some so of bark-like granola, yogurt, juice, and tea.

I sat down to scrambled eggs, two sausage patties, two slices heavily buttered toast, orange juice, and coffee. It was heaven. Tw forkfuls later, I envisioned the fruit and cereal I had seen on Lil table Saturday morning.

Stop thinking about her. Harry's right, you're obsessing abo her. Duh! I am obsessive-compulsive. My silence during th internal dialog attracted Harry's attention. I am rarely quiet.

"Gracie, please. Are you still chewing over Lily?" I hated t way he could seemingly read my thoughts. I accused him once being part Druid.

"Stewing," I corrected automatically. Harry had been in th country for years but our slang still tripped him up on occasion. "A no, I'm not. Maybe a little. Not enough to matter." I stopped talki and started chewing, leaving Harry to smile at what he called r *Laura Petrie Logic*.

I carried my plate to the sink and rinsed it off before putting it the dishwasher. Everybody tells me the pre-rinse isn't necessary, t appliance can handle tiny food fragments, but I figure it's less we and tear on the dishwasher and it will last longer. Logic derived fro growing up in a house with four brothers and no dishwasher, exce me. They thought clearing the dishes was a personal favor to me they banged out the screen door while I washed up from dinner. remember offering to buy paper plates out of my allowance.

Harry refilled our cups; he had given me a new one, and carri them over to the breakfast nook. Harry waited for me to sit dow He placed a mug decorated with a garden angel on my place mat. guess he was hoping for a complete reversal in attitude.

"I will hit the highlights of the day and give you all the details the night if you promise to not interrupt until I finish." My hope w to avoid any mention of the catfight. Harry exaggerated agreement by pantomiming zipping his lips shut. I laughed at lightheartedness; I prayed he would maintain his composure after ale.

He was good to his word and didn't verbally interrupt during my lengthy discourse. I watched his face tighten at the mention of Ric and soften to a smile as I glossed over my *argument* with Lily. I had feeling Harry already knew the full extent of that debacle. I told him about finding the strange box in the garage filled with items I'd never seen before. I explained my surprise when Sergeant Peterson and I checked the contents and the camera and lighter were now missing. I sensed how difficult it had been for him to sit still as I explained the break-in. His entire body tensed and he leaned forward as my voice trembled with remembered fear when I described hiding in the priest's hole.

"I should have been here." He moved to my side of the nook and held me in his arms, not speaking, letting his body absorb the tension and fear that had resurfaced in mine. I felt myself relax and flow into his comforting strength. Harry had a reaction of his own I had been anticipating. I lifted my mouth to his ear and whispered a suggestion. He answered with a soft brush of his lips on mine; a whisper that became more urgent as we both responded to the raw emotions of the last forty-eight hours. Our bodies spoke volumes and said all the right things.

Chapter Twenty-Three

We had muted the telephone as a precaution. I did not intend
have a beautiful mood sabotaged by the exuberant voices of family
friends checking in with us. The reality of calls to be made a
returned became urgent as we played back seven messages, one fro
my father, one from my brother, one from Gertrude (we both f
guilty we hadn't thought to check on Walter), one from Ric, two fro
David and one from Leo DeFreest. We divided the calls.

I called my dad on my cell phone while Harry returned Davi
calls. My father answered on the first ring.

"Hello."

"Hi Dad, it's me."

"Honey, what's going on? I heard about Harry. Why didn't y
call me? What's happening with that crazy neighbor of yours? A
you okay?"

It took several attempts at getting a word in edgewise to fina
stop his questions. "I'm sorry I didn't call you. Things were movi
too quickly to keep up with everything. I'm fine. Harry's home;
was a misunderstanding. *I'm certainly not telling you my husba
went to jail to try and cozy up to the cellmate of my erstwh
assassin,* I thought to myself as I tried to find comforting words
assuage my dad's nerves. "How did you hear about any of this?"
hadn't thought to ask earlier but there was no way this had been
the news and I hadn't called anyone.

"Gertrude told me."

"Gertrude?" I was puzzled by the connection.

"Yeah. Walter told Gertrude and she told me when she call
me for Nonna Santa's recipe for pizziola. She was having a f
people over for dinner last night and wanted to cook Italian."

*That answered the question I was about to ask Walter before he
eled over from the poison parsley. Wait 'til my dad hears.*

"Dad. About last night; I don't think Gertrude had her dinner
rty. Walter was here for dinner and *uh*, he ate something that didn't
ree with him and had to be taken to Good Sam." I felt terrible for
ing to my father, but as long as he couldn't see the telltale shade of
y *lie detector* eyes I felt confident he believed me.

"Excuse me, honey, but what in the name of Sam Hill is going
out there? And, how do you explain wrestling on the lawn with
at woman? Mike and I are coming out there this afternoon. Has he
lled you yet?"

"Yes, he has. I was going to call him back next. Dad,
erything is fine. You and Mike don't need to rush out here."

"Really? Your husband is arrested, you get into a brawl with his
-girlfriend, Walter rushes away from a dinner party to be with you,
d no one answers the phone for three hours this morning."

"Dad, I've a good reason for not answering the phone. As for the
her things I don't have as good an answer. Really though,
erything is back to normal." Harry had been listening to the one-
ded conversation alternately smiling and frowning at my responses.
motioned for the phone.

"Mike? Good morning. I know things seem a bit up in the air.
n here and I have some fellows helping out. Grace is fine. I won't
anything happen."

I saw the look on Harry's face and suspected my father was
ving him *what for*. Harry walked out of the room as he continued
listen. I couldn't hear his response.

He walked back into the room and handed me the phone. "We're
ing to stop in at your father's house this evening." I smiled at his
pression. "That's the best I could do. Otherwise, he was calling
ur brothers." Now, I laughed at *his* discomfort.

"Sounds like you bought us some time. How did your calls go?
w's Walter?

"He's going to be fine. Recovering nicely, Gertrude says. I told
r we'd stop in later today." Harry's voice was tight with emotion,
s bond with Walter so special.

"What did David want? Everything is set with your release, isn't it?"

Harry's face turned more serious. "Yes, everything is in order.

"You don't look happy about it. Did you want a rap sheet?" N
question was rhetorical.

"Sorry. Thinking how stupid I've been about all this. I'm r
even sure what the game is or who the players are and I've already r
off half-cocked in the wrong direction. I was trained to be bette
Harry muttered more to himself.

His reference to his previous vocation, when he only pretend
to be a publisher, still made me uneasy. I knew in my head he w
finished with any subterfuge for his beloved Britain. What my he
felt was another matter. I shook off the old feeling and concentra
on his statement.

"What do you mean? I thought the whole reason for yc
charade was to buddy up with Derek's old cellmate."

"Of course it was. Odd thing though, the day of r
incarceration was the day of Jackson's release."

"Talk about lousy timing and even worse luck," I said. "Y
spent a night in jail for nothing?"

"It would seem, except luck had nothing to do with this. Oh, r
Some anonymous benefactor hired a top gun attorney who manag
to get Jackson released on bond. Same generous chap paid the b;
Timing was everything in this case because the entire process w
done in chambers and the paperwork wasn't made public until t
morning. Kramer's call was to apprise me of the situation. Davi
first call was for the same reason. He's never seen anything like
before. His second call was to tell me he had been able to trace t
money for the bond to the owner of an upscale, extremely popu
New York restaurant."

"Are you saying Derek's killer, immediately guessed what y
were up to and made arrangements to put this guy out of reac
Harry, this is getting crazier by the minute."

"I know, Darling. I can't get a handle on any of this. Each ti
I think I have a direction I run up against a brick wall. I thought t
Jackson fellow might be able to shed some light onto what was
Derek's contract with Sheila Walsh. Derek could never keep l
mouth shut. I never wanted to admit to it to myself, but I'm fai

rtain the reason our mission failed and we were detained is because
:rek bragged to the wrong person, probably a *senorita* wearing a
ht dress and flaunting loose morals."

"Harry, that's horrible. I had no idea. Maybe knowing he
trayed the mission pushed him over the edge."

"He was a lunatic by the time Sheila hired him. I'd hoped to find
t if he had a partner on this. He'd been arrested for driving on an
pired license and for non-payment of hundreds of dollars of parking
kets the week after Sheila and Richard's deaths. He was released
o days before he was killed. Apparently, he went to wherever or
1oever had his money, bought what we found him with and set up
op to wait to get to you."

Harry moved his head from side to side and rolled his shoulders.
walked behind him and started kneading the tight muscles at the
se of his neck. I picked up the thread of the hypothesis. "He wasn't
lled there. Why would someone dump his body on the path? Why
't leave it in the sauna?" Harry twisted his head to look up at me, a
1zzled look on his face. He turned his head forward encouraging me
continue by two quick shrugs. "I don't care where he was killed.
s over. I want to go forward from here and go back to where we
:re before that damn letter showed up." I was stressed; my
ammar, my muscles, my psyche needed adjusting. "God, listen to
:. I can't even say if I'm coming or going."

"I understood you perfectly." Harry switched places with me
d started massaging my shoulders. He leaned his lips next to my
r, deftly pushed past my thick hair, and gently nibbled at the lobe.

"*Mmm*. Equal time," I murmured and cocked my head slightly
indicate my right ear.

"My pleasure."

I felt the tiny tug in my ear as Harry's lips brushed against the
st on the back of my earring. We both registered the same thought.
arry straightened up quickly and my hand flew up to touch my left
r. The earring was gone.

"Oh, no." The panic in my voice betrayed my feelings. My
other had given me these earrings a few months before she died.
1e pair of tiny gold crosses was special not only because of the giver
t because she had them made using her original wedding band.

"Oh, no," I repeated. My voice was smaller now with t
realization of the loss.

"We'll find it. When is the last time you remember having it i
We'll go from there."

I crinkled up my eyes to concentrate and visualize seeing
feeling the precious metal on my ear under the heavy curtain of ha
Unless I pushed my hair behind my ears, most people never saw t
set. "*Ah,* I know I had them on Saturday morning. I rememb
pushing my hair back at the hospital and feeling the post. It was r
left hand because I had a coffee in my right hand. I remember resti
my elbow on the window of the car and leaning my head on my l
hand while I was driving home. I felt it then. I drove to Lil
house…"

"Why did you go there?" Harry's question interrupted r
stream of consciousness.

"I thought she might know something about you. Harry, I
sorry. I didn't choose Ric over you. Ric was bleeding so badly. S
said you needed someone in your life and I wasn't there…"

"Oh, Gracie. How long will it take you to know how much
love you? She was out of line. I hope you gave her one of your ac
retorts."

"Not exactly." I 'fessed up and told Harry about the *brawl*.
watched alternating expressions slip across my husband's face as
told him the tale.

"Wait till your dad finds out." Harry's childlike taunt turned t
atmosphere from tense to jovial. We laughed uproariously; it f
wonderful.

"He already knows," I sputtered between gasps. "I'm gonna he
it tonight." Our laughter was out of control. Everything w
hysterical. "Gertrude told him when she called for the pizzic
recipe."

"The one with chicken and tomato? I love that dish," Harry sa
between subsiding chuckles.

"No, pizziola is veal. The *chicken and the tomato* were me ar
Lily on the lawn." I laughed 'til my stomach hurt. Harry's laught
renewed and he put his arms around me. It felt so good to
laughing and hugging with Harry. Our laughter slowed and stoppe

felt the mood shift and lifted my face. A moment from contact, I ccupped; yet another quirk when I laugh or cry too much. We both irst into laughter again. Harry held me tighter as I held my breath to spel the hiccups.

"There is a good possibility you lost the earring on the lawn," arry spoke to the top of my head. I nodded agreement. "We can e a metal detector to sweep the lawn. I'll call DeFreest and ask that ey postpone their lawn service until we can search. What did you then?"

Harry's arms loosened around me and I looked up at him. "I me home, found the strange box, spent time with Walter, then, the truder, then the police..." Harry held up his hand to stop the flow. iood Lord, I was only gone one night." Harry smiled, but his eyes ere serious.

I continued my timeline. "I was everywhere, including the iest's hole." I shivered. Harry felt the tremor and tightened his ip.

"We'll have to search the house from top to bottom. You take estairs; I'll start down here. But first, I'll return the call to DeFreest.

I went up the stairs with the faint hope I might find the precious epsake in the tangle of bed sheets recently vacated. I carefully ited and shook the sheets looking for a glimmer of gold. I made the d and shook open the comforter; nothing there. On my hands and nees, I searched around the base of the platform the bed rested on d eased my way out from there to the perimeter of the room. My pe was waning as I checked the closet floor and the clothes I had orn since Saturday. My steps were slower coming down the stairs report my lack of success. Harry was on the couch holding mething in his hand. My heart filled with joy.

"You found it!" I rushed toward him holding out my hand. "Oh, y God, I'm so happy. Thank you, thank you," I practically pranced ward him, Thank you." Two steps away from Harry I noticed he isn't smiling; I noticed he was holding a lighter. I felt my joy aining away and a pinprick of annoyance poking toward Harry. He as supposed to be looking for my earring. Instead, he went looking the box I told him I'd explain later. Had he even called Leo eFreest to stop my keepsake from being destroyed in the blades of a

power mower? My thoughts must have been an easy read becaus
Harry looked confused at the anger growing on my face. His word
turned my anger into fear in a heartbeat.

Chapter Twenty-Four

"I found this on the floor in the priest's hole." Harry was holding the lighter with his thumb and forefinger at the top and bottom with one of my pieces of braid protecting the metal from his fingers. His face was closed. I couldn't read the expression.

"The priest's hole. How?" The explanation hit me at once; my legs turned numb and useless. I sat down hard on the chair opposite Harry. My hands gripped the smooth wooden arms to keep from shaking with fear. Harry quickly transferred the lighter to his handkerchief and placed it on the coffee table. He moved to my side, bent down, and cradled my face with both his hands. I must have looked wild with fear. My head filled with a rushing sound that threatened to explode through the top of my head. I couldn't find my voice to speak. Harry's voice was soothing, calming the clamor in my head. My breath tore through my lungs as though creating new pathways with each painful gasp. Harry moved his hands to my shoulders and held them steady as I slowly brought my breathing into range.

He knelt before me and placed his hands over mine transferring his warmth to my frozen fingers. I felt the warmth seep into my numb fingers as he gently rubbed the tops of my hands and massaged my wrists. He never took his eyes from my face during the entire time. My gaze never wavered for to do so would have been immediate relapse into panic.

"He was in there?" My question croaked through a throat filled with tightness on the verge of tears.

Harry nodded his head. His quiet voice laid out what had penetrated my brain. "He probably hid there when the police searched the house. They didn't search there, did they?'

I shook my head no, not trusting my voice.

"Why would they? You'd told them you'd been hiding in the[r] Gracie, how could this be?

"I don't know. How did he know about the priest's hole? H[o] did they know how to operate it? In the dark," I added as my bra[in] started expending gray cells. "Harry, how many people know ab[out] the priest's hole?"

Harry's eyes dulled as though turning inward on an unpleasa[nt] thought. His eyes were no longer filled with love and protection. [I] moved my hands under his to break his fugue. His eyes slow[ly] focused on me and sharpened as he must have realized he w[as] upsetting me more than comforting me. He stood up and held [my] hands forcing me to rise also.

"Let's move into the kitchen. I want to make a quick call. T[he] police need to know about this. Put the kettle on for me plea[se.] We've lots of thinking to do."

He squeezed my hands before he let go. I walked into t[he] kitchen and began preparing tea for Harry and coffee for me. I kn[ew] Harry had assigned me this task to keep my mind occupied w[ith] routine actions, for at least a short time.

My hands needed rescuing. The turn of events left me shak[ing] and feeling as though I was jumping out of my skin. I knew I had [to] braid before I could touch the kettle or the coffeemaker. I settled [on] twenty square knots. I had a length of yarn tied around the wood[en] dowel of the upright paper towel holder. The loops formed quick[ly] under my fingers; just as quickly, I felt the granting of permission [to] relax.

By the time Harry walked into the kitchen his kettle w[as] whistling. He took over the preparations from that point, making [a] selection from a well-stocked tea box, pouring the boiling water ov[er] his choice, and setting it off to the side to steep. My coffee maki[ng] was rote; put the water in the top, put the grounds in the middle, pu[sh] the button.

"I called Sergeant Peterson. He's concerned, talking ab[out] sending a man out to watch the house. He'll call to let us kn[ow.] They'll pick up the lighter for analysis."

"Is he going to…"

Harry guessed my question and answered quietly. "Yes, he's
lling Kramer." My sigh apparently said it all because neither of us
oke for a long moment. Harry's voice broke the silence. "Gracie,
is whole thing doesn't ring true anymore. I mean, it was shaky at
st from the start, but nothing is squirreling together."

Harry picked up our cups and moved to the breakfast nook. We
t down next to each other on the bench side. The sturdiness of his
oulder against mine comforted me. I was still pondering my
estion about who knew we had the hidden chamber. My fingers
ere worrying a simple braid into a fuzzy length of yarn, as I undid
e braid. My family jokingly called it *reverse psychology*."

"Who knows about the priest's hole? I mean, through the years
ts of people have seen it, heard about it, played in it." I realized
w long this list could become. The priest's hole had been part of
e original plan for the library Harry had wanted. It was a replica of
larger library he visited once in an English country house. The
rary and the gardens were the only two areas Harry had much say
when we were building. We thought it a clever conversation piece.
o, how many?" I put down my yarn and started counting off names
my fingers. "My side, my dad, my brothers. Five. My nieces and
phews, four more. My cousin, Dominic." Harry's eyebrows shot
. "Remember, he was here to repair the French doors?" Harry
dded and muttered, "The entire Morelli clan."

"Shush. I only showed him. He doesn't know where the catch
Anyway, my cousin is not a suspect here." I sat up straighter.
hat's about all for me. Oh, Karen knows. *Ah,* Ric knows too."
ying aloud what we both knew, brought an awkward moment. At
e point in my marriage to Harry, when I thought he had been killed,
urned to Ric Kramer for a chance at a new life. Ric knew the house
d its secrets.

Harry shook off the tension. "All right. My side then." Harry
ld up his fingers and closed each into his palm as he accounted for
ople who knew. "My parents, Hannah, Walter, Max, Sergeant
terson, who knows on his staff, John Holter." It was my turn to
ok surprised.

"The publisher? How would he know? Why would he know?"

Harry looked sheepish as he explained. "John has a hidden

room in his New York home. I guess it was a matter of *can you t*
that syndrome."

"Whatever," I muttered.

Harry continued. He seemed nervous. "Lily knows too,"
said.

The name exploded from my mouth. "Lily? You told Lil
Why would you tell Lily?" I bit my lip to stop the rest of wor
forming. I lifted my mug, realized my hand was shaking, and put tl
mug down.

"Grace, I don't want to argue with you on this. She is an o
friend. I was showing her the house. I knew she'd find it interestin
I'm not apologizing for showing her. For God's sake, Grace, you'
shown innumerable people that room."

"But they weren't ex-lovers." As the words rushed from n
mouth my heart thumped hard against my chest. Again, I bit down
my lip, but this time too late; the words and their damage had be
released. Traitorous thoughts of a passion filled afternoon spent wi
Ric years before in this house snaked along the corridors of my min
My eyes reluctantly turned to Harry, the righteous bluster of
moment before deflated like a week old party balloon. He star
back at me, anger hardened his face, but an expression of resignatio
lingered at the corners of his eyes. I felt the same frustration wh
events from our past, reopened the wounds to our marriage we had
carefully sutured and salved.

Harry seemed to bring his emotions under control quickly. I
slid out from the bench seat and poured himself another cup of tea.
knew he was upset because he usually started his brewing proce
from the beginning when he went for seconds. Now,
absentmindedly doused already soggy tea leaves with, at be
lukewarm water. The grimace on his face when he sipped the bre
confirmed my thoughts. He dumped the liquid in the sink.

"It seems we are condemned to always have *the ghost of lo*
past gliding between us when we least expect it or seem to be able
handle it. I propose we call Ghostbusters."

I stared at Harry in disbelief. I looked for the telltale signs t
doctors had warned me about after his rehabilitation. No pu
throbbing at his temple, no tremor in his hand, and certainly

xtreme fatigue. My husband looked the picture of vigor, standing in he kitchen, back lit by the sunshine pouring through the French oors, his hands on his hips as though waiting for me to jump up, ollow him out the door and on to an adventure.

"Harry, I don't understand. You were upset." What I wanted to ay was he was upset as all hell a minute ago, now he was acting like commercial for the old Dan Ackroyd movie.

His broad smile didn't clear up anything. On the contrary, I ould have felt better if he were frowning. Frowning I could nderstand; this bucolic smile confused me.

"I'm sorry, Darling. I know I'm doing an about face. The tea set e straight."

Now I *was* confused.

"Grace, it became so clear to me. Whenever we stray the course, on't follow what we know works for us; like my not following the eps for tea, we start to second-guess and worry over the wrong ings. We've not been talking to each other. We've set off without cluding the other. I know I am the main offender. I should never ve cooked up that scheme with Kramer."

He made an excellent point. I hadn't been totally honest with m either. "And Ghostbusters would be?"

"Oh, just an expression. Surprised you never heard of them. merican comedy, very funny." I knew Harry was baiting me with s dry sense of humor. His smile lessened as he sat down across om me. "Let's spend some time right now telling each other what e think the other shouldn't know."

I nodded my agreement.

Harry continued, "Do you want more coffee?" I shook my head ainst the offer.

We sat across the table for next forty minutes telling each other w seeing and interacting with each of our pasts made us feel. We th expressed similar feelings of excitement tinged with guilt at ing with that person again, a bit traitorous to each other since eing Lily and Ric again brought back feelings better left unfelt.

Harry pronounced those feelings weren't based in true, current otion, but rather in the perfect plastic that encased memories.

I agreed.

By the time we finished talking, we were both hungry. Breakfast had long since passed. Confession apparently was as good for the appetite as it was for the soul.

"We're supposed to stop in at your dad's place later today. If we don't, he'll be on our doorstep with your brothers. I want to visit Walter, see how he's doing. Maybe we could get lunch on our way to Berkeley after we see Walter."

"That'll work. After we leave Good Sam we can hop on the tollway and get off at York Rd. I want to stop at Cottage Hill Diamonds. The Heidelberg Restaurant is on the way." Harry smiled at my roadmap. He was continually amazed at how every destination included my intimate knowledge of a great eatery *on the way*, or *down the street*.

I ran up the stairs to change clothes and pick up the jewelry box. I stuffed the box in my purse and realized I hadn't told Harry about the treasure. I would tell him on the way. No, I would tell him now. I marched down the stairs determined to never keep anything from Harry again. He was hanging up the phone as I entered the kitchen. His face wore a thoughtful expression.

"Harry, " I started, "I want to tell you about the box."

"Grace, we've another stop on our itinerary." He continued as though he hadn't heard me. "That was Lily on the phone. She has your earring." Harry seemed subdued. I was thrilled.

"Great. Did she find it on the lawn? What are the chances of that?" I was smiling from ear to ear, but Harry was still solemn.

"Actually, it was caught in the webbing of a strap on one of her cameras."

Chapter Twenty-Five

"Oh, my God, Harry. She came back for the box? It was her?"

"I don't know. We can't assume it's the same camera. We're going to find out."

The ride to Lily's house was short but not silent. We argued over our approach. I wanted to read her the riot act and call the police. Harry wanted to act as though we were happy she found the earring and not accuse her of breaking in.

"Grace, why would she volunteer she had the earring if she were the one who broke in? That would be stupid. She's not stupid."

"Maybe Miss Genius doesn't know I already found the box and looked inside. Maybe she doesn't know we know, first there was a camera and then there wasn't." I felt my Laura Petrie logic was impeccable.

"Gracie, please. I think I've had more experience with this sort of thing, don't you?"

I wasn't sure if he was referring to his past life with British Intelligence or his past life with Lily. Either way, I didn't like admitting he might be right.

She greeted us at the door with an appropriate smile settled pleasantly under a smooth carefree brow. She looked cool and calm in a jogging suit of sage green, a color that accentuated her eyes into a stunning focal point. In a snit of jealousy I wondered if she had changed her clothes when she knew we, or rather Harry, would be coming over for a chat.

"Please, come in. I've put on the kettle. Tea should be ready in a few minutes." She motioned us inside and into the now familiar great room. "Sit down. I'll only be a moment." Harry did not offer to help in the kitchen this time. He leaned back in his chair and stared

151

out the window. I followed his gaze to the area at the bottom of th hill; remnants of torn, yellow police tape sagged from branches. shifted my sight line to look sideways toward the shed and patio the back of the house. I could see a tripod set up with a camera with long lens that seemed pointed up, rather than across to the trees. idly wondered if Lily had focused on a constellation last night. Had been a clear starry sky? My thoughts jumped into sharp focus as caught movement out of the corner of my eye. Harry must have se it too; he turned in his chair for a better view.

"DeFreest?" I asked.

"Don't think so; looked taller and thinner. Can't tell for sure." Harry was on his feet at the window when Lily entered the room carrying a tray. She put down her burden and looked at us.

"Is something wrong?"

"We saw someone at the back of the patio near the shed. Do you have company?" Harry's question sounded off hand. I knew the tilt of his head and the way he was leaning forward meant his question was anything but casual.

"No. I'm certain it was my father. He's always out there, setting up shots, checking the equipment. He's the one who started me in photographing wildlife. When he no longer live-trapped or took groups on safaris, he developed a great interest in photographing the animals of the savanna. Of course, the animals most intriguing to me are somewhat smaller and much closer to home." Her narrative tone was blithe and light but the delivery had been rushed and a shade tight. Her words might be true but her purpose was to stall or deceive.

Harry kept her fixed with an interested gaze that apparently made Lily feel she was accomplishing her goal. She kept babbling about her father's enthusiasm for picture taking in all lights, at all times of the day and night.

Maybe he was the one taking pictures of stars. I followed my thought with action and turned my head away from her to look back at the camera angle. The camera was gone. I casually turned back to Lily and her soliloquy; her glance flicked toward me. Our eyes held for a second. She continued talking, finally winding down with, "I'm sure he was checking something. He's probably in his room. I'll call im."

Harry had been calmly fixing tea while Lily rambled. He had kept his eyes on her face but deftly poured and placed three cups of tea. I think his routine task had totally thrown Lily off her *ice queen* throne. I imagined she felt as though she had talked more in the last five minutes than she had in the previous entire day. She seemed unsettled, more so than if it was her father out there.

"No need to bother Leo. I'm sure he'll come down in a jiffy when he gets a whiff of the wonderful aroma coming from your kitchen; some sort of beef, isn't it?"

Harry's innocent question elicited the most unusual response from our hostess. She positively blushed to the roots of her too blonde hair.

Harry continued. "If we are keeping you from your supper preparations, please go ahead. We came for the earring."

"Yes. I have it right here." Lily walked over to the sideboard and picked up a small cellophane slip, the kind you'd use to keep a film negative safe. "Here it is." She handed the packet to Harry, totally ignoring me. Of course, after our last encounter the less we interacted was probably a good thing.

Harry fingered the cellophane. "How odd it should catch on your camera strap. What are the chances of that occurring? We thought we'd be scanning your front lawn with a metal detector. Do you have that camera here? May I see it?"

The request caught Lily off guard. She glanced out the window for a split second and then started looking about the room as though she had misplaced something. Her glance settled on a camera perched on top of several books on the trunk next to the coat tree.

"Here. This is the one." Lily smiled triumphantly as she plucked the camera from its spot and handed it to Harry. "I noticed it yesterday. Actually, our mutual neighbor, Barbara Atwater noticed it first. She had stopped in to offer information on the locations of the local market, cleaners, etc., since I am so new to the area.

Offer information, I bet. Why is Barb getting cozy with her? In the tenth of a second after that thought, my nicer side kicked in. Why shouldn't she be nice to Lily? I was the only one with the problem. She went to my school first; she dated my husband first. She slept with my husband first. I knew I had to stop that kind of thinking or I was liable to reach up and yank her long hair just for grins. I was obsessing. I felt a familiar tingle in my wrists moving toward my fingers. I needed to braid something, anything. Her long, silky hair hung a mere twelve inches from my itching hands. *Oh, no. Not the hair.* I could feel the sensation of braiding those lengths of golden strands in my fingertips. *Not the hair.* I struggled with the urge until I forced myself up and away from the table.

The abrupt movement startled everyone, including me. My movement also tipped my cup, sloshing liquid across the place mat and onto the oak table.

"Grace, what's wrong?" Harry's voice was three parts concern, one part annoyance.

Lily's eyes widened at my actions. She moved to the sideboard to get more napkins to sop up the spill. When she put down the camera, the strap shifted and flopped onto the wet table. I lifted the colorful canvas strap. The bright turquoise, purple, and royal blue colors registered in my brain and my hand stopped its rescue mission. Harry continued staring at me. Now, he placed his hand over mine to help me complete the job. He blotted at the strap with another napkin. I looked at him and nodded my head slightly toward the camera. He understood immediately. He picked up the camera and ran his fingers over the canvas.

Lily had returned with enough paper towels to soak up the Red Sea. "What are you doing? Stop. You'll expose the film." She spoke in a panicked voice.

"Calm down, Lily. I checked to see if there was any film. See, no card in the slot.

That was a trick Harry taught me about keeping tabs on what type of film you were using. He always ripped off the top of the film box with the speed and type of film printed on it and placed the small square into the similar sized frame on the back of the camera. Once you removed the exposed film, you removed the box top. It would seem he taught that to Lily, or perhaps she taught him.

"I'm sorry. I'm touchy about my equipment. Anyway, when Barbara was over here we had tea and she noticed the camera and asked advice about settings and film for bird photography. When she handled the camera she spotted the earring stuck through the strap. She was startled by the find and blurted out immediately that the earring belonged to you. Imagine my surprise. I was certain it must be mine, an occupational hazard you know."

Lily glibly flipped her hair away from her ear to reveal a small, silver Celtic knot earring.

"When I looked at it, I knew it wasn't mine. She was adamant it was yours. It is lovely; I love old gold. Is it an heirloom?"

"The earrings belonged to my mother. They're not valuable except to me. She's gone now." My voice exposed the sadness that overcame me when I thought of my life without my mother in it. My brain felt quiet. I registered a shift in Harry's posture and the sound of a door closing in the house. I took a deep breath to quicken my spirits and my mind. I hadn't wanted to show Lily my grief. Her response was unexpected.

She reached out and touched the cellophane packet under my hand and in doing so brushed against my fingers.

"Then they're priceless. My mum died too young; she left me too soon. I never imagined how much I'd miss her. I never imagined she wouldn't grow old with me and…"

Her voice broke off, her head jerked up quickly as though she too had opened up too much to a stranger, perhaps a rival. I couldn't dislike her as much now as when I walked in the door thirty minutes earlier. The bond of maternal loss and ache had pulled us closer in spite of our protests.

I suddenly felt the need for fresh air. The atmosphere in the room was tense and unclear and made me feel queasy. Harry must have sensed my discomfort. He stood up facing Lily.

"Give your father our regards; tell him his Bourgionne smells first class."

Lily looked confused by his comment.

"Unless you've hired a cook, Lily, your father must be in the kitchen. I've been hearing puttering from in there these last ten minutes. After all, I do remember quite vividly your attempts at the culinary arts." Harry smiled at the shared joke. Lily tried to respond with an appropriate smile, but her face seemed stuck on panic.

I wanted Harry to call her bluff, to call out to Leo DeFreest or to walk into the kitchen. I was about to handle that myself when my husband's radar pegged my intent. He put a restraining hand on my arm as I moved around behind him. To the casual observer it appeared he was reaching out to take my hand as we left the room. I knew he was signaling me to stay put. We left Lily at the door looking relieved, confused, and I thought a little scared. Something was happening in there and I'd bet it was related to what had happened to me.

I waited until we were in the car before I started a barrage of questions. "Why didn't you ask to see her father? Why didn't we go into the kitchen?"

Harry interrupted my inquisition. "I didn't need to go into the kitchen to know her father wasn't in there."

My raised eyebrows asked my unspoken question.

"I knew she must know who was in the yard because she wasn't the least bit concerned to make certain it *was* her father. If someone had experienced a body being found in close proximity to their home, with the killer presumed at large, wouldn't you think they'd be a little concerned about a strange man in their backyard?"

"She was *blasé* about who it could be. So she must have known who it was because he is staying there?"

"I think so," Harry responded. "Was that the camera in the box?"

"I can't be sure about the camera but the strap was the same. The colors are so distinctive. That wasn't the camera she had with her on the lawn; at least not the same strap. I would have remembered something so colorful swinging inches from my face." I smiled wryly at the instant replay in my head."

"Then she lied about the earring being caught in that strap. So, if the earring wasn't lost on the lawn, it could have come off while you were handling the camera in the box in the garage or when you were hiding.

Perhaps whoever hid in the priest's hole set down the camera while he waited for the police to leave and it hooked the earring." Harry's thoughtful expression seemed to be showing more concern.

"Oh, the camera! Harry, I forgot. When I first looked at the tripod there was a camera on it tilted upward. Later, I looked back and it was gone. What does that mean? Who removed it?"

"That's another reason why I know there are at least two others in the house with Lily. I heard the oven timer turn off at the same time I heard an outside door shut. One person on the timer; one person at the door."

"Who would she be hiding? Why wouldn't she tell us? Maybe you should go back and talk to her alone." That last comment was more of an internal musing that reached the outside world in error. My head swiveled to the left to see if my husband had heard that part and to note his reaction. He kept his eyes straight ahead, but I could see a tiny pull on the corners of his mouth. He'd heard.

"*Hmm*. Perhaps I should." He nodded his head as though convincing himself my suggestion was the only course of action. He turned toward me slightly. "I mean, if you think that's the only way." He stayed the sputter about to spew from my mouth with his forefinger against my lips. His smile broadened. "Don't worry darling, I think Lily has drawn her line in the sand and both of us are on the other side. She's not going to confide in me, but perhaps she will open up to a visit from the convalescing Inspector."

I couldn't believe this was the same person who had chastised me for treating Lily so coldly a mere seventy-two hours earlier. On the verge of another sputter, I looped five taut line knots before I trusted my voice.

"I thought you didn't want to sic Ric on her." I spoke softly not wanting to start another Lily War between us.

"That was before. This is now." His terse answer filled me with joy. He reached over to take my hand. "She knows something about who put you in danger. Kramer will want to know."

"Harry, what if someone is in the house forcing her and her father to hide them. Maybe Lily is there under duress." I couldn't believe my own ears. My husband was content to throw his ex-lover to the wolves and I was rushing to her rescue. *Gracie, girl, you seriously need help.* My inner voice was despairing of ever guiding me through life.

"Darling, you read too many mysteries. Please don't use your Nancy Drew cunning here. Not when your well-being is at risk."

"I do not. I haven't read Nancy Drew since I was a kid. I'm the last person who should like Lily, and I'm not saying I do, but she doesn't seem the type."

"Which type; the type that plots against the wife of her ex-lover? The type to hide information if it implicates her father?"

Great. Now it sounded like he was moving back to her side.

"Yes. No. I mean, I don't know." I massaged my right temple. "My head hurts from trying to figure this out. Can we put this on hold until we get through seeing my dad tonight? If I don't stop with the *what ifs* my dad will take one look at me and know something is *afoot* as your *compadre* would say."

"We were hardly contemporaries," he said with a characteristic arched brow. I smiled at his comment and knew we wouldn't be discussing Lily for a while.

"Where did you want to eat before we stop in at your dad's house? And tell me at least two blocks before we have to turn." Harry was accustomed to my characteristically hastily given directions which could cause heart palpitations in other drivers during Harry's attempt to follow my lead.

"Let's stop at Portillo's for a quick bite." The exaggerated martyr look was evident even from his profile. "C'mon. One beef sandwich won't kill you or clog you."

Harry's aversion fast food was inconvenient at times. "We don't have time for sit-down, scrutinize the menu, request everything on the side, food. We need 'gotta go, can't wait'…"

"Fast food," Harry finished for me.

"Exactly," I beamed at Harry. "Now you've got it."

"Righto, Professor Higgins. One sliced cow on soggy bread coming up," Harry quipped in his worst Cockney.

He knew the route to the closest Portillo's. We decided to order out and eat in the car. Harry might tolerate fast food, but hated the noisy, pushy atmosphere of most chain restaurants. I was enjoying my sandwich redolent with the aroma of Parmesan cheese and the spicy accent of giardiniera peppers. Harry ordered an Italian sausage sandwich without the bread and asked for a side of tomato and slaw. He pulled a small rectangular plastic box from the glove box and removed his treasured scout knife and proceeded to slice up the sausage and arrange it amongst his tomato and slaw. He carefully wiped the short blade, closed the knife, and returned it to its box. A further rummage in the glove box revealed a baggie with plastic forks.

By this time, I had wolfed down my sandwich; you can't let Italian beef get cold and congeal. I rolled up the empty pepper and salt packages into my waxed sandwich papers and carefully pushed them into the brown paper sack. My stomach satisfied, I turned my thoughts to the rest of the contents of Harry's glove box. Actually, I was looking for one of those moist towelette packets you get with take out from KFC. Silly of me. Harry wouldn't be cruising through for fried chicken.

"What are you looking for?"

"Those hand wipes you get from restaurants. My hands are oily from the giardiniera."

"First of all, don't mistake this venue for a restaurant, and I don't have any. There is a small bottle of hand sanitizer in there somewhere."

"Don't be a snob," I scolded. Harry finished his fine dining and stuffed the remnants into the bag. He started the car and maneuvered past the trash receptacle so I could toss our lunch waste into its yawning mouth.

"Before we go by my dad's, I mean *to* my dad's, (Harry always called me on my Midwestern Americanisms) I want to stop at Cottage Hill Jewelers. It's in Elmhurst on York Road, north of the tracks. I want to check out something I found in one of the boxes."

Harry was moving across one lane and around two slower moving cars so he could get onto I-355 and then to I-88 heading toward the York Road exit. Harry turned slightly to look at me.

"This wouldn't be a clever way to drop hints about an upcoming birthday would it?"

"Not necessarily, but I like the way you think."

We joked about my birthday patterns. Growing up the only girl with four brothers, somehow my birthday received more attention. I think because when I was a little girl the toys were more gender separated and my brothers had a plethora of boy toys to share. The only time my brother Mike played with my Betsy Wetsy doll was to throw her over the railing of our second floor back porch. He said she committed suicide because she hated her name. Nonna Santa yelled at him in virulent Italian. She tried to conceal the crack in the dolly's head by making her a variety of bonnets.

Of course, the obsessive-compulsive behavior that reared its annoying head in my early childhood caused more attention to be lavished on me. A cadre of aunts and older cousins watched me twenty-four seven practically to be on call to distract me from twirling my long hair until it pulled out. A decision was made to cut my middle of the back banana curled hair to a pixie. My father moped for two days and wouldn't speak to my mother for several more. The haircut forced the twirling to evolve to tugging. Relatives were losing sleep and patience. My mother finally decided if she couldn't stop the obsession, she could channel it. She taught me how to finger braid and made my older brother Joseph, a Star Scout in Berkeley Troop 14, teach me all the knots he had learned.

"You were such a spoiled little girl." Harry had heard all the stories from my brothers.

"I know." I smiled beatifically. "And I love how you continue the process."

Harry parked in front of Cottage Hill Diamonds. York Road is one-way north at this point. We were parked on the west side of the street. He reached his arm around me and pulled me closer to him. "I'm happy to do so." He lowered his head, his lips closed over mine. *Hmm. Why hadn't we stayed home? I could have checked this later. Could have gone by, ah, I mean to, oh, hell.*

"*Hmm.* I think we're drawing a crowd." I said into his lips. I had opened one eye, checking to make sure no one was looking; Catholic school guilt. Someone was. Actually four *someones* were staring quite openly at us. *Gee whiz. It was just a kiss.*

"Let them get their own date," Harry joked as he released me and slid back to his side. When he turned to look out at our *crowd* they immediately dispersed. I straightened my top, retrieved my purse from the back seat, and pushed down the handle. During my quick preparation to exit the car, I had looked over my right shoulder for any traffic. I pushed open the door and slid out quickly, timing my exit with oncoming traffic. Harry had come around to open the door, but I had moved too quickly.

"Sorry sweetheart. Thanks anyway."

He took my arm and escorted me behind the Jaguar. We entered the store and were greeted by a young lady behind the counter.

"Good afternoon," I started. "Is Mr. Hill available. I don't have an appointment."

"No problem. He's in the back. I'll get him for you." She smiled and walked down the hallway.

"Why are we here again, Gracie girl? I may have missed something on the way in." Harry's jaunty smile told me he hadn't been listening. I couldn't be too upset. Sometimes I didn't listen to everything I said. Of course, I knew what wasn't important.

"Never mind, it won't take long. There's a Breadsmith a few blocks up. Maybe you'd like to check it out. In fact, I have a coupon for a free loaf of bread from the last time I shopped there; I bought cheese bagels. It's in my wallet." I opened my purse.

"Oh no. Not the Black Hole of Calcutta. I'll pay full price. If I wait for you to find the coupon, their bakery will be day old status." Harry loved to tease me about my wallet. He called it a leather file since I carried my folding money in a zippered compartment of my purse and dropped my change into the bottom. My wallet bulged with receipts, photos, scraps of paper, coupons, sandwich cards, hosiery cards, cleaners ticket, lottery tickets, business cards and other important papers I needed on a daily basis.

The owner walked up to the counter during our banter. He stood leaning against the glass case smiling at us. The first time I met him I noticed his friendly smile. In his casual clothes, which he filled out admirably, he hadn't seemed like my idea of a jeweler; a wizened, older gentleman who spoke with an accent and carried his jeweler's loop attached to a watch fob. Kurt wore his light brown hair short, almost a crew cut. It reminded me of my brother Marty's hair when he played football for Proviso West High School. Maybe that's why Kurt didn't seem like a jeweler to me; he reminded me more of a coach.

"Hello, Grace. Nice to see you again."

"Nice to see you. Kurt, this is my husband Harry Marsden. You met last year at Elmhurst Memorial's Casino Gala. Harry, this is Kurt Hill." Both acknowledged each other and shook hands."

The Lion Tamer: A Caged Death

"I hope you have a few minutes to look at something. It looks real, but I get fooled by cubic zircon." I playfully put out my left hand and moved it closer and farther as though trying to get it in focus.

"It was the best money could buy. I had the devil of a time trying to hook it with that claw." My husband's sincere tone and smile cracked up the jeweler and the woman who had first greeted us. Harry continued, "I think I will walk down to Breadsmith. I'll wait for you in the car." Harry reached his hand out to Kurt Hill. "Nice to see you again. Don't show her anything unless it comes in one of those plastic pull-apart bubbles."

Kurt joined in. He winked broadly and said, "Oh, the good stuff? We keep those pieces back there," he motioned behind him, "in the bubble gum machine."

Harry leaned toward me and gave me a peck on the cheek before he left.

"Your husband is quite a character. I guess I have the stereotypical view of Englishmen. The few I have met in the course of business have been humorless."

I smiled at his take on Harry. I would have liked to take credit for developing the interesting, dry sense of humor in my husband, but his sense of timing and humor was one of the big reasons I was drawn to him.

"He is indeed." I lifted the antique looking turquoise box from inside my purse. Kurt accepted the box with a look of mild interest. He lifted the lid and snapped to attention as though a jolt of electric current ran from the box to his body. His eyes flew up to my face with renewed interest.

"Where did you get this? Is it yours? I mean, in your family?" His questions were fast and tense. I had a sudden feeling of dread. What could spark such a reaction in this otherwise seemingly calm person?

"What's wrong? Is it valuable? Do you know what it is?" I wished Harry were here and not off buying sourdough. He was much better at not panicking. All I could think of was the old time movie where the shopkeeper makes an excuse to go into the back room to call the cops.

162

"I think I know what it is." He seemed to be backpedaling from his initial outburst. "I'll have to take a closer look at it under a stronger light. I'll be right back."

As he turned to head to the rear of the store, I was certain he gave his assistant a look. I looked at her hands to see if she discreetly pressed a silent alarm. She glanced behind me at the door. I turned hoping to see Harry at the window. There was no one there. *Damn, I'd taken my eyes off her. Maybe that's what they're taught to do in jeweler school. Oh, heaven's sake, Grace, get a grip.* I mentally chastised myself and watched, I hoped, calmly as he disappeared down the hallway. *Make small talk with her. Show her you're not worried.* I half expected to hear the distant wail of police sirens at any moment.

As quickly as he had walked away, the jeweler was approaching the glass case dividing us at warp speed. "Grace, where did you get this? I'm afraid if it's what I think it is there will be questions, lots of questions."

"You're scaring me. I found it two nights ago in a box in my garage. A box marked for the jumble being held by several area churches. When I found it, I thought it odd since no one had given it to me directly. Is it valuable?"

The jeweler shook his head slowly. "Grace, maybe we should talk in my office." He motioned me to follow him. His office was a small room off the hallway on the left. The workroom appeared to be straight ahead. "Please, sit down."

I sat in the chair in front of his desk. I couldn't help but wonder if he had already called the police. "Tell me about this jewel."

He did not sit down, but rather half sat, half leaned on the front edge of his desk closest to me. He held the red jewel in a cloth in his right hand. He opened the sides of the cloth and leaned his hand toward me so I might get a closer view. The jewel gleamed even brighter against the soft maroon shade of the material. He cleared his throat. "This is a red diamond, the rarest of all fancy-colored diamonds. This one is especially rare since it is the full red color of ruby. In fact, if this is what I think it is, it is the Red Diamond Duet. This particular gem is one of two flawless red diamonds that, at last report, belonged to a private collector in New York."

"You must be mistaken. How could this diamond end up in my jumble box? Please, check again. Couldn't there be lots of red diamonds like this one?"

"No. There is only one other–its mate. The original Red Diamond was discovered in 1927 at the Lichtenburg diggings of South Africa." He shifted the diamond to his left hand and reached behind him on the desk for a slim hardcover volume. The dust jacket showed pictures of beautiful diamonds in colors and shapes I never connected with the precious gem. The book was simply titled, *Diamonds*. "I favor fancy-colored diamonds. I've seen pictures of the Red Diamond Duet and recognized it immediately. I hesitated because there is only the one, but when I saw the box, the two small nests, I knew I was right. The necklace is an add on. The setting looks original but the loop and chain were added later. When this diamond was discovered, it was a 60-carat black bort rough, which is the lowest quality of diamond; the ultimate *diamond in the rough*. Borts too badly flawed are routinely crushed into abrasive powders for industrial purposes. This bort was sold for $160.00. The buyer was advised by a Dutch diamond expert to send the rough to Amsterdam for cutting. There, two flawless blood red, emerald-cut stones of 5.05 and 5.10 carats were cut from the center of the rough. It was first sold in 1947 for an unknown price and later reported stolen during repatriations after World War II. In 1968, it was revealed it had never been stolen but had been sold to the New York collector. So why am I holding one of the most beautiful diamonds in the world, and where is its mate?"

I wondered the same things and then some. How did it get into my garage? Who put it there? Why? I looked from the book to the diamond to the man. "I can't answer that question or the dozen more swirling through my head right now. I suppose you have to call someone about this." *Where was Harry? Oh God, he said he'd wait in the car.* I made a quick decision. I stood up and moved toward the door. "Why don't you contact who you think should know about this. I'm going to step out and get my husband.

"No need, darling. I just stepped in. Couldn't imagine what was keeping you. Actually, I could imagine and decided to get back here as soon as I could."

What normally would have been a funny line fell flat. I was relieved to see him but couldn't muster a smile.

"What's wrong, Grace?" Harry looked from me to Kurt and back to me for an answer. I swallowed and took a deep breath to begin an explanation I didn't have. During my preparation, Kurt had replaced the red diamond in its nest inside the box. Before I could say anything, he handed the box to me with the lid still open.

"Grace," he began. "I wouldn't even know who to call. Take–"

"Where did you get this?" Harry reached out his hand and intercepted the box. He stared at the contents, snapped the lid shut, and shoved it into his coat pocket. He swung full round on the jeweler. "Where did you get this?"

Kurt looked totally confused at the confrontation. Harry must have read the look as genuine. He turned to look at me. I saw the pieces fall into place in his eyes as he realized this was what I had wanted checked. "This was in the box?" His voice had a strained quality that seemed overdone for the circumstances.

I nodded my head not trusting my voice. Something was wrong. Harry didn't behave this way unless something was seriously wrong.

"Mr. Hill, forget you saw this. This is not your concern. I will handle it from here." Harry was anything but the humorous chap Kurt had admired thirty minutes earlier.

He seemed more than eager to turn the clock back and erase our visit. He agreed to not initiate any calls, but he explained that if he were ever asked about our visit he would not lie. Harry thanked him and we hurried from the store. I rushed around the back of the car anxious to get in and talk to Harry. I was reaching for the thin leather strip I had looped over my purse handle. I never looked over my right shoulder.

Chapter Twenty-Six

I rounded the back of the Jag with a purposeful stride. Harry's shout stopped my forward progress and glued me to the spot. In the next flash of memory, Harry was sliding head first across the top of the car toward me with his hands outstretched. I felt his left arm snake around my waist and lift me onto the trunk as his momentum carried him across the back of the car and onto the street with me awkwardly in his grasp.

The sound of metal scraping metal screeched in my ear. I felt the movement of the heavy car as the sideswipe impact pushed it farther into the curb. Harry was already on his feet pulling me up onto the sidewalk. I saw the back end of a black or dark blue car as it sped up York Road.

We stood staring in the distance, Harry's left arm still tight around my waist. He slowly released me and turned me to face him. His face could only be a reflection of how shaken I looked.

"Are you hurt? His voice confirmed his emotional state. I shook my head no and stepped closer. He put his arms around me and pulled me close to his chest. "Oh, God, Grace. I could only see the car smashing into you, pinning you." His voice stopped abruptly. He held me tighter as I trembled uncontrollably at the picture in my mind.

Several people rushed out of various stores and gathered around us. A woman who said she saw the whole thing told us she had already called the police. Right on cue, a police officer pulled up and parked parallel to our car. She killed the siren but left on the lights. A forty-something woman about five feet, two inches with short brown hair walked toward us. A sprinkling of freckles across her nose gave her a youthful appearance. Her light stride fit her slender, proportioned body. The uniform hat she had donned as she exited the squad sat square on her head, the bill shading bright blue eyes.

It was easy to spot the victims; I was still clinging to Harry, like clematis to a post, and we both looked disheveled. The officer introduced herself, Pat Corrigan, and wrote down our names. She asked if we wanted medical treatment. We both assured her we were shaken but not injured. Harry's right hand was scraped and bleeding. I felt him wince when he hugged me. I knew better than to say anything. If Harry needed medical attention, he'd get it on his terms.

"You both seem shaky, especially you ma'am." She suggested we sit down on one of the sidewalk benches dotting the downtown area. I followed her suggestion immediately; my knees were still rubbery. I listened as she called for a tow truck after her cursory exam of the right rear wheel determined the car couldn't be driven. Her accent was Midwestern, but there was a hint of something. She pronounced corner like *cauhner* maybe an Irish speech pattern from immigrant grandparents.

Once we were seated, Officer Corrigan proceeded to take our information and our statements. Mine was useless since I had my back to the car. Harry seemed to be getting angrier as he explained what he saw.

"This one way through a busy downtown area seems a bit chancy doesn't it? I mean, this bloke probably tried to cut out in front of traffic and lost control. I was a few paces behind my wife and looked up to see the car coming right at her. It was a late model '91 or '92, navy blue Chevy Impala. First letter of the plate was J. All I could think about was Grace. Didn't get anything else."

"Mr. Marsden, most people who are only witnesses and not involved don't get this much." Officer Corrigan looked impressed. So did some of the people near the scene. One of them spoke out. He was one of the young men who'd been on the outside looking in at the *old folks* necking in the car. He looked to be about seventeen with shoulder length, light brown hair. He wasn't tall; maybe five feet eight inches, but had the muscular build of someone who worked out. His clothes were neat but the typical teen style of black jeans, black T-shirt, and black *Nikes*. The other three onlookers weren't with him.

"Dude, you were cool. Where'd you learn that move?"

Officer Corrigan fixed the young man with a quieting glance.

"If you have a statement pertaining to the accident give me your name and number and I'll talk to you later."

"I didn't see nothing. 'Cept this guy flying over the top of the Jag and sweeping her up like some Tarzan stunt. Right before the car hit." *Smack*! He punctuated his comments by one loud clap of his hands. I jumped at the noise. Harry glared at the young man who was skating too close to the imaginary line Harry draws around my well-being.

Murmurs from the people standing around validated the teen's observation. A woman stepped out from the crowd and approached the officer. She was maybe in her early thirties, wearing a navy blue pantsuit and low-heeled navy pumps. Her shoulder length hair was styled in a smooth variation of a pageboy. She could have just come from her hairdresser.

"Officer, I was in my car right behind the hit and run driver. I saw him back out of his space and start forward. It looked deliberate to me."

The murmured speculations, background noise to her narrative, stopped as though E.F. Hutton had spoken.

Officer Corrigan turned her full body toward her. "And you are?" She poised her pen over her notebook.

"My name is Shannon Smith. I'm an attorney in town. I'd be happy to give a statement for the, the…" She leaned around the officer trying to wrangle an introduction to her potential clients.

Officer Corrigan moved with her, running interference for us still seated on the bench behind her. Harry stood up and moved around the policewoman. I noticed he didn't extend his hand to the attorney but nodded an acknowledgment.

"Ms. Smith, I'm Harry Marsden. Thank you for coming forward. Were you able to get a look at the person driving?"

"Mr. Marsden, I'm the one taking the statements." Officer Corrigan wasn't pleased with this turn of events. Another complication drove up in the form of the tow truck. She spoke to the attorney. "I have your name and I'll be with you in five minutes. Please stand over there while I handle the tow. Mr. Marsden, why don't you rejoin your wife for a few minutes? Thank you." She went to speak with the tow operator.

Ms. Smith produced a business card from her pocket and scribbled something on the back before handing it to Harry.

When Officer Corrigan returned, Ms. Smith claimed she was due in court and gave her a card where she could be reached, but didn't add a note.

The earlier witness had been sidling closer to me as the officer's attention had moved elsewhere. The teen leaned toward me with a hurried apology. "Didn't mean to upset you. Sorry." He straightened quickly as he realized both Harry and Officer Corrigan were looking at him.

"Young man, what's your name and phone number? If you can't wait to make your statement I'll call you." He dutifully gave his name, Justin Peerce, and phone number to the police officer then moved off down the sidewalk with the others who had been dispersed. I realized most of the bystanders were merchants when they ducked back into doorways up and down the sidewalk.

"Mr. Marsden, is there anything in the vehicle you need?"

"Not really." He queried me with raised eyebrows. I shook my head no. "Wait a minute. Let me use the car phone to call someone." He moved toward the car and then stopped. I suspected his dilemma. Walter was in the hospital. Karen and Hannah were both out of town.

I stood up and walked to the curb. "I'll call my dad. He's minutes from here. We don't have to tell him where I was when the car was hit." Harry nodded as he opened the driver's side for me. I slid in and lifted the phone. My father listened carefully to where we were and promised to be there in ten minutes. I returned to my perch on the park bench to wait for my dad. I didn't remember benches on York Street when I was a kid waiting for my dad to pick us up after going to the show at the York Theatre.

The car parked directly behind us had pulled away and the tow operator was able to coax the Jaguar up onto the platform. Harry signed some papers and gave the tow operator a deposit to deliver the Jag to Helmut and Vito's Garage on Ogden Avenue.

Officer Corrigan stayed until the tow truck drove off. She handled the accident quickly and professionally giving us the proper paperwork and phone numbers for both insurance and follow-up.

"Mr. and Mrs. Marsden, you're certain you don't require medical attention?"

"We're fine. Thank you for all your help."

"I'll follow up with those two witnesses to see if we can get a better description." She shook hands with both of us and said good-bye.

We sat on the bench. The only evidence of an accident lay near the curb, glass and plastic trim from the headlight of the Chevy. Harry was reading the back of the business card.

"Is Ms. Smith personal injury?"

"Oh, yes. Quite. At least personal." He passed the card to me. The message said, "Call me when you're wife isn't around."

My temper attempted chagrin, then fury, but all I could manage was a burst of laughter. Harry feigned an indignant look. "What? You think it far-fetched a young, attractive, professional woman would come on to me?"

A fresh burst of laughter greeted his *professional* comment. Harry couldn't hold the mask in place any longer. He joined in my laughter. Harry shifted his position so he could put his left arm around my shoulders. We hadn't noticed the light blue Bonneville swinging into the recently vacated parking space.

"Let me in on the joke or you can both walk home." Mike Morelli was seated behind the wheel, his left arm leaning on the open window. He opened the door and walked out to meet us on the sidewalk. My dad was first generation Italian; his parents came to America in 1903 to search out their piece of the dream. He wasn't much taller than me, but his wiry, slim build made him appear taller. His close cut hair was more gray than black.

"Hi, Dad. Thanks for coming to get us." I hugged him with the same intensity I had used as a child. I always felt unconditional love inside his bear hug. We swayed from side to side, left, right, left, a routine from my childhood.

"Yes, thanks Mike. Didn't suspect you'd be pressed into service as a taxi." My dad turned to Harry.

"Hey, with five kids I did a lot of driving," he joked. "Especially this one. Float meetings, play rehearsals, dance recitals, library, roller-skating, Hillside Shopping Center, choir practice. She was always joining something or going somewhere."

"She hasn't changed much." Harry stepped toward Mike. My father's handshake was a two handed approach, the right hand grasping the person's right hand, but then his left hand clamped on at the top of the shoulder in a more familiar greeting. Harry's pain was apparent as soon as Mike grabbed his hand. It escalated as my father's left hand found its mark.

"Geez, Harry! What's the matter?" Mike dropped his hand from Harry's shoulder like it was a red-hot poker.

Harry's face looked gray and pasty. Mike stepped to Harry's left side and steered him toward his car. "C'mon. Get in the car." He opened the back door and guided Harry into the back seat. "Grace, get in the front." I slipped around the back of the car this time looking over my right shoulder for oncoming traffic. Mike had leaned into the back and secured Harry's seatbelt before getting in the driver's seat.

"I'm taking you to Elmhurst Hospital and you're going to tell me what the hell is going on."

This voice was the one I had heard frequently growing up with four brothers. This was the *don't bullshit me or it will go harder on you* voice. I was trained to respond to this voice. Before I could blurt out the truth, Harry told a whopper of a lie. My dad was glancing in the mirror at Harry during my husband's story.

"It was stupid of me," Harry said. "We came out of one of the stores and as we were feet away from the car, this moron comes out of nowhere and sideswipes the Jag. You know how I feel about that car, Mike. I lost my head; tried to rush out to catch a plate number and misjudged the curb. Caught the fender of the car in front of mine and couldn't stop the fall. Must have jammed my shoulder when I hit the ground. Lucky thing I didn't break my bloody leg."

Gee, if I hadn't been there, I would have believed Harry. He had the right touch of indignant anger and sheepishness to sound totally authentic. Was my dad buying it? Harry's gaze was positively guileless. As long as my dad didn't look into my, no doubt, pansy-purple eyes we'd be home free.

"You *were* lucky. I know that's your baby, but it's just a car."

"I feel foolish now. Hate to have to repeat my story to the nurse at hospital; women don't appreciate fine driving machines like we do."

I wondered where this was going. I soon found out.

My dad accepted Harry's story without reservation. I could tell by his next statement. "Tell the nurse you misjudged the curb and put your arm out to break your fall. She doesn't need to know *why* you were jumping off the curb."

"Great idea, Mike." Harry had led my dad to the idea he already had. I'd seen my husband produce these results many times. It amazed me how he arrived at a decision, then led others to it, yet made it appear that he was the last one to get there. Now, there would be no mention of an accident and my dad would not become suspicious about why.

I felt a sense of *de ja vu* as we pulled up to the hospital building. Different hospital, different man, but *de ja vu* all over again. My dad dropped us at the entrance then left to park in the already full lot. We walked into the ER. There were three people in the waiting area. Two people were already talking with nurses. I motioned to chairs near the windows. Harry nodded and followed me.

"I'll go sign in and see what the wait is like." I felt like I was checking in at some trendy restaurant. Harry nodded again and shifted in the molded, one-size fits all, chair. Two steps away from the triage desk I spotted the top of a streaked blonde head over the edge of the next cubicle.

"Tracy?"

Conversation halted and the blonde turned and apparently stretched up on tiptoes to track down the voice. It was whom I suspected. One of my college friends was the head ER nurse at Elmhurst. She had pursued her nursing degree at Rush Presbyterian Hospital after we graduated from Regina. Her first job had been working for a hand and wrist specialist in Elmhurst. I had gone to him with severe thumb pain and weakness. The orthopedic doctor who first saw me recommended surgery. Tracy's guy fitted me with a plastic cast for eight weeks to relieve pressure on a nerve. She worked for him until the hospital lured her away with an offer she couldn't refuse. She joined the staff fours years ago and moved into her current spot when that nurse retired.

I hadn't seen her since our last Regina Luncheon. A group of us still get together every year for a Sunday afternoon brunch. The last one was held at the Jefferson Hill Tea Room in Naperville.

She came around the corner of the cubicle, reached my side in two long strides, and engulfed me in a genuine hug. Regina girls did not give air kisses and shoulder squeezes. "Hi, Grace. You look great. Why are you here?" Tracy was a to the point kind of person; wide smile, booming voice and no chitchat. During my college years, I hung around with Karen and Tracy, both of whom are five feet, ten inches tall. My family would laugh at the sight of the three of us, with me in the middle. I smiled and pointed to Harry across the room. "It's Harry. We think he jammed his arm or something when he fell."

Tracy absolutely adored Harry. She had been with me the day I met Harry at a college function. It had been a chance meeting over a glass of champagne, although Harry insists he had maneuvered the encounter, and when I returned to the table where my friends were seated they had gushed about how suave and handsome he looked. Now, she walked over to where he was seated.

Harry stood up when she reached him.

"Ah, my favorite Florence Nightingale." Harry smiled and hugged Tracy with his left arm. "How are you, Tracy?"

"I'm fine. Apparently, you're the one with the problem." She carried a clipboard with her; she appeared to make a show of taking notes. "Hurt right arm breaking fall." She paused in her paperwork and fixed Harry with a serious look. "So, why did Gracie push you?" She grinned wickedly, setting us all to laughing. "Or was she twisting your arm to go to our reunion this year? Arm twisting is the only way I'd get William to go."

"Actually, I haven't been approached–yet." Harry smiled cautiously at me. "I'm certain it's a conversation we'll be having soon. No, this was due to clumsiness. I misjudged a curb, teetering off onto the street. Felt like Paddy after one too many pints." He winked and joked with Tracy, who was 100% Irish.

"If you'd been Paddy, you'd have melted off that curb and been fit as a fiddle, laddie." Tracy and Harry always teased and poked fun at each other. She turned serious now. "However it happened, let's get you to an exam room." She directed me to fill out the form on the clipboard and told Harry to follow her. Harry gave me a thumbs-up signal with his left hand; his right thumb was hooked inside his belt thereby keeping his arm motionless.

I did my part filling out all the pertinent information and turned in the form to the desk nurse. By this time, I was wondering where my father had parked. I found the vending machine and purchased two cups of black coffee reasoning if he didn't show up soon I could drink his coffee too. I had settled into a chair next to a table and placed my cups between two piles of magazines. Two sips into my coffee I looked up to see both Tracy and my dad converging on me from two directions. Tracy was moving quickly holding Harry's jacket and some papers in her hands. My dad was moving cautiously through the chairs holding a cup of coffee in each hand. Me, my dad and my brother Mike were the coffee fiends in the family; anytime was coffee time. Tracy spotted my dad first.

"Mr. Morelli, how nice to see you. How are you?" Dad noticed Tracy three steps before they would have collided. He liked Tracy's spunk. At my wedding, she took off her size 10 pink podesua pumps and placed them prominently on one of the band's speakers, offering them as vehicles for champagne. I don't think anyone was drunk enough to use them. Tracy and Karen had been two college chums who were always invited to the Morelli's *home improvement* weekend every summer. My parents would gather their children and their children's friends and assign home repairs and or improvements. Our reward was my father's fabulous Italian cooking, my mother's baby-sitting service, and my Uncle Jimmy's homemade wine.

"Hi honey. I haven't seen you in months. How are those two little guys?" My dad was referring to Tracy's sons, Benjamin and Matthew.

"They are growing like weeds and just as tough to control," she said smiling. "Gosh, it's good to see you."

"Let me put these down and give you a real hello." My dad placed his coffee next to the others and turned back to Tracy. He gives those bear hugs where you rock from side to side. He sat next to me and Tracy took the chair next to him. She motioned at the table. "I see neither one on you has cut down on your caffeine intake."

"Hey, it's the only vice I have." My dad lifted his hands palm up.

"Hey, it's genetic." I mimicked his voice and gesture.

Tracy laughed and accepted one of the coffees. She took a sip and made a face. "This is much better with cream and sugar." She put the cup down on the floor next to her feet. "Here's the scoop on Harry. In plain English, it appears he has jammed his shoulder, strained some ligaments, bruised his elbow, and lacerated the hell out of his wrist and hand, but nothing is broken. How fast was he walking when he fell off this curb? I mean was it a normal curb or two feet high?"

My dad and I both laughed; I was pretending her questions were funny and rhetorical. When neither of us spoke, Tracy told us Harry would be out in a few minutes.

"He should wear the sling for a few days to give the arm some time to heal. I don't think he'll need any physical therapy, but that's not my call. He should see his own physician and probably an orthopedic guy for further diagnosis." She stood up. "I'd best get back to work."

I stood and gave her a hug.

"Speaking of work, I'll be in your neck of the woods tomorrow night. I'm attending a presentation on some new equipment at Edwards Hospital."

"Come over when you're finished. You're less than ten minutes away. We can have a glass of wine and catch up. You can check up on your patient."

"You're on. It should be over by seven o'clock. Not too late?"

"Of course not. We'll see you then. Thanks for your help. I mean for getting us through all this." I waved at the waiting room in general.

"No problem, what are friends for? I hope someday you'll explain what Harry was really doing." She grinned and walked away.

"She doesn't miss much, does she?" my dad asked in admiration.

"With her two boys she can't afford to miss a trick. Anyway, she always dramatizes Harry's life ever since he was, you know, away."

"You two don't make it easy not to. People shooting at you,

driving you off the road, rigging your electrical appliances..."

"Dad. I get it." To hear him tell it there was a conspiracy behind every tree. Harry's approach stopped the conversation. He was moving better than he had earlier and was sporting a navy blue sling. His color was better, his smile looked easy.

"Hi Sweetheart. You look loads better. How do you feel?"

"Ridiculous in this thing." He lifted his injured arm away from his body like a wing. The movement caused him to wince. He lowered his arm slowly. "Maybe they do know a tad about healing." He turned to my dad. "Mike, might we impose on you to drive us home?" We started walking toward the exit. His answer stopped us in our tracks.

"No. I'm sorry, I'm not taking you home." Our heads turned around so quickly we might have been admitted for whiplash. "I won't take you home cause I know you haven't eaten, I know you won't be comfortable sitting in a restaurant, pointing to Harry, and I know you," sweeping his hand toward me, "aren't in the mood to cook."

"Talk about not missing much," I mumbled.

"Mike that's kind of you but we..."

"Are coming to my house for dinner," my dad finished. "What are your choices?

We looked at each other and shrugged. "What's on the menu?" My father rubbed his hands together in glee. I thought he'd say *goody*. We walked to the parking lot. It was already dark. He had a great parking spot only seven rows from the entrance. I wondered again what had taken him so long to come in. It wasn't long before I found out.

Chapter Twenty-Seven

We pulled into my father's driveway after passing several parked cars on both side of the street. Harry and I both recognized some of the vehicles.

"Seems like a few of the family have come calling. Perhaps now isn't the time for dinner guests." Harry's smooth voice didn't fool me. He was annoyed. "Mike, I'm tired and this arm is starting to hurt like the devil. I know what you're up to. Not tonight, sir."

My father turned to face Harry in the passenger seat. "Anyone else, any other time, okay. But this is Gracie we're talking about; my little girl." My father spoke with a resolve I'd never heard before. Harry must have thought the same. He didn't argue.

We entered the small brick house through the back door knowing from the parked cars my brothers Mike, Marty, and Glen would be inside. No one seemed surprised at Harry's sling so my assumption that my dad had called the gang while we were in the emergency room seemed correct. A car we didn't recognize belonged to my cousin Nick, my father's godson. Hellos, hugs, and handshakes crisscrossed the room until everyone had acknowledged everyone else. My brother Mike had been making coffee when we arrived. He suggested we all move into the living room and he'd bring in the pot. Harry asked Mike for a glass of water and my dad for anything stronger than an aspirin. We hadn't stopped to fill the prescription for pain pills Tracy had given me along with other papers. My dad seemed to realize how inconvenient this powwow was; too late now. My brother Marty was a pharmaceuticals salesman. He overheard Harry's request.

"What do you want?"

"Something to deaden the pain. It feels like my arm is on fire from my shoulder to my finger tips."

"Dad invited us for dinner. We didn't stop to fill the prescription; I thought I'd run over to Tiechen Drugs while dad cooked dinner."

"Show me the prescription. Maybe I've something in the car."

I handed Marty two slips of paper. "She said one was for pain and the other was an anti-inflammatory."

"Yes. The Vicodin is for pain. I can fill this. I've the generic in my case. Take me a minute." My brother shrugged into his leather jacket and headed out the back.

Nick approached Harry. "What'd they tell you? Sprained, dislocated, jammed?" My cousin was an EMT for the Elgin Fire Department. He had spent two years at a chiropractic college pursuing certification in sports medicine before he shifted his focus and goal to community service.

"Jammed is what they said. Strained ligaments and various degrees of scrapes."

Marty returned holding a small packet. He pushed out two of the foil wrapped pills and handed them to Harry who readily popped them in his mouth and washed them down with a long drink of water.

"You should start feeling relief in ten minutes or so. Shouldn't take them on an empty stomach though."

"Maybe I can heat up some of Dad's leftovers."

My brother Mike smiled. "Dad's leftovers put our first meals to shame. Let's see what's here." He pulled open the refrigerator door. "I don't believe my eyes." My brother's look of incredulity spread to my face as I peered around his head to look in. "Dad, where's all your food?" Mike's bellow brought everyone who had gone into the living room back to the kitchen at a fast walk. You'd think he had body parts on the wire shelves the way everyone jockeyed for a better view.

"Geez, what's all the hullabaloo?" My father stood with his hands on his waist. "Close the door before you let all the cold out."

"Dad," my brother Marty piped up, "You're fridge is our dream. Where's all the food. The salami, the provolone, the prosciutto, the lasagna, the…"

"Marty, stop. I'm starving and you're not helping." I meant it.

It was well beyond my mealtime and my personality wasn't perky anymore.

"Oh man. I forgot about Gracie's time bomb stomach. She'll blow if we don't feed her." Glen was the brother closest to me in age and we had always teased each other. But, I was serious about eating.

"Would everyone please relax." My dad's pleasantly husky voice calmed the crowd. "Food is on the way; I'm having pizzas delivered. I didn't have time to shop today and I had some friends in earlier in the day who *raided the ice box* you might say."

"Might say?" my brother Mike questioned. "Who'd you have over, a football team?" We laughed at Mike's query. We stopped laughing at the look on Dad's face. "You're kidding, right? Where'd you find a football team to feed? And why?"

"Berkeley started a Pop Warner league and some of the kids who play touch football on the street are on the team. I read in the local paper that they needed adults to help out and I don't do much at the senior center so I'm the team manager." Dad stood up straighter, daring anyone to comment.

"I thought the team manager made sure they had equipment, towels, water, that kind of stuff." Glen smiled at our dad.

"Hey, growing athletes gotta eat. Remember when you guys would bring your friends over? Your mother and I would empty the fridge and the cabinets to feed all you bottomless pits. Don't tell you're jealous I found a new team to feed? Same deal. I'll tell you what's different though. We got two girls on the team. You should see them pack away the prosciutto."

We were laughing at his commentary. He beamed as he continued holding center court.

"Wait, wait. You gotta hear their name. They're mostly kids from Victoria Street, both blocks, but because they've got females their team name is Victor-Victoria, so everyone calls them Vic-Vic."

We howled, laughing so hard we didn't hear the bell ring. Heavy pounding interrupted the play by play. Marty was closest to the door. He ushered in Walter. Harry and I exchanged surprised looks, but no one else seemed to think his appearance on the scene unusual. I soon realized why. Walter, looking fit as a fiddle, for which I was thankful, was carrying six pizza boxes into the kitchen.

The Lion Tamer: A Caged Death

Dinner. No wonder Dad said not to worry.

We greeted Walter enthusiastically. Then set about opening boxes, passing around plates, napkins, and toppings. I noticed Harry and Walter stepped away from the ravenous crowd. They stood apart for a few moments talking quietly. I can only imagine the conversation. Maybe Harry was apologizing for not checking on Walter personally and I'm sure he filled him in on the car incident.

After the initial flurry and *clinking* of dishes and cutlery, calm befell the kitchen as most of us chowed down. Mealtimes at the Morelli house had always been a ritual of speed and silence. My dad would come home from work at Western Electric, change his clothes and relax before dinner. We always ate late. Many a baseball or football game on the street would be interrupted twice, once when all the other kids went in to eat at 5:00 p.m. and then again when the Morellis went in at 6:00 p.m. My dad liked quiet after working in a factory all day and we would just as soon gulp and go. The problem was whoever's turn it was to clear had to wait until my dad finished eating. The more we fidgeted, the slower he ate.

We rushed through the pizzas in silence pulling each empty carton from the table until we were down to two pizzas. We seemed sated so the noise level crept up again. But not so loud we didn't hear the doorbell this time. I was nearest and opened the door in a grand *come one come all* gesture. My preparatory smile froze on my face.

Ric Kramer stood in the doorway. Voices dropped off as people realized the identity of the visitor. Unlike before, the quiet in the room now was not calming. My brothers were obviously curious about his reason for being here, heck we all were. My father stepped forward removing me from the role of hostess.

"Hello, Ric. Come in. We were working our way through some pizza. Hungry?"

My dad's graciousness eased some of the tension in the room. My brothers Marty and Glen acknowledged Ric with a nod.

"No thanks, Mr. Morelli. I came by to talk to Mars…Harry." He stepped into the room and turned to face Harry. "I tried your home and then called Walter. Gertrude told me Walter was on his way here, so I figured you might be here too."

When Harry turned to square off with Ric, they looked liked

mirror images, each with opposite arms in slings. There was the imminent danger that I would burst into laughter at this sight. I looked over at my brother Glen. I think he saw the same irony. His mouth was curving into a smile. I was certain he would come out with some wisecrack. My dad spoke first.

"Why don't the two of you go into the front room? You'll have some privacy there." Both men nodded and turned toward the hallway. Glen couldn't leave it alone. "Hey, Gracie," he called in a stage whisper, "Looks like a set of bookends."

My face flamed. I looked at both backs but couldn't tell if they had heard. Marty reached over and punched Glen in the arm.

"What the hell's the matter with you?"

"C'mon. What the hell's the matter with you? You know they're crazy about Gracie."

My eyes were filling with tears. Sometimes Glen didn't know when to stop teasing. This was definitely one of those times.

"Dammit, Glen. I'd send you to your room if you still had one here." My dad glared at my brother.

"There is the basement, Dad," Mike offered.

"All right, all right. I didn't mean anything by it. C'mon, Gracie girl; don't be upset." Glen put his arm around my shoulders squeezing me to him. At this point, I was furious with myself for getting emotional. I wanted to know what was going on in the next room.

In what seemed a short time Ric came back into the kitchen. "Thank you, Mr. Morelli. I'll be going now." He shook hands with my father and turned to say a separate good bye to me. The last person he looked at before the door closed was my brother Glen; if looks could maim.

"How'd he know it was me? Does he have eyes in the back of his head?" Glen looked uncomfortable.

"He asked me the name of the *jerk* who'd spoken." Harry explained as he walked into the room. His look wasn't any less violent than Ric's had been. "I told him."

"Geez, Harry. I'm sorry. You have to admit you two looked silly standing together." Glen was trying to wiggle out of this current gaffe. We all let him twist a little until he looked apologetic. Harry took him off the hook. "Think of your sister's feelings next time, okay?" He couldn't shake hands with him so he clapped his on the shoulder. I think harder than necessary if the wince on Glen's face was an indication.

"All right folks, I'm serving coffee and Aunt Edna's pizelles and biscotti. Take some and go sit in the front room." We all dutifully lined up to fill our plates with my aunt's excellent cookies. The last three people in were left with only carpet room for seating. Of course, Walter, Harry, and my dad were those three, my dad because he served, Walter and Harry because they hadn't dived into the feeding frenzy. My dad raised us right, Mike gave his seat to our dad, Marty moved to the floor for Walter, and Glen about shot out of his chair to offer it to Harry.

Once seated, we all turned toward my dad as he called this meeting. "Everybody ready." He waited for nods. "Good. We're here because a series of events have occurred to cause them trouble," he pointed to us, "and may continue to cause them trouble." The room remained quiet as my family leaned forward to concentrate. My father looked directly at me. "Everyone in this room is ready to help you. We need to know what's been happening. Don't keep us out."

I looked from face to face. My brothers, my cousin, my dad returned my gaze with strong affection and it seemed, a glimpse of resolve. I looked at Harry, whose expression was masked by pain. I saw the slight nod.

I started the explanation with the arrival of the letter and the feeling I had and the flash of light I saw the next morning while riding. Harry described finding Derek's body and discovering the new neighbor we were headed to meet was an old friend of his. We left out the argument.

Harry continued with the scheme he and Ric threw together at Lily's house. He explained Ric agreed they needed to find out if Derek was acting alone or with a partner who was still *on the clock*.

I quickly glossed over bringing Ric to Good Sam and the rest of that afternoon. I left out the brawl, even though I knew they knew. I took more time explaining the evening events with the intruder and the police. I left out finding the items in the box. I recapped visiting Harry, skipped driving Ric home, and moved right to dinner with

Walter.

Harry picked up the line explaining how once Walter had passed the information about the break-in to him in jail, he pulled the plug on the scheme and contacted Katernak to arrange his release. He didn't mention what he found in the priest's hole.

I picked up the narrative explaining our trip to Cottage Hill Jewelers, under the guise of purchasing a gift, and finishing with the crazy motorist who sideswiped our car. I didn't include where I had been standing at the time.

"Now you know what we know." I smiled and held my hands out, palms up to emphasize my comment. I was amazed all five of them had stayed quiet and not interrupted. My father must have laid down the rules of engagement before we arrived. Released from their vow of silence, my brothers immediately shot questions at us. I answered what I could as honestly as I felt I should. A glance at Harry told me he was sinking fast but managing to stay alert by tapping some deep reserve of strength.

"Are you sure?" I had missed a question from my brother Glen who, when he wasn't tormenting me, was an excellent dentist with a flourishing practice. I turned to him, raising my eyebrows and shoulders to indicate I hadn't heard.

"Are they certain it's Rhodes? Harry said the face was bashed in. Did they check fingerprints or dental records or what?"

Or what, was more like it. Do I tell my suburban, Dr. Painless Dentistry, Derek Rhodes had his prints altered because of where he once worked and for whom he worked?

My thoughts swirled in my head. Harry took point on this question and answered for me. "Forensics followed up on the teeth. Apparently, there was some issue with the fingerprints and they decided the bridge and partial they found in the mouth would do nicely for identification." Harry paused for a moment; a strange look crossed his face. He seemed anxious to leave now. "Don't want to be an old sponge, but your meds haven't exactly dulled the roar." *I'd never heard that colloquialism before.* I don't think they had either, but we all got the message. Walter stepped forward to say he'd go get his car to drive us home. He said a hurried good-bye to everyone. Marty handed me a small vial. "Give him one of these before bed.

It'll help him sleep, guaranteed." I smiled a thank you and kissed him good-bye. Each Morelli in turned was bussed on the cheek. Harry was already out the door when I hugged my dad. "Dad, I know telling you not to worry won't mean anything. But, Derek is dead. He was the bad guy. The break-in was just that. Remember last year the Bishops were burglarized? I guess Pine Marsh looks pretty good to a burglar. We've made an appointment with Mike to beef up our security."

My oldest brother owned his own consulting company. They did high-end security systems for corporations and individuals interested in the latest technology at *unaffordable* prices. I was hoping for the sibling discount.

"I remember the Bishops moved too. Smart people. You said they moved to Hinsdale. Nice place, sidewalks, street lamps, next door neighbors who can hear you if you scream."

"Okay, Dad. I get the point." My father had never liked Pine Marsh, said it was too isolated. Couldn't even chat over the fence while you were hanging out your wash. He was right about that. *Who hangs out wash?* I hugged him harder and promised to be careful.

Harry was in the back seat leaning back against the headrest. His eyes were closed. Walter had already turned his Rover around in the drive. I climbed into the back next to Harry. "Sorry."

Harry stirred. "No problem, darling. I know your dad is worried; your brothers too. You know how fortunate you are to have them?" Harry came from a small family, his twin sister Hannah, parents, William and Dorothy, and a few distant cousins. Hannah spent a lot of time here, but his folks were still and would remain in England.

I climbed in on his left side. I reached over and squeezed his hand. "We'll be home soon. I'm beat; you must be exhausted. You need to soak some of those aches out. I'll run a bath for you, after which I'll massage the parts that don't hurt too much." My voice had taken on a soft, coaxing tone. "Sound good?"

"*Mmm.*" A murmur and sigh told me I was on the right track.

Chapter Twenty-Eight

Walter insisted on coming in with us to check the house. He told Harry he'd be back at 9:00 a.m. to work on his sore muscles. I knew whose ministrations Harry would prefer. I locked the door behind Walter and turned to favor my husband with a wicked grin. He wasn't standing where I'd left him.

My first stop would have been the kitchen; I was hungry again. I knew my husband's M.O. He was in his office, awkwardly trying to hold the receiver between his left ear and his injured shoulder to take notes. I heard him ask for a call ASAP; then he hung up.

"Who were you talking too?"

"Following up with Kramer. Loose end is all."

I knew when Harry was being vague and this was one of those times. The idea of Harry and Ric even talking was unsettling, but the thought of their hatching plots and working together was frightening. I had seen their anger and animosity burgeon into a terrible rivalry. An unfounded one since I had chosen to stay with Harry. This alliance upset me.

Harry moved passed me dismissing the call as easily as walking out of the room. "I seem to remember a promise of bath, massage, something along those lines?" He placed his hand under my chin and lifted my face. His lips closed over mine with a softness of what I hoped would follow. "Be patient with me." He nodded slightly to his injured arm. "I won't disappoint you."

I thought I knew what he referred too, but there seemed to be an underlying meaning to his words. *Was he telling me something else? About? About Ric?* I focused on his words and followed him up the stairs. Harry stood near the Jacuzzi while I fiddled with the faucets and temperature. This was my territory. I had the tub filling with soothing hot water in no time. Harry wrinkled his nose at the scent released from the eucalyptus cubes I crushed and added under the running water.

"Eucalyptus will promote healing of sore muscles. I'll do the rest." I smiled seductively. Harry's smile widened, then became sheepish.

"I can't seem to do a thing with my left hand. The undoing of these buttons and such are so awkward." He ran his left hand down his shirtfront and settled at his belt buckle. "So awkward," he murmured. Harry slipped the sling off his shoulder and let it drop to the floor. He hooked his right thumb in his waistband and let his left arm hang at his side.

I stepped toward him and easily undid his top button, and then the next two. I let my fingertips rest lightly on his chest for a moment before continuing. *Buttons and such* were no problem for me.

Our lovemaking stayed hot longer than the water in the *Jacuzzi*. The second tub full of Eucalyptus enhanced water eased the day's aches and soothed our spent bodies. Harry's eyes shone with a mixture of pain and euphoria. I knew as he relaxed from our lusty coupling the pain would again gain the upper hand. I handed him the meds my brother had provided. We snuggled under smooth sheets layered under a feather light comforter. Pillow talk was minimal. Harry's slow, heavy breathing signaled his fast dive to deep sleep. I wanted to ask a million questions. I had so much on my mind; I knew I'd be up early to walk with Barbara. *I'd rather ride April and sweep up the meadow to the field overlooking the lake. Maybe I could beg off.* Those were my thoughts as I drifted to sleep.

My internal clock roused me from a troubled sleep shortly before six o'clock; enough time to put the coffee on before I met up with Barbara at the back door.

I dressed quickly and quietly in a pair of lady Wrangler jeans and a turtleneck sweatshirt combo from Park City. I checked to make sure Harry was covered. Not to worry; he looked as if he hadn't budged a bit. Apparently, Marty's elephant dropper sleeping pill had worked. I had a few minutes to spare so I retrieved our clothing from various quadrants of the room. Harry's sports jacket hung lopsided on the chair. I remembered the diamond and his strange behavior when he saw it. That was one of my questions. I dumped the clothes in the laundry room on my way down to the kitchen. Two minutes later, the coffee was set to go and so was I.

"Good morning." Barbara was outside leaning against the boot cleaning post.

"Hey, early bird. How are you?"

"Freezing, I didn't realize how cold it was. It must have dropped last night."

"It is only April. It might even snow one more time." I enjoyed teasing her.

Barb and Harry, the Pine Marsh gardeners, loved spring and summer for the obvious horticultural reasons. I knew Barb couldn't wait for the weather to stabilize. In Chicago, you could need a parka on Thursday and only a shawl by Saturday. Or vice versa.

"Let's walk to my house so I can get a jacket."

"Don't be silly. Wear mine. I won't need it with this sweatshirt." I lifted my black plaid shirt jacket from the peg in the mudroom and handed it to my neighbor.

"Are you sure you don't need it?"

"I've this double layer thing going on," I pulled the material away from my neck to demonstrate. "I'd be sweating bullets with my jacket."

"Thanks." She slipped into the warm wool and visibly relaxed.

"Coffee is brewing, and we're moving out."

"Grace, are you talking or thinking today?" Barb liked to set the pace both physically and mentally on our morning outings.

"*Mmm*? Thinking. I've gotta think this morning."

"Thinking, it is." Barb adjusted the headset she had around her neck to her ears. The wire wound under the loaner jacket and into the Walkman clipped to her belt. I followed her lead toward the back of the property to the band of pecan shells that designated the walking paths. I knew once the thinking lamp was lit we would not speak. She swung out onto the path; her walking shoes crunched the chilled ground cover. I moved in step next to her and settled into the fast pace Barb had set.

The Lion Tamer: A Caged Death

Why had Harry reacted so strongly to the diamond? Had he seen it before? Where? Why had someone dumped it in my garage and then broken in to take it back? That lawyer, with the hots for Harry, told the police officer that the driver of the car looked as though he was trying to hit me. With Derek dead, who would want to hurt me?

The wind picked up as we crossed an open stretch from one leaf covered copse to its mirror image across from the third fairway. I pulled up the hood on my sweatshirt. Swirling winds mimicked the thoughts in my mind. The pace was brisk; I used the solitude and muscle strain to clear my mind in an attempt to organize the events of the last week.

Lily arrives in town. Derek is murdered. We discover Derek's body. Harry reunites with Lily. Harry and I argue over Lily. Leo DeFreest arrives in town. Harry and Ric argue over Lily. They fight; Harry is arrested; Ric is hospitalized. Lily and I argue, *okay, fight.* Strange items are in my garage. Someone breaks into the house. Walter is poisoned. Harry's jail time is a scheme. Lily is lying about her whereabouts. We learn the diamond is some rare gem. I'm almost compacted by an errant car. Harry is hurt saving me. My family is upset and is getting involved.

Hmm? Whose name keeps popping up? I can't move three spaces in this web without tangling with Lily. Speaking of tangling...

My hands automatically sought the comfort of the snaps on my walking jacket. I could repeatedly snap and unsnap the bottom fastener on my jacket without breaking stride. *Oh, damn.* Barb was wearing my *comforter* and this sweatshirt was a pullover. I touched the neckline searching for the drawstring on the hood. The string was missing; probably pressed into service once before. My mind demanded action and I had none to take. I reached for my belt loop– no yarn hung from the cloth circle. *I snap when I walk.* At times like this a burst of heat would seize my neck and face. An involuntary clamp tightened around my chest. My brain betrayed me now ordering a panic attack. *Unless, unless. Braid, dammit.* My brain would not clear the white noise filling my head and obstructing sane thought. *My jacket; the pockets.* I always had something in my pocket; string or Kleenex that I could knot or shred. I had fallen off the brisk pace and was now a few yards behind Barb. When we walked in our thinking mode, to each his own space. We didn't always walk abreast on the path.

I noticed Barb making entries into her recorder. She seemed calm, focused. I was in a meltdown. My only thought was to reach those pockets bobbing ten feet ahead of me. A quick burst of speed and I was within an arm's length of my jacket.

Barb must have heard or sensed my hurried movement. She stopped abruptly and whirled to face me. I couldn't stop quickly enough and collided with her. I put my hands out to keep her from falling.

A noise ripped through the morning stillness like a teeth rattling crack of thunder. I felt Barb jump from the shock then felt her full weight as she slumped against me. I lowered her to the ground frantic to run and hide in the depths of the woods we had just left; I recognized the noise as a gunshot. We were so exposed on the fairway. I lifted her hand to chafe her wrist to increase the circulation. My fingers felt the wet warm blood in the same instant my brain registered my friend hadn't fainted. My fingers held her wrist; I couldn't feel anything but the mounting panic now surging through my stomach, which threatened to explode along with the scream forming in my mouth.

A shout from the fairway stayed my voice and forced me to look away from my friend's ashen face. I dropped her hand, jumped to my feet to motion to the caller. *This isn't too smart if he is the shooter.* I couldn't worry about that now; Barb was unconscious and bleeding.

The cart drew closer. Harry was racing toward me steering the golf cart badly with his left arm. I was relieved and confused. *Why is he coming from that direction? How did he know to come after us?* I shrugged off the questions and knelt down next to Barb. I gently picked up her other hand and squeezed it. "Hang on, Barb; Harry's here. You're going to be fine."

Harry was out of the cart and on his knees next to me. He used his left arm to grasp my right shoulder and pull me into his chest. "Grace, what happened?" He looked down at our neighbor and then noticed the blood on me. "Are you hurt?"

"No, no. I touched Barb. I thought she had fainted. But it was a gunshot. It must have hit her. Harry, call 9-1-1." My voice hit a frantic pitch as I thought about how still Barb lay on the ground.

"I called. I called everyone. This place will be swarming with Sheriff's Police, Pine Marsh personnel, emergency medical staff, everybody." As good as his word, within seconds of the end of his sentence I saw the first vehicle coming across the fairway, an ambulance. Not far behind was a Sheriff's squad car. Harry stood up to move the cart away from Barb's inert body. It was then I realized he had purposely parked the cart as a shield on one side of us, had come around and blocked us with his body from the other wooded area.

Harry turned to the first officer on the scene. "I called it in. They were shot at. One shot only. I may have frightened off the shooter."

"Yes, I have your name from dispatch. Mr. Marsden, would you and your wife sit in my squad. This will take some time and I have some questions for you, both of you." I smiled a thank you at the young man and took note of his nametag, Manelli. Wow, how close was that? I looked at him more closely. Definitely Italian. Dark brown hair, brown eyes, strong chin, slightly wide nose. He was about 5 feet, 10 inches tall and solid. He appeared to be in his late twenties. I did a mental search of eligible cousins, but came up empty. Maybe, Jolene. I shook myself from those matchmaking thoughts. Harry mistook the movement for a shiver. He tried to use his injured arm to cover more of me. I felt the wince in his muscles.

"You're not wearing your sling." My tone was accusatory. "You should be wearing it. Your arm won't heal properly. Let's get in the car. You can prop up your arm on the armrest." I slid in first and waited for Harry. Once inside, he turned to me. "Grace, I was so worried I wouldn't reach you in time. I know which way you two walk but I didn't know how far you'd gone. I couldn't ride April with this," he motioned his limp arm, "so I drove your car round to the clubhouse and took one of the carts. I told them to call 9-1-1. I called the police. I wasn't sure what I'd find, but I wanted everyone here after Kramer's call this morning."

"Ric called you? Did his call have anything to do with your call to him last night? Does it have something to do with what happened here?"

"I'd like to know that myself." Manelli's voice startled me. He was leaning against Harry's open door. I swear he hadn't been there a moment before.

Harry twisted slightly on the seat to look at the young man. "Ric Kramer is a police inspector who is working a related case that might help the Pine Marsh police with a murder investigation."

On cue, Sergeant Peterson walked up to his brother in blue. "Officer Manelli, I'm Sergeant Peterson. Thanks for the quick response on this."

"I was practically at the entrance to the course when the call came in. The ambulance driver told me he was going back empty after arriving second at an accident about a mile from here. Dumb luck we both were nearby."

"I'd rather be lucky than good," I heard Harry say softly. I smiled at the expression. Sometimes it was just luck and sometimes... I let that thought go.

"Excuse me, either of you. What about Barb? Is she okay?" I was leaning across Harry to look out the door.

"That's one of the reasons I walked over here. She's conscious and stable. EMT says it looks like the bullet went clean through the top part of her arm. Sergeant Peterson touched his left arm between his shoulder and elbow. "She bled a bit, but she'll be fine. I called her husband to meet her at Edwards. "One inch to the right and it would have missed her completely."

"Yeah, but two inches to the left and she'd most likely be dead." Officer Manelli shook his head. "One lucky lady."

There was a comment on luck again. I didn't want to leave life to luck. I wanted to believe I had some say in what happened. But did any of us have any control? This time I shivered from the chill my thoughts generated. Harry pulled me next to him with his good arm.

"Officer Manelli, have you a blanket in your car? I'm afraid the shock of all this is catching up to my wife. I'd like to take her home."

"Yes'sir." He moved quickly and returned with a blue plaid wool blanket. "Here you are, ma'am." He leaned in and handed it to me.

"Thank you." I draped the blanket around my shoulders.

"As far as leaving," his attention was back on Harry, "I'm turning this over to the sergeant here, so whatever he says goes. I'm going to stick around and help them look for the bullet. Mrs. Marsden, it would be a big help, if you could tell us where the two of you were standing when Mrs. Atwater was shot. Did you move away from the spot?"

"No, we didn't move at all. When we heard the shot, we both jumped. I thought Barb fainted. I laid her down. Then I saw the blood. I didn't know." My voice quieted. I pulled the blanket closer.

"Thank you, ma'am. I'll be here awhile, so feel free to stay in the car as long as you like." He turned away from us and walked toward a technician who appeared to be taking measurements of the area.

Sergeant Peterson slid into the front seat passenger side and turned sideways in his seat. "I was on my way to your house when I heard the call. I had news for you and your husband." He directed his next comment to Harry. "The fact you're out here tells me you already know." Harry nodded solemnly.

I didn't like the somber look that passed between them. I turned to Harry. "How did you know there was trouble?"

"Something one of your brothers said reminded me that Derek had a partial. He'd pop it out every so often when he was first fitted, couldn't get used to the feel of it when he was eating. I remembered Kramer commenting on the autopsy report. He made mention of how lucky we were to have that partial since the mouth had been so damaged most of the teeth were missing or broken. I already knew they'd have no luck establishing his identity from his prints since surgical obliteration of finger ridges was mandatory with his previous employer."

My small gasp stopped his explanation. I looked at *his* hands resting palm down in his lap. *Were his fingerprints altered? What else didn't I know about my husband? Would we ever be rid of his past?*

He followed my glance to his hands. He looked at them in an odd way, like they were someone else's hands left with him until the owner could claim them. *What a strange look. What was he thinking?*

Peterson cleared his throat and both of us looked up. Harry rubbed his left hand along the top of his thigh a few times, as he picked up the thread of his story. "Kramer called the medical examiner's office, explained the urgency, and asked them to try to match the partial to where it would be in the corpse's mouth. No way was that partial made for that mouth. He called as soon as he heard. I was still groggy from the pills I had taken. I was afraid I'd be too late."

He stopped talking and shifted his body more toward me. "From a distance, with that hood up, I didn't recognize you. All I saw was your black plaid jacket on the ground. My God, Grace, I thought it was you."

My eyes were no doubt wide and purple. It never struck me that Barb was shot because she was wearing my jacket. My stomach lurched as a lump of guilt settled in.

"Excuse me, Mrs. Marsden. Why was Mrs. Atwater wearing your jacket?

I had forgotten about the sergeant in the front seat as I struggled with the enormity of what I was hearing. *Derek was still alive. Out there, wanting to kill me. My friend could have died because of me.*

A slight pressure of Harry's hand on my thigh brought me out of my thoughts. "*Ah*, when she walked up this morning, she realized it was colder than she thought. Rather than walking back to her house I offered her my jacket."

"Walk me through your morning. Did you see or hear anything unusual?"

I quickly sketched the morning walk. There had been nothing out of the ordinary. I explained that we were in a *thinking mode* and that Barb had been several yards ahead of me. I even explained how my thoughts had put me in a panic to find something to braid and how I had nearly bowled her over when I speeded up, eager to get to the snaps on my jacket.

"Your need for that jacket at that moment and the action you took saved your friend's life. I have no doubt that if we are dealing with Derek Rhodes he wouldn't have missed." Peterson looked to Harry for confirmation. I saw the nod of his head.

Reliving the past hour brought my original urge to the foreground. I sat up straighter viewing the interior of the squad car. Peterson was asking Harry some questions. I was hearing less talk and more noise as my head began throbbing with a mission. I could feel the nerve endings in my fingers twitching as they waited for release.

Harry noticed my discomfort and reached down to his sneaker for the lace. His face crumbled when he apparently remembered that without two hands to tie shoes, he had slipped into loafers. They did me no good. He kept talking to Peterson, but I could see now that he had become a little distracted trying to satisfy my need.

Finally, even the sergeant noticed my increased fidgeting. He rolled a long rubber band that stretched around the clipboard he was using to take notes and handed it over the seat to me. I snatched the offering and smiled. "Thank you." My mind raced with the possibilities and settled on a series of loops and pull throughs that calmed me within minutes. I tuned back in on the conversation in time to hear mention of some trouble at the DeFreest home. Peterson was saying, "Called out last night, domestic dispute, anonymous caller."

"Male or female caller?" Harry's concern piqued my jealousy.

"Whispered. Couldn't tell."

Harry shared what we had seen the other night and what we had thought about the mysterious guest in the kitchen. Sergeant Peterson nodded his head.

"That family keeps their secrets close. Apparently the argument was a round robin with the three of them shouting and accusing each other of several crimes, including the murder of our John Doe."

Harry and I leaned forward at the same time closing the gap between Peterson and us. "Do you have anyone in custody?" Harry asked. "Have you charged anyone?"

"We've detained the younger man, your *mysterious guest*, on a previous warrant that came up when we ran his identification. The DeFreest's refused to press charges on anything, called it a misunderstanding. I'd love to know who called it in. That family keeps close."

"You said that before. Who is the younger man? Is he family?"

Peterson shrugged his shoulders. "He's Ben Jackson, Ms. DeFreest's ex-husband. I guess that's family of a sort."

Harry stiffened and sat back. He moved as though he'd been slapped in the face. Even his cheeks heightened in color. His reaction was so strong, Peterson commented on it.

"Mr. Marsden, is there something else about this? You seem more upset than I would have expected."

"How many years of clinical psychology brought you to that conclusion?" Harry's unnecessarily sharp comment caught Peterson and me off guard. I snapped my head sideways to stare open-mouthed at Harry. Peterson looked like the one who'd been slapped now. His years of training enabled him to recover faster. Before I could sputter any question he spoke.

"I don't need years of psychology to tell me when someone's holding back. I can feel it here." Peterson gestured to the middle of his stomach. "Do you want to tell me what's going on, or do I need to get Kramer involved again?"

I think Harry had been about to apologize. His body had relaxed and the slightest expression of regret had begun to form on his face. That was before Peterson threw the gauntlet and Ric in his face. I sensed the anger in Harry escalating. The vein at his temple throbbed visibly and his body stiffened next to me. He used his injured arm to open his door, an action that must have hurt like hell, but he didn't flinch. He took my hand and began moving us both out of the vehicle.

"We're finished here. Charge me or leave me alone." His voice was low; he was exceptionally calm for the turmoil I could sense in him. He didn't wait for an answer. We walked to the golf cart. I still had Officer Manelli's blanket, but thought better of trying to return it. Instead, I left it on the fairway. Harry turned the cart toward the tee and never looked back. I couldn't resist. Officer Manelli was folding the plaid blanket. Sergeant Peterson was retrieving some papers that must have slid off his clipboard. They both stopped as though sensing they were being watched and stood together looking after the cart.

When we reached the clubhouse Harry, leaving the key in the cart, walked toward my Jeep. I saw him fumbling for the keys in his pocket.

"Let me drive." I took the keys from his hand. He gave them up willingly and climbed into the passenger side. I resolved to not say a word until we were home. He held his arm against his chest, leaned back, and closed his eyes.

Chapter Twenty-Nine

Of the five cars parked in our driveway, four belonged to people I knew: Ric's Porsche, Hannah's Explorer, Walter's Land Rover, and Marty's Park Avenue. The unknown vehicle, a cream colored Mercedes, occupied a middle spot on the tarmac.

"Are we having a party, darling?" He smiled at me in a most innocent manner that made me suspicious. He couldn't have orchestrated this gathering; he had been with me all morning. Harry's about face in mood surprised me as much as his attack on the sergeant.

"Let's not stop. Please. I don't have a good feeling about this. Let's keep driving, go to a hotel."

"*Shh*, *Shh*, it's all right, Gracie." Harry placed his left hand over my hand on the wheel.

I vaguely wondered if he would try to turn the car if I tried to drive past our driveway. There was room to park one more vehicle. I slipped into the spot and turned off the car. I turned in the seat and took a deep calming breath. I undid my seat belt and noticed the blood on my hands and my sweatshirt. "I can't go in like this." I reached into the tray on the console and pulled out a moist towelette packet. The sheet cleaned my hands, but rubbing at the stains only made them worse. I quickly pulled the sweatshirt over my head and tossed it into the backseat. My skimpy sports camisole would have to do. I might raise eyebrows with this get up, but at least I wouldn't raise any questions. One glance at Harry told me I'd raise more than eyebrows.

I retrieved my *inside out* garment and put it on that way. The stain hadn't soaked through; I felt inside out, I might as well look that way. "What's going on? Why is everyone here?" I must have looked in a panic. Harry cradled the right side of my face with his left hand. He gently stroked my cheek with the tip of his thumb. He moved his thumb down the bridge of my nose, over my upper lip, and across my parted lips all the while murmuring, "It's okay, it's okay."

I captured his thumb with my lips and touched the tip with my tongue. *Fingerprints surgically altered.* My eyes flew open; I pulled back from his hand.

Harry's soft moan of pleasure changed to an exclamation. "Grace, what's wrong?" He looked past me, behind him, out the window, searching for the reason for my abrupt behavior.

"We'd better get in there. They know we're here by now." I hid my embarrassment by hurrying from the car. I reached the passenger side and threw open the door before Harry had time to reflect on my lightning turn about.

The front door opened and Walter ushered us into our own home. A strange feeling. I expected someone else to say *so glad you could stop by* or something equally inane. The Fellini feeling continued as I entered the living room and surveyed the scene. I learned that Hannah had brought Karen, Walter had brought Gertrude, (who I heard in the kitchen), Ric had a stranger in tow, Lily and Leo, (the rented Mercedes, didn't know you could), and Marty brought my father.

My head swirled. For one moment I came close to bursting into laughter thinking of the old nursery rhyme, *The cheese stands alone.* I felt like the cheese. I must have looked as weird as I felt.

Harry moved across the room to greet his sister. Hannah Marsden was an attractive, feminine version of her brother. Her blonde hair was cut in a short smooth bob with the edges skimming her jaw. The same cornflower blue eyes, unencumbered by glasses or contacts, filled with affection as she hugged her brother. Hannah was a few inches shorter than Harry and had the same slim body style.

"Hullo, Hans. Didn't know you were back."

"I flew in to meet Karen at her conference in Toronto and we came back together. Mum says you haven't called in a while." She delivered the gentle chastisement with a sweet smile that was only belied by the mischievous gleam in her eye.

As pleasant as it was to watch their reunion, homecoming was not the purpose of this gathering. Apparently, everyone had been introduced around the room; only Harry and I were ignorant of the newcomer's identity. Ric handled that introduction.

"This is Ben Jackson, Ms. DeFreest's ex-husband, who is currently out on bond. Mr. Jackson has agreed to explain what he knows about all this. He has already made an official statement in exchange for consideration on earlier warrants.

"Why are all these people here?" Harry asked.

"Because no one can keep anything to themselves." Ric seemed exasperated as he continued. "He," pointing to Jackson, "called them," pointing to the DeFreests, "to tell them he was making a statement. Then they wanted to make one too, but not at the station." Ric turned toward the other side of the room. "I came here first, assuming you'd both be home after what I told you this morning. Walter and Gertrude were here to check up on you. They called Grace's dad thinking you were there. Mike called Karen and so forth."

"That still doesn't answer my question. Why are all these people *here*?"

"Don't worry, Marsden. Some of them won't be much longer. I paged Sergeant Peterson to come over and sort them out." Ric waved a hand toward my houseguests.

Harry and I looked at each other across the room. Ric caught the eye contact.

"What's up? I thought you two liked Peterson; he's over here as much as some of your neighbors." Ric's attempt at sarcasm was lost on half of the room.

"Peterson and I had a run in at the golf course earlier. That's where we just came from." Harry nodded toward me.

"What were you doing golfing after what I told you this morning?"

"What did you tell him this morning that's so God awful important?" My father who had sat quietly now spoke up. "What aren't you two telling us? Again," he added under his breath.

"Dad."

"Mike."

"Mr. Morelli," Ric stood and assumed authority. "The body in the woods was not Derek Rhodes. I called here this morning to warn Grace."

The room exploded into a cacophony of voices crisscrossing the room with questions and concerns. This seemed to be the time to let them know what had happened to Barb. I sat numbly waiting for the noise pendulum to swing closer to normal. My only movement was the fifty corner crossovers I agreed to braid before I spoke. The bright yellow yarn I pulled out of a close by drawer grew in pattern under my nimble fingers. I knew I was close to finishing because the tightness in my head eased as I looped and pulled the last two knots. I glanced up from my hands and realized that everyone had stopped talking. I seemed to be the center of attention.

Harry crossed the room and stood next to my chair. "I took the call from Kramer this morning. Gracie had already gone walking with Barbara. I knew their usual route. I drove to the golf course and took a cart to intercept them. I was too late."

Murmurs of confusion broke the silence. Harry continued. "Apparently, Rhodes was waiting for Grace, but Barbara was wearing Gracie's jacket and he mistakenly fired at her."

A stunned group greeted Harry's comments. I watched the three people I knew the least and suspected the most. I saw genuine surprise in all three faces. Lily's eyes reflected a horror at what she was hearing.

"Barbara's fine. It was a superficial wound. She's at hospital now; probably will be home this afternoon."

Any further explanation was obscured by multiple questions from Ric and my dad. The doorbell rang, adding further confusion to the already out of order mix. Walter opened the door to Sergeant Peterson and one of his men. A curt nod to Harry was his only greeting. He moved to the center of the room and immediately asked that all non-essential visitors leave.

It's not easy telling my dad he is non-essential when it comes to my well-being. The sergeant had quite the time assuring Mike Morelli that his daughter would be protected; that the twenty-four hour guard he ordered would keep me safe. He finally convinced my dad and Marty to go home, but only after both of them extracted promises from me to call daily. I was hoping that would satisfy them, but I was feeling they might mount their own "Morelli Security Force" and show up here in shifts.

When the room cleared, only Ric, Ben Jackson, and the DeFreests remained from the original cast of characters. The others left after securing Harry's promise that he would keep them up to date.

The results of what Gertrude had been attending to in the kitchen came out now on two trays filled with a carafe of fresh coffee, a pot of hot water, mugs, rum baba pastries (they looked like Edna's) and an apple strudel from Gertrude. No wonder Peterson didn't mind shifting his office to our living room. This beats doughnuts any day of the week. If word spread at the department, policemen would be jumping on any calls from our house just for the goodies.

God, Grace what are you thinking? I needed to focus on the events of the day not on the menu. I also needed to focus on reclaiming my position as mistress of this house. Lily had stepped into the breach I had left wide open and was offering to pour for everyone. I bristled at the thought of how quickly she stood in for me. Then I paled at the thought of how quickly she would step in for me with Harry. For a change, I didn't charge ahead with the first thought that came half formed into my brain. Instead, I let her play hostess and sat back to watch the tableau. Could she have more to do with Derek Rhodes and his determination to kill me? Maybe Derek took Shelly Walsh's money and disappeared. Then who was the body in the woods? And why did someone leave Derek's partial in a corpse's mouth? Derek could have killed him that way to try to set up his own death so he'd be free from further pursuit. Or maybe he was crazy enough to want to be *dead to the world* so he could be a better spy. Maybe the House was involved in this charade. Maybe Lily took advantage of the murder to plan one of her own–mine. Then she could have Harry. She certainly fit well next to him.

I shifted my gaze to Leo DeFreest. His eyes were never still in his face. Even as he sat back, comfortable in his chair, his eyes paced the room, touching faces, gestures, furniture, walls. Was that a habit from his days as a famous wild game hunter? I had read up on him and was amazed and impressed by his biography.

He had been a highly accomplished wild game procurer in the

The Lion Tamer: A Caged Death

1940's before the war. If the animal lived on the continent of Africa, he could secure one for a generous donation to his wildlife foundation based in Johannesburg. His specialty was big cats. Many zoos throughout the world still carry a DeFreest cat's gene in their animal collection. Why would he wish me harm? Our few encounters had been as pleasant as one could expect given the circumstances. Was he Lily's cohort? Could he fire a rifle with one hand? Would he kill me to secure his daughter's future?

His eyes locked on mine. They were like green marbles with no depth, flat and cold. In that instant, I knew he could kill.

I broke the contact and looked at Ben Jackson. What was his role? Was he trying to reconcile with Lily? Did he know Derek? When did he arrive on the scene? Was he here when the body was discovered?

I stopped my assessment when I realized that Harry had called my name. I looked at him and for a second time in less than an hour everyone was staring at me.

"Grace, are you all right?" Harry was walking toward holding out a mug to me. "Coffee, then?" Apparently, I'd missed the question on bakery preference. Fine with me. My stomach hadn't returned to its rightful spot since this morning.

"I'm fine. Just tired. Coffee is perfect. Thank you." I accepted the mug and gratefully sipped at the Rain Forest Nut thankful to be doing something normal instead of touring the room for my would be killer.

Ric ordered everyone to be seated, then quickly recapped what he learned from forensics. "The victim was Charles Costello. Once we determined the partial was a plant, the doc went in and found some dental work he could track. It wasn't an easy find. Rhodes is a twisted bastard. He smashed this guy's face in so he could remove the teeth and plant his partial. We know he was killed somewhere else, hours maybe even a day earlier. The blow that killed him wasn't one of the first ones administered. When we told the doc on the case what we suspected, he played a hunch and checked the back of the throat and trachea for pieces of teeth that the victim may have swallowed during the bludgeoning."

Lily gasped and clamped her hand over her mouth. She jumped

up and ran into the kitchen. Ben followed on her heels with Harry a half step behind. Leo had risen from his chair, but sat down again thinking his daughter was in good hands. Whose hands?

Unpleasant sounds of retching followed by running water confirmed her condition. One too many *babas*. Better to have heard Ric's reports on an empty stomach. Of course, I had the advantage. I had heard Ric recount autopsy reports before. He never pulled punches. I looked over at Ric now. He seemed amused by the events. *I wonder, was he that graphic on purpose? Was he trying to get a reaction? He certainly got one!*

As much as watching the ice queen puke in my sink held a certain middle class satisfaction for me, I refrained from smirking and waited until the trio rejoined us. She looked more pale than usual. Ben sat next to her holding a glass of water with a lemon slice in it. Harry looked like a fifth wheel as he watched Lily accept ministrations from her ex. *Wonder how that made him feel? Not too good, I expect.*

Ric's voice continued. "I told you this Rhodes was twisted. My hat is off to the Sheriff's department and their lab on this one. We knew that the victim had to have some recent connection to Rhodes so they started with his most recent cellmate. That first look was a match. They served time together at county a few months back, no connection before that. Who knows what story Rhodes fed him."

"That explains why Rhodes waited so long and why he'll keep trying. It's personal with him now. That doesn't explain who was in the house that night or who tried to poison Grace." Harry looked at Ric for answers he didn't have.

"What makes you think this Rhodes person wasn't in the house or that he didn't doctored the parsley?" Leo DeFreest spoke for the first time that afternoon.

"If Derek had been that close to Grace he would have snapped her neck on his way out of the house. He wouldn't have let that opportunity slip through his fingers even if it meant he might be caught."

Harry's answer didn't appear to faze Leo DeFreest. He accepted the statement of fact and reiterated the last half of his question with a calmness that made me queasy.

Ric answered. "From his M.O. Poison doesn't do it for him. He would want to feel the kill, be more involved."

God, they're talking about me, ways to kill me. Only Lily seemed to understand my discomfort. She looked at me with wide eyes that reflected the horror I was feeling. I felt helpless to stop all this chatter about ways to commit a homicide, my homicide.

"Derek wouldn't know parsley from plankton. He couldn't have switched herbs." Harry had spoken when Ric turned to Ben Jackson.

"Perhaps Mr. Jackson could enlighten us on that count."

"Ben?" Lily turned to look at him. "What do you know about this?"

"Apparently a lot more about fool's parsley than Derek ever could." Harry had been moving, fist formed, toward Ben as he spoke. "You bastard. You tried to kill my wife."

Peterson and his officer were ready for this. I'd forgotten they were in the room. They both moved from their innocuous positions against the wall to block Harry from reaching his target.

Sergeant Peterson placed a hand lightly against Harry's chest. "We can all agree to sit quietly or we can leave with those three and you can get the news when hell freezes over."

I guess the sergeant was still rankled by Harry's earlier behavior.

"Aren't you going to arrest him? He tried to kill Grace." Harry's plea was directed to Ric.

"He is under arrest. We lifted a print of his from the murder weapon. He's not going anywhere." Ric's comment ignited another salvo of questions.

"I thought you said Rhodes killed Costello?" Harry voiced my question.

"I didn't kill anyone and I wasn't trying to kill her." Ben jumped up to add emphasis to his denial. Peterson placed a hand on his shoulder and eased him back onto the loveseat.

"Rhodes did kill Costello. This idiot is guilty of conspiring with Rhodes to blackmail DeFreest." Ric held up his good hand to stop further questions. "Mr. Jackson has already made his statement and is assisting the police in any way he can concerning Derek Rhodes. He wanted to make his peace with Ms. DeFreest." Ric favored Lily with the tiniest of smiles before he continued. "Jackson and Rhodes have a history. I'll let him tell you."

Focus shifted to Ben Jackson. He leaned forward and sideways away from Lily. I thought for a minute he wasn't going to say anything. His face looked chalky. I wondered if he felt as though he was about to lose Edna's babas too.

"This is all a mistake. I never meant for anyone to get hurt. I should have known he was crazy." He stopped talking after his disclaimer.

Lily's voice rang out crystal-clear and icy cold. "What did you mean to have happen?" Her face turned sharply to fix her ex-husband with eyes that may have mirrored her father's cold stare. I didn't envy Jackson that view.

Jackson's answer was in a lower voice, directed totally to Lily. "I know it was stupid, but I wanted to get it back for you. I never meant to keep it; I was hurt, I wanted to hurt you."

"I'm not interested in this sophomoric display. My daughter and I are leaving." Leo DeFreest stood up and moved toward the couch.

"I'm staying. I want to hear what Ben has to say." Lily turned her head toward her father. I could see her eyes; they gleamed defiant, but rimmed with fear at her own audacity. Her eyes, except for the color, weren't at all like her father's. They glowed with a soft light and a brightness that rivaled the perfect green of spring herbs.

"Lily, we're leaving." DeFreest had taken two steps toward his daughter. Ric, Harry, and Sergeant Peterson all started moving at once. Thank goodness DeFreest stopped or the three would have collided mid room. No one, except me, seemed to see the humor in their rush to rescue. I knew better than to laugh aloud. My sense of humor didn't always have a sense of timing.

"Dad, this has been a secret too long. I want to know the truth. I'm not leaving." Lily turned back to Ben. "Well?"

Chapter Thirty

Four men were left standing awkwardly in the middle of my living room. There was a moment of confusion then resignation as DeFreest sat down, cueing the others to do the same.

Ben started his explanation, talking only to Lily. The rest of the room disappeared for him as he searched her face for understanding and perhaps absolution.

"I know now how stupid I've been. When I thought you left me for Marsden, I wanted to get back at you. I knew the one thing you cherished was the necklace your mother had left you. I took it from our apartment the last time I was there. Remember that day, Lily?" His tone turned bitter; an expression of pain settled on his face. "On most Sundays, we would stay in bed reading the papers until past noon. Then I would slip out of bed and make a huge breakfast for us. By two o'clock we'd be dressed and out to the park or walking uptown to search for locations for the restaurant you were going to help me open. All that changed after you met your jetsetter. You exercised your option since the lease was in your name and threw me out. That Sunday you were anxious for me to leave with my box of things. I think you had an *engagement*," Jackson exaggerated the word and pinned his gaze on Harry, "with him."

Lily reached out in a flash of movement and slapped him hard across the face. The three men tensed to move if Jackson looked like he would retaliate. The shock of her action made him lean away from her. Her words seemed to shrink him even more.

"How dare you spout this drivel? You and I were through before I met Harry, and even if we weren't, you wanted my father's money for *your* restaurant. It wasn't my dream, you never listened to what I wanted."

"That's not true. I loved you." His protest was quiet and made while looking down at his hands.

"I want to know why he tried to poison Grace. Forget about ancient history." Harry was losing patience with the melodrama unfolding in our living room.

"I told you I never meant to hurt anyone. I transplanted the parsley to make the two of you sick enough to go the emergency room, not kill you. I figured if you had these herbs at your fingertips you probably cooked with them. I didn't know that older guy would be eating with you and that he has a mild heart condition. I wasn't trying to kill anyone. You have to believe me."

"How did you know about the herbs? Were you the one in the garage that night?" I finally asked.

"Garage? No. I've never been in your garage or your house. I've kept up with you, Marsden." He looked at Harry. "Every article, story, news piece about you. I knew you dabbled in flowers and food, being the *country gentleman* and all. I was in your yard and saw the plantings of herbs in the sarcophagus. I recognized the fool's parsley and switched them."

"Why now? For God's sake man, if you wanted to even the score with me why not come after me?"

"I didn't want to even the score. I wanted to get into your house and search for the necklace. This was my last chance to get it."

"Get it? I thought you said you stole it?"

"I did steal it but it was stolen from me."

"What, no honor among thieves?"

"Shut up, Marsden. You should talk about honor. Your partner was the insurance investigator that picked up the case."

"Rhodes?"

"None other. He knew it was me from the beginning. I wasn't a thief. I must have smelled guilty from his first meeting. I thought for sure I was going to jail. I was desperate to save myself. It was a stupid thing to have done, but I couldn't get out of it now. Rhodes told me point blank he knew it was me and that I was going to serve time because Lily's old man was rich and he'd make sure they'd throw the book at me. I didn't know DeFreest had already called off the insurance claim his daughter had filed. Apparently he didn't want any investigation."

"Is that true?" Lily asked her father. Leo DeFreest sat straighter in his chair.

"You would believe *anything* he says at this point? He's obviously trying to make his case look more sympathetic. I find him now, as I found him when you first brought him home, pathetic."

That barb seemed to weaken Jackson. He shifted uncomfortably in his seat.

"Interesting enough, Mr. DeFreest, I did check out what I could of his story and there was a claim filed by your daughter with Midwest Insurance and that same claim was withdrawn by you stating the necklace had been misplaced not stolen." Ric's comment brought us all to the edge of our chairs; the shift in everyone's posture so apparent that Ric paused before continuing. "Care to explain, Mr. DeFreest, or shall I continue with Jackson's statement to the police?"

DeFreest sat motionless. He didn't look panicked or furtive. He sat and seemed to be considering his own plan of response. His cold, hard attitude chilled me. Like a premonition of evil, I shivered and shook off a bad feeling.

"All right. I'll fill you in. Rhodes convinced Jackson that he could fence the necklace and that he would then split the money with Jackson. You can imagine Jackson's surprise when Rhodes disappeared with the necklace. What could he do? Report a robbery?"

"Why did you cancel the claim? That was my mother's necklace, it meant the world to me." Lily's voice was steady and low as she questioned her father. He remained silent and stared past Lily to Ric.

"Why?" Her voice trembled.

"Perhaps, it's time to enlighten everyone to Leo DeFreest's interesting past. Perhaps he'd care to tell us about his career before he became a lion tamer to the highest bidder; about his days in South Africa and the diamond trade. About 1947 and two rare red diamonds that disappeared."

Harry stepped forward. I saw the box in his hand. Jackson, Lily, and DeFreest saw it a moment later. All three reacted with widened eyes, but only Lily lifted a hand to her mouth.

"I believe this belongs to you." Harry bent low over Lily as he held out the box to her. She held out both hands, palm up, as though accepting communion and slowly lowered the treasure to her lap. Her eyes, filled with tears, never left Harry's face.

"Thank you," she whispered.

"Wait a minute, Marsden. Where'd you get that?" Ric looked as if he were ready to grab the box from Lily's lap. She tightened her grip and pulled it in closer to her body.

"Ric, I found it in the garage Saturday night when I came home from the hospital. It was in a box on the workbench. I thought it was for the church jumble until I opened it. I brought it in with me. Later when Sergeant Peterson was checking the garage, I noticed that the other items that had been in the box were gone. I don't know who put the box there in the first place. Or who emptied it." I shrugged my shoulders when all eyes turned toward me.

The sergeant had something to say about that. "You didn't think that was important to tell me?"

"I'm sorry sergeant. I was tired and confused. I should have told you. Harry, what does Mr. DeFreest have to do with this? Was he the one in the house?"

"No, darling. I suspect he was the one bumping about in the garage that you heard."

"What about it, DeFreest, were you in the garage?" Ric and Peterson waited for an answer.

Leo DeFreest seemed to come to a decision. He straightened his shoulders and crossed his left leg over his right. "I was in the garage. I didn't mean to frighten you, Mrs. Marsden. I had observed someone take a camera from Lily's set-up table and carry it off through the woods. He had it in a small cardboard box. I followed him and saw him enter your garage. I couldn't imagine why he'd done that, but I wanted her camera back. It was daylight so I had to keep back quite a distance. That Atwater woman almost caught me at the back of your property. I was off the path when she came up to your back door. I moved around to the side to avoid her return trip. It was then that I noticed a car pulling into your driveway. I decided I'd wait until dark to retrieve the camera. I came back later and entered the garage by the side door. I wasn't certain where he had put the camera but I found the box I had seen him carry on the workbench. I searched the contents and removed Lily's camera. I'm a bit clumsy with this," he held up his right hand, "and I knocked over the box and in my haste to leave bumped into a bin next to the door. I didn't know if you heard. I left immediately."

Sergeant Peterson spoke now. "You'll have to come to the station and give me all this again. You are certain you want to stick to your story that you didn't enter the house?"

"It wasn't him." We all turned to look at Harry.

"What else do you know that you aren't telling us, Marsden?" Ric seemed annoyed.

"It's not what I know, it's what I feel. After listening to DeFreest, I think I know what Derek was doing."

"We know he was trying to kill Grace."

"No, I don't think he was, at least not then. Listen to me. I know him better than anyone else possibly could. You don't spend months with someone thinking you'll die together and not get to know the way they think." Harry paused and looked up at the ceiling as though collecting his thoughts.

"This has been about framing me for his death. I should have seen it sooner, but I was focused on Grace because of the letter. Even when you found that scrap of paper with the date and my name and number on it in the dead man's pocket you thought it was Rhodes pinpointing a date he'd try for Grace or maybe a phone call to lure her out." He looked at Ric.

"That's right. We never suspected you because of the letter. If that letter hadn't arrived when it did, we'd have focused on you. His bad luck that my aunt had to have the last word. I'm sure he had no idea that she *communicated* her intent to you."

"You mean she didn't hire Rhodes to kill Mrs. Marsden?" Sergeant Peterson asked.

Harry answered, "Oh, she hired him all right. Derek thought he'd tweak the contract. By killing some poor indigent and planting his identity and evidence against me on the body, he was aiming for the ultimate revenge, my conviction for his murder. He could wait to dispose of Grace at his leisure then. He was the one in the house that night. I was wrong in thinking that he would have killed Grace."

I interrupted his thought process. "Did Derek know about the room? You didn't mention his name when we were adding up how many people knew about it."

"I didn't name him because I thought he was dead. Seemed a moot point. The night of the break-in he must have been watching the house and saw DeFreest go in and come out with the camera. He knew the only things left to incriminate me would be his lighter and the necklace. He must have been furious when he realized the necklace was gone. I'm sure he believed that DeFreest had taken that with him as well. He knew the initials on the inside of the lighter would identify it as his. He probably guessed that Jackson here would spill his guts about losing the necklace to him years earlier. The question then would be how I got his personal effects if I wasn't the one who killed him."

"But why my camera?" Lily asked. "Why was he trying to involve me?"

"To tighten the noose around me. He was only involving your camera, the camera that I think I handled at your house. Derek has been in the woods watching all of us. He must have seen me through the window. The strap was distinctive, easy for him to spot. He must have felt the case against me would be more airtight if I ended up with a piece of the apparent murder weapon. Your tripod had been treated with the victim's tissue and blood and I think if a lab checked that camera they'd find bits of blood and tissue from the dead bloke smeared into the niches. Keeping some of the victim's wound samples is the kind of twisted behavior I'd expect from him."

"This is all theory, Marsden. We can't prove any of this."

"May not be proof, but we might get closer on some of the pieces. For instance," Harry swung around to face Ben Jackson, "How did you know the necklace was in the house? Did you follow Rhodes?"

"He's clean there, Marsden." Ric interrupted. "He's been keeping tabs on Lily's career. He knew she had moved back to the Chicago area. He drove out here from New York three months ago. Two days after he arrived, he was pulled over for speeding and the officer found that Jackson's license had been pulled for a DUI conviction. So, Mr. Jackson has been a guest of the county until last

Saturday."

"Well then, he's clear there, but how did he know the necklace was in the house?"

"Good question. Jackson, you'd better have a good answer."

Ben Jackson had regained some of his bravado while the spotlight had been off him. Now he puffed out his chest before he spoke.

"It was my destiny to have that necklace. When I ended up in jail, I renewed an old acquaintance. I spotted Rhodes in the mess hall the first week I was there. He pretended not to recognize me, but kept after him. He finally decided to acknowledge me. That man was crazier than the first time I crossed paths with him. After a few weeks, I couldn't shake him. He became obsessed with telling me about his incarceration in that South American prison. When this Costello person was released, Rhodes must have worked something out because the next thing I know is I'm his new cellmate. He'd spend every opportunity talking about what they did to him, reliving each painful and disgusting treatment. I wished I'd never approached him. One day he stopped. He started telling me about this nutty old broad who'd hired him to kill Marsden's wife. His eyes gleamed with some kind of freaky light, like from inside, when he talked about it.

First, he said he'd get even with Marsden for leaving him to rot in that prison. He was going to frame him for his own death. He was going to kill himself to get Marsden. I knew then that he had lost any grip he had on sanity. I figured we'd all be better off with him dead. He was the one who told me where Lily was living. He talked about planting evidence against Marsden and connecting him to Lily through the necklace. But first, he said he'd blackmail the old man into paying him not to use the necklace. He needed money to get lost after he killed her." Jackson leaned forward, warming to his story.

"That's when I started listening. I thought he'd fenced the necklace years ago. Now was my chance to get it back. He kept laughing and saying he'd *plant it where they could smell it right under their noses.* When I sneaked up to your back door, the first thing I noticed was the sarcophagus. I started digging into the soil between the herbs and under the plants remembering what he'd said about planting it. That's when I spotted the fool's Parsley and made the switch. I'd noticed that the parsley plant nearest the door had leaves cut from it. I figured that you used it often. I knew I had to get into the house to find my necklace. I was thinking he'd hidden it in the houseplants."

"Your necklace?" Lily's voice exploded from three feet away. "How dare you. You are pathetic. That necklace belonged to my mother, a gift to her from my father. How dare you think you had any rights to it?"

"Rights? You want to talk about rights? I had a dream to open a restaurant. You knew that, Lily. You were going to help me get the financing. Instead, you divorced me for your rich boyfriend. I've spent the last ten years *working* in restaurants that I could run better than any of those owners. You stole my dream. I had a right to get it back any way I could."

"I should have left you in jail." Leo DeFreest's pronouncement startled everyone.

Jackson looked stunned. "You?"

"Dad, why did you do that?"

"Yes, Mr. DeFreest why did you do that?" Sergeant Peterson asked.

Leo DeFreest faced him calmly. He shrugged his shoulders. "A poor decision on a caring father's part. I didn't want my daughter to be embarrassed by him." He shrugged. "Poor decision," he murmured.

"Spare us the paternal bullshit. You hustled him out of there because you didn't want me to find him." Harry stared at DeFreest. "What tipped you off, DeFreest? How did you know I wanted to be arrested?"

"Nothing *tipped me off*. It was a feeling. When you've tracked as many wild things as I have, you learn to use those feelings. Doing so has saved my life on more than one occasion."

"So, is he working with Rhodes?" Sergeant Peterson asked the question I had on my lips.

"Not directly, although I don't think he much cares if I would have gone to jail for killing Rhodes. He was more concerned with hiding any connection between Jackson and Rhodes which would lead us to the theft and questions about that necklace."

"Why? What's the big deal with the necklace?" Ric asked.

"It's stolen," I answered quietly.

"You're a liar. It was my mother's."

"Not originally, Lily. I'm sorry." Harry moved to take the seat vacated by Jackson who had moved to the chair near the window and away from Lily after his confession.

"This stone is one of the rare Red Diamond Duet, a diamond mined in South Africa in the late 1920's. It was stolen and later reported not stolen but in the possession of a New York collector who wished to remain anonymous. There's no doubt as to the identity of this diamond. The doubt is in your father's ownership when he gave it to your mother."

"Dad?" Lily's voice was small and tremulous. In that moment, I felt a bond forming with her. I couldn't imagine the pain of finding out from my father that a treasured keepsake of my mother had been ill gotten. I prayed that Leo DeFreest had an answer for his daughter.

He wasn't made of granite. Leo DeFreest turned his face to his daughter. The flat marble green eyes were moist. His voice as he began what had to be a painful explanation, wavered before it found it's calm frequency.

"Lily, I was young, foolish. I worked with several exporters and couriers in the course of many years. Two of us developed a scheme to deliver uncut diamonds to buyers around the world. Whenever a zoo or private collector wanting to secure a cat contacted me, I would alert my cohort. He would discreetly find interested parties in those cities. When I arranged to ship the animal to that location, I would secret a shipment of diamonds in a compartment specially built into the cages I used. Part of our service included my partner at the receiving end to insure the animal's safe arrival and, of course, to remove the diamonds and deliver them.

It was right when the war was starting. It was getting dangerous to continue. We heard about the Red Diamond Duet and agreed to make that our last heist. With our credentials, it was easy to be where we needed to be and the theft went off without a hitch. We split the booty and went our separate ways. I ended up fighting Germans; I don't know what happened to him."

"How could you give it to mom as an engagement present?"

Lily's voice was flat. Her shoulders slumped and her eyes wouldn't meet her father's face.

DeFreest moved to her and knelt next to her. He tried to lift her hands still holding the box. She jerked back as if burned.

Now she lifted her eyes to his. They blazed with anger. "Don't."

"You two can sort out your relationship later. I want to know when you knew the body wasn't Rhodes, DeFreest?"

Leo DeFreest stood and turned to face Ric Kramer. "I don't like what you're implying, Inspector."

"I don't care what you don't like. I want to know your involvement. When did you know the body wasn't Rhodes?"

"Oh for God's sake, he didn't know until I told him." Jackson had turned from the window. "I had no where to go once I was released. I knew Lily lived here; I called her and gave her my sob story. She let me stay at the house. It wasn't until I reached her house that she told me about the body in the woods. I figured Rhodes' plan to frame Marsden was working until Lily mentioned that Rhodes had been bludgeoned to death. I knew he was insane and a schemer but even he couldn't beat himself to death."

"Shut up, you fool." DeFreest hissed through clenched teeth.

"Hey, I'm the only one in this room with an alibi. I'd rather plead guilty to blackmail than murder."

"Blackmail? I don't understand." I couldn't follow all the twists and turns.

"Ben here thought he could run a deal with DeFreest. He'd keep quiet about DeFreest's possible motive for murder in return for either lots of money or the necklace. He wasn't sure if DeFreest had killed Rhodes before or after he retrieved the necklace." Ric faced Jackson during the entire explanation. "Is that about it, Jackson?"

"Pretty close, Inspector. I figured the old man killed Rhodes."

"You're insane. I didn't kill him." DeFreest swung around to face Lily searching her face for a verdict. Lily didn't look at him. "I wasn't even in town."

Lily lifted her head. "That's right. I picked him up at the airport that night, after the body was found."

"Anyone can walk out of arrivals at the airport, Lily. You didn't meet his plane at the gate."

"Harry, no. What are you saying?"

"I'm saying that Rhodes could have sent the dead man to meet your father to get the money. Your father had never met Rhodes. He didn't know he was killing the middle man."

"Bastard. What are you trying to pull? I'm an old man with one good hand." DeFreest waved his gloved appendage. "You think I could beat a younger man to death? That's ridiculous."

"Not so ridiculous, DeFreest. We've been keeping this area under surveillance and some of the photos show you going through the paces of a strenuous work out complete with one arm-push ups. I'd say you're in good enough shape to swing a blunt instrument at an unsuspecting target."

"Inspector," a calm DeFreest asked, "If I killed this man to protect my *secret*, why would I use my daughter's tripod to kill him."

"Oh, I don't think you used the tripod. I think you killed him with the blow to the back of his head that the coroner's report states could have been the fatal blow. We know that Rhodes is an opportunist. He discovered your handiwork when he returned to the sauna. You left the body there hoping it wouldn't be found for a while. I can imagine your surprise when the body turned up in your daughter's backyard in that condition. Rhodes probably used the same weapon to demolish that poor devil's head and then kept some of the tissue for the final clues on Lily's equipment. We haven't found the weapon you used yet, but we will."

"This is all conjecture. I'm not staying here another minute. Charge me or release me, Inspector. I believe those are your only choices." DeFreest's calm impressed and frightened me at the same time. I could believe the scenario Ric and Harry had presented. At the same time, I could see how there was nothing concrete to link him to anything.

I studied the tableau of faces. Emotion moved across their faces, expressions forming, dissolving and reforming as accusations and absolutions must have rolled through their minds. The only face I couldn't see was Ben Jackson's. He had turned his back on the room and was again staring out the window. His voice broke the uncomfortable silence as we waited for Ric's response.

"Jesus, no!" Jackson's exclamation gave us scant time to react to what he saw. I glimpsed his face white with terror as he turned from the window a second before Harry pulled me from my chair and pushed me in front of him into the next room.

Chapter Thirty-One

The blast that followed shook the room with such force that anything not nailed down in the room took flight. The heavy decanter from the bar cart launched across the room and smashed into the wall. Pictures flew off the walls and landed into the furniture. The solid metal torchiere teetered and then toppled to the floor. Seconds after the explosion, it seemed as though all the air in the room was sucked out through the hole that must be where Ben Jackson had been standing.

I heard a weak call for help from someone behind me. The black acrid smoke filled my nostrils and mouth. I couldn't get a fresh breath of air. I heard another sound that filled me with terror. Crackling and an odd swooshing sound came from the living room.

"Fire!" I heard my own voice weakened by smoke and the weight across my back. The plea for help came again, stronger this time. It was Ric.

"Ric. Where are you? I can't see anything." My voice erupted into to spasms of coughing.

I realized the weight across my back was one of the dining room chairs. I lurched onto all fours to try to shift the weight. The effort was enough to allow me to wriggle out from under it. I stayed on my hands and knees.

"Grace, are you all right?" Harry was next to me. "Can you walk? We have to get out of the house before–"

Another explosion rocked the room. Harry crouched over me as the debris and whatever hadn't shattered in the first blast rocketed around us.

"C'mon, get up. Move fast."

"Wait. I heard Ric call for help. He's hurt. I think he's still in the living room."

"Grace, we can't help him. The living room is gone."

Harry pulled me toward the bay window. Part of the glass had blown out and Harry used the leg from one of the chairs to break out enough glass for us to climb out. He hastily threw the runner from the table over the sill to give us some protection from the shards of glass.

The smoke and heat seemed to seek out the fresh oxygen.

"Hurry, Grace. Stay low to the ground and run toward the front of the house. Help will be there." He was right. I heard the ear-splitting sirens as the fire trucks screeched to a halt. A new sound, popping and then a low roar, drowned all other sounds out. I realized that things were exploding in the house. I stopped at the corner of the house to wait for Harry. He wasn't behind me. Instead, Lily was a few feet from the window and her father was lifting his leg over the sill and dropping to the ground. He limped toward us.

"Keep moving, get away from the house. Get out front." His directions made sense, but I wasn't moving without Harry.

"Where's Harry? He was behind me at the window." I looked from Lily to her father.

"He helped me out the window," Lily said. "I thought he was right behind me."

I looked at DeFreest. "Where's Harry?"

"I don't know, Mrs. Marsden. There was no one there. I barely made it out before something blew up behind me. Please, we need to move away from here."

On cue, a window shattered and glass blew out over the bushes. Hungry flames licked greedily at the space beyond, anxious to devour anything hapless enough to remain. I let Lily lead me out of the smoke and toward the front of the house.

Paramedics rushed to the three of us and guided us to the ambulances. My heart leaped with joy as I realized there was a man in the back being treated. As quickly, I recognized the uniform. Sergeant Peterson had made it out. His face was grim and covered with small cuts still bleeding. Sergeant Peterson's shirt had been cut away from his body. I could see several angry red splotches on his skin. On one area, the size of my hand the blue material from his shirt had melted onto his skin. One paramedic was applying wet gauze to the affected areas. The other medic worked on a deep gash on Peterson's right forearm. He carefully sutured the wound and covered it with a sterile bandage. During all this, the sergeant had been trying to give his report to the police that had answered the call.

"The first bomb came through the living room window, northeast corner of the house. Only had seconds of warning. The second one hit through the next window. I thought the bastard was going to circle the house and lob them through all the windows. The second blast blew me through the bay window."

I wanted to ask him about Harry. I started to walk toward him but the paramedic guided me to the back of another ambulance. I felt as though I were floating. That couldn't be a good sign. He led me to a small cot and had me sit down. He gently lifted my chin and examined my nostrils and the inside of my mouth. Satisfied with his cursory exam he placed an oxygen mask over my face and adjusted the dial and the strap. He asked me a few questions. I nodded yes or no. He left me to assist the other medic. The oxygen cleared my head. The sensation of floating disappeared, replaced by a meticulous attention to detail.

Leo DeFreest's gloved hand seemed charred. I didn't know if the glove covered a total prosthesis or there had been flesh under the leather. They had him stretched out on a gurney, applying ice packs to his ankle.

Lily's hands were being bandaged with sterile gauze soaked in something. Her chin wore a similar covering; her golden hair was scorched and frizzed around her face.

I alone seemed untouched. No burns, no cuts, no broken bones. My injury was devastating. I lifted the mask from my face, left it on the gurney, and walked away. I couldn't bear to look at the house. I couldn't bear to think about Harry being inside, trapped, burning, or dead. I stopped walking when I couldn't hear the shouts of the firemen and the crackling of the fire. The inequity that I was unscathed and he was gone overwhelmed me. The wail sounded inhuman. I knew it was my pain and guilt that I had lived and he had not that rent the already chaotic atmosphere. Tears gushed from my eyes, finally released to express anguish at my loss. I slowly slipped to the ground; felt the coolness of the spring forest floor against my body. My tears mixed with the dirt and wild violets that grew in abundance. Daylight was waning. The fire no longer lit the sky with orange flames eerily illuminating the treetops. The darkness comforted me in a strange way. It suited my mood, my thoughts. *How could there be sunlight and blue skies without Harry? How could I lose him again? And now Ric, too.*

My heart beat loudly in my chest, a mockery that I was strong, that I had survived. The velvety night slipped more securely around me and I realized that I hadn't heard noise of any kind for several minutes maybe longer.

Good, they're gone.

I felt a comfort in the solitude, as though by staying in the woods Harry and Ric would still be here. In the confusion of the fire, I was certain that no one looked for me. After all, the only two people who would come looking for me were gone. An overwhelming sense of loss flooded my body. I didn't care if I ever left that sod. Let it be my grave as the house is theirs. Hours seemed to pass, yet time seemed to standstill. The cold ground leached my human warmth until I felt as numb as a log on the forest floor. Still, I didn't move. The damp had sapped my strength; the loss of Harry sapped my will to live. My thoughts spiraled up from my brain asking my mother to welcome Harry to heaven. Now, my body felt light and in motion. I spiraled from the damp clod of dirt to somewhere a few feet above. All I had to do was turn my head toward the sky and my mom, or maybe even Harry would be there to beckon me home.

I'm ready. Why stay? Dad has the boys. I'm ready.

A scraping and cracking on the path snapped the spell; I plummeted to the ground and startled myself awake. I heard the noise again, furtive and stealthy. My fear factor leaped to high alert in a split second. Somehow I knew what was out there was evil. My head was pounding with fear, but no plan for escape. I no longer wanted to slip quietly to follow Harry through eternity. At least, not yet; I wanted to live.

Chapter Thirty-Two

The cracking of pecan shells under heavy feet sounded closer than before. Whoever was out there was moving closer. *Should I stay still? Am I visible from the path?*

In my confused state, I had walked aimlessly into the woods. I wasn't exactly sure of where I was, which path he was on, even which direction I faced.

"There you are." A light shone in my face blinding me to owner of the voice. I put my arm up to block the beam. "Grace, I thought I'd never see you again."

The words were right, but the voice wasn't. Not Harry's, but English like Harry's.

"C'mon, Grace. Everyone else left you. I waited for you. We've a little business together."

My senses kicked into gear and my lungs sucked in a volume of air for the scream that never came. Derek Rhodes covered the few feet between us and clamped his hand so hard over my mouth that my teeth cut into my lip. I tasted blood along with the piece of rag he quickly stuffed into my mouth. In an instant, he had covered my mouth with tape. All this and I was still on the ground. His face leered over me.

"Up now, Gracie, girl." He manhandled me to my feet placing one hand under my left breast and the other hand between my legs. I struggled and squirmed to be free of his grip. He squeezed until my eyes teemed with pain.

"Be nice to me, Gracie, and I'll be nice to you." He shifted one hand to my left arm, twisting it up behind my back. He stayed off the path and pushed me ahead, unmindful of the branches that hit me, or the roots that tripped me. Each time I stumbled he squeezed me harder and laughed.

I screamed into the filthy rag until I felt the vomit inching up my throat. I gagged and swallowed hard trying not to choke. My eyes blurred with anger and humiliation. Each step I took brought an increase of pressure on my arm until I thought it would break.

"Nearly there. They won't be back 'til the morning. Paid some sod to roar out of here and lead them on a merry chase. Tonight is all we need."

I recognized where we were. He was insane. Derek Rhodes opened the door to the Rowe's sauna and pushed me inside. The heat was stifling. My nose hairs prickled as I inhaled the superheated air.

"They've been and gone from here Gracie; no one to interrupt us. I'll strike a tiny light, enough to see you and for you to see me. Because my face is the last you'll be seeing on this earth."

His laugh was low and conspiratorial as though I were in on his scheme.

He removed his jacket and shirt. His pale chest glowed like the flashes of marsh gas on humid summer nights. He poured some water over the rocks and steam rose up in a strong wave. I felt the steam on my thighs and then on my chest. The thin gold chain around my neck attracted the heat like a magnet; it felt as though my neck were being burned.

"I tinkered with the electronics on this unit and cranked it up beyond the max. I'm good with tinkering." He stroked my thigh. I jerked my leg away. He grabbed both my arms and pressed me to his sweaty body. He crushed me against him while he continued.

"I was positioned to fire my last bomb into that window when I saw you climbing out. I'm happy you did survive. I figured old Harry would have got you out. Not like he did for me. I realized then that there was a reason I hadn't been able to kill you. That's when I nipped back here to turn this on for us. I wanted it so hot we wouldn't sweat."

I squirmed and tried to move away from him. The heat burned the hair in my nose. My eyes itched and hurt all at once.

"So, I owe the bastard for getting you out for me. Enough about Harry. I don't want to speak ill of the dead." His chest heaved with hollow laughter.

The Lion Tamer: A Caged Death

Even through the tape, he heard my cry.

"Take heart, Gracie, I'm with you. All the time I was in that filthy hellhole your husband would stare at the wall and imagine you were on the other side waiting for him. Thinking of you kept him whole up here."

Derek released me and pointed to his own head. I moved away from him. He didn't notice.

"Not me though. No, they said I'd lost it, gone bonkers, you see. I'm going to find out tonight what was so special about his bird that kept him sane. Cause, you know, Gracie girl, no normal person could have come out of there in one piece." Again, he tapped the side of his head.

The unholy light gleaming in his eyes scared me more than I've ever been scared in my life. My stomach twisted and churned. I didn't know how I'd live through what he had planned. Then I realized I wasn't supposed to live through it. He seemingly read my thoughts.

"Now for you. I'll tell you how it's going to be. I am going to kill you. I have too. I was hired and paid. A man can't go back on a contract. A man shouldn't go back on his word. Not like some. Before I kill you I am going to have you tonight, like Harry would have you. You make it memorable for me and when it's time I'll make it easy on you. If you don't bring the walls down with your lovemaking, Gracie then I'll have to get off on your screams while staring into those purple eyes of yours. Your choice." He shrugged and waited.

I gagged behind the rag feeling the bile collect in my throat. My head ached from the heat. I couldn't think, I couldn't breathe.

"Well then." He reached forward and hooked his hand in the front of my shirt. My left arm was limp at my side, but I raised my right arm instinctively. He ripped the front of my shirt open and in the same movement pushed away my raised arm. He pulled me sideways, used his right hand to yank the back of my shirt down to my waist. He turned me toward him and slapped the side of my face. I felt blood seep down my throat from the inside of my cheek.

His hand grasped the front of my waistband; he used that hold to leverage me toward him.

He was on me in that instant pushing me into the corner between the bench and the rocks. I could feel the heat from the rocks so close to our heads. I tried to roll him onto the superheated rocks. He was too strong. I couldn't pull away, couldn't push him off. His hands were tugging at my pants forcing them down over my hips. Heat from the cedar floor burned my exposed skin.

I didn't want to die, and I sure as hell didn't want to die after being raped by this murdering lunatic. My only chance would come when he shifted his hands to his own belt and trousers. In that instant of inattentiveness, I would make one last attempt.

He grunted and pulled at his own clothes, keeping one arm across my chest to pin me. His zipper burned my stomach as he shifted to free himself. I felt clammy skin against my belly and again fought down the revulsion.

Wait, wait. He's going to move his arm to position himself. Wait. Now!

I felt the pressure ease up from his arm as he moved it to the floor to prepare himself for possession. In that moment I reached up and pushed the bucket of water over onto the superheated rocks. I turned my head away from the rocks in the same movement.

Rhodes, caught off guard, turned his face to the rocks to follow my hand movement. He screamed now as the full force of the steam engulfed his face and neck. He rolled away from the rocks and off me clawing at his face and eyes.

I jumped to my feet, pulled up my pants, and bolted for the door. The steam blurred my vision and burned my lungs. I held my breath until I was outside. I ripped off the tape and pulled the rag from my mouth. Gulps of cool air filled my lungs and fueled my need to distance myself from him. I knew he wouldn't be down for long. I also knew he wouldn't make it easy for me. I had made my choice. My hope was that I knew this area in the dark better than he did. My resolve faltered a little when I realized that he'd been living out here for several days getting the lay of the land.

I knew I should run for the road, but I was afraid to come into the open; I couldn't outrun him on even ground. I didn't know how long I had before he'd be after me. I stayed on the path and raced back behind Lily's house and then Barb's until the silhouette of my own house loomed ahead of me. I hoped that maybe fire or police personnel were still there. No one was there. Then I heard a low neighing and I knew I wasn't alone.

I ran to the barn, threw open the door. I didn't dare turn on any light. April greeted me with a soft whinny, but immediately grew anxious as she sensed my fear. Her eyes widened, she rocked against her stall. I'm sure the noise and smoke from the fire had already tensed her nerves. My state of abject terror didn't calm her one bit.

I unlatched her stall and jumped out of the way as she almost ran me down in her haste to get out. I wanted to soothe her jangled nerves with soft words. None came. My mouth felt like gritty cotton and my throat ached from the screaming and burned from the retching.

Without warning or preparation, I grabbed a handful of her mane and swung up onto her back. She shied then thrust sideways slamming me into the front of her stall. I pulled up my leg. The movement unbalanced me and I knew I was headed for the ground if she did that again. In a moment of pure desperation I threw my arms around her neck and two words, "Whoa, girl," managed to escape. "Whoa, girl." Again and again, I whispered the words until I felt the twitching and spasms stop. I knew we were once again a team.

"Easy, girl. Let's get out of here." I pressed my knees against her sides. We walked to the door. I planned to turn her toward the meadow to put as much distance between Rhodes and me as I could.

April sensed him before I saw him. She shied and shimmied sideways moving away from him. I felt his hand brush down the side of my leg as he missed yanking me off the horse. He loomed in front of me. What little I could see in the ambient light looked gruesome. His face and neck oozed with what looked like red gel. He waved his arms trying to spook April into dumping me.

She didn't buck. She backed up, then paced forward forcing him to back up. This equestrian *cha-cha* went on until April backed him hard against the door of the barn. He reached out for balance and wrapped his hand around the inside of the frame. He steadied himself and came up swinging April's lead in his hand.

He caught her under her left eye. She whinnied in pain and lunged away from him. Her sudden movement almost threw me. I had to get out of the barn.

He came at us again swinging a bridle he had plucked off the wall. I turned April at the last second and felt the sharp pain as the metal landed full force right above my knee. Thank God, it missed my kneecap. I could feel the stinging and burning in the muscle of my leg.

Rhodes screamed obscenities and charged at us swinging both pieces. I buried my face in April's mane, stretched my arms around her neck, and gave her the knee command to gallop. I felt the metal hit against my forearm the moment before I felt nine hundred pounds of terrorized horseflesh leap under me.

We exploded from the barn, horse and rider so close it was difficult to say where I stopped and she began. I turned her toward the meadow in a frenzied gallop until I thought we were safe. It took half the length of a football field to get her to a controlled pace. My body language to her screamed *run* while my voice checked her. I turned her onto the fairways where I knew the ground was even. The deep breaths started to work; my heartbeat slowed from ramming against my ribcage to a simple jackhammer staccato. My hands felt the long strands of her mane and a familiar braid grew under my twitching fingers. April calmed down as my body eased and released the tension held in every fiber. I walked her across two more fairways and finally up the first tee to reach the darkened clubhouse.

I knew they had a phone near the putting green. I leaned down, lifted the receiver, and punched 9-1-1. The receiver slipped from my hand as I slid from April's back to the hard ground. I remembered a nervous whinny.

Chapter Thirty-Three

Sounds filtered through the clouds in my head. Slowly, the sounds translated into words.

"Oh God. This is Grace Marsden. Call for an ambulance. Get that blanket out of my car."

Car doors opened and closed. I felt welcomed warmth as the blanket touched my cold skin. The edges tucked under me, I lay safe and cozy, as in a cocoon. "Hold on, Mrs. Marsden. Help is on the way."

The voice sounded familiar, a nice voice, but not his voice. I drifted away.

Someone lifted me onto a soft bed. The bed bumped over the ground. More lifting. More voices. None his.

"One, two, three." I felt a shift, movement, then a different bed. "Grace, can you hear me? Grace, open your eyes. C'mon, Gracie you can do it."

Someone who seemed to know me rubbed her hands briskly around my wrists, first one then the other. I felt a tingling sensation through my arms and then neck.

"She's getting some color. That's it Grace, you're doing great."

I wasn't doing a damn thing except getting aggravated with this person who had pulled me back from a quiet fuzzy place in my head. The tingling had turned to pain in my left arm. God, it felt as though she was rolling cookie dough.

"Stop." That's all I could muster. I hadn't opened my eyes, yet.

"That's it, Grace. C'mon back." My cheerleader continued to knead my arms. I figured she wasn't going to stop until I opened my eyes.

I tried opening my eyes, the bright light forced them closed. More chaffing. I scrunched up my face and opened my eyes to a slit aperture. Several frantic blinks later I stared up into Tracy's beaming face.

"Hey, Morelli, where have you been, girl."

The familiarity and affection I heard in her voice cheered me. I think I managed to smile; my face hurt when I moved my lips. I tried to talk but my throat ached with the effort. I reached my hand up to hers.

She squeezed it. "You're going to have a sore throat for a while. They had to intubate you when you first came in. Your vitals are strong; you're going to be fine. No lung damage from the smoke or heat. You've some scrapes and bruises on your face and hands. We stitched up a cut on the inside of your cheek. You are one lucky person."

My eyes filled with tears; my throat ached even more with the emotion I couldn't control. Tracy leaned over my bed.

"Gracie, take it easy. Try to relax. It must have been horrible but you're safe now. Your family is on the way. They know you're here now. I'm going to give you something in your I.V. to help you sleep."

I realized I had a needle in the back of my left hand that led back to the I.V. apparatus. I watched Tracy empty the syringe into the tubing.

"We'll all be here when you wake up. C'mon, close your eyes now."

My eyes felt weighted; I sank deeper into myself rather than floating away. I didn't like this sensation. It felt unnatural and desperate. Maybe Tracy was wrong. Maybe I wasn't fine. I knew she was wrong about one thing. Not all of my family would be here. Not Harry. The thought brought no fresh tears only a weight on my chest that pushed me further into the darkness.

No one sleeps in a hospital, not even those they've drugged. My door swished opened and closed more times then I had family members so I knew people were checking me on a regular basis.

Was something wrong with me? Why all the visits? Why wasn't

I asleep? I needed sleep.

I recognized the mounting panic. I looked around the room. Nothing.

Oh, damn. Why now? Why not now? The call button. Press the call button.

I ran my right hand up and down the side of the pillow. *Where is it? Where is the damn button? Grace, calm down. The button is here somewhere.*

My self admonishment worked temporarily, at least long enough for me to find the cord to the button wrapped around the bar of the right side rail to keep it from falling onto the floor and out of reach. I managed to loosen the cord and push the call part through the loop without actually pushing the button. I didn't need them. I had their cord. I pulled the length of it across my body so my left hand could reach.

You want knots? You got knots.

The feel of order from routine soon calmed me. As I looped by rote I took a physical inventory. I felt much better; even my left arm seemed improved. My head had stopped aching and my throat felt cooler; swallowing didn't hurt like hell. I pulled my legs up so that my knees made a tent of the bed linen. I lifted forward from the shoulders in a lazy man's crunch; nothing hurt too much. Sometime during the process I fell asleep and one of the door swishers must have undone my tangle and repositioned the cord.

The next time I woke up the room glowed with subdued sunlight through the peach tinted blinds on the window across the room. I stared at the rosy hue wondering how I would get through this day.

The telltale *swish* alerted me that someone entered my room. Nurse? Morelli? I didn't care.

"Grace, I never thought I'd see you again."

The words. The voice. I turned my head so slowly I barely felt motion.

"Harry? Oh, God, Harry. Harry."

He sat next to my bed in a wheelchair propelled by a nurse. His hair was singed to the scalp in some spots, the left side of his face seemed swallowed by a triangle of gauze, and several black stitches held together a portion of his lower lip. His hands were wrapped from fingertips to above the wrists. An I.V. tube snaked out from under the edge of the wrappings and led up to two bags hanging on a split I.V. pole. I could only guess at further damage. *Is that why he's in a wheelchair? Are his legs burned?* I didn't care. He was alive!

The stitches made the smile more a grimace, but his eyes shone through a mist I felt growing in mine.

"It looks worse than it is, old girl." Harry's eyes smiled and held me with tenderness.

He was real. I rolled toward him unmindful of the I.V. attached to me. His nurse tried to warn me. Too late. The needle pulled out of my hand accompanied by a spurt of blood. I didn't care. He was alive. I reached both my arms through the side rail and touched the sides of his face. He was real. Tears streamed down my face, relief lifted the stone that had weighed on my chest. I pulled my arms back through the rail and moved down the bed to climb over the metal brace.

"Wait, Mrs. Marsden, wait. I'll lower it for you."

Harry's nurse moved around the wheelchair and worked the catches that lowered the bar. My feet hit the floor before the last click. I knelt next him and tried to embrace him. The best I could manage was to lay my head in his lap. I could feel his awkward hands patting my back trying to console me as I sobbed into the folds of his robe. Neither of us spoke.

"Mrs. Marsden, you shouldn't be out of bed." She reached down to help me up. I slipped my arms around Harry's waist. I felt Harry lean forward and use his forearms to hold me. This would be a tug of war she'd lose.

"Give us a few minutes, please?" Harry's voice strained with emotion.

I eased up when I heard her leave the room. Harry rested his arms on the padded arms of the wheelchair. He winced during the transition.

I let go of him and sat back on my feet. "Did I hurt you? What else is wrong? Your legs?"

"*Shh*, Gracie, no. I'm fine. What you see is about all that's damaged. I'm damn lucky."

It seemed that he wanted to say more. His eyes grew serious.

Ric. In my joy to find Harry alive, I'd forgotten Ric.

I swallowed several times before I could ask. "Ric?"

"He wasn't as lucky, Darling. You were right; I heard him call out when we were at the window. I followed his voice back through the smoke and found him pinned under the sideboard in the dining room. So much smoke." Harry shivered as he relived the hell that must have been. "The wood was burning on top of him. I managed to push it off and drag him back through the living room. He was unconscious by then. Too much smoke. We made it out through the French doors. I must have passed out. Didn't know a thing until I woke up in the ER. No one knew where you were. My God, Gracie, I was so worried."

"How's Karen? Is she all right? I have to go to her."

"She's fine. She's with the doctors making arrangements for Ric."

Oh my God. Arrangements. Poor Karen.

"Where's Hannah? Is someone with her?"

"Hannah was here last night. She's the one who told me they'd brought you in. These sods tried to stop me from seeing you last night. Finally someone with good sense wheeled me down here so I could see you. You were asleep with that cord," he motioned to the call button on the rail, "twisted around your hands. I knew you were okay. That's all I wanted."

"But who is with Karen. She shouldn't have to do this alone." I was on my feet and searching the closet for a robe. I yanked it off the hanger and hurried into it.

"Gracie, wait." A new expression filled Harry's eyes. "Grace, Ric is alive."

"He's alive. But you said..." I put my hand on the bed and slowly sat down.

"Oh my God, Grace. I'm so sorry. You thought he was dead? Oh, darling. Come here." He opened his arms for me. I stayed where I was; the room was swaying.

"Grace, are you all right?" Harry was trying to get up out of the chair without using his hands.

"Don't get up. I'm okay. I thought you were both dead. Lily said you helped her through the window but her father said you weren't there when he climbed out."

"I heard Ric call out after I helped Lily. I didn't even see DeFreest; there was so much smoke. I only found Ric because of his screams–"

My gasp stopped Harry. "Screams? But he's alive?"

"Yes, he's alive. He's still unconscious and his legs are badly burned. They don't know the full extent of the smoke damage to his lungs. They're arranging a transfer to the Loyola Burn Unit in Maywood. They wanted to stabilize him first."

"I didn't know. I thought you had both died." My voice sounded flat. "I heard a fireman say it looked like a war zone. I didn't care anymore. I walked away; into the woods. I never knew."

"I asked for you as soon as I came to. Tracy was here; I thought I was dreaming. She said you were probably in the other ambulance that went to Good Sam. Your dad and brothers went to Good Sam and then showed up here looking for you. That's when we realized no one had seen you since the fire. The paramedic that treated you at the scene said he thought you were in one of the other ambulances."

"I'm sorry you worried."

"A whole bunch of other worried people will probably be pushing through that door as soon as visiting hours allow. Your dad and Marty assumed you were still out at the house, maybe hurt, maybe dazed. They called all available Morellis, the Pine Marsh Police, and the Sheriff's office. Marty says they started a line, arm's length apart, stretching a hundred yards on either side of the house and worked their way down through the yard and woods. When the police found you at the golf course, someone radioed one of the Pine Marsh policemen in the search party and he told your family. By the time they arrived here you were already sedated. All they could do was peek in one at a time to see for them selves that you were safe and sound. I don't think they would have left without a fight if they couldn't see you."

That sounded like my dad and brothers. I smiled realizing all those nocturnal visitors had been my family. I felt calm enough to stand and move closer to Harry.

"How badly burned are your hands?" I stared at the white bandages so thick they looked like mittens.

"It looks worse than it is. I've some spots that burned in, probably need some grafting there, but the rest of this," he lifted his hands, "is for protection against infection."

Harry's nurse had given us exactly a few minutes. She returned with reinforcements.

"Geez, Grace. Can't you ever follow orders? You're supposed to be in bed." Tracy's scolding set off a lopsided smile on Harry's face.

"I tried to tell her, boss," Harry said.

"You're no better, Mr. Marsden. You threatened to crawl here if I didn't help you."

Now, I was grinning at his nurse's rebuke.

"Both of you need to get back to bed."

"I feel fine, Tracy. Honest."

"I'm not leaving Grace."

Our nurses took a quick huddle. Before they could decide a course of action, the door pushed open and five Morellis streamed in followed by a sputtering nurse.

"I said two visitors at a time." Her instructions went unheeded.

"Honey, we were so worried." My dad's face filled with relief the moment he saw me. The fact that I was out of bed, in a robe and standing confirmed my heartiness.

"I'm fine dad. I'm sorry you worried." I stepped into a bear hug that seemed a little tenuous. I squeezed him harder and he responded. Without leaving his arms, I looked over his head at my three brothers and cousin.

"Hi guys. Sorry you had to worry too."

My brother Mike spoke first. "We weren't worried. We were in the neighborhood, thought we'd form a search party, something to do. Pity it's not Snipe Season. Thought I saw a couple." Mike's dry humor prompted laughter, even from the nurses. He ruffled the top of my head as he leaned in to kiss my cheek. Glen and Marty followed suit, each walking forward to give me an arm lean and kiss on the cheek. My cousin Nick held back. He was the youngest of the first cousins.

"Well?" I prompted moving one hand to motion him forward.

When Nick came forward I noticed his eyes seemed moist. I

realized too late that he hadn't laughed at Mike's quip. Nick stepped toward me.

"Gracie, I was so scared for you." He swallowed hard trying to hold back tears. "We didn't know what happened and then when we found that man–"

"Nick!" My father's voice was sharp.

The memory of last night seeped into my body starting in my stomach and spreading like steam through my tissue until I imagined heat in my lungs. The throbbing in my head threatened to topple me.

I felt Tracy take my arm.

"What man?" Harry had about stood out of his chair trying to get an answer. His nurse firmly held him down. "What man, Nick? Mike? Somebody start talking."

"Enough. That's it." Tracy's low authoritative voice filled the room. "You," sweeping my family with one arm, "outside now."

They reluctantly filed out the door. My dad turned to us. "I'll wait until I can come back. I know you need answers."

"You," her finger pointed at me. "Back in bed, you can sit up, but in bed."

I climbed in trying to unravel the hastily thrown aside sheets. The second nurse followed my family out. She was probably standing guard. Tracy efficiently smoothed out the linens and fluffed up the pillows. She shook her head when she noticed the I.V. dangling from the stand. She turned to Harry.

"You…"

"I'm not leaving Grace," Harry interrupted. His face settled into stone.

"Of course you're not. I know that." She turned to Harry's nurse.

"Mr. Marsden, Nurse Moore seems to think we should place another bed in here." She hesitated until Tracy nodded. "I have to check with the floor nurse, but I don't think that will be a problem."

"I'll redo her I.V. and check his while you call for that bed."

The nurse seemed happy to leave us in Tracy's care.

"Thanks, Trace. I owe you one."

"No, you owe me several," she smiled. "But who's counting."

Harry's face softened as he addressed her. "Tracy, it is

extremely important that I talk to Mike Morelli."

"No visitors for now. You two may think you're fine, but you're not. Harry I can see the pain in your eyes. You're due for meds. You," she turned to me, "were dehydrated and in shock when they brought you in."

Tracy lifted a tray from the bedside cabinet and prepared another needle. She deftly positioned it in the back of my hand and secured it with tape. She checked the connection and seemed satisfied.

"Tracy, I need to speak to Mike," Harry pleaded with her.

"First, you need to take this. If your color and eyes are any indicators you're about three minutes away from a lot of pain. I don't know why you're not unglued now. I brought this for Grace but she doesn't seem to be in pain." Tracy looked at me for confirmation and I nodded. "I checked your chart. You're able to take this." She poured a small amount of water and a straw in a glass and placed the pill on Harry's tongue. Tracy held the straw to his lips. Harry swallowed the pill and looked expectantly at Tracy.

"Now let me talk to Mike."

"Talk about a one track mind. You gotta love this guy." She grinned at me.

"I do." My eyes felt moist. I swallowed and cleared my throat. "I also know him well enough to assure you he won't stop until you let my dad back in."

Tracy's smile vanished. She moved the visitor's chair closer to Harry and sat down. She could look at both of us now. "You don't need to talk to Mike. I was here when they came in last night. I was here when they brought him in."

"Brought who in?" Harry asked.

"Derek." My voice sounded loud and nervous.

"Rhodes? He was out there? You saw him?"

"He waited in the woods. He said he saw me come out the window. He was going to fire another bomb, but he didn't. He watched me leave the ambulance and then he waited until everyone left." I stopped and swallowed several times trying to erase the bitter taste in my mouth.

"Easy, Grace." Tracy stood up.

"I'm okay. Truly." I didn't know how much to tell Harry in his condition. It was over; he couldn't do anything about it. Why torment him? I knew he'd blame himself.

I looked Tracy straight in the eye before I spoke, cautioning her not to mention my condition or lack of clothing when I was brought in.

"I ran away from him through the woods and made it to the barn. He followed me but I was up on April already and she knocked him down getting out of the barn. We rode across the meadow and several fairways to get away. I think we owe the course some maintenance work." I kept my story as brief and uneventful as possible. "April. Oh my gosh. I forgot about April. I don't remember what happened to her." My voice rose with panic and concern.

"She's fine, Grace. One of the officers that answered your 9-1-1 call took care of her."

"Good. I owe her my life. I'm thinking big bag of carrots."

"What about Rhodes? Have they arrested him? You said they brought him in."

"Apparently, April did more than knock him down. He took a hoof to the head. He was DOA." Tracy smiled at me. "Better double those carrots."

Chapter Thirty-Four

Tracy was a good nurse and an even better friend. She waited until the extra bed was delivered. Harry and I were both exhausted from the excitement of finding each other alive and trying to fill in the blanks. Tracy ran interference for us when the police asked to talk with me, explaining that I had been sedated and they should come back later in the day. She helped the nurse change Harry's dressings and made sure that we had fresh water, the TV remote and reading material. She even left the belt to her trench coat for me.

"Okay you two. You're set. I have to go home and find out if my house is still standing and if William has filed papers yet."

"Tracy you've been an angel. I don't know what we would have done without you. Thank you so much." Harry spoke softly.

"Like you two wouldn't do the same for me." She brushed off our thanks and promised to visit tomorrow. "I'll send your dad in on my way out."

Swish, she left. *Swish,* my dad appeared.

"I know you're both beat. Tracy told me she filled you in on Rhodes. It's over now. You need to rest and heal. When you're released you'll stay with me until your house is ready. Don't worry about that either. We have people lined up to start rebuilding."

"Mike, I don't know if we're going back to in Pine Marsh."

"What? You guys love it there."

I was stunned at Harry's statement. I knew he was exhausted, knew he was trying to hold it together for my sake.

"Dad, I have bad feelings about Pine Marsh. Harry and I need to talk."

"Sure, honey. Everything's on hold 'til we hear from the two of you."

"Thanks, Mike."

"Rest. I'll see you tomorrow." My dad leaned down and kissed my forehead.

The door closed behind him and Harry turned to face me.

"I know that was sudden. I'm not sure how I feel about the place. I didn't want Mike to get the clan moving on it too soon."

I smiled at his reference to my family. "I'm tired. Let's sleep and talk about it later." I blew him a kiss through the bars and closed my eyes. I didn't know if sleep would come, but I figured my silence would allow him to sleep.

Within a few minutes I heard the steady rhythm of his breathing. I tried matching the rise and fall of his chest but couldn't calm my mind or my heart. Too many emotions, too many thoughts filled me to the point of confusion. I couldn't seem to catch an easy breath. I wanted to scream, I wanted to leave my body. I realized why I couldn't settle down. I wanted to see Ric; had to see Ric.

I carefully climbed over the rail that had been left up and removed the I.V. bag from its hook. My robe had been placed over the back of the chair. I held the bag and slipped the loose-fitting sleeve over my left hand, bag and all. The rest was easy. I found slippers lined up under my bed. I opened the door a crack to check for nurse activity. No one was out there, at least from my limited view. The nurse's station was empty. I thought I could do like in the movies and check a chart to see where Ric was. I couldn't find a roster or room assignment or anything with his name. It always worked on TV.

"What are you doing?" I jumped and dropped my I.V. bag. Karen stood on the other side of the desk staring at me in disbelief.

"*Shh*. You scared me half to death." I walked around the desk and guided her with my free hand. "Come over here where they won't see us." I led her to an alcove at the end of the short hallway. There were two tan couches, assorted chairs, and a coffee table. The excitement and short, brisk walk tired me more than I thought possible. I sat and pulled her down next to me.

"I was trying to find Ric. How is he? Harry told me he was being transferred to Loyola."

"He's already there. They transferred him this morning. I was coming to find you and Harry."

We hugged each other. "No one knew what happened to you. I didn't realize you were missing until hours after they brought in Ric and Harry."

"I know. It was stupid of me to walk off. I thought they were dead. I didn't think anyone could get out of there. You didn't see it, Karen. It was horrible."

Karen held my hand between hers. "It's over now. They're alive, and so are you. That creep is dead. I feel so horrible that all this happened because of my aunt. Grace, can you ever forgive me."

Karen's eyes filled with tears and my vision began to blur. I leaned toward her again and hugged her as best I could with one arm. I released her and wiped at my eyes with the sleeve of my robe.

"This wasn't your fault. Your aunt was sick and she managed to hook up with another sick mind. Don't blame yourself." She seemed to brighten a little. I realized she hadn't answered my question. "How's Ric? Please tell me."

Karen swallowed and straightened her shoulders. "It doesn't look good." She hurried as she looked at my face; I felt lightheaded and I'm sure I lost color. "He's in a drug induced coma and on a respirator to keep him calm and comfortable. His legs are badly burned and his back was broken when the sideboard fell on him. They don't know the extent of the damage to his spine."

I winced and sobbed as I thought of that heavy piece of furniture crushing Ric under its bulk and weight.

Karen shook me by the shoulder. "Stop it. He's alive and that's what counts."

I stopped and cleared my throat. How stupid and insensitive could I be? Karen was holding on to that thought and not going beyond the moment. I hadn't seen her fear; I only felt my pain.

"That's what counts. Nothing else. When can you be with him?" I made a final swipe at my eyes and vowed not to cry anymore in front of Karen.

"Hannah is meeting me here. She was already her way to Toronto when I received the call about Ric. I called her on her cell phone. She was on her way back before I knew about Harry. After she checks in on Harry, we'll drive to Loyola."

I was glad that Hannah would be here soon. She was devoted to Harry and Karen.

"Which room is Harry's?" Karen asked. "I wanted to thank him. The fire chief said he'd never seen anything like it; didn't think anyone could have made it out. They were stunned to see Harry crawling away from the house on his back with his arms under Ric's armpits dragging Ric on top of him. He used his legs and feet to push across the lawn until someone spotted them. Ric would have burned to death."

Karen paled and I feared she would faint. I snugged my arm around her shoulders and swayed to my feet.

"C'mon, let's get some water or juice. I'm still a little dehydrated. I don't think this thing works without the principle of gravity." I motioned to the bag in my left hand.

"Oh my gosh, Grace. Sit down, I'll get you some juice." Karen bustled off to find juice. My distraction worked. When she returned she handed me a large cup of orange juice and placed an even larger glass of water on the table.

"I'm sorry, I wasn't thinking."

"It's okay." I took a sip to complete the charade, but ended up drinking the remaining orange juice in three gulps.

"Here, take this." She handed me the water and I drank half of that before putting it down.

An alert nurse had followed Karen around the corner. She stepped into view. "Mrs. Marsden your husband is awake and asking for you."

The way she emphasized *asking*, made us smile. We followed her down the corridor to my room. Apparently, Harry wasn't the only person asking for me. A uniformed police officer was talking to the nurse at the desk. Several nurses were making notes in charts. It must be a shift change. The one talking to the officer glanced up as Karen and I approached, she pointed to me. Hannah Marsden walked up rapidly from the other direction. She and Karen embraced and said a few words to each other. I knew only two visitors were allowed at one time. I told them to go in and visit; to tell Harry I was going to the bathroom and that I would be in after their visit. I realized I did need to use the bathroom after all the liquid I drank, but

I wanted to make my statement to the police about last night away from Harry. He didn't need to know what I had to tell.

Chapter Thirty-Five

A week hardly seemed enough time to heal body and soul, but the human spirit is indomitable and equally amazing. I was released from the hospital after one complete day and night of observation. My family worked around the clock to get my old room in my dad's house ready for us. I spent the next four days, before Harry's release, puttering around trying to make everything right. Difficult to do when you've downsized from a twelve room home into a 10'x12' bedroom.

My brother hired ServiceMaster to come out and clean our clothes and the upstairs bedrooms. The bombs demolished the living room, dining room, and part of the library. As bad as it looked, the house was still structurally sound. Dad told the boys about Harry's comment. They took it upon themselves to clear out the rubble. As soon as the Fire Marshal and the police released the building Marty, Glen, and Mike ordered a dumpster and hauled out every piece of broken, charred or smoke and water damaged item they found. My sisters-in-law, Carolyn and Eve, packed the entire kitchen into storage.

Marty offered to drive me out to the house with him. I couldn't make myself go. Eve sent clothes that ServiceMaster had cleaned back with him. I filled my old dresser with our clothing. The scent of lavender lingered from the old liner paper my mom and I had placed in the drawers when this dresser had been new.

I hadn't attended the funeral service for Ben Jackson, the only death from the bombing. I guess his warning saved the rest of us. In a surreal way, I recalled the movements that seemed so fast that day. I sat in wonder at what had frightened him as he turned from the window. In my memory I could see DeFreest, Ric, Peterson, and

Harry reacting immediately, moving away from the window and pulling Lily and me with them. In their own ways all four had been trained to act in an emergency. I know Lily and I, left alone, would have moved toward Jackson or at the very least sat there until we knew why he was so upset. Those precious seconds would have meant our deaths too.

I found out that Lily had attended the funeral. Her father had been absent. A few of Ben Jackson's friends from the old days when he lived in Chicago came to pay their respects. Both DeFreests had been released the night of the fire. Leo DeFreest required a new prosthesis and flew to New York to be fitted by his specialist.

Suellen Rowe and Barb Atwater drove out to visit with me. Barb had been released and returned home the morning after the fire. I was happy to see she seemed fully recovered. I promised her lunch at her favorite spot, the Jefferson Hill Tea Room, as soon as things were settled.

Dave Katernak stopped by twice, once with, and once without the police. The police had more questions. Dave was there because he's a lawyer and he wanted to make sure there were no inappropriate questions about Derek Rhodes' death. The second time he stopped in he tied up loose ends about the insurance claim. It was then that he told me Derek's body had been sent home to his family in England. I knew it could have as easily been Harry's body returning to his English soil. Talk of death and sadness took its toll.

Harry would be released tomorrow. I puttered furiously to prepare our one room to his liking, but nothing I did lifted the stone I felt in my heart. My dad tried cheering me with Edna's pastry. I noticed he had a tray arranged on the counter. I hoped he was going to his Senior's Club with that caloric death wish.

I heard the doorbell.

"Gracie, company's here." My dad's voice sounded jovially staged. At least I knew he wouldn't sound that way if it were the police or even Dave on the doorstep.

Karen and Hannah stood smiling in the living room. From the looks that passed between them and my dad, I knew he must have called them when I didn't seem to shake my funk. I greeted both of them with huge hugs.

"Sorry we didn't get here sooner. Tracy wanted to come too, but she has one of the boys home with a cold." Karen scrutinized my face. "You look great. Those scratches and cuts are barely visible."

"Ladies." This from my dad as he walked in with the tray of pastries. "Follow me," he said as he motioned toward the dining room. He had already set the table with place settings, cups, and a tea box. What a sneak. He put down the tray and returned with hot water for tea and coffee for me.

"Thanks, Mr. Morelli. I love Edna's bakery."

"*Mmm*, me too. Looks heavenly." My sister-in-law beamed as she contemplated her selection.

Once we settled in, I asked about Ric.

"His prognosis is better than they first thought. He's off the respirator, breathing easily and fully on his own. His back will heal with no damage to his spine." Karen seemed happy, yet cautious.

"He joked about his back injury being the same type as 49ers' quarterback Joe Montana, who came back to lead his team to a win in a Super Bowl after his recovery."

Karen giggled, then continued. "As soon as he said it we both thought of the comedy line, 'doctor, doctor, will I be able to play the piano after the surgery?' doctor answers, 'Yes, of course.' Patient says, 'that's great, I could never play before!' *ba-da-bump*!"

The three of us roared with laughter at Karen's lighthearted poke at her brother. I reminded myself to hug my dad later for calling them. Karen still seemed reserved.

"What else, Karen. You're not telling me everything."

Her face grew serious, the laughter of a minute ago faded.

"It's his legs, Grace. They've already done two surgeries, two of many more to come. There's been deep tissue damage to one leg and it's become infected."

My heart froze in my chest. I didn't want to hear more. Karen continued in a softer tone. I noticed that my dad had come to the archway to hear the news or maybe watch my reaction.

"He's on high dosages of antibiotics. They have to clear the infection before they can do more surgeries on that leg."

I didn't know how to ask. "Could he..." My voice wouldn't say it.

"Lose the leg? If they can't stop the infection, yes." Karen's eyes filled with tears. Hannah's arm moved around her shoulders to comfort her.

Mike Morelli to the rescue. He sat down at the head of the table and spoke in a calm, assuring voice. I had heard this voice all my life when things didn't turn out like I wanted them to. He had used this voice when I was a little girl to tell me that my nana had gone to heaven. He had used the same voice to talk about my mom's cancer and what would likely happen.

Now he used that voice with us. "Let's not lose sight of what's important here. Ric is alive and will survive his injuries. Don't go borrowing trouble thinking about what could happen. Look at what is and accept what will be. Seems to me from what you say about your brother that he's done that. If he can, you must." His steady gaze included all three of us.

Unexpectedly, I began to laugh. Hannah and Karen looked at me with concern.

"Dad, you're like Yoda." I pictured my 5 foot 4 inch father with those sincere brown eyes and big ears. I couldn't stop giggling. Karen and Hannah stared at me, both of them slack-jawed and appalled at my comment.

My father sat still with a slight smile forming on his face. He knew I fought anguish with humor.

Karen, who knew my family better than Hannah did, began to chuckle and then outright laugh. Hannah looked at her as though she'd succumbed to whatever craziness I suffered.

My dad spoke. "Is that a short person joke or an oversized ears joke?"

That did it. Even Hannah caught the giggles.

Gloom banished, we covered general topics of interest. That was my dad's cue to leave.

"If you ladies will excuse me, I need to pick up a few things for dinner tomorrow."

"*Ugh*," Karen sighed. "We have to do that when we leave here. I hate grocery shopping."

"Do you have a list made up? I'll shop for you too. I don't do Jewel, too expensive. I make the rounds between Aldi's, Sam's Club, and Cub. Not going to Sam's today."

I could see that Karen was tempted. Her hand started to reach for her purse. Hannah answered first.

"Mike, that's a lovely offer, but we've quite a list and some of the items are at a specialty store."

"To each his own," he said as he doffed an imaginary cap and left the room.

"Your father is such a sweetheart. Does he do windows?"

We burst into laughter again.

"I'm so happy you came over. I haven't laughed since this whole thing started. This is good for Harry too. I'm thrilled he'll be here tomorrow, but I was worried about my mood dragging him down."

"Now that you're in the right frame of mind…" Karen smiled at Hannah before she continued. "We want you to come with us to the *Whirl* this Saturday." Karen held up her hand before I could say anything. "I know what you're going to say, but I think this is what you need. You've been cooped up here moping about for a week. You need to get out."

"I know what you're trying to do. I appreciate it, but I'm not in the mood–"

"Exactly," Hannah interrupted. "You need to get in the mood. We already checked with Harry; he's all for it. We invited Barb and Tracy to fill in our table. C'mon now, they've never been."

Harry's twin argued as persuasively as he did. It was weird to hear a different voice from a similar face using the exact words he would. I couldn't fight them all.

I grinned at them. "Oh, all right. I'll go. Wait, I don't have a dress that's right for the occasion. Eve and Carolyn only brought over regular clothes. I don't want to go out there."

"*Ah,* we thought that might be the case. I'll be right back."

Karen grabbed her car keys and took off out the front door.

"What's going on?" I looked at Hannah. She flashed a Mona Lisa smile.

"You'll see."

I suspected the answer. Karen and I had been shopping the malls together since we were in college. She knew my taste and size.

She was back in a few minutes with a garment bag. She held it by the hanger and started unzipping the bag.

"Lord and Taylor. It's perfect for you." Karen pushed the shoulders of the garment bag off the hanger to reveal a stunning evening gown. The burgundy bodice shimmered with hundreds of tiny black beads. The long, black skirt reflected swirls of the same beads. The dropped waist, fuller skirt and tea length all complemented my shorter, fuller figure.

"Well?" Karen spoke, but both she and Hannah waited for my reaction.

"It's exactly what I would have picked out. Thank you." I stood up and moved around the table to hug both of them.

"And in the event that these were needed," Hannah rummaged in the oversized bag she carried. She pulled out a pair of black evening shoes and held them aloft.

"What, no evening bag?" I laughed at their crestfallen faces.

"All settled then. We will collect you at six-thirty. Cocktails are at seven o'clock," Hannah said. "We have to run now. See you Saturday." Hannah hugged me good-bye.

Karen moved in for her good-bye. When I hugged her whispered, "Say hello to Ric for me. Tell him I'm…" I hesitated, not knowing what I wanted Karen to tell her brother.

"I'll tell him you send wishes for a speedy recovery," Karen said.

"That sounds like a sappy greeting card."

"You don't have many choices here."

"Yeah. Say hello."

"Will do. See you Saturday night.

As they were leaving out the front door, my dad was coming in the back door carrying two small bags of groceries. I stood in the doorway and watched as he pulled item after item from the bags and carefully put each product where it belonged on the shelf or in cabinet. After over thirty years, he still cut the Italian bread cut in half and wrapped each piece inside another paper bag; the American bread went into the metal breadbox that my nonna had used in her kitchen. The extra canned goods (he had to have two in the pantry went down into the basement on shelves built under the stairs. Only the *Contadina* tomato paste and stewed tomatoes were all housed in the kitchen at the ready to make emergency gravy. He straightened up after he tucked the last item, *Bon Ami* cleanser, behind the half full container already in use.

"The girls invited me to the *Whirl* Saturday night. They even bought me an evening dress and shoes. I said I'd go, but I'm not sure. Harry's coming home tomorrow."

"Right, he's coming home tomorrow, Thursday. You'll have three whole days to fuss over him. By Saturday afternoon, he'll need a break. The Bulls are playing the Bucks, Mike and Marty are coming over and the three of us can certainly keep Harry company."

I smiled at the plans he had for Harry, a devoted soccer fan. "I thought Joseph was in town. Isn't he coming? And what about Glen?"

"Joe's been invited to say grace at some event that night."

We both smiled momentarily as we remembered how confused I had been when I was a little girl and my family would gather to say *grace*.

"And Glen has a second date with Ms. Two-Cubicles-Away in his office."

Glen worked in a dental partnership that had several dentists and hygienists in one large suite.

"Didn't he date Three-Cubicles-Away last month?"

My dad laughed. "No, that was Down-the-Hall, one floor up. Maybe I missed Three-Cubicles."

We laughed at Glen's crazy love life. Since his divorce, he had dated many, but no one more than twice. When we asked him why only two dates he had said he was getting too old to invest more time than that if he didn't get that *I think I could love you* feeling by date number two. We joked about it but all of us hoped he'd find the right one.

"Here." My dad handed me an envelope. From Carolyn and Eve.

"What is it?"

"Your name's on it, not mine."

The envelope looked familiar. I used a butter knife from the utensil holder in the dish strainer to slit open the paper.

I waved the gift certificate for a manicure and pedicure at Mario Tricocci under my father's nose. "Everyone was pretty darn sure I'd go to this *Whirl*. I don't know if I like being that predictable."

"We wanted you to relax and enjoy yourself. Harry suggested that place. Said he used to be jealous of how you'd get all doe eyed and say *'Oooo*, Mario' when you'd get one of those gift cards."

"He didn't say that and I never looked doe eyed." I picked up the dishtowel and threatened to snap him. He was laughing so hard I don't think it would have mattered. I dropped the towel on the table. It wasn't fun if he wouldn't run.

I executed my best flounce when I left the room. "I'd better call Mario and set up my hot date."

Chapter Thirty-Six

Harry hurried me out the door for my one o'clock appointment at the salon in Naperville. I had added a facial and massage to the plan. I felt like putty under the firm fingers, knuckles, and elbows of Madeline, the masseuse. Of all the services, I enjoyed this one the best; lying still and savoring each palpitation and manipulation. She paid special attention to my hands and feet, stretching and massaging each digit. She asked me if I had carpal tunnel in my left hand; she could feel the wrist bone and it seemed out of place. She kneaded each hand naming the bones as she moved over them from the *carpals* across the *hamate* and *capitate* to the *trapezoid* to the *metacarpals* on up to the *phalanges*. I didn't care what she called them as long as she kept rubbing.

"They teach you all of that in massage school?"

Her laughter was genuine. "No, pre-med at Benedictine. It helps me study if I name all the parts as I go. Hope I didn't annoy you."

"No, this was the most informative massage I've ever had."

She bent back too her task. Too soon my time was up and Madeline encouraged me to visit again. I wished her luck in med school. She left me to get up, don my robe, and move on to the next stop. After a manicure and pedicure I would be back in time to dress for the *ball*.

I entered the house to pretend fanfare as Harry and my dad sounded *ta da's* as they held out their arms pretending to hold trumpets. I felt like Cinderella, except I was leaving Prince Charming at home.

"Thank you, my loyal subjects. Your princess appreciates your thoughtfulness and you will be rewarded." A soft couch pillow caught me in the back of my head. I giggled and picked up the pillow and turned toward the living room. Marty sat on the couch ready to lob another pillow.

"*Ah, ha*, the spoiled brother prince." I threw the pillow at his head then ducked behind Harry. Marty's pillow bounced off Harry's chest and skidded across the hardwood floor.

"No throwing stuff in the house. You're gonna break something. Geez, you guys knew that when you were little." My dad shrugged his shoulders in a what's the use gesture. "I'm gonna put in the pizzas."

Marty and I grinned at each other as I put the pillows in order on the couch.

"Mario did right by you, Sis."

"He did indeed, but then he had so much to work with," Harry added.

"Thank you gentlemen. Now I must dress for the ball." walked regally from the room expecting another pillow any moment.

I heard Harry before I reached the hallway. "She'll probably need help with a zipper. I'd better see to it."

"Yeah, you'd better," Marty said.

I slowed down to wait for Harry.

"Help with a zipper?" I laughed as he followed me into my childhood bedroom. "With those hands?" Harry's hands looked like white fluffy ping-pong paddles.

"What would you have me say? Excuse me Marty, but I going down the hall to make love to your sister in her girlie girl bedroom?"

I smiled at his dilemma.

"Gracie, it's been so long, I'd use my teeth to undress you if I had to." He stepped closer to me. "You won't make me though, will you?"

"An interesting experiment for another time. You're sister will be here in thirty minutes. You know she's never late."

"Yes, but Karen is always late. I'm willing if you are."

I could see he was willing.

Luisa Buehler

Chapter Thirty-Seven

We arrived at the *Whirl* ten minutes later than planned, a combination of Karen's tardiness and my own *whirl* with Harry. I had playfully blown kisses at the men in the house.

"Good bye my darlings. I'll be home by midnight."

Karen snorted a giggle as she and Hannah whisked me down the steps and into my carriage. I kept thinking in fairy tale terms.

Hannah deplored being late; she tapped the steering wheel and gnawed at her bottom lip the entire drive. *They say I'm obsessive-compulsive.* I kept my thoughts to myself and enjoyed the short ride to the zoo.

Jolene greeted us at the South Gate. She directed us to the left toward Tropic Zone where the cocktails would be served. My niece's eyes lit up when our tiny evening bags revealed sizable purchases of raffle tickets. The bag I carried was an old-fashioned drawstring affair; enough room for compact, lipstick, yarn, and folding money. Hannah's bag was red silk and the size of a number ten envelope and almost as thin. The purse matched her dress perfectly. Blondes are stunning in red. Karen's gown, a creamy fawn color, set off her particular coloring to a tee. All in all, we looked fine. Karen's bag was too small for whatever bulged inside it. Maybe she was carrying stuff for Hannah.

The path to the three-story building was illuminated by tiki torches spaced two to three feet apart alternating from side to side. I liked the symmetry of the zigzag design.

We followed the path leading high into the canopy of the rainforest and began our journey through South America. We crossed the bridge spanning the fifty-foot chasm to the jungle floor below. Spray from the waterfalls cascading on both sides of the bridge

253

delighted most partygoers as the *oohs* and *aahs* increased at this point. I say most were delighted. One woman tried to screen her hair from the slight moisture and seemed perturbed that her group, in which she was stuck in the middle, had stopped on the bridge to admire the falls. Her coiffure seemed sprayed into place, but she held her hands with fingers stretched out and gently cupped over both sides of her head.

I grinned as I thought of the *hear no evil monkey*. And of course, she chose that moment to look right at me. Her face, which also looked sprayed, questioned my obvious glee at her dilemma. She dropped her hands to her side and gave me a rather nasty look.
hadn't noticed her gown before. It was a simple strapless sheath in gradient shades from dark buff to light brown to cocoa brown to black at the hem. She wore long black finger-less gloves and a choker made from similar colored thin wooden beads around her neck. The effect was either squirrel monkey or spider monkey.

My eyes must have widened with surprise; her look became a glare. Her group moved forward and she turned and walked off the bridge. Thankfully, that group kept moving, apparently anxious to get to the bar in Asia, the next exhibit. Jolene told us the bar was there because that was the area without a waterfall and conversation was easier. We waited in South America for Tracy and Barb to arrive.

Barb walked toward us from the other direction carrying a glass of wine.

"I drove here in record time. Thought I grab a drink before the lines reached back to Pine Marsh."

I saw Tracy's head and shoulders above a small group coming across the bridge. She spotted us about the same time.

"Hi. Sorry I'm late. Matthew needed, Benjamin wanted William ignored. You know, the usual *how can we slow down Mom cause she wants to be on time* stuff."

Only Barb laughed from knowledge; we laughed at Tracy' recounting of her escape. We spent a few minutes at the railing watching the monkeys watch us from their tree top perches. decided, Monkey Madam, as I thought of her now was definitely in the spider monkey family.

We walked across a darkened hall through double doors and found ourselves in Asia. The bar was set up against the high cliff on the right. Small, high tables were stationed throughout the exhibit, placed so one could nibble at *hors d'ouvres* and sip champagne comfortably while watching the gibbons, river otter, and orangutans. Each table displayed a pewter monkey in a sitting position with its arms wrapped around a votive candle.

Since Hannah and I seemed to hang at the rail and read the graphics and watch the animals while the group wanted to move on, we agreed to split up and meet at the trolley cars at seven o'clock. They would transport us to the dining tent at the other end of the park.

Barb and Tracy went in search of more nibbles. Karen decided to stay with us. I knew she'd be bored and sure enough after ten minutes I noticed her against the wall on a small wooden bench. She had removed the bulge from her purse. Curiosity won out over nature. People who knew me would say curiosity was my nature.

"What did you do, bring some light reading with you?"

"Oh, this. I've been picking up Ric's mail at the house. This came by messenger as we were leaving tonight. I carried it with me and automatically stuffed it in my bag. I'm contemplating running it out to the car so my purse doesn't look like it swallowed a suckling pig."

"Or a pewter monkey." I pointed to the centerpiece.

"You don't think anyone would think that? See, now I do have to take it back to the car."

"Don't be silly. Personally, I thought you were taking advantage of a quiet moment and grading some darling's paper."

I grinned at her until she broke into a smile. "As long as you've taken it into custody for the night, what is it?"

"Grace, it's addressed to Ric. I can't open it."

"When did you develop scruples?" I teased. "C'mon. Who is it from? That's on the outside of the envelope."

"It's from Andy Mays at the State Police Forensics Lab. Andy and Ric met at some continuing ed classes a few years ago. He's the tall red haired guy whose wife owns that gallery, *It's all about View*, in Naperville."

"There you go. You know him. Open it."

"Grace, you're impossible." Her eyes gleamed with excitement during her reproach. She slit open the envelope and pulled out three standard size sheets of paper and one smaller piece of paper attached with a paperclip. Karen's eyes widened as she read the note.

"Oh my gosh. It's the preliminary report on the skeletons. knew I shouldn't have opened this. Andy says in the note that the brass would roast his chestnuts if they found out he gave this out. Karen started to fold the sheets.

"Don't do that. It's open. Ric will know you opened it. Let's a least read it." I took the papers out of her hands before she could change her mind.

"Don't tell anyone else."

"Tell what?" Hannah had walked behind Karen and was peering at the envelope in her hand.

"Karen opened the report on the skeletons from the forensic lab."

"What does it say?"

"Will you two stop." Karen tried to grab the papers from my hand. "I should put those away–unread."

"What good will that do? I vote with Grace." Hannah smiled.

"This isn't up for a vote. We shouldn't be reading it. We…oh what the hell." Karen resigned herself and shrugged her shoulders.

"That's the spirit. Move your purse so I can spread this out." unclipped the three pages and set them side-by-side on the tabletop. started skimming the first page aloud. "This page has information of the man, 5 feet ten inches tall, medium build, approximately thirt years old. Old break on left femur. No wound apparent. Leaning toward cause of death as drowning. That's odd." I turned over the sheet. "Here's stuff on the lion. Male approximately seven years old Talk about weird."

"What? What is it?"

"It says here the cause of death for the lion was a bullet to the head. Andy scribbled something in the margin. Looks like millimeter from a Luger."

"A what?"

"Luger. It's a German automatic pistol. Popular during and after World War II."

Karen and I stared at Hannah.

"My dad fought in Germany. He brought one home. Harry and learned to shoot with that gun, light, accurate, good balance."

Karen continued to stare at Hannah. "You never told me that. How old were you?"

"Oh, c'mon, Love, you know I competed in shooting when I was younger. Still do. I've taken you with me."

"I know you shoot those terra cotta thingies. I never thought about when you learned."

I poked Karen in the arm. "It's a sport. Shooting is big in England especially in the rural areas, just like the rural areas in this country. I'm certain Hannah didn't flounce into grade two and announce, 'Hi I'm Hannah. Want to see me shoot an apple off your head?'"

Hannah burst into laughter. "I think that happened in Austria to the guy who wrote the *William Tell Overture* after he survived the demonstration," she said between fits of laughter.

"No, no. That was the theme song for the Lone Ranger, '*ta da dump, ta da dump, ta da dump, dump, dump*." I gasped with laughter and tears.

"I'm surrounded by illiterates. Anyone with a grasp of literature would know that it was Robin Hood who shot the arrow that split the apple equally so those two women wouldn't argue about who was entitled to the produce."

We howled with laughter, so much so that people looked around for the reason.

"*Shh, Shh*. Security will probably show up. We're having too much fun for a black tie event." I cleared my throat and dabbed at my eyes. Hannah and Karen followed suit. We all took a deep breath to regain our composure. We looked at each other and burst into laughter again. It felt like we were at a dressed up pajama party.

I shuffled the top sheet to the bottom and looked at the next page. "Look at this. Andy's note says this is the inventory of everything found on the floor of the cage. *Egh*."

"What's wrong?"

"It's an inventory of the human bones. Look at this:

* * *

The Lion Tamer: A Caged Death

1 Mandible	*2 femur*	*1 clavicle*
2 patella	*2 humerus*	*2 tibia*
1 sternum	*2 fibula*	*2 radius*
11 metatarsals	*2 ulna*	*18 phalanges*
7 metacarpals	*3 hamates*	*3 capitates*

"That's gross." Karen took the sheet from my hands. "This goes on and on. How many bones are in the human body?"

"Don't look at me, I majored in English, like you did."

"Honestly, I can't believe the lack of a well rounded education in the American school system. The human body has approximately 200 bones," Hannah intoned in a classroom voice.

Karen and I grinned at each other. "Tell that to Sister Hillaire. She tried her best."

"Most of those 200 must be on this list, it continues on the back."

"Not really, if it says seven metacarpals you're missing a few," Hannah wiggled her fingers, "Five on each."

"Some bones may have washed away or been carried off by a critter."

"Look here," Karen continued. On the back they couldn't even identify them all. It says 'non human, non bone' in this column. Looks like small rocks and pebbles. They even measured and inventoried these. Must be pea gravel, they're approximately the same size. Report says these were found with the lion."

Karen was pointing to another column of figures.

"And something called *indigenous debris*."

"Your closet, perhaps?" Hannah's raised eyebrow in Karen's direction caused more laughter.

"Anyway, we know the main ones, right Gracie?"

Karen started singing, "*The humerus connected to the radius, the radius connected to the ulna, the ulna connected to the ham bone...*"

"Ham bone? I didn't learn much, but I don't think we have a ham bone."

"Okay, so I took poetic license. It's a hamate and we have three of them. I just don't know where." Karen's smug response set us off again.

Something niggled at the back of my mind but I couldn't place it. Karen scooped up the papers, folded them back into the envelope, and tuffed it in her evening bag.

"You're still here. I told Barb I'd back track to find you. Do you want to ride or walk to the other side of the park? Trust me, I've done in sneakers but I don't want to try it in these." Tracy lifted the hem of her dress to reveal high heels. "I'm a mom and a nurse; I'm out of uniform."

"Sorry. We were side tracked by Karen's lesson in anatomy."

"Karen's lesson? I thought she only memorized the fun parts when we were in Sister Hillaire's class."

Hannah burst into laughter. Karen tried to salvage her dignity.

"We were discussing bones and the ham hock came up."

"Hamate," both Hannah and I corrected.

Tracy looked confused. "Why were you discussing a bone in the hand?"

That's it. The masseuse talked about carpals and she said hamate.

Karen hesitated. She didn't want Tracy to know about the report. "We were reading something about bones in the body and we didn't know where the three hamate bones are located. Just light reading."

Tracy shook her head slightly. "I don't know what's going on but we better get to the trolley unless you want to hike across thirty-four acres."

We walked toward the next exhibit and the exit. The bar had closed down. There were a few other stragglers following the same path.

At the double doors Tracy paused. "About those bones, there are only two, one in each hand, about here." She pointed to an area between the wrist and little finger.

Since Karen chose not to inform Tracy of her source, I didn't feel I could say anything. The note did say it was preliminary. I suppose they could miscount or misidentify one or two bones out of that whole pile. A thought occurred to me.

"Tracy, do animals have hamate bones?"

"Animals? What are you three up to?" Tracy shrugged. "Some

primates, but nothing else. We're talking about a hand, not a paw or hoof."

Barb greeted us with waving arms. "C'mon, hurry, this is the last trolley. The driver was willing to wait until this patron kept insisting he leave immediately so she could be seated with her party." Barb nodded toward the trolley.

Through the window I spotted *Monkey Madam* from the bridge. I considered walking.

"Oh, dear." Karen spoke softly. "That's Fifi Chaney, a trustee. Worse yet, I think we're at her table."

"Oh, great."

"What's wrong?" Karen asked. They all waited for the answer.

I told them about the encounter on the bridge and the *hear no evil* pose.

"Geez, Grace. How am I supposed to sit across from her and not crack up laughing? Did you have to tell me?"

"You asked."

Hannah's voice, filled with amusement settled the problem. "Don't worry ladies. Karen put your napkin on your head over your eyes, and Grace, tie yours around your mouth. Then you'll be a matched set."

The roar of laughter caused heads to turn from those few guests boarding the trolley. *She* turned her head and fixed us with a malevolent stare. We hurried and stepped in quickly moving down the aisle to open seats.

The short ride brought us to the newest exhibit, Zone Africa. A large tent stretched at least the length of a football field and about as wide. Our nametags were on the table outside the entrance, most had already been collected. We followed Trustee Chaney aka Monkey Madam into the tent and toward a table of distinction.

My heart tightened as we approached the table. Lily and Leo DeFreest were seated and chatting amiably with others at the table. They hadn't seen me yet. I wanted to turn and run but I kept walking like an automaton toward the group.

Mrs. Chaney was introducing Karen. Leo DeFreest and the other gentleman had stood to greet the women. He spotted me there. His smile was fixed in place. I didn't know how he felt. I hadn't alked to either of them since the afternoon of the bombing. I saw him touch his daughter's shoulder and she looked at me. A slight nod, but no smile. Her hair had been trimmed and layered to remove the singed parts. The new style covered most of the small patch of gauze that still protected tender skin near her left jaw. The golden colored gown matched the darker blonde streaks in her hair and provided the warm backdrop for her single piece of jewelry, the Red Diamond. The gem lay against the thin shimmering fabric; the effect was stunning. The soft red glow enchanted me. I understood why she would have mourned its loss.

I heard my name. Karen's voice seemed strained as she introduced me. I'm sure she felt as badly about this seating chart as I did.

"Fifi Chaney, Adam and Nancy Triska, this is Grace Marsden. Grace, this is Fifi Chaney one of the zoo's longest-serving trustees, and Adam and Nancy Triska, corporate contributors to Zone Africa. You already know the DeFreests."

We all acknowledged each other and moved to be seated. DeFreest held the chair on his right for Tracy. I slipped in next to her to avoid sitting anywhere near Lily. A server appeared at my elbow to ask if I wanted a cocktail. I ordered a Vodka martini with double anchovy-stuffed olives.

The conversation centered on the coincidence of our all being assigned the same table.

"I had no idea that you were neighbors when I reserved the table. I knew Adam and Nancy would enjoy meeting Leo DeFreest," Ms. Chaney explained.

We were saved from further conversation as the chairperson of the *Whirl* approached the microphone. We had missed the first welcoming announcement.

"At this time I would like to introduce Father Joseph Morelli who will lead us in the invocation."

So this is where he was saying grace.

Karen looked at me across the table. "Did you know about this?"

"My dad said he was saying grace at some event tonight. He just came into town today. I thought it was odd he agreed to *work* on his vacation. Now I get it. Jolene must have volunteered him."

Monkey Madam shot me a two-eyebrow raised look. The last graphic I remembered reading in Jungle World was about similar facial expressions made by primates and humans.

My grin was irrepressible. She started to say something, but I put my forefinger up to my lips and nodded toward the podium. She looked like she contemplated putting up a finger.

"Let us bow our heads," my brother's deep voice instructed.

Joe was the most handsome of my brothers. His genetic code lavished thick dark brown hair, mile long eyelashes, a Cary Grant dimple, and sky blue eyes on a 6'2" frame. Joe's sport in high school was gymnastics. Even now he had that *Body by Jake* build.

"Lord let us be mindful of our stewardship, let us be grateful for our friendships, and let us give thanks in your name for our blessings. Amen"

Echoes of *amen* murmured throughout the tent.

"That's what I like about Joseph's style, short, sweet and to the point," Karen said.

"Do you know him," Ms. Chaney asked.

"Grace knows him better, he's her brother."

"Really?" Ms. Chaney looked at me with new eyes. "I'd be most interested in meeting him."

I bet you would. It's the damn dimple. It gets them every time.

"I'll be sure and introduce you after dinner."

The introduction came sooner than expected. I heard Joseph's voice behind me.

"Are you surprised to see me, Gracie girl?"

I turned in my chair and smiled up at my big brother. "Yes, I am. This *Whirl* has been a surprise." I realized that Karen, Hannah and Tracy were smiling. They had known he'd be here just like my dad had known. I wasn't upset.

Joe leaned down and kissed me on the cheek, then proceeded to greet Karen, Hannah, and Tracy in the same manner. I glanced at my dinner companions and realized that the other women looked like they hoped he'd continue around the table.

I waited for the smooching to cease and introduced Joe in my favorite manner, "Everyone, this is my brother, Father Joseph

Morelli. Joe this is Fifi Chaney, Adam and Nancy Triska, and my neighbors, Barb Atwater and Lily and Leo DeFreest."

"Nice to meet all of you." He turned his attention to me. "I wanted to catch you early in case I don't stay for the entire event–jet lag. I'll see you back at Dad's if I miss you later."

He leaned down for a good-bye kiss. I whispered in his ear, "Check with me before you leave, I'm kind of tired already."

"Will do." He squeezed my shoulder.

Several pairs of female eyes followed his progress as he made his way back to his table. I was saved from answering the questions and hearing the comments about my gorgeous big brother by the arrival of baby bib lettuce, flanked by quartered hearts of palm drizzled with a raspberry vinaigrette. The conversation geared toward passing the baguettes and butter.

The entrée bore no resemblance to the meals I whipped up. The non-traditional surf and turf consisted of a thin filet of snapper prepared with a paprika type seasoning and a small medallion of veal Oscar. I liked the substitution for the more common lobster and steak. The entrée was a healthier choice. Hannah, being a vegetarian, enjoyed surf and surf. Her fillet was larger and was accompanied by a half dozen tender shoots of asparagus.

Between mouthfuls, dinner conversation began.

Nancy Triska asked the question probably under discussion at most tables. "Do they know anything about the wagon and the skeleton yet?"

Fifi seemed hesitant to answer. She had been given the canned response by the board, but here was a corporate sponsor asking. I mean, why donate thousands of dollars if that doesn't entitle you more than the *film at eleven* version. I sensed her dilemma.

Karen came to her rescue. "The entire cage and contents was shipped to the state's forensics lab. They will be able to study the skeletons and determine all types of information. It would be inappropriate for them to release any information until the venue is cleared as a potential crime scene."

Nancy looked at Karen with some skepticism. "How do you know all this?"

Karen smiled. "Shop talk. My brother is also a man of the

cloth. He's a police inspector."

Nancy nodded her head slowly. I was praying that she hadn't caught Karen's words. She looked satisfied.

Whew. Dodged that one. Karen seemed unaware of her gaffe.

"What crime scene? I thought they found the remains of a lion in an old circus wagon."

Karen's eyes widened as she realized what she'd said. She looked at Fifi for help. Fifi Chaney looked green. She fidgeted with her napkin, dabbing at her lips and then smoothing it across her lap.

"Yes, what did you mean?" Adam Triska asked. Only Lily and Leo DeFreest seemed uninterested in the conversation.

"Oh, that's police procedure. I'm a nurse at Elmhurst Hospital," Tracy rushed to offer her credentials, "and the police invented red tape."

I smiled since most of the tape I'd seen at crime scenes was yellow.

"Even when we are convinced of the cause of death, if no one was present to see the person expire before they're brought in, we can't list a cause of death until a police investigation is completed and the coroner makes his call."

I thought Tracy was laying it on a little thick, but Barb, Nancy and Adam looked convinced. Only Fifi looked suspiciously at Karen. She may have caught the look of gratitude on Karen's face.

"So they'll spread out the contents, the bones, the debris," Tracy continued, "check it by the book, and then issue a report. Probably want to make sure there aren't any ham hocks in there." Tracy grinned and looked at Karen.

The look of gratitude was replaced by one of guilt. She fingered her purse on the table.

"Ham hocks?" Fifi's suspicious gaze included Tracy now. I think Fifi thought she and her corporate donors were being made the butt of a joke.

Tracy sensed the same. "An inside joke from an earlier discussion. Karen called a hamate bone ham hock." Tracy again demonstrated where the hamate bone was located in the hand.

Everyone inadvertently touched the spot on one hand or the other. Except Leo DeFreest. He sat perfectly still, both hands on the able. I glanced at the gloved hand and froze. My stomach lurched and my head filled with noise. I forced my eyes to look away. Instead I looked up. His eyes locked on mine and in that instant a shock of evil gripped me. I shivered and jerked my hand against my water glass. Tracy grabbed at it.

"Grace, what's wrong? You look like you've seen a ghost. Are you okay?"

I felt like the ghost of evil had gripped me. What could I tell them?

"We may have overdone this," Karen said. "C'mon, I'll take you home."

Fifi spoke up. "Ms. Kramer, you are one of the presenters tonight. Did you forget?"

You could tell by the look on her face that she had forgotten.

"Maybe you could fill in for me. My friend is ill and I need to take her home."

Monkey Madam looked about ready to howl.

"Karen, stay. I'm going to splash some water on my face and then look for Joseph. He was going home early. I'll catch a ride with him. Besides, looks like dessert is crème brûlée. I'd never forgive myself if I made anyone miss that."

I smiled what I thought was a genuinely hearty smile. It must have looked so to everyone else as they cleared places for the dessert that was being served.

I stood up and said my good-byes. I couldn't walk away from that table fast enough. Thoughts swirled though my head, snatches of previous conversations came back to me to add to the turmoil. *It fits! Kurt said it wasn't always a necklace. Not earrings. I kept thinking jewelry for a woman. Cuff links! Rich men, famous men, have always worn cuff links. His cuff link, his bone.*

I jostled several people as I tried to distance myself from Leo DeFreest. He knew I knew when he saw me staring at his hand. I wanted to stop moving and think. I also wanted to find the restrooms. *Where the heck was the bathroom?*

I had walked the length of the tent and through the flap that I thought hid the fancy port-a-room facility. The only thing out there was the caterer's truck.

Darn. Now I'll have to go back in and go all the way to the other side.

I thought of *Makundi Boma,* and the bathroom Jolene had pointed out near that exhibit. The tent was set up at the east end of Zone Africa.

I'm closer to that than going all the way back. No lines, either.

I smiled to myself and headed into the brush to *Travelers' Rest.* The round building was discernible from the lighted area. I followed the path past it to the outhouses with indoor plumbing. I flipped on the light and eagerly used the facilities.

I stared at my face in the mirror above the sink. My eyes were purple with excitement at my discovery. I dried my hands and reached for my cell phone to call Harry. My tiny evening bag mocked me with its inability to hold more than my compact, brush, and lipstick. I pulled out the length of yarn I had stuffed in there. Without rhyme or reason I suddenly needed to tie knots before I could leave.

Don't argue, just do it. "Wish I knew what made me tack instead of tick."

I lamented my condition out loud in an outhouse. At least I could be talking to those wild dogs. I laughed and quickly finished my tenth knot. I flipped the switch down and heard the solid *click.* Up, *click*; down, *click*; up, *click*; down, *click.* I needed ten of those before I could leave.

The night seemed darker than before. I decided not to sit and talk to wild dogs, but rather go back to the tent. With my physical need removed from my mind I chastised myself for walking out here instead of staying in the tent. Harry would tell me it wasn't a wise choice; Ric would tell me I was acting stupid, again.

I felt better just thinking about those two, as if I had conjured up their presence. A noise in the path ahead of me startled me; it stopped me cold. What if I had conjured up someone else? Would DeFreest have followed me?

God. This isn't a bad choice; this is the stupidest one I'd ever made. Of course he'd come after me. If he thought I hadn't told anyone my suspicion, he could kill me and his secret would be safe.

The thought that I was alone, in the dark, with Leo DeFreest between me and safety prompted me to act. I quickly moved to the left and stepped into the shadow of the outside wall of Makundi Boma. I could hear someone coming. I opened the door slowly, ready to stop if it made noise. I slipped inside and eased the door closed behind. Just in time. Someone hurried past the building toward the bathroom. By the sound of the footsteps I knew it was a man.

What an idiot! I've been flipping the light on and off. Why don't I just paint a target on my back?

I didn't want to stay put in case he decided to check out this building on his way back. He knew I was out here somewhere.

The icy finger of terror touched my spine, a second before I understood, a second before he spoke.

"Don't move, Mrs. Marsden. I'm pointing a pistol at you." He stepped forward from a deep shadow near the other door. "I hid in here when I heard someone coming up behind me on the path. How convenient for me that you thought to do the same."

We both heard the sounds of footsteps at the same time. He moved close to me and whispered, "It's your brother. If he walks in here, he's a dead man."

I didn't doubt for one minute that he'd keep that promise. I prayed that Joseph wouldn't stop to look for me in here. I held my breath as the footsteps approached, paused on the other side of the thick wall. I released my breath slowly only after I heard my brother move to safety.

"Very good, Mrs. Marsden. You're a bit too clever for your own good I'm afraid."

I could see him clearly in the ambient light coming from the ceiling to floor plate glass windows. He held a nasty looking gun in his hand; the long, narrow barrel seemed more sinister than other guns I'd seen.

"We're going to walk outside and toward Iroquois Lake. You won't call out because whoever comes to your rescue will die with you tonight. I don't expect anyone to be at the marsh. With your husband and Inspector Kramer sidelined, your only salvation just walked away. Perhaps he can save you in the afterlife with his prayers."

His words chilled me, but the tone of his voice filled me with terror. He spoke calmly, as though debating a philosophical treatise. I feared his emotional void would keep him focused on task and give me no opportunity to escape.

I needed him to keep talking.

"Don't do this. You could turn yourself in. That happened fifty years ago. There could be circumstances. What you're doing now is pre-meditated." I nodded toward the gun.

"Oh this? I never go anywhere without this. I had no idea when I dressed for dinner that I'd have to kill you, Mrs. Marsden. I made a quick trip to my car. I saw Mrs. Atwater on my way back. She was leaving, said good night to her. I stopped by the table on my way out here, mentioned I saw you catch Mrs. Atwater for a lift."

He paused for a moment. His face reflected his own brand of humor; a smile slit the bottom half of his face.

"Such irony," he said. "My last visit to this zoo ended up much the same way. It was a bit different; that night I did dress to kill someone."

So much for a self-defense plea.

We were at the bridge between the giraffe exhibit and the main path, moving further away from any possibility of help. He hadn't been in the zoo for fifty years. His dead reckoning of Iroquois Lake failed him. We were headed in the right direction but the landmarks he'd navigated by decades ago were long gone. We started across the bridge. I purposely put my weight on my heel and forced one leather spike between the planks. I faked a stumble and succeeded in a realistic twist and spill.

"*Ow*!"

"Be quiet and get up."

He pointed the gun directly at my face. The round black hole at the end of the barrel seemed to expand to the size of my head. I swallowed hard to keep from crying out.

"My ankle. I can't."

"I think you can. Get up or I'll shoot you right here and take my chances."

I stood and limped to the rail. *I needed more time.* I put my full weight on it and winced for his benefit. "Give me a moment. What does it matter?"

"It matters because the zoo's soirée will be winding down soon and I need to be where people can remember seeing me."

He forgot about walking. His face seemed lost in thought; maybe of his last zoo visit.

I needed to keep him talking. I took a long, slow breath to steady the pounding in my chest and asked him a question in the calmest voice I could muster.

"The park is developed now. How was it that night, out here?" He stayed still for so long I thought maybe I hadn't spoken out loud but only in my head.

His voice seemed to come from another place in his head. Not like a ventriloquist, but more like a sleepwalker.

"Yes, the park has changed. But the night is the same; warm for April, a sliver of a moon that barely illuminated our work. We agreed to meet that night to split up the diamonds that were cached in the bottom of the wagon. My *signature* was the elaborate wagon that I used to ship all my animals. No zoo would dismantle and destroy a wagon as they would a shipping cage. I explained the idea as beneficial to the animal during shipping and during the acclamation process. Zoo curators acclaimed me as a true conservationist."

He paused. I worried that he might stop. He looked beyond me. I knew no one was there. His view was of the past. He seemed to be rousing himself. I couldn't afford that.

"Maybe you started out that way." My voice sounded calm and soothing; my brain was seething with thoughts, none too pleasant.

He spoke from his past but addressed me. "Maybe I did."

I breathed a little easier.

"But I didn't end up that way, did I, Mrs. Marsden? You are tricky indeed. Let's continue our journey, shall we?"

His brusque, back to business tone cut through me. I thought I'd found the *chink* in his armor. He waved the gun to move me off the railing and across the bridge.

"Nice piece of psychology for an English major." He chuckled at his own joke. "Lily's major. You two have much in common, especially your husband. Your death will make it easier for Lily to reclaim him. They belong together, a bond you might say."

A bond? I didn't have time to pick his psychotic brain about his take on Lily's love life. He seemed to slip back to the past.

"Yes, indeed, the park has changed," he continued as though he'd never mentioned Lily. "Not so much that I can't find my way. Had no trouble that night either. The zoo had forced a change in plans. They sold one of my lions to St. Louis the day he was delivered. He was due to be shipped the next morning. My partner was in charge of re-routing the lion. Keepers, trustees, workers had been in and out of the Lion House all day excited for a view of the magnificent creature. My partner couldn't get to the diamonds until after the zoo closed and most everyone had left. He told the grounds manager and the keeper that he'd be spending the night to prepare the wagon and its passenger for a pre-dawn departure to avoid traffic. I met him at the building."

He stopped talking and seemed to hesitate about direction. We had reached a t-intersection that I'm sure hadn't existed before twenty years ago. We had walked to the Thirty-First Street end of the park. A right turn would take us to Australia and the North Gate. He knew enough to turn left. He seemed satisfied with his choice.

"Stupid fool. Things would have been fine. This was our last deal. He raged at me when he spotted the cuff links. Stupid of me. I shouldn't have worn them. I offered him a bigger cut of the diamond sale. I argued that one couldn't split up the pair. Nothing worked. He wouldn't listen to reason. He was out of control. I told him to get the diamonds out and he could have the entire sale. That seemed to appease him, but I saw him look at the cuff links and the greed in his eyes was unmistakable. I made my decision and swung at his head with this," he turned his gun hand palm up, "as he was climbing out from the bottom with the diamonds. The angle was bad and the blow glanced off his shoulder. We struggled with the gun, ramming up against the cage. I broke free and told him to turn around and lay the pouch inside the cage where I could see it. I couldn't risk a shot so I knocked him out and stuffed his body into the cage bottom."

I slowed my pace and barely breathed; I didn't want to distract him from his story. He had slowed down as well. *As soon as Joseph gets home, he'll realize I'm still here. He'll be back with everyone.*

He stopped talking. "Very clever, Mrs. Marsden. Let him talk

270

d lose his way. Was that your plan? No matter. By the time nyone realizes you're not there, you won't be here either. I see the ath to the marsh."

Had he read my mind or had I spoken out loud?

We had circled back and were at the bridge near the giraffe yard.

"That way." He waved the gun toward the Thirsty Animal Trail. Go through there."

He didn't know that this trail looped out and back to the same pot. I wasn't about to tell him. We were entering the end of the trail.

I was prepared, he wasn't. In the still of night, the lion's roar that y steps activated startled him. He whirled and set toward the sound, nsing for the leap he expected.

I took that instant to plunge into the thick woods on the left side f the trail. I heard him curse as he realized what had produced the und. I ran as quickly as I could; the shoes weren't as much of an npediment as the darkness.

Hyenas howled, I knew he'd stayed on the path to make better me. He was parallel tracking. I ran faster. Branches flew at my ce, slicing my cheeks and grabbing at my hair. I turned slightly to nd an easier way through the trees. Thick bushes loomed in front of e. I turned again, a little the other way making slow progress.

I stopped moving. No other animal sounds. Had he stopped on e path or was he coming toward me through the woods? I tried to alm my breathing so I could hear something other than the beating in y ears. I heard a tiny rustling. Too small for a person. Wings oove me. Owl? Bat? No big sounds came to my ears. But he had een a hunter. He didn't make big sounds, any sounds.

I can't stand here much longer. I have to move. Which way?

My head ached with life and death questions. I had lost my earings. I didn't know if I'd be running toward or away from him.

Move, Gracie, move. Which way?

My brain demanded a price for the answer. *Step left, step right, nce; step left, step right, twice; step left, step right, three times, hoose! Left! I choose, left.*

I moved slowly to my left, trying to make as little noise as ossible. My dress rustled with each step. It sounded like paper eing crumpled; deafening in the quiet. The nylon zipper made a

The Lion Tamer: A Caged Death

breathy sound as it released me.

My full slip wasn't much protection against the cold or the branches, but I could move through the woods as quietly as DeFreest, I hoped. I thought I should be close to the path again; unless I had crept in circles.

A hyenas' shrill howl broke the silence. The sound seemed behind me. That was good as long as he was moving away from me.

Set off the next animal and I'll know where you are. I think Warthogs are closer to me. Let the lions roar. He'll be at the end. I can cross the path here and go through the woods on the other side.

Warthogs grunted and I smiled to myself. I moved forward and stepped out of the trees.

Lions roared and I froze, exposed in the weak light from the moon.

"You've led me quite a chase, Mrs. Marsden. Bravo."

I heard his silky voice from the darkness of the tree line on the other side of the path. I couldn't see him.

"Such a pity. I do regret killing a worthy opponent. I didn't enjoy killing that magnificent lion that night. I grew careless as I quickly tried to hide my crime.

A plan formed in my head. A plan to make it appear that my partner had left with the lion as planned. No alarm would be raised to do that I needed to dump the lion, the wagon, and the carrier. lured the cat into the wagon from his cage with chunks of raw mea from the commissary; the blood stained my hands and jacket. The wagon was already on the low carrier used to transport crates. hitched my partner's truck to the carrier. I didn't know the area. didn't want to be stopped on the street. I had toured the park earlier in the day with the director and remembered Iroquois Lake. I drove the short distance to the marsh and backed the carrier down into the wate as far as I could with the truck hooked up.

My plan was to turn the truck around and push the carrier out to deeper water. I realized in my hurry to cover my crime, I had left the diamonds inside the cage that now held an upset lion. The diamond were no more than twelve inches inside the cage. I should have left them, but then I was Leo DeFreest, the great lion tamer. I inched my hand inside, all the while staring straight into his savage amber eye. My fingers made contact, but even then instead of pulling the pouc oward me with my fingertips I moved my hand over the bag and lifted it. In that instant I saw the reflection of what my hand covered in blood holding a chunk of leather looked like to him. An instant was all he needed. I felt the searing pain and screamed in agony. I heard the crunch of bones splitting in his jaws and I knew in another instant he'd have my arm up to my elbow.

The shift in weight when he pounced caused the wagon to move further out. The carrier was starting to sink in the unstable marsh material beneath it. My choices were death by mauling or death by drowning. Big cats don't let go. It's not their nature. The pain was excruciating; the animal was backing away forcing my shoulder against the bars. I feared I would pass out before I could shoot. I pushed the gun between the bars and fired.

The water swirled around my waist before I could pull my mangled hand from his mouth. I dragged myself out of the water and tied strips of my ripped jacket around what was left of my hand, using the barrel of this gun to make a tourniquet to stop the bleeding."

My face must have reflected the horror of his story. He stopped talking. He stood staring at me.

"I am sorry, Mrs. Marsden. It's time."

A cacophony of animal sounds burst into the night, snarls, snorts, and roars. The animal voices were followed by human ones shouting my name. Footsteps were coming fast on the path from both sides and through the woods behind me.

DeFreest was gone; the spot he occupied less than two blinks before empty.

"Grace!" My name exploded from Harry's mouth. "Oh my God."

His arms were around me pulling me into the warmth and safety of his body. I heard voices shouting, calling for help. I heard a gunshot and flinched in Harry's arms. I couldn't speak. My emotional roller coaster had taken too many loops. It crashed.

I felt a jacket snugged around me and then arms lifting me, then hurrying me down the trail. I head the lion roar and then nothing.

Chapter Thirty-Seven

"Gracie, Gracie." Someone kept repeating. I floated closer and recognized my father's voice.

"*Mmm*, Dad?" I opened my eyes slowly and focused on my father's worried face.

"She's awake." His announcement brought more faces looming in my field of vision; Marty, Karen, Hannah, and some I didn't recognize. I didn't see Harry. Had I imagined him holding me? I turned my head to enlarge my view. I was stretched out on the stage in the tent. Several tablecloths were folded under me and a few more covered me from head to foot. I was warm, too warm. My eyelids felt heavy; the wave sliding toward me.

I tried to lift over it to find Harry. I spotted Joseph standing across the room. He was on one knee next to the body of Leo DeFreest. I knew he was dead. Joe was wearing his priest's stole around his neck and I could see from his movements he was administering the last rites. He made the sign of the cross over the body, "*In nomine Patris, et Filii, et Spiritus Sancti, Amen.*" I found myself mouthing the words. He pulled a tablecloth over DeFreest' head and stood up. I watched the still form thinking of the irony of my brother praying for his salvation tonight.

Only when I made my mental peace with him did I renew my search for Harry. He sat on a folding chair fifteen or twenty feet away from the body. Lily sat next to him. Joseph leaned down to Lily. He spoke a few words to her then left her with her grief. Tears rolled down her face and gentle sobs moved her shoulders under Harry's arm. He tried to lift a strand of hair that clung to her wet cheek. The attempt was awkward; the gesture heartbreakingly sweet. *What had DeFreest said? That they belonged together, a bond c sorts.* I let go and slipped back into myself.

"She's just asleep. Conked out." Someone assured someone.

The voices were blurred in my head as if I were dreaming or slurred in my ears as if I were hearing underwater.

I think I'm asleep. I would be more asleep if people would be quiet. The room droned with voices, occasionally one or two louder, demanding.

"Can we move her, take her home?"

"Of course. The doctor who examined her said she needed rest. Let me ask for a wheelchair."

I'd better wake up; I don't want a wheelchair. Did the doctor check my ears?

"That's not necessary. I'll carry her. Lift her into my arms."

I felt a shift and then a draft as I left the warmth of the make shift bed. A blanket dropped over me and then I felt strong arms cradle me to a familiar chest. The softest kiss brushed my forehead.

I woke up in Harry's arms.

"Harry."

"Welcome back, darling. You had us worried. I can't lose you, you're my life."

My hearing was perfect and so were his words.

"Was I dreaming? Is he dead?"

"*Shh.* No one can hurt you. He's dead. You're safe."

My brothers and dad walked on either side of us as we left the *Whirl* Tent behind.

"I wish we could go home." I felt orphaned with no nest of my own.

"Tonight we're sleeping in your room, but tomorrow night we'll be sleeping in my old room."

I looked blankly at Harry.

"I'm taking you home to my Mum and Dad and my childhood room. Seashore, fresh air, and my Mum's peach cobbler. That'll set us both right as rain."

A nest was easy to build; a mate was the tricky part. I smiled and closed my eyes.

The Lion Tamer: A Caged Death

Meet the Author:

A native of the Chicago area and owner of her own staffing services corporation, Luisa Buehler attended Rosary College during the seventies and graduated with a B.A. in English. Even then, the stories of spirits, sightings, and the supernatural intrigued her. Since then she has spent time 'giving back' to her community by volunteering as a Docent at Brookfield Zoo and as a trained leader in the Boy Scouts of America. With her debut novel, she has realized a dream that has been on hold while raising her son and running her company. Luisa lives in Lisle, Illinois with her husband, Gerry, their son, Christopher, and the family cat, Martin Marmalade. In her free time, Luisa loves to garden and wishes she could play golf better.

Echelon Press Publishing

Echelon Press Publishing

Celebrating Five Years of

Unique Stories

For

Exceptional Readers

2001 -2006

WWW.ECHELONPRESS.COM

Also available from Echelon Press Publishing

Situation Sabotage (*Global Adventure*) Graeme Johns

*Contamination...sabotage...*terms feared by food industry executives around the world. They prefer to announce the problem as a potential...*situation.* Now, Investigator Barton has been called in to solve the case before word leaks out. A frantic dash across the Pacific uncovers three murders before he discover the mastermind behind the sabotage.

$15.99   ISBN 1-59080-477-5

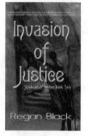

Invasion of Justice (*Women's Adventure*) Regan Black

In 2096 an empath with a penchant for all things retro, Petra Neiman is making a good name for herself reading crime scenes for the judicial system. That is until a serial killer drags her into his crimes and pins a gruesome murder on her brother. Now she must sort through myriad feelings and memories to unravel a plot that began before her birth.

$12.99   ISBN 1-59080-443-0

Dangerous Affairs (*Romantic Suspense*) Kelle Z. Riley

A man fighting his past. A woman fleeing hers. When fate throws them together they form an unlikely—and temporary—alliance. Soon real passion infuses their fake marriage and they begin to dream of more. But someone has other plans. Someone who would rather see them dead than happy.

$12.99   ISBN 1-59080-468-6

Fractured Souls (*Suspense*) T.A. Ridgell

*People aren't always what they seem...*Terrifying accidents have Dr. Benita Kyser on edge. Teaming up with private investigator, Sean Turner, they work against time to identify the threat. *Cracked Minds Lead to Fractured Souls...*One man wants more from Beni. She's the reason for his success--or failure. He will have her as his own. And if he can't--then no one will...

$12.99   ISBN 1-59080-471-6